Pop, Fizz, Clink

a novel by
Jenna Beall Mueller

For my mom, Wendy,
a fearless nurse who has never hesitated
to help someone in distress.
I'll never forget the afternoon you pulled the
Honda Odyssey over on Bridgetown Road
to help the runner you saw collapse.
You are the bravest person I know.

For my husband, Adam,
who has shouldered so many tears,
loved me when I wasn't feeling very lovable,
and always said yes to that next rescue dog.
No one rocks a flannel better than you,
and no one makes a better roast chicken.
You're the bee's knees.

And for my daughter, Marigold,
who gives me strength and joy,
so much joy, on my hardest days.
Even before you were born,
you astonished me with your tenacity.
I love you with every bit of me!

Author's Note:

Multiple sclerosis is often referred to as the snowflake disease because every case is different. Bea's multiple sclerosis story is based on my own. MS symptoms vary greatly, and every MS sufferer's story is a unique one. Certain details, particularly the timing regarding neurologist apointments and the arrival of Bea's MS medication, have been expedited to fit within the time-frame of this plotline. Because jeez louise, things don't move quickly in the medical world!

This is a work of fiction and should not be taken as medical advice. I was a Creative Writing major, so I'm not your gal for any sort of medical guidance. I encourage everyone to find a doctor they trust and can talk to about their concerns.

Unless otherwise stated, all names, characters, businesses, places, events, and incidents in this book are either the product of the author's imagination or used in a fictitious manner. Any resemblance to actual persons, living or dead, or actual events is purely coincidental.

Chapter One

hy haven't I heard from Dr. Macaulay?

I refresh my Internet browser like I've done every five minutes since arriving home from my eight a.m. MRI.

No new MyChart messages. Only Black Friday promotions and a reminder from my dentist's office that I'm overdue for a cleaning.

I stare at the construction paper turkey that my niece, Violet, mailed me. Even though he arrived a bit wrinkled—it's a long journey from Santa Fe to Cincinnati—I'd proudly stuck him to my fridge with two magnets. But his once cheerful smile and lolling tongue now look like a teasing, manic smirk.

Does this Thanksgiving turkey know something I don't?

It's quarter past four, and Dr. Macaulay's office will close soon. Even worse, it's a Friday, so an anxiety-filled weekend potentially looms ahead of me.

Maybe no news is good news?

I shake my head, that's not it, and close my eyes while I draw a concentric circle. When I determine a good stopping point, I count my number of lines. Seven. Counting in sevens, I go through the process of elimination until I'm left with a snapshot of my future life.

It's the last night of my twenties, I'm nervously awaiting an important phone call, and do you know how I'm coping?

By playing M.A.S.H.

Yes, *that* M.A.S.H. The one you played at sleepovers or covertly passed between desks in the fourth grade.

There are a lot of ways to play M.A.S.H. depending on your age and

geography, but here's the template I stick to: Future Husband (where you must list a guy you're swoony over, one who is perfectly nice but maybe lacking a certain spark, and a dude in your life you'd *never* want to exchange words with, much less vows); Number of Kids (again, follow the Future Husband structure of best, okay, and worst—this is how each category works); Future Career; Future Car; Future Husband's Job; Future City.

Here is tonight's forecast.

I'm going to live in an apartment. (What else is new?) I'm going to marry Ian, the electrician I dated for three weeks who was kind and had a giant sheepdog but got bored too easily. ("Only boring people get bored," my mother has always said.) We are having one child. (*How will we avoid spoiling our only child?* I worry.) I'm going to be an accountant. (Yikes. Between us? I wouldn't hire me.) I will drive a powder blue VW Bug convertible. (MY DREAM CAR!) Ian will be an art museum docent. (Charming!) And we're going to live in Nantucket. (I don't know how we'll afford it, but we'll do what we must.)

I shrug. This isn't half bad. And it's certainly taking my mind off scary medical possibilities and my doctor's ominous silence.

The front door groans with its exhausted creak, interrupting my musings.

Curious, I twist around in my seat.

My across-the-hall neighbor, Janet Shapiro, has a habit of inviting herself over. I usually don't mind, though. Janet's an excellent storyteller, and she often comes bearing colorful cocktails.

But the apartment is quiet.

Janet's not here, and the front door is now wide open.

"Tony Soprano!" I shout the name of my blind dachshund, shooting up from my chair and lumbering down the stairwell in a panic. I grip the railing as I go, my legs tingly and weak.

Thankfully, I spot him just a floor below, sniffing the new welcome mat in front of recently vacated apartment 3A. It features an illustration of Yoda and reads *Welcome You Are.*

Unfortunately, apartment 3A's new tenant doesn't spot Tony moseying around his doorway. Probably because he's carrying a very large cardboard box and wandering dachshunds aren't on his radar.

"Oh, shit," I breathe before shouting, "Watch out!"

But it's too late.

Apartment 3A's new tenant trips right over Tony's torso. I wince, bracing for a terrible fall, and am relieved when the man catches himself against the wall. Only the box topples to the ground, spewing kitchen supplies across the terracotta tiled floor.

Chapter Two

"Oh my God," I say, hurrying down to help. "Are you okay? I am so, so sorry. I swear my dog getting loose isn't a normal thing. This has never happened before."

I fall short in many aspects of my life—for example, I rarely vote in primary elections, I usually forget to bring my reusable shopping bags to the grocery store, and I consume way too much sugar—but dog ownership is an area where I positively shine.

I don't play this card often, but now seems like a good time. I hold Tony up. "He's blind," I say. "He doesn't have eyes."

But the new tenant isn't angry. Honestly, he doesn't even look peeved.

"I accidentally trip people all the time, and I have both my eyes," he replies, an easy smile tugging at his lips.

And what big eyes you have! I swoon, before remembering this is a line from *Little Red Riding Hood* regarding a wolf disguised as a grandmother. Cool, Bea. Not creepy at all.

"Your dog, on the other hand, has a very valid excuse," the neighbor says.

I smile back. My new neighbor is kind—and handsome, too, with dark, curly hair and a single dimple in his right cheek.

"I'm Chris Little," he says, extending a hand. His skin is tanned, despite the gray of the late fall, and covered in coarse hair. *A manly hand,* I think. "I'm moving into 3A."

Quickly, I try to flip my shoulder-length hair out of my face and give my most charming grin. "Bea Parker, 4A," I tell him.

"Pleasure," he says. "And did I hear you say your dog's name is... Tony Soprano?"

"It sure is. And while he answers to Tony, he really prefers you call him by his full name. *Or else*," I tease, inwardly cringing at my lame attempt at a mobster joke.

Chris gives me a charitable chuckle. *Good manners*, I note.

"When I adopted him, he had been through a lot," I explain, choosing not to elaborate. It's a tale as old as time, really. Just another couple who lost interest in their fur baby the moment they had a human baby. But when I talk about it, my face gets fiery hot, and I actually start to stutter. It's not exactly becoming, if you catch my drift.

"I named him Tony Soprano, so he would never forget how tough he is," I say.

"It's an excellent name," Chris says, and I'm pleased to have his approval. "May I?" He nods towards Tony.

"Pet him?" I interpret. "Of course."

Cute, charming, *and* an animal lover? Be still, my heart!

We both grin at one another in that sort of dopey way, where your whole face is beaming, and it feels like your nose, your chin, *even your eyebrows* are smiling, and only break our trance at the sound of squeaky sneakers coming up the stairwell.

It's an attractive woman wearing matchy-matchy athleisure. She's even got on those tall athletic socks that make my stocky legs look like tubes of Lip Smacker lip balm. "Meeting neighbors already?" she asks Chris cheerfully.

He nods, and I gamely stick my hand forward, disappointed but not all that surprised. Of course a handsome, sweet guy like Chris has a girl-friend. Better to find out now than after I've spent hours daydreaming about the man.

"Hi. I'm Bea, and this is my dog, Tony Soprano."

"Tony Soprano! That's amazing," she laughs.

Beautiful and great taste, like I could expect anything less.

"I'm Maria," she offers.

"New to town or just the neighborhood?" I ask them.

"Neither. I grew up in Pleasant Ridge, but I haven't lived here since high school," Chris says. I pick up on his use of the singular and determine he and Maria don't live together just yet.

"I, um, had a somewhat abrupt end to my previous accommodations..."

My eyes widen, and I take a subconscious step backward. "Bed bugs?"

He shakes his head, looking amused. "No, not bed bugs."

"A messy breakup," Maria volunteers.

"*Maria,*" Chris murmurs, his ears growing red.

"Trust me, I wouldn't be here helping my twin brother if he moved 'just because,'" Maria says.

Twins, I marvel, noticing their physical similarities, like the shape of their brown eyes and the slope of their broad noses.

"When a relationship crashes and burns after six years though—" Maria continues, only to be elbowed by Chris.

"Maria, seriously. Not now," he says, his voice low.

But Maria isn't done yet. "I told Chris he should take a hiatus from the dating scene," she says. "Doesn't seem like the worst idea, right? Spend some time alone, figure out what he really wants..."

"Totally," I say, as if I have any idea what that's like. I've been trying to get myself *into* a long-term relationship since I was thirteen years old to no great success.

"Since Maria was born a whopping two minutes before me, she likes to boss me around," Chris grumbles.

"Have I ever steered you wrong?" she quips. "I like to consider myself a sort of expert on my brother's life. I've been there since the start and all."

Now worried they're the sort of codependent twins who communicate via ESP, I give a small smile before kneeling down to pick up the contents of the fallen box. "I hope nothing broke," I say, gathering a set of nested mixing bowls and a bunch of those silicone sandwich bags.

Chris and Maria both join me on the dusty floor. "It's just random kitchen stuff. It's all good, really," Chris says. "Quick question: does the building offer composting?"

I stare at him. "As in this apartment building? The Amelia?" I often wonder about the architect of our historic apartment building, who chose to name the practical brick structure after his wife. Wouldn't she have preferred a trellised gazebo? Or maybe a fountain?

Chris nods, squinting behind his thick-rimmed glasses.

"Have you *met* Stanley?" Our seventy-something landlord has a sun-spotted, oily scalp, and since he refuses to wear hearing aids, only hears about half of what you say. He exclusively calls me "missy," which is sexist, but probably just because he can't remember my name, and drives a 1989 Cadillac DeVille. "Just be thankful we can recycle."

"My brother is sort of an environmental...enthusiast?" Maria says. "During a family trip to D.C., we had an Al Gore sighting, and sixteen-year-old Chris nearly passed out from excitement. I'm pretty sure we had to fan him to prevent a fainting episode."

I laugh while Chris blushes.

"You're quite the comedian today," he tells his sister.

I cock my head at the faint sound of The Lovin Spoonful's "Do You Believe in Magic." (I was recently informed by my Gen Z colleague that ringtones are incredibly cringe. It made me feel ancient.)

Is it Dr. Macaulay calling?

But why would she be calling instead of sending a MyChart message?

"I've been expecting an important call," I stammer, already hurrying up the steps. "It was, um, nice meeting you both. See you around."

Chapter Three

Back inside my apartment, I set Tony on the floor, shut the door *tight,* and lock it for extra measure.

Where did I put my phone?

I hurry through the living room and bathroom, I live in a shotgun-style apartment, and into my bedroom with its periwinkle walls and hodgepodge of antique furniture. *Aha.* My phone's resting on the nightstand. I must have left it there after my twenty-minute power nap.

I pick up my phone, and there it is. A missed call and voicemail message from Dr. Macaulay's office.

This is just like that Regina Spektor song, I think. Do you know the one I'm talking about? It's called "Laughing With" and includes this line, "No one laughs at God when the doctor calls after some routine tests." I say a quick Hail Mary, but considering I only go to mass on Christmas, Easter, and whenever my mom guilts me into attending, my prayer request probably goes to the bottom of the stack.

I glance at the inside of my elbow, where a cotton ball is still taped. I required contrast with this morning's MRI, and it took the poor technician multiple sticks to finally reach my tiny veins. Why haven't I taken the bandage off by now? The prick stopped bleeding hours ago. I pull down the sleeve of my plaid dress, covering the evidence.

My primary care doctor, Dr. Macaulay, had requested I schedule an MRI following an especially severe migraine headache. But I hadn't been expecting this call. I had been expecting a MyChart message saying everything was fine, that I was simply doomed to this sort of headache-filled life, just as I'd been told countless times before. Sometimes, the note asked if

I wanted to change my migraine prescription, but there was never a call.

Why did she call?

I think back to the cluster headache that started this whole mess, remembering the sudden, intense pain on the right side of my head that was astonishing in its severity. I was home when it happened, sound asleep in my bed of mismatched sheets and crocheted blankets. The stabbing sensation actually startled me awake and had me scrambling for the bathroom where I promptly threw up.

It was so unlike my typical migraines, it warranted a visit to Dr. Macaulay.

Between us? My primary care doctor's office has become a pathetic sort of hangout spot for me this past year. Not exactly as fun and charming as being a regular at the local watering hole. And while there's no bartender named Sam, I can tell you that everybody knows my name.

But when Dr. Macaulay suggested an MRI, my mind immediately went *there*.

You know where.

"Do you think I have a brain tumor?" I asked, my eyes wide.

"We'll look for any masses or abnormalities," she said, which I interpreted as yes, it was a possibility. "Better to be overly cautious."

My breath caught somewhere deep and painful in my chest, I sit on the edge of my bed, the tired mattress exhaling a sad sigh. "Hi. This is Bea, err, Beatrix Parker. I was just, um, returning Dr. Macaulay's call?" I stumble, fighting the urge to bite my nails.

"I'm glad you called!" says the receptionist, suspiciously perky. "We close at five, so you just caught us. One moment."

My heart pounds. Why didn't she pause or request further clarification? Has the office been talking about me? What the heck did they see on my MRI?

After only a few seconds, Dr. Macaulay comes on the line. "Bea, hi."

I know Dr. Macaulay well enough to know when something is wrong. A former college softball star, she has a low, raspy voice and buoyant disposition. But when she has unfortunate news to deliver, say my heart rate is too high or she's listing off the serious-but-rare side effects of a prescription, her voice becomes just a little softer, like a piece of taut velvet.

"Hi, Dr. Macaulay," I babble. "I got your voicemail. So, what's up?"

What's up? I cringe.

She clears her throat. "I received the results from your MRI," she says. "Let's start with the good news."

Wait, what? Start with the good news? Does that mean there's bad news?

She called, I remind myself.

She did not send a MyChart message.

Dr. Macaulay always sends a MyChart message.

I wish I had carried Tony Soprano back here with me. Instead, I reach for a decorative pillow and hold it against my stomach, clutching the embroidered fabric like it's a teddy bear.

"You don't have a brain tumor," Dr. Macaulay says, and my entire body relaxes.

But my relief only lasts for a single beat before the other shoe drops.

"Unfortunately, there's a chance you have MS." Dr. Macaulay pauses. "Multiple sclerosis."

I stop breathing and stare at my knees.

"Are you near a computer?" she asks.

"No," I say, the tremor audible in my voice. "I'm in my bedroom," I add lamely, as if that has anything to do with my access to a laptop.

Dr. Macaulay begins reading me the MRI notes, but it's hard to focus.

"Mild scattered foci of hyperintense..."

Multiple sclerosis. MS. There are a lot of terrifying diseases and syndromes whittled down to acronyms: ALS, COPD, WPW. I'm not entirely sure what multiple sclerosis *is*.

"The findings are suspicious for underlying demyelinating disease/multiple sclerosis..."

Isn't MS a disease where people end up dependent on walkers or confined to wheelchairs? Do I know anyone with MS? Are there any celebrities with it? Oh my God, what a stupid question!

"The findings would satisfy McDonald's criteria for dissemination in space..."

McDonald who? Who the hell is McDonald?

Dr. Macaulay clears her throat. "You'll find this all in your MyChart account."

How can *I* possibly have a disease? I'm an independent, nearly thirty-year-old woman who works a demanding full-time job—would someone with a disease be able to do those things? And I certainly don't look sick. My gray eyes are bright, almost lavender, and I have smooth, clear skin. My face is round and apple-cheeked, far from gaunt, and I have a spirited smattering of freckles across my nose. Shouldn't there be a physical sign of the disease?

"Are you okay?" Dr. Macaulay asks. "Do you have any questions for me?"

"Just a little shocked." Isn't that the correct way to respond? What do patients on *Grey's Anatomy* say after receiving scary diagnoses? Truthfully, I feel both numb and scared.

Okay, I'm more than scared.

I'm pretty terrified.

Even if I don't know what MS is, I know it's bad. I continue onward, ridiculously trying to end this conversation on a positive note. "But, um, there are *way* worse things to show up on an MRI, right?"

Cue the awkward laughter.

Dr. Macaulay does not join in.

Chapter Four

I sit in my dim bedroom, my brain lost in a dense fog. Finally, a thought forces its way to the surface. *I need my mom.* My mom is a nurse, for Pete's sake! And God knows she will burn rubber if one of her kids needs her.

I reach for my phone just as the downstairs buzzer crackles from the living room. My heart lifts, marveling at a mother's intuition.

I hurry toward the intercom, wiping the raw area beneath my eyes as I go. "Hello?" I say, and then, as if my muffled voice hasn't already given away the fact that I've been crying, it actually cracks as I ask, "Mom, is that you?"

"What? No, it's Mattie," I hear in reply.

Super. *Mattie.* My perfect older sister. A woman who is the absolute portrait of good health.

"Are you okay? You sound funny," she continues.

"Everyone sounds funny over an intercom," I reply.

After a pause, Mattie asks, "Well, can I come up?"

I shake my head but say, "Yeah, of course."

Mattie is bounding through my doorway only a few minutes later, which is quite remarkable considering I live on the fourth floor and my building doesn't have an elevator. Or, at least, I think it's my sister. It's hard to tell considering the extravagant floral arrangement she's carrying.

"Mattie," I stutter, bumping into an end table and nearly toppling over a ceramic lamp. (1950s Delft, no less. What a tragedy that would have been.) "What a surprise! Did you get off work early?" Mattie's office is nearly an hour's drive from my apartment, and it's only a quarter after five.

"Happy birthday!" she replies, heaving the flowers toward me. "And yes.

We've actually been doing four o'clock Fridays to improve morale."

I place the bouquet on the countertop where it takes up most of the modest real estate. The lavish arrangement includes white spray roses, red dahlias, hot pink peonies (Where did Mattie find peonies in November?), blue thistle, and lots of eucalyptus. It's absolutely spectacular and stunning, and it must have cost more than two weeks' worth of groceries.

Mattie reaches into her tote and retrieves a bottle of fancy champagne, thrusting it in my direction.

"Wow," I say, my voice unsteady. I hold up the champagne, studying its label and pretending that the information means something to me. "Bottled in 2015!" I manage to say. "Gosh, Obama was still President then."

"A special occasion champagne," Mattie smiles before studying my face so intently, I turn away. "Are you okay?" she asks, her voice low.

Mattie and I don't share clothes, much less our feelings.

I'm an awful liar, so I share another upsetting incident of my afternoon. "Tony Soprano got out, I guess I didn't shut the door tightly when I was bringing up a load of laundry earlier, and it really freaked me out. He was just a floor below, thank God."

Mattie gives a sympathetic hum, but I doubt she understands. She isn't much of a dog person. Dogs are too messy for Mattie's neat world. "I'm glad he's okay," she says. "So! How are you spending the last night of your twenties? Heading downtown with your pals?"

Even though Mattie is only three years older than me, she manages to make everything sound overly formal, like your dad asking a hotel for its "wireless fidelity" password (true story) or your grandma referring to tights as pantyhose.

"I'm pretty tired from the work week," I reply. "But, um, Hannah organized a nice dinner out tomorrow," I add, referring to my best friend and colleague, Hannah Nielsen. You know, so I don't seem completely tragic. "It'll be nice to take it easy tonight. I'm going to watch *Sleepless in Seattle.* Slip away to Nora Ephron's world."

"Well then, shall I stay for a drink?" Mattie asks, dropping her leather handbag and starting to slide out of her parka. "We can order a pizza, split a big salad..."

Everything wrong with my apartment suddenly glares at me, like the basket of unfolded laundry sitting on a dining room chair and the pile of cardboard boxes I still have to break down and recycle. The only company I want this evening is WebMD and Google.

"I feel like we haven't really chatted in a while," Mattie continues. "It would be nice to catch up."

I desperately want to be the type of sisters where there's no need for scheduled "catch-ups." I'd love to be the kind of sisters who don't ever have to say "hello" when we call or text because that's way too formal for us, because our conversation is ever going. Even though Mattie asked me to be her maid of honor in her upcoming wedding, I know she must have done it out of obligation rather than fondness. Mattie is all about etiquette and rules, and if you have a sister remotely close in age, I think it's mandatory or something.

"And you can't spend the eve of your thirtieth birthday alone!" she insists.

I really don't need Mattie's pity party, but she's stubborn. "Let's do a drink," I say, thinking this is the path of least resistance. Have a quick glass of wine and then get rid of her. God knows a bit of booze won't be the worst tincture for my current nerves. "Should we open the champagne you brought?"

The shake of her head is immediate. "Don't waste that nice bottle on me!"

"How about a chenin blanc then?" My voice sounds breezy, but I'm hiding a grimace. Why does she make everything so difficult?

"Great!" she says.

"Great," I echo, reaching for a vintage pink coupe and knocking it over with my trembling fingertips. The crystal makes a high-pitched peal when it hits the tiled countertop, and we both wince. "Sorry about that," I stammer.

"Is everything all right?" Mattie asks for a second time. "Cute glasses by the way. Another one of your flea market finds?"

"I'm just being a ditz. I'm fine." I've chipped a neat triangle from one of the coupe's edges. *Ugh.* "And yeah, sort of. Facebook Marketplace."

But when I try moving the damaged glass to the trash, the coupe slips out of my hands again. This time, it crashes toward the checkered floor, shattering upon impact.

"Shit," I murmur, lowering myself to the ground. "Do not walk over here!" My movements are spastic as I try to gather the tiny pieces in my hands.

"Are you drunk?" Mattie whispers. Her tone is stuck somewhere between playful teasing and genuine concern, which is a tremendously awkward place to be. She's bent down beside me, and I want to shout at her to stand back up. You can see just how filthy my floor is from this angle, see where the cheap linoleum is peeling up and cooking splatters have congealed against the cabinets.

Self-conscious, I shake my head. "Jeez louise, Mattie. *No.*"

I stand up too quickly, losing my balance and slamming a hip against one of the brass cabinet pulls. *Ouch.* That is going to leave a bruise. "Thanks again for the flowers and champagne," I say between gritted teeth. "But maybe it's best if we do that drink another time."

Mattie frowns, genuine worry in her green eyes that makes me feel all the worse.

"Seriously, I'm exhausted," I continue, ushering her toward the front door.

But Mattie stops in the entryway, her body physically blocking me from shutting the door. "I'm sorry. I shouldn't have asked if you were drunk. It was a rude and stupid question," she says. "You just don't seem like yourself, and I don't know... It's basically your birthday, so I figured maybe you got an early start... Anyways, I'm sorry. Are you okay?"

I nervously shift my weight from side to side, debating whether I should confide in her.

"Just some dread over turning thirty tomorrow," I finally say.

I can't remember if I told Mattie about today's MRI. Did Mom mention anything? I hold my breath, wondering if she will bring up this morning's test.

Thankfully, she doesn't.

"The best is yet to come," Mattie says, which couldn't be further from the truth.

Chapter Five

I stand in the hallway, watching Mattie make her way down the stairs with her confident, capable gait. I feel guilty for not trusting my sister with my news, but how could she ever understand?

Mattie is a marathon runner. She eats and drinks in moderation, she gets enough sleep each night, and she never forgets to wear sunscreen. She never finds herself caught in the rain without an umbrella. How could Mattie comprehend the panic of your body potentially failing you? Plus, she is such a motivator, such a doer. I can imagine Mattie setting a 30-second timer for wallowing ("And...stop! Crying time is over!") before making me research therapies and medications.

How exhausting.

But before I can power up my laptop—because like any millennial worth their salt, my immediate reaction is to consult the Internet regarding my prognosis—I'm hit with an almost painful urge to pee.

These intense urges have become typical over the past year, and I practically sprint towards the bathroom. I sit on the cool toilet, and the relief is immediate even though the output is just a trickle. I stare at the retro pink and green tiles that line the walls and think about the urologist I consulted a few months ago, a man with swoopy blonde hair who looked more like a frat dude than a medical specialist.

Dr. Sigma Guy (not his real name) performed an ultrasound of my bladder that didn't result in any brilliant insights. "Overactive bladder syndrome, I guess," he shrugged.

It felt like a throwaway diagnosis.

But this evening's possible diagnosis doesn't feel wrong in my gut.

Tony Soprano pokes his head inside the crack of the bathroom door. Similar to toddlers (so I'm told), dogs don't have much respect for privacy.

"Something might be wrong with me," I tell him somberly, my bottom lip quivering. "I might have MS."

Tony cocks his head curiously, and I appreciate the attentiveness.

"That stands for multiple sclerosis," I say. "We won't know for sure until I see a neurologist. But between you and me? Plus some guy named McDonald? It seems pretty definitive."

I scoop Tony into my arms and sink into the sofa with my laptop. I *love* this sofa. It's actually the denim loveseat I grew up with, a treasure Mom was going to set on the curb for the garbage truck before I intervened. I take a moment to bury my nose into the fabric and breathe in its comforting scent, a smell I'm convinced is still bottled from my happy childhood, though no one believes me.

"What does your childhood smell like?" Janet once asked me. (For the record, she does believe me. Because she's that sort of friend.)

"Fruit Loops, fabric softener, and Mom's Earl Grey tea," I replied.

I relax a little, at least I think I do, until I notice my hands trembling.

I type "What is multiple sclerosis?" into Google and press enter.

The National Multiple Sclerosis Society provides the following definition: "Multiple sclerosis (MS) is an unpredictable disease of the central nervous system that disrupts the flow of information within the brain, and between the brain and body."

"The cause of MS is still unknown," the website continues. "Scientists believe that a combination of environmental and genetic factors contribute to the risk of developing MS. The progress, severity and specific symptoms of MS in any one person cannot yet be predicted. Most people with MS are diagnosed between the ages of 20 and 50, with at least two to three times more women than men being diagnosed with the disease."

The next query takes more moxie.

I assumed the disease's definition would be high-level and clinical, but the answer to this next question could get personal.

"What are the symptoms of multiple sclerosis?" I type.

As my eyes land on each symptom, I actually feel the room start to spin and darken. My heart is racing, and I wonder if I might faint or even throw up.

Fatigue.

Walking difficulties.

Numbness or tingling.

Dizziness and vertigo.

Weakness.

Bladder problems.

The tears are immediate, and I swallow hard, trying to push them down.

I hoped to see foreign symptoms pop up, ailments I've never experienced before. "False alarm!" I would laugh, delirious with relief. "There's no way I have MS." Then, I would close my computer and reclaim my thirtieth birthday, my life.

But I know these symptoms.

These are some of the reasons why I've been in and out of Dr. Macaulay's office so often this past year, from suspected UTIs to undergoing bloodwork to determine if an underactive thyroid was the reason why I felt impossibly tired so much of the time. As for the other symptoms, like walking difficulties and tingling, I'd rationalized they were the effects of being exhausted, of sitting in an awkward position...

They were all so easy to explain away.

I slam my laptop shut and pace the length of my living room, feeling hot and agitated. Panicked. Is this a panic attack? I've never had a panic attack before. I open the fridge with too much force, the door hitting a cabinet with an unhappy clatter of glass condiments, and pull out the bottle of nice champagne. Fumbling with the foil and cork, I pop the "special occasion" sparkling wine and pour it into a juice glass. I take a sip followed by a painful gulp.

Will I need to use a cane someday? A walker? A wheelchair?

Another swallow of champagne.

What if these things happen fast? What if this is all just on the horizon for me?

I down a fresh pour.

Do you know what another symptom of MS is? *Blindness.* This disease could rob me of *my vision* someday. I think of Mary from *Little House on the Prairie.* Will that be me? Will I be like poor Mary Ingalls?

I'm a graphic designer! How am I supposed to do my job without my eyesight?

When the first sob escapes my throat, I press "play" on *Sleepless in Seattle.*

If I'm going to slug champagne and cry, I want Tom Hanks and Meg Ryan to be there with me.

Chapter Six

Brrrrrrring! Brrrrrrring!

I bury my face deeper into the pillow, unable to place the aggressive noise. Did I leave the TV on? Is it my mercurial 1940s alarm clock malfunctioning again?

Brrrrrrring! Brrrrrrring!

It's the buzzer.

I try to blink, to open my eyes, but the mascara I was too lazy to remove before bed stubbornly holds them together. Finally, I'm able to squint at my phone. Why is someone buzzing me at nine-thirty on a Saturday morning? If it's Mattie delivering fresh orange juice and an egg white omelet after her morning run...

Brrrrrrring! Brrrrrrring!

Since whoever it is isn't leaving, I trip towards the intercom. "Hello?" I say, my voice sounding like it belongs to one of Marge Simpson's sisters.

"Hey. It's your DoorDasher," the fuzzy voice replies. "I have a delivery for Bea Parker?"

"Oh," I say, unable to piece together basic words and form a complete sentence. Who sent me a DoorDash order? "Be right down." I need to pee first (of course) and leash up Tony Soprano. Because God knows if I'm going down those stairs now, he's coming with me for his morning bathroom break.

After throwing on a baseball cap and sunglasses (yes, sunglasses!), I struggle down the staircase as quickly as my hungover self can manage. I struggle on the stairs on a normal day, having to intensely focus on each careful step I take, but on this foggy morning, they seem like an obstacle course. My mouth is dry. My head is throbbing. My stomach is gurgling and upset with me. And everything hurts. Even my freckles.

When I open the door, I'm met with a burst of crisp November air and a blessedly quiet sidewalk. If I'd had to make small talk with bright-eyed, lululemon-clad moms pushing their UPPAbaby strollers, I think I'd have melted into a puddle of shame.

"Are you Bea?" a woman calls, exiting a beat-up Ford Taurus. Her hair is pulled into a messy bun, and she's wearing polar bear pajama pants. "I got cold, so I was waiting in my car."

The DoorDasher's eyes widen at the sight of me, and I think, *How pathetic is this? A woman wearing polar bear pajamas thinks* I *look tragic!* She hands me a coffee cup and a small bag from my favorite local coffee shop. I peek inside to see a slice of banana bread. "Thank you," I say.

I'm tempted to add, *I only look this way because my doctor called last night, and I might have a chronic disease.*

"Looks like you need it," she replies. She studies Tony, finding him much more appealing. "Cute dog. My grandma used to have a dapple dachshund."

Once Tony and I are back upstairs, I pop two Ibuprofen tablets and guzzle an entire glass of water. As I slump against a bathroom wall, swallowing the terrible salty taste in my mouth, I scroll through birthday messages. The coffee and banana bread were surprises from Hannah. **Wanted you to have a sweet start to your day!** she's texted me. **HAPPY 30ᵀᴴ BIRTHDAY!!! Love you! See you tonight!**

My mom has already called three times, which is impressive considering it's not even ten a.m. yet. I press the phone against my ear and listen to her voicemail. She loves leaving voicemails, as many moms do.

Good morning, sunshine! How can it be that my youngest is thirty?

My mom isn't an overly sentimental parent—she's far from the mother who has bins full of our childhood artwork and toys stashed in the basement—but birthdays always make her dewy-eyed and doting.

Happy birthday, bumblebee! Call me later, okay? You never told me how your MRI went yesterday. Aunt Julie and I have yoga, and then we're delivering Meals on Wheels this afternoon. Mass is at four thirty, of course, so anyways. Lots going on today, but call when you can. Bye, honey! We love you!

Even though Mom still works part-time, she has more extracurriculars than a student set on attending an Ivy League university.

But when I go to call Mom back, my thumb hovers over the phone, hesitant and unsure. I might have MS. *Might.* Is it worth telling her, worth telling *anyone*, at this point? You don't go around telling people when you might land a new job, or you might be asked on a second date.

And shouldn't I tell Mom in-person? Isn't this the sort of news that deserves to be delivered face to face? I can talk to her and Dad tomorrow at my family birthday dinner. What's the point in upsetting them today?

I know this is all a terrible idea—*of course* I should tell my parents, especially my mom, now, ASAP—but somehow, I'm able to convince myself otherwise. Because apparently I am both diseased and delusional.

I reach for the cup of coffee and take a drink.

"Shit!" I yelp, the liquid still scorching hot.

I immediately lean over and spit the scalding coffee into the bathtub, but my entire mouth is already throbbing. *Fantastic.* I've surely burnt my tongue. There goes the ability to enjoy good food on my birthday.

"I can't even get coffee that hot when I pick it up myself! Did that DoorDasher have a microwave in her car?" I seethe, stalking into the living room. I can feel last night's panic igniting all over again. Except today, it feels a thousand times worse combined with my hangxiety.

"Why is it so warm in here?" I say, my heart racing and my forehead starting to sweat. Is my apartment stuffy, or is this the heat intolerance symptom I read about last night? (This could be why my mind gets all foggy during the hot and humid Cincinnati summers. At least if I have MS, that is.) I fling open a window, causing the ancient screen to nearly topple out of its frame. "And why is this place so junky?"

Tony looks put out by my dramatics and tucks his little head behind his back legs, choosing sleep over witnessing an existential crisis.

My eyes go from the wonky screen to the chipped windowsill paint to the cracks in the plaster walls. I don't even have a kitchen sink disposal, much less an actual dishwasher. Sure, I love old things, but why am I still renting an apartment like this one? It's essentially falling in around me.

From there my mind spirals.

What have I *really* done with my life at this point? What have I achieved? What do I have to show for three decades on this planet? My parents were raising kids by the time they turned thirty, and my dad was running his own business.

Kickerville.

I close my eyes, my headache pangs growing sharper, and retreat to my bedroom.

Kickerville Cabin Co. is the modular home and log cabin business my dad built from the ground up, laying its foundation in his early twenties and finally retiring a few years ago in his mid-sixties. My older brother, Justin, has come and gone since then, choosing New Mexico and a career in solar energy over the family business, and now Mattie is at the helm.

Ever since Mattie took over Justin's responsibilities, she's made it clear this is *her* prize, *her* exclusive club that I am not invited to join.

Whenever I volunteer my design services—"It's on the house, pro bono," I awkwardly add with each desperate offer—Mattie quickly declines. "We've got things under control," she says, which is code for, "We don't need you."

Despite a childhood spent sweeping sawdust and peering longingly over Dad's shoulder as he sketched rustic log cabins, I have no involvement at Kickerville. None whatsoever. And it's my sister, the Parker kid who was much more interested in her Girl Scout troop field trips and volleyball matches, who grabbed the torch.

I pull a sleep mask over my eyes and slide into the cool sheets.

Instead, I'm a mid-level graphic designer at an advertising agency. It's a good job: I have decent benefits, smart colleagues, and occasionally interesting projects.

But it isn't my *raison d'être*.

What even *is* my *raison d'être*?

Here I am on my thirtieth birthday, without a house, a husband, a kid, or a job at the family business.

All I have is a hangover and a potential chronic disease.

And all I want to do is go back to sleep.

Chapter Seven

"You are Emma Thompson's character from *Love Actually*," I tell myself, gliding each hanger aside as I search for a tunic. "Your world is crumbling—your beloved husband is cheating on you, and you know it—but the children have their nativity play tonight, and the show must go on. You've got to act like you're thrilled over that ridiculous Joanie Mitchell album and that everything is fine."

Yes, Emma Thompson will get me through the evening.

I actually cue up Joanie Mitchell's "Both Sides Now" for effect.

I'm heading to Hannah's for early evening apps and cocktails before a nice supper out with a small group of friends. My pals will be expecting the cheerful and chatty Bea Parker, and I'm determined to deliver. Again, why burden everyone with a medical diagnosis that might not even be true?

God, this is all turning into such a mind game.

I find the tunic I've been searching for, a gauzy black one with velvet, floral embellishments, and I slide it over my black top. Despite a closet full of colorful vintage clothes, I've found myself reaching for darker, more muted items this past year. I've gained twenty pounds since January, and dark clothing beneath drapey tunics or oversized cardigans hides it well.

While my diet hasn't changed, my exercise routine has become nonexistent.

It's difficult for me to stick to class commitments, or even complete a solid thirty minutes on the treadmill, when I feel so impossibly tired most of the time. And when I'm not exhausted, those seem to be the days when the dizziness hits.

C'est la vie, am I right?

Do you believe in magic in a young girl's heart?

How the music can free her, whenever it starts

I hear my ringtone echoing from the bathroom and hurry towards it. I left my phone propped against a jar of makeup brushes since I was listening to a true crime podcast while getting ready.

You know, nothing like a cold case to set the tone for my thirtieth birthday celebrations!

To my delight, it's a FaceTime call coming from Justin, which means it's more likely coming from my niece, Violet.

Violet is four years old and my favorite person in the entire world. Her current interests include swimming, grilled cheese sandwiches, coloring on objects she shouldn't, and everything *Bluey* and *Pinkalicious*. She thinks Tony Soprano is the cutest dog ever (duh!), and much to my brother's horror, she says she wants to be just like me someday.

"Hello!" I answer, heading into the living room.

"Happy birthday, Aunt Beezus!" Violet shouts in such a way, I know she's rehearsed. I love that Justin still calls me by my childhood nickname, a reference to the Beverly Cleary books I adored, and that he passed it along to his daughter. "You look *sooooo* pretty. Are you wearing purple eyeliner? I want to wear purple eyeliner! Did you know purple is my new favorite color?"

"Purple is an excellent favorite color. Especially for a gal named Violet," I reply. Spending time with my niece, even over a video call, always lifts my spirits. "But you don't need any eyeliner. You have the best brown eyes, and they're perfect just the way they are."

Unsatisfied with this response, Violet changes the subject. "Did you have any birthday cake yet?"

"Not yet," I say. "But I'm going to my friend Hannah's apartment soon, and we're going out to dinner with a bunch of friends. I suspect there may be a cake at the restaurant."

"I hope it's chocolate on chocolate." I am now staring at Violet's chin. She's not the best videographer, easily distracted by her stuffed animal collection and Magna-Tiles. "What will you get for supper? My mama is having supper with her friends tonight. So Dada is making us mac and cheese."

I love the way Violet says "cheese," replacing the "s" with an exaggerated "z."

"That sounds tasty. Maybe I'll eat mac and cheese, too."

"No. If I were you, I would get mozzarella sticks," she says with such authority, I wonder if my niece is the next Padma Lakshmi. "Can you put Tony Soprano on?"

"Of course." I wander into my bedroom where Tony is napping. "He's sleeping," I stage whisper, pointing at his snoring, gently vibrating body.

Violet lifts the phone, so I can now see her button nose and long eyelashes. "He's the cutest dog in the world. Will you tell him I said that when he wakes up?"

"Hey Vi?" I hear Justin in the background. "Can I have a turn with the phone? I'd like to wish Aunt Beezus a happy birthday."

She gives a long, dramatic sigh that communicates, *Ugh, dads! Am I right?*

"My dad wants to talk now. I love you, Aunt Beezus!"

"I love you more!" I reply before my brother's bright face fills my screen. His green eyes look small and decidedly tired but his smile remains larger than life.

"Happy birthday! The big 3-0!" he grins. "Welcome to the club."

"Is that even more gray I see in your beard?" I tease. Justin is nearing forty himself.

"Probably. Guess what Violet asked us for the other night?"

I frown, thinking this over. "A TikTok account?" I'm no Luddite, but I can't say I'm the savviest social media person around. Honestly, I think we should all go back to rotary phones with their curly cords. Weren't those charming?

"A baby brother or sister," he replies.

I laugh. "What did you and Katie tell her?"

"Katie said that every family is different, that some families have multiple kids and others only have one, and that everyone can be happy in different ways." I watch Justin head into the kitchen with its turquoise backsplash and clean, white cabinets. Justin, Katie, and Violet live in Santa Fe, and their house features all the colors, textures, and sheer magic of the Southwest. "Violet wasn't satisfied with that answer, so I told her to write a letter to the stork."

"Nice. What's his mailing address these days?"

"Funny you should ask." Justin opens a bottle of beer. "I gave her your address."

I snort. "So, the stork lives in Cincinnati, Ohio, huh?"

"Please write her back and say something like, 'You and your parents make a happy trio, and I believe things are great just the way they are.'" He takes a long first drink. "I don't know. You're creative. You'll think of something better, I'm sure."

"You're absurd," I say. "Can't you at least get her a shelter cat?"

"Allergic," he says matter-of-factly, and I realize I have no idea which family member he's talking about. "So, how have you been celebrating today?"

I bite my bottom lip. Should I tell Justin about yesterday's conversation with Dr. Macaulay? He'll be a good first person to confide in: easygoing, rational, and optimistic. Before I can lose my courage, I decide to plow onward.

"Honestly, my birthday got off to a pretty bizarre start." I look at the ceiling as I say this next part. "I had an MRI yesterday, and they think I might have MS."

But when I look back at my screen, Justin's face is frozen in his earlier smile.

The screen gives a spastic flicker before my brother's face becomes animated once more. "Sorry, Beezus. What was that? You were cutting in and out," he says, though now it's impossible to hear him over the sound of Violet belting a *Peppa Pig* song. God, she's even nailing the British accent, that star.

"I'll tell you later," I say quickly. "I'd better get going."

Chapter Eight

The Uber drops me off at six o'clock in front of Hannah's stately brick and sandstone apartment building. The sun's already set for the evening, and the night is black and cold. I should have worn boots instead of mules, but slides and flats have become yet another dependency this year. Regular shoes require too much balance and too much coordination. I teeter as I try to slip my foot inside a bootie or even a gym shoe, toppling this way and that. I wish I could pinpoint when such simple tasks became insurmountable feats. Even taking a hot shower leaves me dizzy and disoriented these days. But there is no clear before and after for me, just a bunch of gray.

MS, MS, MS! my brain sputters.

"Thanks for the ride," I tell my driver, a middle-aged woman named Sandra who chatted excitedly about her pet hedgehog named Watson. Honestly, I learned quite a bit. Did you know hedgehogs are nocturnal? "Have a safe night. And give my regards to Watson."

"He'll like that." I imagine a tidy hedgehog giving a gracious bow. "Thanks, sweetie."

Hannah and her boyfriend, Arthur, live beside Washington Park in Cincinnati's Over-the-Rhine neighborhood. They have a spectacular view of historic Music Hall and can walk to dozens of restaurants, shops, and cafes as well as their respective downtown offices. The entry to their Queen Anne-style building is already decorated with twinkling white lights, and there are holiday fir branches and pinecones in all the ground floor window boxes. Their landlord is an interior designer and basically the exact opposite of my landlord, Stanley.

I press the button for apartment #3 and wait for Hannah to answer.

"Bea? Is that you?" she asks, her voice fuzzy over the intercom.

My teeth chatter in the cold. "Were you expecting Chinese food?"

"Oh, stop it. Come on up, birthday girl!"

At the sound of the buzzer, I grab the vibrating door handle and enter the toasty lobby. The radiator hisses against a plaster wall, and a group of twenty-somethings practically spills down the stairs in a sea of laughter, flared jeans, and expensive-smelling perfumes. Between my new thirty-something age and probably diseased status, I feel ancient in comparison.

I stare upwards at the wide staircase the whippersnappers just came down and opt for the building's creepy elevator instead. It's one of those ancient models with accordion doors, but I'm thankful not to have to slog up three flights of steps. I don't want to show up at Hannah's all sweaty and dizzy.

As the elevator croaks up, up, up, I find my spirit doing the same.

I'm not going to worry about MS or whatever the future days or weeks have in-store for me. It's my thirtieth birthday, and I'm going to clink champagne flutes with my best friend and have an overly indulgent night out.

It's my party, and I won't cry if I don't want to! So there, Universe!

I'm touched to see a handful of balloons tied to Hannah and Arthur's front door. It's adorable and totally something my mom would do. I give a few perfunctory knocks. "Hi! I'm here!" I announce.

"Come on in!" Hannah calls.

I open the door and am met with darkness. But before I can think *Surprise party?* the lights come on, and a room full of people shouts, "SURPRISE! HAPPY BIRTHDAY!" A few kazoos sound, and confetti poppers spray colorful squares through the air.

"Oh, wow! *Wow,*" I breathe, suddenly a bit lightheaded and my balance unsteady. Hannah tackles me with a hug, and I hold on to her tight, both out of love and for sheer physical support. "Hannah! What the heck? I had no idea you were up to something like this!"

"I'd call it a successful surprise party then," she beams. Arthur walks over next, giving me a hug and a flute of champagne. "Notice anything?" Hannah asks, her brown eyes excited and playful.

"Give me a minute to catch my breath!" I say, taking a sip of my drink. With my heart beating wildly, I look around Hannah and Arthur's apartment, wondering who all is in attendance tonight.

The first guests to catch my eye are Mattie and Peter. Ah yes, the blonde and the beautiful. Honestly, I'm surprised my sister and future brother-in-law have graced us with their presence. Surely they have some other fancier event to make an appearance at tonight.

Mattie looks radiant with her hair swept into a low chignon. She's wearing a satin yellow dress that hugs her delicate curves just so. Honestly, she looks more fitting of the guest of honor designation than me. Come to think of it, she's a dead ringer for Kate Hudson in *How to Lose a Guy in 10 Days*.

Wait a second...

My cousin Allison is wearing a pink two-piece suit and has a stuffed animal chihuahua tucked inside her shoulder bag. *Elle Woods*. My friend Dave, a mild-mannered financial analyst, looks hilariously edgy in a black tank top and black jeans while his wife dons blue jeans and a white shirt tied just above her stomach. Johnny Castle and Baby! My other friend, Kristen, and her long-time boyfriend, Paul, are dressed as Sally Albright and Harry Burns, complete with two very amusing wigs.

"Oh my God!" I squeal. "Everyone is a different rom com character!"

I glance back to Hannah and Arthur, taking a closer look at their own ensembles. Hannah has her braids pulled into a variety of high ponytails and is wearing a silky, rainbow swing dress that shows off her mile-long legs. A giant butterfly necklace rests on her chest, and there are strokes of heavy pink blush across her chestnut-colored cheeks. As for Arthur, he's wearing gray slacks and a light blue shirt as opposed to his standard flannel and jeans.

I point at them. "You're Jenna and Matt! From *13 Going on 30!*"

"Well hunky-dory, that's impressive," Arthur says in his ridiculously charming British accent. "I feel like I look like any random dude you'd see on the street." Honestly, Arthur *does* look like any random dude you'd see on the street, but when he's standing beside Hannah, it's easy to deduce.

"Is it weird?" Hannah asks, sounding slightly unsure. "Remember how much we loved that scene from Mindy Kaling's *Four Weddings and a Funeral* remake? I thought it would be fun to recreate it for you. I *wanted* Arthur to be Quincy, and I'd be Monica, from *Love and Basketball*—"

"—but there was no way I was pulling that one off," Arthur says with a wry smile. His short, boxy stature and reddish hair admittedly don't give off Omar Epps vibes.

I give Hannah another hug. "This is honestly the best birthday present you could have given me. Thank you."

Hannah is the greatest. She's the sort of friend you can tag in an Instagram contest to win a dog version of a Baby Bjorn, and she won't be annoyed (or, you know, weirded out). She is such an optimist, she reports the weather as "partly sunny," and she always fills out those associate surveys the grocery store cashier hands you at checkout. Whenever she takes her first sip of morning coffee, a beatific smile spreads across her face before she gives a happy sigh, and you half-wonder if you've stumbled into a Folgers commercial. But it's all genuine with Hannah. She is just that sweet.

"Well, you obviously need a costume yourself." She nods toward her and Arthur's bedroom. "I set out two options. One is Mia Thermopolis—I asked your mom for that strapless dress you wore to prom, and then I found white gloves and a tiara. And the other is Vivian Ward. My aunt had a polka dot dress from the 80s she let me borrow. It even has a matching hat! I know how much you love 80s fashion."

"So, my choices are a princess or a prostitute?"

Hannah and Arthur laugh.

"I'll try on both and see what looks best. Seriously, Han. Thanks." I pause, bringing my friend in close. "I'm wearing natural deodorant tonight. Do I stink?"

Hannah gives me a few sniffs. "You're good. I only smell lavender, I think."

"Who knew quitting aluminum would be so tricky?"

"Detox is a process, babe," Hannah says. "Now go get changed!"

Hannah and Arthur's bedroom is less polished than the rest of their apartment, which boasts exposed ductwork, brick walls, and Hannah's extensive art collection, but I like it back here. There are the same floor-to-ceiling windows and gorgeous city views as the living room, but the furniture is mismatched and well-loved, like Hannah's childhood four-poster bed and the pair of nightstands Arthur and his father built when he was just a boy. A standing desk with an expansive oak top is positioned in front of one of the windows. It's where Hannah makes her polymer clay earrings, which she sells at various art fairs and from her Etsy shop.

Maybe now that I'm thirty, I'll start a side hustle, I muse.

Blessedly, Hannah didn't set my costume choices across the bed, now covered in guests' coats. Instead, she hung them on the back of the closet door.

I finger the white satin dress longingly, wishing I could be Mia Thermopolis tonight. I would love to wear an elegant gown and a sparkly tiara. But there is no chance my prom dress, with its pretty silver threading, will fit, so I'm stuck being Vivian Ward.

Or at least I *hope* I'm stuck being Vivian Ward. What if that dress doesn't fit me either? With my eyes squeezed shut and a silent prayer, I step into the frock and let out a huge sigh of relief once I realize it zips. Hannah's aunt must be pear-shaped like me. Thank Christ.

The brown polka dot dress is admittedly very lovely, so is the matching hat, but really? A prostitute "saved" by Richard Gere? There are so many better leading ladies! I could have been hardworking and brave Lucy from *While You Were Sleeping* or kind and smart Iris from *The Holiday.*

With a sigh, I pull on the white gloves from the Mia Thermopolis ensemble and twist my dark hair into a low bun. I gamely grab my drink and walk back out to mingle with my guests and celebrate.

"*Pretty Woman!* I love it," my sister says, giving me a kiss on the cheek like we're French or just plain fussy. "Remember how Mom wouldn't let us rent that movie until we were in high school? She always made us pick a Mary-Kate and Ashley movie instead."

"We were so deprived," I smile, pleased Mattie remembers those Blockbuster trips. It's the warm satisfaction I feel whenever Mattie remembers just about anything remotely personal about me or us.

"Happy birthday!" says Peter, giving me a warm hug. Peter has wispy blonde hair and kind eyes. He smiles easily and has a relaxed disposition that complements Mattie's rigidness. Opposites attract and all that jazz. "How was your day?"

I woke up feeling like I was going to hurl and spent most of the afternoon in an existential crisis as I contemplated my own mortality and failures!

"Not bad!" I reply instead.

"It was nice of Hannah to include us tonight," says Mattie, sounding like your proper Great Aunt Delores. "And I love the theme. Very festive."

"Did you listen to this week's episode of *You're Wrong About?*" Peter asks, referencing our favorite podcast that re-examines past people and events and gives listeners the true story. "Pretty mind-boggling, huh?"

"I did! Totally mind-boggling," I reply. How bizarre is it that my future brother-in-law and I share a favorite podcast, but my sister and I don't? "Mattie, you should really listen sometime. I think you'd love it. The hosts are hilarious, and they cover tons of topics from our childhood."

She gives a good-natured shrug as Peter says, "Mattie claims she only has time for *The Daily* and *Up First*."

"I like those shows, too. I'm very interested in current events," I volunteer weakly, proving there is no person I act more awkward around than my very own sister. "So, where did you find a dress like that? You look gorgeous."

"Nordstrom," she replies, before spinning the subject back to me, since it's my birthday and that is the polite thing to do. "Hannah told me she'd gotten your prom dress from Mom. I'm shocked you didn't choose the Mia Thermopolis costume! You were obsessed with *The Princess Diaries* and the idea of a foot-popping first kiss."

I've gained twenty pounds this year! I want to scream. *Why did anyone think a dress from twelve years ago would fit me? Are my drapey clothes really working that well?*

Instead, I try to smile. "Polka dots are so cheerful! I couldn't resist."

From there, I visit with various cousins, friends, and colleagues. Everyone has dressed up. Everyone! Even my team's curmudgeonly copy director is dressed as Mr. Darcy, which I find especially fitting. Arthur has a fire roaring in the massive, wood-burning hearth, and Hannah manages to find a playlist titled "Nancy Meyers' Kitchen" that instantly conjures the warm, cozy feelings of the director's iconic film sets.

There are all sorts of apps spread across the kitchen counter, from tzatziki and pita chips to cocktail weenies, and there's even a three-tiered birthday cake, "a layer for each decade" according to Hannah. (It's chocolate on chocolate. Violet would approve.) Metallic balloons are tied to various pieces of furniture, and around midnight, we pull out the karaoke machine.

"Okay, Bea," Arthur grins, his freckled complexion ruddy and merry. He has some sort of app pulled up on their TV and is ready to cue the music. "What's it gonna be?"

"Britney Spears!" I exclaim, not needing a second of thought.

"Yes! Britney Spears!" Hannah cheers.

Hannah and I croon classics such as "Baby One More Time" and "Oops!... I Did It Again" to the amusement of our fellow (very tipsy) party revelers. But right when I decide that yes, I *am* having a rather wonderful time, I feel a sharp jolt in my right arm and drop the microphone. A painful screech sounds throughout the apartment, and everyone covers their ears.

"Nice one, Bea!" A guy from the animal rescue where I volunteer calls out. Everyone laughs, me loudest of all, before returning to their drinks and conversations.

But Hannah's eyebrows are furrowed. "You all right?" she asks. "You looked like you got electrocuted."

"Just a random arm spasm," I reply, my voice too high, too bright.

"What did it feel like?" she asks.

"I think I need a fresh drink," I say, even though another boozy beverage is just about the last thing I need right now.

Before Hannah can ask any more probing questions, I make a beeline for the crowded kitchen. "Any chance I can get in there?" I say to the couple, AKA Cher Horowitz and Josh Lucas, who are making out in front of the wine selection. Once they stop swapping saliva, I realize Josh is actually David, Hannah's little brother.

"Oh. Hey, David," I say, finding this tremendously uncomfortable. "How have you been?"

When I first met David, he was a nerdy high schooler with a high voice and low self-esteem. Now, he is a sinewy twenty-two-year-old *man* with dreadlocks. And apparently, he's someone who makes out in public places.

It's been quite the transformation.

"And..." Oh, no. What's David's girlfriend's name? She's been around for years now. There was even a night last summer when we drank too many margaritas, and she showed me her secret Pinterest wedding board. "Leslie!" I stupidly take a guess, which you should never do when it comes to someone's name, relationship status, or maybe baby bump. "Hi."

"It's Lisa," she frowns, swinging her long, black hair over her shoulder with understandable sass.

My hand trembles as I hold up the half-empty bottle of red wine. "Too much of this," I say, even though I know alcohol isn't the reason why my brain struggled to remember the girl's name. "Sorry about that."

I stick a fresh Solo cup under the kitchen tap and fill it with water. I swallow the lump in my throat.

I probably have MS.

How dare I forget it.

Chapter Nine

I spend the next day dodging Mom's calls. It is completely out of character for me and totally immature.

And yet, I switch my phone to "do not disturb" mode, turn on *Derry Girls*, and try to lose myself in my tiny house drawings instead.

Ever since passing a tiny house being towed on the highway, I've been completely obsessed with the astonishingly small and outrageously adorable homes. I watch all of the shows—*Tiny House Nation, Tiny House Hunters,* you name it—and follow dozens of tiny homeowners' Instagram accounts and YouTube channels.

But my most favorite activity is sketching my own tiny house creations.

Sometimes the houses are ridiculously over the top, with built-in espresso machines and hot tubs on roof decks. Other times, they include features I haven't seen before, like a second-story greenhouse or a hidden library behind a moving wall. But mostly, they're simply cozy illustrations that make me feel happy and inspired.

But even tiny house dreamland can't calm today's panic.

Should I tell my family about my *maybe* MS? I mean, of course I should, but how do I go about telling them? You never hear stories about people summoning their loved ones to announce they "might" have cancer or they "might" have an incurable disease. What is the etiquette for possible diagnoses?

You do have MS, a small voice says from somewhere deep inside me. *You do have MS, and you know it.*

"I don't know it, though. I won't know until a neurologist sees my

MRI scans," I reply, officially reaching a new level of crazy by conversing with myself.

After feeding Tony Soprano an early supper, I lock my front door and hustle down the stairs. My parents are expecting me at their west side Mc-Mansion in twenty minutes, and I have a nearly forty-minute drive ahead. The numbers are not in my favor.

My heart skips at the sight of the new tenant, Chris Little, in the lobby. He's pinning a piece of paper to the bulletin board no one uses. Before he can see me, I smooth my dress and give my hair a quick tousle. "Hey there," I say, excited for him to see me cool and composed and not chasing down a wayward wiener dog.

"Ope!" he startles, literally jumping backward. The sheet of paper floats towards the floor followed by the delicate *ting* of the push pin.

Not exactly the reaction I was hoping for.

I pick up both the flyer and push pin. "Sorry about that. This is becoming a bad habit of mine. First, my dog nearly trips you, and now it's me taking you by surprise. I promise we don't sneak around waiting to scare people."

"I have a bad habit of getting lost in my own head," he says, smiling so that his one dimple shows.

Damn, that dimple is cute.

I examine the piece of paper. If Chris plans on displaying it for the entire apartment building to read, I may as well look at it now.

COMPOSTING NOW AVAILABLE AT THE AMELIA!!!

Hello. My name is Chris Little, and I recently moved into 3A. I'm passionate about composting, but I know it's a tough task for many apartment dwellers. I'll be leaving a bin outside my door starting tomorrow (11/23) to collect compost for the building. Check out the approved list of compostable items below and then drop in whatever you've got! I'll take it to my parents' composter whenever it gets full, so don't hold back. I can empty it as often as we need! Thanks! Let me know if you have any questions.

"Composting, huh?" I hand him back his flyer.

"Nearly 40% of the food produced in the United States is thrown away each year. I figure the least I can do is compost as much of that waste as I can. Keep it out of landfills, you know?" He pushes his tortoise glasses back on his nose, and his brown eyes gleam with a sort of intensity. "Even worse, more than 44 million Americans struggle with food insecurity. What a terrible disconnect."

"I didn't know the numbers were that awful," I admit, not quite sure what to say. Also, how does this dude retain stats like that? Even before my body started acting weird, I wouldn't have been able to report numbers and figures on demand.

"Well, um, thank you for bringing composting to the Amelia," I stumble. "I think it's great, and I'm sure everyone will appreciate your efforts."

That's a bit of a lie. I consider the college-aged guys in 2B who are constantly throwing their beer cans into the garbage cans rather than the recycling bins. Even well-intentioned Janet might need a composting primer.

"It's the least I can do." Chris's face relaxes. "You look very nice tonight."

I blush, surprised by his compliment. "Thanks. This is my favorite dress and my favorite coat. I found them both at a vintage shop in Northside. They're from the 40s." I run a hand along the mink collar. "Sometimes I feel bad about the fur, I would *never* buy a new piece of fur, but I figure what's done is done. This mink's been gone for nearly eighty years now."

Chris smirks. "I think you have a point there. And buying vintage is the way to go! I exclusively wear secondhand clothing."

"Yeah?" I am amused.

"Yeah, but for environmental reasons. The fashion industry is responsible for around ten percent of annual global carbon emissions. Isn't that horrible?" Chris cringes.

I nod, it is horrible, but I'm also wearing a new pair of tights and booties from a department store that are decidedly fast fashion. I'm not sure I can cast a stone here.

"Oh, and I'm a climatarian," he offers somewhat shyly.

"I'm sorry, but *what?*" I ask, intrigued.

"It's a diet that's focused around the climate crisis," he explains. "A lot of people mistake me for a vegan, but I do eat animal products when they're locally and sustainably sourced. Oh, and organic, of course. There's a lot to consider when you're a climatarian."

This guy is *intense.*

"Wow. It certainly sounds like it," I reply, trying to wrap my own mind around it all. "But, um, that's very admirable of you, eating that way."

I look down at our feet. Chris is wearing a pair of suede moccasins, and I wonder if he only buys used shoes as well.

"Well, I'd better get going," I say. "I'm running late for dinner."

"A date?" Chris asks, surprising me. He shakes his head. "I'm sorry, that's none of my business, I don't know why—"

I'm flattered, and the skip in my heart spreads to a warm feeling in my belly. "No, just a small birthday celebration at my parents' house. My sister and her fiancé are coming, plus my weird aunt Amethyst who invites herself to everything."

Chris smiles. "I think we've all got a weird aunt Amethyst. Have a nice evening."

Chapter Ten

"You're half an hour late!" Mom welcomes me when I walk through their front door. "I was getting worried." Mom is the most punctual person I know, arriving at every engagement fifteen minutes early. Definitely one of those *if you're not early, you're late* types. "Did you run into traffic?"

I give her a hug, breathing in her vanilla-sugar scent. I want to bury my face in her cardigan and tell her everything that's happened since Friday. "No. I got caught up talking with a new neighbor," I say instead, blaming my tardiness on the five-minute encounter rather than the hours of *Derry Girls* that preceded it.

"Is that any way to greet the birthday girl?" Dad booms, rounding the corner from their gourmet kitchen. He's wearing the apron Mattie and Peter bought for *his* last birthday, a posh Hedley & Bennett one that replaced his kitschy *Kiss the Cook* apron, a downright tragedy in my opinion, and wipes his hands on his thighs. "Hey sweetie. Happy birthday! You look beautiful."

Dad gives me one of his warm hugs. If Mom smells like vanilla and sugar, Dad smells like sawdust and garlic. Since retiring, Dad splits his time between the workshop and the kitchen. He is a creator, through and through, and I like to think I've taken after him in that way.

The doorbell rings.

"That must be your sister," says Mom to Dad.

"I'll go get it," says Dad to Mom.

Mom ushers me into the living room where she's hung the traditional foil birthday banner across the fireplace mantel—I swear it must be from the early 90s—and has apple-scented candles wafting a sweet, crisp scent into the air. A small pile of presents sits beside one of the armchairs, and a jazz album is playing on the Sonos. Mattie and Peter are curled up in the loveseat with glasses of iced tea, and they get up to greet me.

"Long time no see," Peter smiles. He can be pretty corny.

"Super party last night," Mattie says. "Your friends and colleagues are lovely."

Lovely? My friends and colleagues are a lot of things—creative, witty, sarcastic, smart, fun—but I'm not sure lovely is the first adjective that comes to mind.

"Thanks again for coming," I reply. Mom hands me my own glass of unsweetened iced tea with extra lemon, a Parker family favorite. "I had a blast. You're lucky you left before Hannah and I busted out the karaoke machine."

"I don't think my skin could have handled any more alcohol." Mattie points to a flawless cheek. "Too much wine never agrees with my complexion," she says, attempting self-deprecation and failing miserably. "Sometimes I miss wearing a mask."

"Watch what you're saying," Mom says, the pandemic's devastation fresher in her nurse's heart than any of us could begin to understand. She plops down on the sofa and pats the seat beside her. "How come you never called me back yesterday or today? A few texts? That's all I get from my daughter on her birthday?"

I start to squirm. "Um, well…"

Mom narrows her eyes, a thought suddenly occurring to her. "Your MRI results were normal, right? All good on that front?"

"Ha, funny you should ask—"

"I brought crudités!" Aunt Amethyst exclaims, entering the living room like a starlet sauntering onto the stage. She sets the veggie tray on the coffee table and gives me air kisses. "Happy birthday, Beatrix, darling."

I thank my eccentric aunt and introduce myself to her latest beau.

"Thomas Buchanan," he says, his eyebrows and mustache wagging in tune with his jaunty handshake. "Pleasure."

"You'll never believe how we met," Aunt Amethyst trills, tossing her lavender scarf over her shoulder and nearly swatting Mom in the face. "We're both long-time season ticket holders with the symphony, and this past year, poor Gertrude—she's the woman who held the seat beside mine— passed away. She was ninety-six, so she lived a good life. Anyways. Thomas changed his seat assignment after Gertrude's seat became available, and that was that!"

"That was that!" Thomas echoes.

"Love at first sight?" I try not to smirk. Aunt Amethyst has a new boyfriend every few months, and every man is The One. If they last longer than four weeks, she usually invites them to move in with her. Relationships are hot and heavy and move very fast in Aunt Amethyst's world. "How romantic."

While Mom, Dad, Aunt Amethyst, and Thomas disappear into the kitchen to make drinks—they all love Tom Collins cocktails; it's probably the only thing Mom and Aunt Amethyst have in common—Mattie, Peter, and I giggle to ourselves.

"She's been chatting about him nonstop," Mattie divulges.

Aunt Amethyst is Kickerville Cabin Co.'s one-woman creative team, a position she's held for nearly thirty years now, and with Dad retired, Mattie has to deal with our aunt more than anybody. Every time Mattie turns down one of my offers to help with Kickerville's creative—Aunt Amethyst has a habit of getting easily overwhelmed and snippy—I can't help but think how pathetic it is that my sister would rather deal with our aunt's quirks than work with me.

"Apparently, Thomas made her a recording of himself playing *Phantom of the Opera* songs on his violin," Mattie continues. "It's what she falls asleep to every night."

"Oh, lord!" I laugh. "Well, he beats her last three boyfriends. He seems pleasant enough. And pretty normal, all things considered."

"So, speaking of new romances..." My sister and Peter exchange *a look* before they both focus back on me. "One of Peter's college friends just moved back from Chicago, and we think you two would have a lot in common."

"He's a terrific guy, Bea," Peter says. "You'd have fun together, I think."

I blink.

"Wait, like you want to fix us up?" I ask.

Mattie and Peter nod.

I stare at them, waiting for the other shoe to drop. *We thought you could groom his dog,* Mattie might say. Or maybe, *We thought you could design his wedding invitations! He's marrying a hot heiress this summer!*

When it doesn't arrive, I hesitantly ask, "On a date? Like a romantic one?"

"Yes," Mattie laughs. "Exactly. Is that so strange?"

Honestly, it *is* strange. I've never asked to be set up before, nor has Mattie ever offered. I figure it's because I don't fit into the perfect world that orbits my older sister. Mattie, Peter, and their pals are fit, fashionable, and flush. Their Instagram feeds are expertly filtered and glamorous, featuring European holidays, designer dog breeds, monogrammed *everything*, and extravagant meals at the latest and greatest restaurants.

Is this friend of Peter's the black sheep of the group? Is he a total weirdo everyone has just learned to tolerate over the years? I imagine a thirty-something nose picker that wears socks with sandals.

And let's be real, blind dates are a lot like one-size-fits-all jumpsuits. The idea of this person (or ensemble) fills you with hope! Excitement! But ultimately? The fit is all wrong. Fabulous in theory, but too good to be true. That's been my experience with blind dates (and jumpsuits).

Despite this, I'm interested.

"I would love to meet your friend," I say, cautiously optimistic. "What's his name?"

"Yeah?" Mattie lets out a little squeal. I love seeing this slightly less polished side of my sister. "Oh, this is going to be wonderful! I really think you're going to like him. His name is John Noble. He's tall, handsome, and has a great job."

"What does he do?" I've harbored a vegetarian firefighter fantasy for years now.

"He works in finance," says Mattie, reminding me that she and I have very different definitions of *great job*.

"He's also a very nice guy and loves dogs," Peter adds.

Mattie squeezes my knee. "Now that we have your blessing, I'll pass along your number. This is exciting, Bea!"

It *is* exciting.

John Noble, I muse. What a chivalrous name. The finance job seems a tad boring, but if he loves dogs, he must have some personality.

Thanksgiving is this Thursday and then Christmas, of course, and New Year's will come charging along after that. It's a nice time to be coupled off, to have a special person. Even if John Noble turns out to be a dud, it would be fun to enjoy the holiday hoopla with a plus one by my side. I think of us snuggled on the sofa watching Christmas movies, our pups cozied up beside us and a half-finished game of Monopoly on the coffee table.

"Kids?" Dad calls into the living room. "Time to dish up!"

Chapter Eleven

We fill our plates with steaming shrimp and scallop scampi in the kitchen before moving to the formal dining room. I smile at the colorful balloons, a single one tied to each chair, and the awkward childhood photos Mom has set on the buffet.

Everything about my parents' house feels larger than life. It's Dad's pride and joy, one of the few custom homes he built during his career, and no expense had been spared. For example, the dining room has a mural of cherubs painted on the ceiling while a Swarovski crystal chandelier hangs over the colonial-style table that seats *twelve*.

It is totally extravagant and slightly gaudy. And it definitely gives off Carmela Soprano vibes.

Now that my parents are well into their sixties and Mom is retiring next spring, they're ready to downsize. "Maybe a condo downtown that overlooks the river," Mom likes to say. "Or one of those cute landominiums near a golf course."

While Dad agrees it's time to find someplace smaller, he's struggling with the likely possibility that he may not live in a Kickerville home. "If that's important to you, make it a priority to buy a piece of land instead," I tell him. "And build one of your smaller modular homes there."

But between us? I think Dad is tired. I don't know if he has another home build in him.

We enjoy pleasant chit chat for approximately three minutes before Mom turns her attention to me. I escaped her earlier question thanks to Aunt Amethyst's dramatics, and she's ready to pounce.

"So!" she says. "Your MRI. I assume all's okay? Because you would have told me otherwise."

I stare down at my lap instead of into Mom's gray eyes, eyes that are remarkably like my own. Oh God, I feel so immature. Why didn't I say anything before this? "Probably," I mumble, taking a generous bite of scampi.

"What was that, honey?" Mom straightens in her chair. I look up briefly to see the concern that has wrinkled itself into her forehead.

I hold up my finger and give an awkward smile, pretending to be too busy chewing to answer. *Shit, shit.* What am I going to say? I don't want to tell my entire family the news over my birthday dinner. I was hoping for a quiet moment alone with my parents. After telling them the news, I planned to tell Mattie and Justin later.

This is too much at once.

"Things are *probably* fine, but they might not be," I venture, hugging the line between healthy and sick, between normal and diseased.

I shrug and reach for my water glass, eager to fill my mouth with anything other than words. I take a long glug. Everyone has stopped eating, even Thomas Buchanan, and all eyes are on me.

I swallow, realizing there is no way out of this.

"I might have multiple sclerosis," I offer weakly.

And there it sits for a beat of excruciating silence.

No one breathes.

The possibility hangs there in the room, sucking up every bit of oxygen.

And then Aunt Amethyst collapses into Thomas Buchanan's arms with a performance-of-a-lifetime sigh. Thomas Buchanan, who apparently works on his HR department's benefits team, begins to rattle off health insurance information. Dad gets red in the face and flustered. Peter looks sad, and Mattie asks too many questions.

"Who called you with the results?"

"How certain are they?"

"Will they do further testing?"

"Do you already have an appointment with a neurologist?"

"Did you find out on Friday?" I see the suspicion pass over Mattie's face before the realization, and subsequent hurt, register. "You found out on Friday, didn't you? Right before I came over. That's why you were acting so strange. Why didn't you tell me?"

I avoid Mattie's wounded gaze and instead look to my ever-calm, ever-capable mother. Growing up, she was essentially the neighborhood's resident nurse. Every kid's parents brought their "Does this need stitches?" and "Is this bug bite a spider bite?" questions to our door. And Mom had the confidence and knowledge to answer those questions, too. She would either provide the care needed or send them to the appropriate place if the skills were outside her wheelhouse. Coupled with her soothing nature, Mom eased so many anxious minds and hearts over the years.

But her eyes are glassy now, and her lips are trembling.

She's scared.

I've never seen my mother look scared before, at least not regarding my health, and her palpable fear makes me feel unsteady and sick.

"I'm sorry, if you'll just excuse me," I say with a politeness that feels uncomfortable for the family dinner table. My movements clumsy and heavy, almost oafish, I shuffle towards the powder room. I run my hands under freezing cold water before pressing them against my face.

My mom slips inside only a few moments later.

I sit on the closed toilet seat, and she kneels in front of me.

"It's okay," she murmurs, running her fingertips through my hair and gently against my scalp, just like she used to do when I was upset as a child. "It's all going to be okay."

"But what if it's not?" I stare at the geometric patterned wallpaper, which immediately makes me dizzier. I close my eyes. "What if I *do* have MS? What if it's not all going to be okay?"

Mom stops stroking my hair. She reaches for my clammy hand, but she is quiet.

It's the first time my mom doesn't have all the answers.

Chapter Twelve

I wake up the next morning to an onslaught of family texts.

From Mom: I'm going to 6AM mass and lighting ALL the available candles. It's going to be okay, sweetie. Did you know the patron saint of multiple sclerosis is St. Lidwina of Schiedam? She was Dutch.

(Does Mom expect me to pray while wearing wooden shoes and holding a wedge of gouda cheese?)

From Dad: Love ya, kiddo. Hang in there.

From Aunt Amethyst: If you *do* have MS, you should consider writing a memoir. I've always thought I'd be a good ghost writer, and I'd be honored to tell your story. We'll split the profits 50/50, but I'm open to negotiations. LMK! Sending you ~*~love and peace~*~

From Mattie: I wish you would have told me on Friday. I could have been there for you.

I throw on a coat, tuck my phone inside my pocket, and then grab Tony's harness, leash, and a poop bag. I slip down the first flight of stairs and hiss a four-letter word.

Thankfully, I'm able to catch myself on the banister, but I've landed right in front of Chris's front door with a low *thud*. I stand there, leaning against the wall, and try not to breathe too loudly, even though it feels like my heart has dropped into my stomach. I can make out the muffled sound of a television and coffee percolating inside Chris's apartment, but it doesn't seem like he heard my tumble.

MS! MS! MS! my brain shouts.

No, I tell my brain. *This is how it's always been.*

My legs always feel wobbly, and very unreliable, after first waking up.

I'm sure everyone feels this way when getting out of bed in the morning. After lying in the same position for eight hours, it isn't the craziest idea that your limbs might feel stiff.

But when I stop into the French-style bakery later that morning before work, I'm hit with another eerie echo of the disease.

Madeleine is located just beneath Polly Feinstein, the ad agency where I work. William, the bakery's owner and a total Francophile, immediately begins filling a small box with jewel-toned macarons for me.

Let's just say I'm a bit of a regular.

"Anything else I can get you this morning?" he asks cheerfully.

"Yes, please! I'll have the, um..." I stare at the chocolate-filled croissants Hannah loves, but the term for them escapes me. What are they called again? Not Danish, certainly not cannoli. *Pane* something... Or pain...

"The pain au chocolat?" William offers, seeing me struggle.

"Yes." Embarrassed, I over-order. "A dozen of them."

"Bien sûr," says William. "You're going to be the office heroine this morning."

That wasn't an isolated innocent, my brain reminds me. *You've been struggling to think of correct words for a while now...*

MS! MS! MS! it seems to scream.

Everyone forgets words sometimes! I want to shout back, though my skin has turned cold and prickly. Because these moments feel different than those slips of mind. It feels like there's this dense fog between my brain and the thought I'm after, and no matter what I do, I can't seem to illuminate my way through it.

Instead, I focus on William delicately setting the pain au chocolate pastries into a pastel pink box that matches the rose and white striped walls. Madeleine makes me feel like I'm inside an *Eloise* storybook with all its fancy, wonderfully fussy details. Globe fixtures cast light across the round bistro tables, and vintage photos of Paris decorate the walls. The countertops are all creamy white marble, and William often has Louis Armstrong or Edith Piaf playing. I love bringing Violet here whenever she's in town. We wear berets and drink tea from a pair of vintage cups and saucers, which I swear William keeps just for us.

I tuck my sweet treats under my arm and give William a dainty wave.

"Merci beaucoup, William. Have a good day!"

The lobby is crowded this morning, and I have to wait a few minutes for an elevator to arrive.

"Dennis! Hi." I'm surprised to see our Creative Director hop on my elevator just before the doors close. Dennis works from the Chicago office and only makes it down to Cincinnati once a month or so. "I didn't think I'd see you until the holiday party. What's new? Did Bella make the basketball team?"

Dennis runs a hand through his salt-and-pepper hair. He's north of fifty but has been gray for as long as I've known him, like Steve Martin. He's a divorced father of two and probably the most down-to-earth creative director in the world. We've always had a good rapport.

"Bea, hey there. That's so nice of you to remember." He looks slightly frazzled, which is typical for Dennis. "She made the JV team. Thanks for asking."

Would someone with MS remember such a detail? I think smugly.

"Oh, that's fabulous. Congrats to Bella!" The elevator dings at floor three, which is where I sit. Dennis will stay on the elevator until four, where the executives work. "Have a nice day!"

Feeling rather proud of my thoughtful interaction with the big cheese, I stow my winter accessories in the coat closet and set out the French baked goods in the community kitchen, saving a croissant for Hannah. Finally, I grab a fresh cup of coffee and head toward my workspace.

"Bon matin, mon ami," I say, placing a pain au chocolat and an accompanying paper towel on Hannah's desk. I settle into my chair and power up my computer. "What's shaking?"

Hannah removes her headphones and claps happily at the sight of the sweet treat. "Aww! What's this for?"

"Thanks again for Saturday," I reply. "I know I've said it a million times already, but I had a ball. And there are more croissants in the kitchen."

She takes a big bite, and flaky crumbs sprinkle across her high-waisted jeans. "Well, something's going down today," Hannah murmurs between mouthfuls. "Christina's been in Gwen's office all morning, and I heard rumblings that Dennis is in town."

"He is," I confirm. "I just rode the elevator up with him."

I look in the direction of our manager Gwen's office. Since our company believes in "transparency," every manager's office has glass walls. As for the rest of us peasants, we sit at tightly sandwiched desks, almost like sardines, with not a cubicle wall in sight. Lucky for me, I have an end desk with my best friend on my right side, but some of my colleagues are stuck in far less ideal seating arrangements.

"Gwen looks slightly flustered but not upset," I observe. "Plus, it's Christina in there, and Christina rocks. It's not like she would be in trouble."

"Maybe Christina is pregnant?"

"I thought she didn't want kids," I say. "Remember that happy hour in June? The one where they brought in the margarita machine?" I'm telling you, agency life definitely has its perks. "Christina had three margs and then started to babble."

"I can't imagine not wanting kids..." Hannah replies, a faraway look in her eyes. Hannah has dozens of cousins around her age who already have children, and I know she can't wait to add her own to the Nielsen brood.

"Me neither, but different strokes for different folks," I say.

"Do you think Arthur will propose soon?" Hannah lowers her gaze, looking into her mug of coffee like it's a crystal ball. "We've been together three years now and living together since last February," she adds, like I haven't been around for their entire relationship.

So, here's the thing—don't tell anybody, but I know for a fact that Arthur is going to propose soon. He started sending me engagement ring ideas in August, and if all is going according to plan, the ring is either being made right now or could even be finished and ready for Hannah's perfect left hand. My guess is that Arthur will ask during the holiday season, which is idyllic for a gal who likes to curl up with hot cocoa and read cozy Jenny Bayliss and Josie Silver novels for hours on end.

"Arthur's crazy about you," I deflect.

Hannah sighs, "I don't mean to sound so desperate. But my parents haven't made things easy, you know? And now they keep saying things like, 'What's the holdup, Han? Is Arthur unsure about something? You deserve a man who appreciates what he has.'"

"I'm sorry." I give Hannah's hand a small squeeze, knowing the uphill battles she and Arthur have had to face and will have to continue to face.

Mr. Nielsen is apprehensive about Hannah being with a white guy, anxious if Arthur truly understands the effects of systemic racism or what it's like being Black in America. It doesn't help that Arthur is British. He only moved here when his father got transferred to GE's Cincinnati headquarters when he was fifteen. ("A terribly awkward time to move countries," he likes to say with a wry smile.)

As for Mrs. Nielsen, she's a very proper woman who wears silk scarves and has weekly tennis matches. Mrs. Nielsen loathes the fact that Hannah and Arthur moved in together before marriage. "You're not even engaged!" she gasped when Han told her the news.

And so Hannah, the ultimate parent pleaser, has felt like she can't do much of anything right lately.

"For the record, I don't think Arthur is unsure about anything," I add.

Hannah nods quietly. She knows Arthur has marriage trepidation since his own parents had an ugly divorce. They've talked through all of this. But I also understand how difficult it must be to think rationally when your parents are breathing down your neck about such big and personal topics.

"It's all going to work out," I tell her. "I just know it." My eyes widen at the sight of Dennis exiting the elevator and heading for Gwen's office. He moves with long, measured strides. "He's here!"

"Ooohhh," Hannah breathes. "The show has begun!"

Chapter Thirteen

We watch for a few minutes longer before Hannah receives a rush job from one of the traffic managers, and I receive client feedback. Darn it. Actual work is calling, and our snooping must wait. I'm relieved though for the morning's distractions, still unsure if I should tell Hannah about my potential diagnosis now that my birthday is behind me. At this point, I figure I'll wait until after I've seen the neurologist.

Speaking of which, I jot down a reminder to schedule an appointment ASAP.

But honestly, I'm starting to feel like a politician avoiding tough questions. "No comment, no comment!" I know it's weird not to tell Hannah about any of this, she's my best friend, but in some perverted way, I relish it. I like getting to pretend like nothing is unusual, that I'm completely healthy, with someone so close to me.

I spend the next few hours working on an email campaign for an organic beauty company. Unfortunately, the client-provided assets are alarmingly dated. "The woman is wearing gauchos," I argue with the project manager. "And her boyfriend has frosted tips. We can't use any of these. Customers will think they've been transported to the early 2000s."

"Isn't that stuff back in-style?"

"I don't think frosted tips are making a comeback," I counter. I press my eyes together, trying to think straight through the fog that's setting in. "But even if they are, this imagery looks dated, okay? It's the color grading, the shadows, the makeup on the models…"

The project manager is annoyed with me. "Well! What should I tell the client?"

Isn't that your job to figure out? I want to sigh. Instead, I say, "Blame me. Say that the designer doesn't believe these photos best convey their brand attributes of fresh, clean, and natural. Tell them we'd be happy to schedule a photo shoot for the campaign."

Thankfully, this pacifies the project manager, and she walks away, leaving me in peace.

Around eleven a.m., Gwen gives one of her sharp whistles. It's the way my manager gathers her design team, like we're a pack of herding dogs she has to call back to the barn. (And guess what? Gwen doesn't like dogs, so do with that what you will.) Ten of us report to Gwen: two art directors, four mid-level designers (that category includes Hannah and me), and then four junior associates. We all wheel our chairs closer to Gwen's office, most of us still nursing lukewarm cups of coffee and tea.

Gwen is standing primly with her delicate hands clasped across her flat stomach. She's wearing a white turtleneck this morning paired with a short black skirt that would look hugely inappropriate on my curvaceous figure. She pulls it off, though. Gwen always looks polished.

"Good morning, everyone. Happy Thanksgiving week." Gwen licks her glossy, pink lips and tucks a strand of ashy blonde hair behind her ear. "I have some bittersweet news to share."

Maybe Gwen is resigning, and Christina is backfilling her position! I hope, nay, pray.

I haven't always reported to Gwen. When I first started at Polly Feinstein, I reported to a hilarious woman named Erica. Erica had a thick Cleveland accent and the most outrageous, contagious laugh, and her grandmother periodically sent in hand-knit scarves to be dispersed among Erica's subordinates. I adored Erica. Unfortunately, Erica got poached by another agency in town (I couldn't blame them; she was a treasure), and now we're stuck with Gwen.

Blergh. Gwen.

Gwen arrived at Polly Feinstein with twelve years of agency experience and two faces: one reserved for the higher-ups and one for the rest of us unfortunate souls. It doesn't help that she has a downright sweet physical appearance, like she cooks up batches of homemade granola on the weekend and volunteers at a senior center.

(For the record, she does neither.)

No, Gwen and I have never jived.

I'm too loud, and I ask too many questions. While I like to get things done and never miss a deadline, I am my father's daughter, through and through, Gwen is a perfectionist. She obsesses over arbitrary details and misses deliverable dates because of it. Gwen thinks numerous tasks are beneath her pay grade, and she places panel appearances above regular check-ins with her direct reports. She also has a bad habit of ducking out of the office early and going on vacation without tidying up loose ends, leaving her team to clean up her messes.

So, yeah. I'm not a huge Gwen fan.

Gwen clears her throat and gives a sad smile. "Christina resigned on Friday afternoon," she says. Everyone lets out a collective sad sigh. Chase, her fellow art director, even boos. "I know, I know. I'm disappointed, too. As you're all aware, Christina has been with Polly Feinstein for ten years now, and she leaves behind very big shoes to fill."

Christina stands up, looking bashful. "Ben's company offered him a position in Philadelphia," she explains. "As most of you know, Ben and I met at Temple, and we always hoped we'd return to Philly someday. I'm sad to leave but excited for this next—"

"We are so excited for you," Gwen says, cutting off poor Christina. She gives a tight smile, deciding to return to business. "Dennis and I plan to backfill Christina's role from within. Mid-level designers, if you do *not* want to be considered, please let us know by end-of-day Wednesday. We would like to have Christina's position filled before the end of the year."

Everyone crowds around Christina after that, but Hannah and I form our own little huddle.

"Well, hot damn," I say.

"I'm going to miss Christina," Hannah says. "But this is a great opportunity for you."

"And for you! And for Carson and Maggie," I say, referring to the other two mid-level designers.

It's rare for someone to leave Polly Feinstein, especially at the director level. As disappointed as everyone is to see Christina go, excitement's also in the air. Not only will a mid-level designer get promoted, but that means one of the junior associates will, too. A long overdue shakeup is brewing.

"But you're the strongest digital designer," Hannah points out. "Plus, you've been here the longest."

I've been at Polly Feinstein for nearly eight years compared to Hannah's six, Carson's three, and Maggie's two. "But Gwen hates me," I say.

"Dennis is also involved, and he doesn't hate you."

Well, that's fair.

Hannah and I take our turns visiting with Christina and wishing her well in Philadelphia before returning to our desks. While I wait for an InDesign file to load, I toss around the possibility of Christina's position.

Maybe this is the sort of change I need.

I've been underwhelmed and slightly bored at work for a while now. But if I'm promoted to art director, that position will come with all sorts of new challenges and responsibilities.

Beatrix Parker, Art Director, I think.

It has a nice ring to it.

Chapter Fourteen

Only a few days later, I sit in a large, modern waiting room in an even larger, modern medical complex trying to focus on a bizarre, seemingly neurologist-specific, issue of *People* magazine. The cover story is about a soap opera actress and her lifelong struggle with migraine headaches.

Migraine headaches, I think. *The good old days.*

I put in a half-day at work, but I can't say it was productive. "I'm sorry. Can you repeat that?" I stammered twice during a morning meeting, though I wanted to ask the question at least three times more. Concentrating on my work was a losing battle, and I ultimately signed off thirty minutes early.

I stupidly decided I'd rather sit here, in this too cold, too crowded waiting room, and carefully study every person who comes and goes.

Dr. Wessels specializes in multiple sclerosis, and I try guessing who the MS sufferers are. Does the woman with the asymmetrical haircut and nose piercing have MS? What about the middle-aged man who uses a walker? What ailment does the mother of three suffer from? Does *she* have MS? Can MS sufferers have kids?

My hands go to my stomach. I hope so.

"Why, thank you, sir!" I hear a man cheerfully exclaim. I look up to see my father holding the door open for an elderly couple, the husband pushing his wife in a wheelchair.

"I just love your sweater," Mom tells the woman, always quick to give compliments.

The woman in the wheelchair is pleased. "It was a birthday gift from my son. He lives in Ireland," she says proudly. "They just don't make sweaters like this in America."

"Isn't that the truth?" says my father.

(My dad has never been to Ireland, and I doubt he's ever worn an Irish sweater. But he's an agreeable person, and he likes making people feel good about themselves and their opinions.)

The sight of my parents makes me want to crumble in relief. It's the sort of comfort I used to feel when first spotting them in a crowded auditorium right as I was about to take the stage, or sitting in the bleachers during one of my lacrosse matches.

No matter what happens, the people who love me the most are here, so everything will be okay.

But that reassurance is quickly replaced by exasperation at the sight of Mattie trailing behind them.

Who invited her?

It's not like I think my neurologist appointment is an exclusive event, but I already feel a bit childish bringing my mom and dad along. Now I have to walk back there with *three* family members in tow? This doctor is going to assume I'm some sort of high-maintenance diva or a pathetic case of failure to launch.

Mom wraps me in a big hug. "How are you feeling today?" She and Dad sit in the abstract-patterned chairs on either side of me, flanking me with their support.

"I hope it's okay I tagged along." Mattie takes a seat diagonal from me, placing her messenger bag neatly at her feet. "I was at Mom and Dad's going over the florist's quote when Mom mentioned your appointment. I thought it might be helpful having another set of ears." She pulls out a leather-bound notebook. Even Mattie's pocket notebooks are somehow posh. "And I'll take notes."

"Of course I don't mind," I lie. "Thank you," I add, so I don't sound like a barbarian.

"Did you have trouble getting off work?" Dad asks. He is "dressed up" for the day, which means khakis and a button-up shirt instead of his usual faded blue jeans and a t-shirt covered in spackling and paint.

"I know your manager can be difficult," Mom adds. "What's her name again? Wren?"

"It's Gwen," I smile. Mom has a habit of mixing up people's names when she doesn't like them. It's her quiet, passive aggressive form of rebellion. "But she was understanding. I said I had a dentist appointment. I don't want anyone to know I'm seeing a neurologist until, well... Until things are more definite."

"Right! Absolutely!" Mom and Dad are quick to agree, eager to hope this has all been a scare, a misdiagnosis.

But Mattie wrinkles her nose. "Hmm. That could get tricky..."

I ignore her. She isn't even supposed to be here! "The excitement at work is around one of our art directors resigning," I say instead. "They're going to backfill her role from within, so that's pretty cool."

Dad pats my knee affectionately. "I hope you threw your hat into the ring."

I imagine throwing my winter cap into a ring...and Gwen swatting it away with a tennis racquet.

"It will be between Hannah, Carson, Maggie, and me," I say. "The mid-level designers. I'm trying not to get my hopes up."

"They would be very lucky to have you in that role," Mom says.

"They certainly would," Dad agrees. "You've always been our most creative child. Remember that tree house we built together?"

Am I imagining things, or does Mattie actually look a bit jealous with her eyes narrowed like that? God forbid I'm awarded one measly accolade!

"After that summer, I figured you'd end up at Kickerville."

My heart starts to race, and my palms actually turn sweaty. I know—dramatic, right? But I get so darn excited anytime the possibility is mentioned. By the time I graduated college, my ever-capable sister was already preparing to take over the company, and there didn't seem to be room for another Parker kid. I certainly didn't want my father to create a superfluous position, I'm no freeloader, but I often daydream about getting a call that Kickerville needs *me*, Bea Parker, for some sort of grand creative endeavor.

"I'm not sure a childhood tree house puts me in the lead for the art director promotion," I smile. I turn to Mattie, choosing my words carefully. "But what's new at Kickerville? Any interesting projects lately? You know I'm always happy to lend a—"

"Everything's fine. Nothing new to report on our end. No art director excitement, that's for sure," Mattie swiftly replies, trying to sound breezy but coming off as guarded.

"Tell her about the A-frame you're building down at Norris Lake," says Dad. He folds his arms across his chest and gives a small chuckle. "Now that's a style I didn't predict becoming so damn trendy again."

"Oh, this is hardly the time to talk shop," replies Mattie. "I'm sure Bea would be bored anyway. Modular homes aren't as flashy as the agency world."

Bored? I spent two hours yesterday photo tagging cat food images for our archives!

"Look at all of these holiday decorations," Mom trills, inadvertently but effectively ending the Kickerville portion of the conversation. "Thanksgiving is tomorrow, and they've already skipped ahead to Christmas. I hate when people skip Thanksgiving."

I sigh, sad the Kickerville door has been closed yet again, and stare at the dwarfed artificial trees sitting on end tables. The glass surrounding the front desk is decorated with garland and gel clings in the shapes of candy canes and snowmen. Paul McCartney's "Simply Having a Wonderful Christmas Time" plays softly, and the cheerful song feels misplaced.

"I meant to pull names last night," Mom says, referencing our annual gift exchange tradition, "but I got carried away packing."

Mattie and I both raise our eyebrows, finally in sync.

"You've finally started packing?" Mattie asks.

"Well, I *thought* about it. I decided I'm going to start in the guest bedroom."

"Right," I smile. Even though my parents plan to put their house on the market in January, I imagine it will be more like June at this point. Mom is adamant about sorting through all of their things before they list the house, and considering they have nearly twenty years' worth of possessions to go through, it's going to take a while. "Well, you've got to start somewhere."

We sit in silence for the next few minutes, Dad resting his elbows on his knees and staring quite intently at his thumbs while Mom flips through the migraine issue of *People* magazine. Mattie is already scribbling down notes. *Patient seems nervous and possibly agitated,* I imagine her writing. *Has dark bags under her eyes and unsightly split ends. May or may not be MS-related.*

A nurse with a no-nonsense bob of gray hair opens one of the office doors.

"Beatrix Parker?" she calls.

Chapter Fifteen

Mom, Dad, Mattie, and I all leap to our feet.

"Which one of you is Beatrix?" the nurse asks, not at all amused.

See? I told you these people would think I'm a quack for having an entourage!

"Me." I raise my hand. "I'm Beatrix. Bea."

(Naming me Beatrix Parker is the one whimsical thing my mother has ever done. Mom was reading *The Tale of Peter Rabbit* to Mattie most nights when she found out she was pregnant with me. Inspiration comes in many forms, you know?)

"My name's Donna," the brusque nurse says. "You're here to see Dr. Wessels?"

I nod.

"Step on the scale, please," she instructs.

I hand my heavy peacoat and purse to Mom and slide out of my shoes because every ounce counts. "No one is allowed to look," I tell my family.

Mattie starts to say something, probably wanting to argue that this is an important metric for her report about me, but she ultimately casts her eyes toward the drop ceiling. I gingerly step on the scale.

Donna narrows her eyes and scowls as she moves both the large counterweight and small weight to and fro.

"Please don't say my weight out loud," I mutter. "I know it isn't a number you want to shout from the rooftops."

I'm surprised when she gives me a smile and a slight nod. "It's just a number," she murmurs, not unkindly. "There are more important numbers."

We follow Donna into an exam room where she takes my blood

pressure. "Dr. Wessels will be with you in a few minutes," she says, disappearing back into the hall.

We wait in nervous silence for five minutes that feel like five hours. The exam room is cold, white, and sterile, like nearly every exam room in the history of the world, but there is a bulletin board in this one pinned with MS-specific events, like yoga, bicycling clubs, and support groups.

Dad wastes no time inspecting the cabinetry. "Particle board," he reports gruffly.

I hope my neurologist is more impressive than her desk.

Finally, we hear two *tap-taps* on the door and Dr. Wessels walks in.

"Hi Beatrix. I'm Dr. Wessels," she says kindly, extending her hand. Dr. Wessels is young, late thirties, I think, and she wears regular clothes rather than doctor's scrubs or a lab coat. She's even wearing a pair of combat boots that looks both stylish and badass. "How are you?"

"You can call me Bea," I say. "And thank you for getting me in so soon."

"Dr. Macaulay can be rather persuasive," she smiles, which makes me smile, too.

"And who have you brought with you today?" Dr. Wessels asks.

I introduce my parents and sister.

"Eileen Parker," Mom says, bright and professional. "This is my husband, Frank, and our other daughter, Matilda."

"Mattie," my sister says. "I'm the notetaker for the afternoon, so just pretend I'm not here."

Ah yes, because beautiful blondes with nice manners and impeccable style simply disappear into the background. They're such wallflowers!

"It's wonderful to meet you all," Dr. Wessels says, returning her attention to me. "You clearly have an excellent support system, Bea. That means you're already two steps ahead."

Ahead of what? I think.

Dr. Wessels starts by asking me if I know much about multiple sclerosis.

I tell her how I didn't know anything about MS when Dr. Macaulay first called with my MRI results. "But I've obviously done a lot of googling since then," I say. "And honestly," I look straight into Dr. Wessels' eyes when I say this next part, partly because I want her to know how confident I feel, but also to avoid my family's gazes, "this diagnosis would make a lot of sense."

I can see my parents are alarmed by the admission. Mom sits up straighter in her chair, and Dad exhales deeply. It's hard to know how Mattie feels because she's too busy jotting it all down.

"It's a disease that's easy to explain away. Invisible diseases are tricky like that. It's frustrating when you look fine on the outside, but you don't *feel* fine," Dr. Wessels replies, her understanding filling me with relief. "What sort of symptoms have you been experiencing that sound like MS?"

I take a deep breath and begin, ready to rehearse the list I've been piecing together for days now. Unfortunately, the self-proclaimed notetaker decides to take on the role of assistant neurologist as well, making it impossible to get through my monologue uninterrupted.

"What does the tingling feel like?" Mattie asks when I describe the pins and needles in my feet and hands. "And what time of day does it occur?"

"It feels like tingling?" I offer lamely. "It isn't specific to any time of day."

"You say your limbs go completely numb—which limbs?" Mattie *tap, tap, taps* her pen against her paper. "And how often do the balance issues happen? Are we talking every day, once a week...?"

"My arms and legs. And I experience balance issues every day." I'm tempted to roll up my leggings and show everyone the bruises that routinely cover my legs. All of my stumbling and tripping isn't without casualties.

"How many times are you peeing each hour?" Mattie wants to know.

"Usually twice, but as often as four," I say with a grimace.

"I read that vision problems are an early symptom of MS." Mattie looks down at her notebook, where she's apparently included some preliminary thoughts. "Have you experienced any blurred or double vision?"

"No," I say, thinking, *Please don't introduce more worries into my anxious brain.*

After Dr. Wessels connects my difficulty with stairs to spatial awareness, Mattie requires further elaboration. When I discuss my fatigue, my sister asks me to rate it on a scale of 1–10.

"It's a 10, Mattie. A *10*," I snap. "Maybe even an 11 or 12, honestly."

Dr. Wessels narrows her eyes at Mattie, but in a way that seems more curious than scrutinizing. "Do you have a medical background?" she asks her.

Mattie instantly colors, setting her pen down. "Me? Oh gosh, no. It's my mom who's a nurse. Am I being obnoxious?" she asks, to which I want to reply *yes, yes you are.* "I'm sorry, I've just been researching..."

"No, no." Dr. Wessels shakes her head earnestly. "I only asked because you're asking smart questions."

My sister beams, pleased with herself. Trust Mattie to treat my neurologist appointment as another opportunity to shine. Who does she think she is hijacking my appointment anyway? I'm annoyed with Mattie for being here and with my parents for letting her come.

"Are there any other symptoms you'd like to tell me about, Bea?" Dr. Wessels asks gently.

I mention my difficulty concentrating and try to describe the heavy fog that seems to hang around my brain so much of the time.

"It's like I'm seeing life through a fogged-up windshield," I finally say.

Dr. Wessels nods.

I tell her about my occasional loss for words and the slip-ups with phrases. "I know everyone experiences those moments from time to time," I say. "But this feels different. I'll call my dog's leash a rope, or I'll ask for a milkshake when I mean to say sundae. The words are close but not quite right. I recognize it immediately, but it scares me when the wrong word spills out like that."

I then give Mattie a look that says, *And I'm taking no further questions.*

"These are all normal MS symptoms," Dr. Wessels replies, and I want to laugh at her use of *normal.* Nothing about this feels normal. "Thanks for sharing all of this with me. Let's pull up your MRI and go over it together."

Chapter Sixteen

Dad pulls me close, tucking me safely under his hefty arm, and Mom reaches for one of my hands. Mattie trains her eyes on my neurologist's laptop screen. Wordlessly, we sit there and watch as Dr. Wessels points out the various lesions in my brain.

Lesions.

The sound of the word makes me think of leeches, of something slimy and predatory attacking me. I picture the Demogorgon from *Stranger Things*. I don't have the superpowers of Eleven, though. I'm just me, Bea Parker, a slightly overweight, mid-level designer whose greatest confidante is her blind dachshund.

"So, here are a few lesions in your cerebellum region," Dr. Wessels says, pointing to the image of my skull, which is equal parts horrifying and fascinating. "And you have two more in your parietal lobe."

"Wow," I breathe. I also hear Mattie inhale, but blessedly, she doesn't offer commentary.

Dr. Wessels takes a deep breath. "Taking into consideration your symptoms as well as the MRI findings, I feel confident diagnosing you with MS. The good news is you don't have many lesions. Only five." She pauses. "We caught this early."

Mattie looks sad and pensive, and I can tell Mom and Dad are stunned, a little confused, and definitely overwhelmed. But I don't feel any of those things. For nearly a week now, I've been suppressing that little voice inside me, the one that's pointed out every MS symptom, each MS likelihood. But I no longer feel that resistance.

I feel relieved.

Because I *finally* have an answer to all the upsetting symptoms I've been experiencing this past year. I have evidence I'm not crazy, that I haven't been imagining things or simply overreacting to uncomfortable sensations everyone else seems to endure just fine.

"We can do a spinal tap if you want further confirmation," Dr. Wessels says. "Is that something you'd be interested in?"

"Maybe you—" Mattie begins. Thankfully, she catches herself and stops, shaking her head. "Whatever you think is best, Bea," she says instead.

"No," I reply, my voice strong. "I don't want the spinal tap. This all makes sense. I trust your diagnosis." *And I trust my body,* I want to add.

Dr. Wessels takes out a toolkit of sorts and does a series of somewhat amusing tests with me. For example, I have to move my finger from my nose to her index finger a handful of times, and she hits a little hammer against various reflex points. Dr. Wessels takes me into the hall and asks me to walk in a straight line towards her.

How silly, I think.

And yet, when I try doing so, I feel my balance falter, and I careen to the left.

She nods, adding this detail to my file.

"I'll order some bloodwork, which you can have done before you leave today, and I'll also be ordering a neck and spine MRI," Dr. Wessels says. "That MRI will tell us if you have any spinal lesions, as well. Do you have any questions for me?"

I gulp. Spinal lesions? This can somehow get worse?

"Not right now," I say.

"Well, it was a pleasure meeting you and your family today. Donna will schedule another appointment for you, hopefully within a week or two, and with the results of your bloodwork and the second MRI, we can choose the best treatment plan." Dr. Wessels gives me a sad sort of smile. "How does that sound?"

"Super?" I offer, which makes Dr. Wessels laugh.

(Finally a doctor who appreciates my lame jokes!)

My parents and Mattie return to the waiting room while I have my bloodwork done, and even though all the pricks leave my right arm sore,

I'm glad to have that part finished. I leave the neurologist's office feeling tired but optimistic. We caught my MS early. It's only going up from here. If everything goes according to plan, my MS will never be worse than it is today. I can live with that.

"Thanks for coming," I tell them, as we stand outside the front doors of the medical complex. It's windy, and I keep having to pull my hair out of my mouth. "I really appreciate it. Having you there made that news easier to hear." I pause. How do you end an afternoon like this one? "Um, careful driving home? See you tomorrow?"

"Do you really think we're going to leave you right now?" Dad asks. "We're coming to your place, kiddo."

"But it's a mess!"

"Sweetheart, you lived with us until you were eighteen. There's nothing we haven't seen before," Mom reminds me.

"I'll make my famous clean-out-the-fridge stir-fry," Dad says. "And we can watch *Planes, Trains and Automobiles.*"

My heart lifts. "That sounds *so* nice."

"Why don't you drive home with me?" Mom suggests. "You must be exhausted. Dad can drive your car."

Relieved, I hand my keys to Dad. He takes one look at my little sedan and declares he's taking it to the car wash on his way back.

"Mattie, are you joining us?" Mom asks. "Maybe Peter can come over after work?"

My sister looks at me, and I know what she must see in my eyes: disappointment and dread. Her own eyes immediately look wounded.

"I have some work to get caught up on," she says, sweeping a hand through her hair. "I'll let you three have some time alone." When Mattie gives me a quick hug goodbye, she murmurs, "I'm sorry if I overstepped. That's just that's how I process tough—"

"I get it. It's fine," I say, exhausted with this afternoon and exhausted with this conversation before it's even happened. "It was overwhelming news to receive."

"I was so impressed with your neurologist. You're in great hands," she says.

"Yep," I smile, again feeling just too tired for all of this.

"Right then," she says. "Well, I'll see you tomorrow."

Once we're back at my apartment, Dad gets busy making an impressive stir-fry from my meager offerings (frozen potstickers, red onions, a bell pepper on the brink of expiration, and microwaveable rice). Mom tidies up the kitchen afterward, she even dusts the chili pepper lights that dangle above my rickety cabinets, followed by a quick sweep of the living room. And then she cleans my bathroom, for Pete's sake.

"Eileen, would you sit down already?" Dad asks.

"I want to be useful," she says, surveying the mess that is my bedroom.

"You'll be most useful sitting here on the sofa with us," he says.

Finally, Mom settles in to watch *Planes, Trains and Automobiles* with Dad and me. I don't last long nestled between my two parents with a satisfied stomach, a relieved mind, and a full heart. Just as Neal Page discovers his seatmate is taxi-stealing Del Griffith, I drift into a deep sleep.

Chapter Seventeen

I wake up in what I can only describe as an adult version of a swaddle. Using my top sheet and down comforter, my mother managed to Mac-Gyver a sort of blanket burrito. Tony Soprano glares at me from his (perfectly cozy) bed on the floor, bitter Mom's expert tucking-in skills left him out in the cold. As I shimmy back and forth in my attempts to break free, I wonder if my mother flipped a quarter off the bed before considering her work done.

Also, how is a woman in her sixties still so strong?

I watch the Macy's Day Parade while I stir together canned corn, a box of Jiffy, butter, and sour cream. "Tony," I say as the thought occurs to me. "I didn't get up to pee a single time last night. Can you believe that?"

Tony doesn't even bother raising his head. He isn't ready to forgive me for last night's sleeping arrangements. Instead, he stares at Al Roker who is wearing a cheerful knit cap and matching scarf. God, I love Al Roker. People like to say Tom Hanks is America's dad, but I think Al is equally deserving of the title.

Anyways, I know a miracle hasn't occurred. It isn't like my bladder issues have been mysteriously cured overnight. Instead, I enjoyed the sort of sweet relief and subsequent deep sleep that come from a major anxiety having been lifted. I can't remember the last time I slept so soundly, my mind so relaxed, I didn't even dream. Yes, I have multiple sclerosis, and that's scary. But at least now I have a name for the invisible monster I've been battling. Plus, I have an ally in my corner. Dr. Wessels is going to help me slay this beast.

I pour the creamy corn mixture into a casserole dish and slide it inside the oven. I toss aside my oven mitts and come eye-to-eye with the seven-dollar bottle of pinot grigio I planned on bringing this afternoon. I *may* have brought two-buck chuck to our family's Thanksgiving last year. I'm no wine snob, but even I have to admit it probably wasn't the best pairing for the organic, farm-raised turkey or the truffle-and-chestnut stuffing.

I consider my options.

Venturing to the grocery store on Thanksgiving morning sounds dreadful. Maybe I can bum something nicer off Janet, though. It's only ten a.m., but Janet is a notoriously early riser. "In bed by eight means you don't sleep late," she likes to say.

"I'll be right back," I tell Tony, who is now resting inside the elaborate dog house I recently finished building.

I went a little overboard on the project, effectively building Tony a miniature Swiss chalet. There's a flower box beneath each window and even a small, carved bird that perches on the roof's peak. Inside is a foam bed covered with one of my old t-shirts as well as a fleece blanket for burrowing.

But Tony Soprano deserves the best, and I hope his little chalet makes him feel comfy and safe.

Still wearing my flannel pajama bottoms and an oversized sweatshirt, I cross the hall and gently knock on Janet's front door. She keeps a wreath of artificial blue hydrangeas on her door as well as a wooden WELCOME sign where the "O" is a heart. Janet has lived in the building longer than any other tenant, since the late 1980s, legend claims. Somewhere north of fifty and south of seventy, Janet refuses to reveal her age.

"What a wonderful Thanksgiving surprise!" she greets me.

"Wonderful surprise! Wonderful surprise!" her cockatiel, Buddy, repeats, while her Yorkie, Minnie, scampers around our feet, barking and occasionally nipping at me.

"Minnie! Stop that. Have some manners," Janet scolds.

"Oh, it's okay," I say, giving one of my feet a little shake. I'm wearing my French bulldog slippers this morning. "I'm sort of asking for it with footwear like this." We both giggle. "Sorry to bug you on Thanksgiving morning."

"Don't be sorry. I'm happy to see you! Come and enjoy a mimosa with me? I was just watching the parade." Janet waves me inside her apartment, which smells like potpourri and citrus and where everything is a different pastel hue. "Or would you prefer a Bloody Mary?"

"Neither, I'm afraid. I've got corn pudding in the oven, and I still need to get myself ready for the day." I gesture at my frumpy pajamas.

Janet certainly isn't still donning her pajamas. No, she's wearing an orange-and-brown patterned shift dress and kitten heels, both of which look like they were plucked from the 1960s. Janet's outfits are always posh and wonderfully unique, each item a treasure from a fancy department store or vintage shop.

"Well, darn!" She props a pink-manicured hand on her hip. "I wanted to dish about the cute new neighbor. Did you see his compost sign? I've never composted before. Can I put my chicken wing bones in there?"

"When did you have chicken wings?" I can't picture tidy Janet snacking on the saucy snack. "And no, you can't. At least not in Chris's composter. They're all a little different in terms of guidelines. He included a list of items you can and cannot compost though."

"I deep-fried a batch last night." Janet shrugs. "And I must have missed his list. Oh, lordy. What happens if you put the wrong thing into the compost?"

"I don't know," I admit before waggling my eyebrows. "Sounds like a question you can ask the cute new neighbor."

"He's young enough to be my son!" Janet pretends to be scandalized.

"Maybe he likes older women."

She swats me away. "Well then, it's a shame I've never been into younger men."

"Do you have a bottle of nice white wine I can have?" I ask. "I'll pay you for it, of course. I just don't think my family, especially my sister, will be very impressed with my current selection."

"My second husband was a sommelier. Gerald. He had a beard that tickled me every time we kissed," Janet says, looking wistful.

You should know that Janet *constantly* brings up ex-husbands and former lovers. For as long as I've known her, she's been single, but judging by her abundance of tales and juicy tidbits, her previous life was an exciting and amorous one. That, or she's an excellent storyteller. I hope it's the former but suspect the latter.

"Anyhow! Why don't we have a look inside my fridge? I have a handful of whites already chilling that would pair perfectly."

Relieved, I follow Janet into her kitchen, where the countertops are crowded with her milk glass collection, Mid-Century Modern Pyrex, and dozens of well-loved cookbooks. She opens the refrigerator door, and we peer inside.

"I would go with a riesling or a sauvignon blanc," says Janet. "Chardonnay is usually a safe bet when entertaining, but it's not the best match for a turkey. Too oaky. A light-bodied red would also be nice, like a pinot noir."

I am impressed with Janet's selection of wines, and even more so, her knowledge of them, but what catches my eye inside her refrigerator is the single plate of Thanksgiving dinner sitting on the top shelf. It looks like a meal she picked up from a local grocery store's deli department, the mashed potatoes too smooth and uniform, the green beans stubby in size and dull in color.

Janet's eyebrows lift, the glitter in her blue eye shadow giving a small sparkle. "I forgot I had this one! It's ready to impress snobby sisters and be enjoyed alongside the perfect Thanksgiving bird."

"Oh, Mattie isn't snobby," I say quickly, as Janet hands me the cool bottle. "She's just...discerning." I study the elegant label. It's a sauvignon blanc from New Zealand. "I owe you big time," I tell Janet, pulling her in for a hug. "Thank you."

"You owe me nothing at all. It's my Thanksgiving gift to you," she says.

I give her a smile. "I'm not sure what your plans are for today, but would you like to come with me to my parents' house?"

"Oh, goodness. I wouldn't want to burden you all with another mouth to feed," Janet immediately replies. "I'm actually preparing a proper Cornish hen today, just like my boyfriend from Wales used to make for special occasions, and potatoes au gratin. My, um, former sister-in-law is probably going to join me."

"Well, if you haven't started any of those recipes yet," I think of the fridge where a Cornish hen is decidedly not hanging out, "and if your former sister-in-law won't be too disappointed, we would love to have you."

"But I don't have anything to bring," Janet says.

I hand her back the bottle of sauvignon blanc. "Sure you do. And it's one of the most important parts of a fancy meal." I glance at her wall clock, which has a round face surrounded by a square of green enamel. "Meet me in the hallway at one-fifteen?"

Janet hesitates, but only for a moment.

"That sounds lovely," she beams.

On our way out the door that afternoon, we run into Chris Little outside his apartment. He's wearing a flannel shirt beneath a corduroy jacket, and his hair is still wet from the shower. He has a reusable shopping bag slung over one shoulder and is holding his own casserole dish.

"Hey there!" Chris says. It's our first time meeting where neither my dog nor I have taken him by surprise. "Happy Thanksgiving."

"Happy Thanksgiving!" Janet and I chorus.

"What are your plans for the day?" I ask, that warm feeling in my stomach instant and exciting.

"Any fun traditions?" Janet adds. "When I was little, my Uncle Abe had us go around the table and say what we *weren't* thankful for, which was delightful for us kids. We used to love complaining about the teachers who gave too much homework and the brussels sprouts our parents made us eat."

Chris and I both laugh. "That's creative," he says. "Maybe I'll suggest we do that this year. We need something to lighten the mood. My sister insisted on hosting, and our mom isn't happy about it."

"Why's that?" I ask, but Janet is already nodding knowingly.

"She's insulted," Chris says. "Mom thinks that just because she turned seventy back in September, everyone's acting like she can't do the things she's always done."

"Is that why Maria's hosting?" I'm genuinely curious.

Chris chews on his bottom lip. He has awfully plump lips. "Sort of," he says. "I think Maria feels guilty having her seventy-year-old mother prepare an entire Thanksgiving spread. Mom would never admit it, but all of the cleaning and cooking puts her in bed the rest of the weekend. Her knees hurt her more than she'd ever let on."

"It's always the darn knees," Janet offers, giving her own a little knock with a balled-up fist. As usual, I wonder how old Janet really is. "It's nice that Maria is hosting. Get a glass of wine, or better yet, a strong cocktail, into your mom's hands as soon as possible. Make sure whoever's cooking asks her a bunch of questions, even if they already know the answers, and bring up lots of past Thanksgiving memories. It'll be a wonderful day."

"Thank you," Chris smiles, and I can tell he is touched. "So, where are you two heading this afternoon?"

"Janet's joining me at my parents' house. She's got the most sublime bottle of sauvignon blanc, and I made corn pudding." I hold up the dish. "I don't really like the stuff, but my dad goes crazy over it."

"It's nice you made it then. I'm in charge of the sweet potatoes. It's the only dish Maria trusts me with since my family likes the marshmallows a little burnt," he says.

Chris eyes my own reusable bag, which I grabbed at the last moment. If Mom has truly started packing up their house, Lord knows she'll have childhood mementos to unload on me.

"Did you bring enough Tupperware?" he asks.

"Tupperware?" Janet and I both repeat.

"Yes, for leftovers," Chris says. "I hate thinking about all the plastic being used today. It just about gives me a panic attack."

"Um, my mom has a bunch we're going to borrow," I say, which is only sort of a lie. My mom does have a bunch of her own Tupperware, but we certainly haven't made a game plan for Thanksgiving leftovers.

I briefly wonder if Chris's ugly breakup was over recyclables.

"Well, we'd better run," I say. "Happy Thanksgiving!"

He reaches for my hand, and my entire body feels an electric jolt. His big, brown eyes lock with mine. Good gravy, what is happening here? For a split second, I imagine us both dropping our Thanksgiving offerings to the floor and making out passionately in the stairwell. Janet would politely excuse herself because if anyone's an expert in love, it's Janet, and then Chris would push me up against the cool wall and...

"I'm not sure if your parents have their own composter or not, but feel free to bring any food waste back here," he says.

I blink a few times.

"Thank you," I finally smile.

Janet and I walk to my car, the wind whipping our hair in wild directions, and slide inside. "He's a looker," Janet says. "But that boy takes environmental issues pretty darn seriously. What do you think he'd do if he ever saw me toss a recyclable in the trash? Tackle me to the floor?"

"You know what? I bet you'd like that," I grin.

The two of us burst into laughter. I'm happy I asked Janet along today. It will be a fun Thanksgiving.

Chapter Eighteen

We pull up to my parents' house at two o'clock sharp.

Mattie's Lexus SUV is already parked in the driveway. My heart sinks in the absence of Justin's beat-up Subaru station wagon. Part of me hoped for a Thanksgiving surprise, that he, Katie, and Violet would all be waiting inside. Even though Justin moved to New Mexico over ten years ago, holidays without him have never gotten any easier.

Once Mom retires, my parents plan on spending lots of time out west. "We can be gone for two, four, even six weeks at a time," Mom marvels, exaggerating just a bit. "Especially if we find a condo that doesn't have a yard that needs maintaining."

"Well, that's one upside of an HOA," Dad grumbles, still adjusting to the idea.

At their current house, a sprawling brick Tudor, Mom and Dad keep a famously neat lawn and landscaping. It all looks even more immaculate now since Dad wants everything to be perfect for when their house goes on the market. "Our house is a reflection of the Kickerville name," he says. "It has to absolutely shine."

"I just hope we can sell this house to a nice family," Mom often replies with a sigh.

"People who will appreciate it," Dad will then add.

"You know you don't have to move," I remind them.

"It's time," Mom declares, resolute.

"We're nearing seventy," Dad says. "There's simply no need for this much space—or this much stuff."

Hannah recently asked if I was sad about my parents leaving my childhood home, but I'm not. Mom is constantly renovating and redecorating, so the house I remember from my youth is radically different from the one today. Besides, we moved to the McMansion when I was in junior high. I feel more nostalgic for the three-bedroom cape cod we left behind, where you had to light a match to use the antique stove, and there was a window seat in the kitchen.

"Bea! I had no idea you were some kind of west side royalty," Janet whistles, admiring the stately home. It's truly the crown jewel in a subdivision that glitters. "Is there anything else I should know before we go inside?"

My stomach turns when I realize there is.

"Actually, yes," I say quietly. "Remember how I had that MRI last week?" Janet gives a slight nod, her brows furrowing and her mouth puckering into a small *oh* shape. "They found something suspicious on it. Lesions. I saw a neurologist yesterday, and as it turns out, I have multiple sclerosis."

The car is eerily silent. We hear kids laughing in the distance and look toward a driveway where a handful of them, cousins probably, have materialized with sidewalk chalk, jump ropes, and a basketball.

"Well, jeepers," Janet breathes. She studies my face for a few seconds. "I'm really sad to hear that," she says. "But this disease has no idea who it's messing with. You're going to be okay, sweetie. You're tenacious. You'll come out on top."

"Thanks, Janet." I reach over and give her a hug, the seatbelts awkwardly constricting our movements.

"And you know I'm just across the hall if you need anything," she says, her signature Janet assurance. "Anything at all, okay?"

"Okay," I say.

"You promise to ask me for help when you need it?" she presses.

"I promise," I smile.

We're quiet for a few more moments before I shrug my shoulders. "So, are you ready to join the Parker family Thanksgiving?"

"Sure am," she murmurs, giving her head a little shake. "No overly political relatives to worry about? No handsy uncle everyone avoids?"

"Nothing like that, I promise," I laugh.

Inside, Mom will be basting the turkey, Dad will be standing over the mixing bowl making his extra buttery, extra peppery mashed potatoes,

Mattie will be efficiently chopping vegetables for a tossed salad, and Peter will be standing there in the middle of it all, unsure how the heck he can help in the midst of all of these doers.

I just hope they haven't been discussing my MS all morning.

Janet and I grab our Thanksgiving offerings and start up the long, brick sidewalk to my parents' glass-paned front door. There are bales of hay positioned on either side of the porch and a pair of cheerful scarecrows in the landscaping.

"Oh! I nearly forgot." I spin around, locking eyes with Janet. "My mom will ask which pumpkin pie you'd like for dessert. Choose the one with the traditional crust, *not* the chocolate crust. Mom will then suggest you take a slice of both. Insist you want the traditional one because it looks so much prettier, especially with the sugared cutouts of leaves and pumpkins along its edges, but then eventually agree to try a small slice of each."

Janet frowns but gives a quick nod of confirmation, sensing the importance of the situation.

"After you've tried both, announce that yes, the traditional pie was much better," I say to a very confused, slightly overwhelmed Janet. I sigh, "Mom's frenemy, Mary Ellen Stooplemeyer, lives just across the street. She brings over her famous chocolate crusted pumpkin pie every year. And any guest who has complimented it? Well, they've never seen another Parker family Thanksgiving, or another Parker family *anything*, ever again."

"Jeez louise!" Janet exhales.

"Yeah, Mom doesn't mess around when it comes to Mary Ellen Stooplemeyer." With an encouraging smile, I push open the front door.

"Helloooo!" I call, walking through the cavernous, two-story foyer and into the kitchen. The house smells wonderful, like turkey and cinnamon and sweetly spiced pumpkin. Mom has the Amy Grant Christmas album playing, which is the official sign that the holiday season has started in the Parker household. "Happy Thanksgiving!"

Mom and Dad's kitchen is huge and impressive, with towering cherry cabinets and green marble countertops that are flecked with gold and silver. They have a six-burner stovetop and two ovens, plus a massive Sub-Zero refrigerator.

It is very extravagant.

"You all remember my neighbor, Janet Shapiro?" I loop an arm around Janet, who suddenly looks shy.

"Thank you for having me today," she says to Mom and Dad, handing them the bottle of wine.

"We're so glad you could join us," says Mom. "And thank you for this! It looks exquisite. Sauvignon blanc is my favorite varietal." She says this about any bottle of wine brought into her home with the exception of moscato.

"Nice to see you again, Janet," says Dad, giving her a handshake. "What can I get you ladies to drink?"

Mattie and Peter are lingering near the island, sipping on tall glasses of water. They're probably parched from early-morning turkey trots. Mom sets out a tray of appetizers that feature little bites of who-knows-what wrapped in puff pastry, and Dad is already carving the turkey. My stomach growls. I'm hungry.

Mattie hops down from her stool and gives me a weird, long hug. It's awkward since we aren't the touchy-feely sort of sisters. Peter offers an affectionate pat on my back. "I'm so sorry, Bea," he says, like Tony Soprano has died or I've lost my job.

"We're here for you every step of the way," Mattie adds. "Whatever you need."

My face burns hot. While I've never been one to shy away from the limelight, I do not like being the center of attention because of a disease. I want all eyes on me as I recount a hilarious story or show off a new craft or woodworking project. I don't want to be some sort of charity case.

"Thank you. I appreciate that." I turn to Dad. "Did you pick up the Thanksgiving beer from MadTree?" One of the local breweries does a fall ale called Pilgrim. Dad nods. "I'll take one of those. How about you, Janet? Maybe a glass of wine?"

"Yes, please," she agrees.

"Did you sleep okay last night?" Mom asks me. She's wearing an oatmeal-colored turtleneck this morning. Like Mattie, she's never worn much makeup. "Did you have a nice morning?"

"Oh, gosh, yes. I slept better than I have in months," I say. Dad hands me a cold can of beer and I give him a peck on his warm cheek. His face is rosy and damp with perspiration. He always gets overheated when he cooks. "Thank you for such a nice dinner. And for tucking me in. Tony couldn't even get under the covers! Where did you learn those sorts of bed-making skills?"

"I'm a nurse," she shrugs. "I can do anything."

The doorbell rings.

"Aunt Amethyst?" I ask the group. I turn to Janet. "Wait until you meet her. One Thanksgiving she showed up with the most insane arrowhead earrings and feathered headdress. It was horrifically inappropriate."

"She's not coming," Dad says, moving the turkey to the serving platter. "She and Thomas are going to his family's Thanksgiving."

Well, that's an interesting twist of events. While Aunt Amethyst is quick to bring her suitors around her own family, she rarely shows enough interest to meet theirs. "It's just another example of how selfish she is," I once heard Mom murmur to Dad.

I should also tell you that Aunt Amethyst was not born with her name. She was Carole until the 1980s, which was when she took a trip to Burning Man and got into all sorts of New Age practices, like healing crystals, incense, and tarot cards. She legally changed her name when Justin was just a toddler, so at least for Mattie and me, she has always been Aunt Amethyst.

I've caught Mom calling her Carole from time to time. I told Mom this was a microaggression and that she should stop, and Mom replied that Aunt Amethyst has doled her plenty of macroaggressions over the years, so she felt no remorse.

Mic drop by Eileen Parker.

"Fran's coming today," Mattie explains, while Mom goes to answer the door. "Her brother and his family went to Disney World for the week, so I told her she should join us instead. She said she prefers our company to her brother's anyways."

"That sounds like Fran," I say.

"I know how that can be," Janet smiles, starting to come out of her shell.

Fran Bosse was Dad's right-hand woman at Kickerville for over twenty-five years and now reports to Mattie. Having grown up on a dairy farm just a few miles down the road from the company, Fran had applied for, and been hired into, the open personal assistant role when she was all of nineteen years old. Even though she's in her late-forties now, Fran still looks like that earnest teenager with her black, tightly curled hair, oodles of freckles spread across her nose and cheeks, and hazel eyes that somehow see every little thing happening at Kickerville. Nothing gets past Fran Bosse.

Fran is an important fixture in our family, just as loved and familiar as a favorite aunt.

"So, I loved Dr. Wessels," says Mattie. "But will you get a second opinion?"

Thankfully, all four-feet-ten-inches of Fran Bosse enter the kitchen just then. "Happy Thanksgiving!" she booms.

I can tell Janet is surprised to hear such a baritone voice from such a tiny person.

"Who's serving up the booze?" Fran wants to know.

"I don't want a second opinion," I mumble in Mattie's direction before hurrying to the fridge. "*I'm* the bartender, Fran. What can I get you?"

It's going to be a long day, and I suspect I'll need alcohol to see me through it.

Chapter Nineteen

After introductions are made between our two very different guests—Janet seems underwhelmed by Fran's no-nonsense jeans, peasant blouse, and ponytail, while Fran is likely wondering if we've all be transported to the 1960s judging by the beehive on Janet's head and her retro shift dress—Dad announces it's time to dish up.

We pile our plates high with the bounty: turkey, cranberry sauce, green bean casserole, rosemary stuffing, mashed potatoes, corn pudding, buttered noodles. "Try the carrots I brought," instructs Fran, elbowing Janet. "They're from my neighbor's vegetable garden. Have you ever seen a purple carrot before?"

Like most people who are given a Fran Bosse command, Janet does as she is told. "I have, yes," she hums. "I once dated a Michelin star chef, and he was fond of colorful produce. I've never eaten so many rainbow radishes or heirloom tomatoes in my life."

There's a basket of fresh dinner rolls at the table as well as a crisp kale salad, and we all settle in with tall glasses of water and crystal goblets of wine. Mom sets Janet's New Zealand sauvignon blanc in a swanky ice bucket, something she hadn't done with last year's two-buck chuck, and Dad cues up a relaxing playlist from his phone.

"Are you using Spotify?" I ask, impressed.

"Justin and Katie bought me a subscription for my birthday," he says. "Did you know they have a playlist for every occasion? This one is called 'Thanksgiving Dinner.'"

"Yeah? That's pretty neat," I smile, pretending this is news to me.

"How are you feeling today?" Mom takes a bite of turkey. "Any tingling or numbness?"

I force a pleasant smile. "A little tingling this morning, but I feel fine right now," I say, knowing Mom means well. I just don't feel like discussing my MS all day.

"That's how I feel when I sit on top of my criss-crossed legs all day," Fran volunteers. I realize Mom, Dad, or Mattie must have already told her about my MS. Word travels fast around this family, and in this case, I'm thankful for it. As much as I love dramatics, it's not so fun giving the "I have MS" spiel.

"Any dizziness today?" Mom wants to know.

"Thankfully, no. Not yet," I say. "I'll lie down if I do get dizzy though." I've learned that one the hard way. If I don't sit down and drink some water when the dizziness hits, it quickly turns into nausea.

"Would you like some salad?" Dad asks. "The bowl's a little heavy, sweetie. I can get it for you..."

"I can lift the salad bowl. It's fine. *I'm* fine, okay?" I appreciate everyone's concern, but this is starting to feel suffocating. "So! Has anyone talked to Justin, Katie, and Violet today?"

After my parents talk about the video from Violet's Thanksgiving play, they quickly return to the topic du jour, the disease affecting my central nervous system. "Are you tired right now?" Dad asks.

"Nope! I'm nice and awake, thanks." Now feeling desperate, I throw my older sister under the bus and venture into dangerous territory. "Did you hear Father Kennedy is doing Stephanie Stooplemeyer's wedding mass?"

It's a lie. Even worse, it's a lie that involves a religious figure, so I've probably just received a serious mark on my karma, but I can't stomach the concern or the questions a moment longer.

Mom's fork, skewered with a piece of white meat, freezes mid-air. "That's impossible," she says. "Father Kennedy is retired."

Father Kennedy is the west side of Cincinnati's most beloved priest. For decades, he's been hotly sought after for weddings, he married both my parents and the Stooplemeyers, but now that he is ninety-two years old, Father Kennedy is officially in retirement.

I'm far from a practicing Catholic these days, but even I would be thrilled to have Father Kennedy officiate my wedding.

"Mattie, do you think it's worth reaching out one more time?" Mom turns to my older sister, her eyes big and intense.

Mattie takes a bite of cranberry sauce, taking her time to chew, swallow, and dab her mouth afterward. Oh my God—is Mom twitching? Part of me wonders if she's going to hop into her SUV and speed to the retirement home where all of the elderly nuns and priests live. "I demand answers!" I imagine her shouting to a bewildered Father Kennedy.

"*Eh?* What was that?" he would ask, craning his good ear in her direction.

"No," Mattie finally says. "I don't think it's worth bothering him, Mom. I'm sure whatever Bea heard was from the west side rumor mill."

"I bet you anything Mary Ellen sent him a batch of her snickerdoodles." It's difficult to tell if Mom is talking to us or mumbling to herself. "And she probably made a donation to the church, too. Oh, she's good all right..."

"Eileen, let's discuss this later," Dad says, giving her forearm a concerned pat.

As if Mom and Mattie aren't already obsessed with the upcoming wedding, Stephanie Stooplemeyer also has a wedding on the books for May. Mom and Mary Ellen Stooplemeyer turn everything into a competition. Who's doing more volunteer work at the church? Who had their first-floor powder room more recently remodeled? Who delivered lasagna to the new neighbors in the cul-de-sac faster? But nothing compares to this matrimony match. It is the ultimate showdown.

"Besides, Peter and I really like working with Deacon Joe," Mattie explains, tucking a strand of blonde hair behind her ear. She's wearing a gorgeous pair of pearl-and-diamond earrings today.

"He's been fantastic." Peter reaches for the basket of dinner rolls and is met with a glare from Mom. He briefly falters. "It's nice talking to someone who is actually married himself, versus a priest who has never had that experience."

"Father Kennedy is lovely, but we're happy with Deacon Joe," Mattie finishes, rounding third base and heading for home. "He'll be a terrific officiant."

Mattie and Peter's wedding day will begin with a proper Catholic mass at the cathedral downtown. From there, the happy couple will take an antique Rolls Royce to their reception at the Netherland Plaza, an elegant venue that absolutely sparkles with Art Deco splendor. Mattie still doesn't have a wedding dress (shocking, I know), but whatever she chooses will probably feature a twelve-foot train that I'll be expected to carry.

It's all incredibly ta-ta-ta, if you catch my drift.

"Deacon Joe is a stand-up man," says Dad, which is quite the compliment in his book. "Fran," he turns to his long-time assistant, still dependent on her to get him out of sticky situations. "Did Julia land a part in *The Nutcracker* again this year?"

"She sure did, boss," replies Fran, steadfast as ever. Fran's niece is a wickedly talented ballerina. "I actually have a spare ticket for the matinee on Saturday the fifth if anyone is interested in joining me."

Janet actually squeals, clapping her hands excitedly. "I would love to go!" she says. "I haven't seen *The Nutcracker* since I was a little girl."

I see the apprehension in Fran's eyes. What would she, a woman who routinely carries around a nail gun, possibly have in common with a gal who runs errands with her Yorkie tucked into her purse? But Fran is a fair person, and Janet quite enthusiastically asked for the extra ticket first.

"Great," says Fran, sounding like she thinks the situation is anything but that. "It's yours."

Peter begins to gather our empty dinner plates because he has excellent manners, but also because I think Mom has totally scared him, and Mattie asks if anyone would like dessert.

"We have traditional pumpkin pie and chocolate-crusted pumpkin pie," Mom says, like this isn't always the case.

"Let me help." I start to stand, and everyone insists I stay put. "I can at least start a pot of coffee," I persist.

"No, no," says Mattie. "We've got things under control."

Maybe they think my legs will give out and I'll break the nice china. Or that I'll experience an arm spasm and send hot coffee into somebody's lap.

"Traditional pumpkin pie for me!" chirps Janet.

"Are you sure?" Mom asks. "Why not try a small sliver of each?"

Per my instructions, Janet emphasizes how much prettier the traditional pumpkin pie looks, what with its intricate cutouts and all, but that yes, she supposes she could give both pies a try. It is Thanksgiving after all!

Unfortunately, things go downhill from there as I haven't prepared my friend for how truly delicious Mary Ellen Stooplemeyer's chocolate-crusted pie is.

Janet takes a delicate bite and her satisfied groans give away her true opinion. "Lordy, that's good!" she sighs, immediately covering her mouth and looking panicked.

"Amateur move," Fran smirks.

Thankfully for me, I don't have to witness the drama unfold as my phone begins to vibrate deep within my dress pocket. Blessedly, it's not a spam call but rather the inimitable Hannah Nielsen, my Turkey Day savior.

"Hannah wants to FaceTime," I explain, wondering if I've ever been so grateful for an interruption. "I'll be just a minute. She hasn't FaceTimed me since the pandemic, so it must be something important."

Mom and Mattie exchange wide eyes, sharing my same suspicions.

My heart beating wildly, the way it only does with excitement for your closest friends, I slip into the front den. "Hello?" I say with a grin. "Are you calling to wish me a happy Thanksgiving? Or do you have some other fun news to share?"

"BEA! OH MY GOD! I'M ENGAGED!!!" Hannah exclaims, her smile giant and radiant. "I mean, *we're* engaged! Arthur popped the question! We're getting married!!!"

"Hannah! Shut up, shut up!" I shout. "How did he ask? Let me see the ring!"

Hannah's hands are shaking, but it's easy to see how gorgeous her oval-cut solitaire engagement ring is. Arthur has done a beautiful job. Tears well up in her brown eyes and she fans them away. "I thought I was done crying. I'm sorry! I'm just overwhelmed with happiness!"

Before leaving for Hannah's parents' house, Arthur had asked her to take a walk with him through Washington Park. "He got down on one knee and everything. There were a few other couples and a family there, and they all started clapping and cheering for us," Hannah says. "It was so romantic. And one lady even thought to take a few pictures for us!"

"Well, I sure hope he got down on one knee! You deserve nothing less," I laugh, wiping at my own eyes. "Oh, Han. I'm just thrilled for you."

"I felt like I was in a movie," she says. Hannah takes a deep breath.

"Um, so! How is your Thanksgiving going?"

Well, I was diagnosed with an incurable disease yesterday, and now my family is treating me like an invalid! So, pretty shitty, thanks! I put on my biggest and brightest smile. "Considering I got news like this, how could it be anything other than amazing?" I say. "And your parents? They're happy?"

"They're happy," Hannah confirms. "We've all got some work ahead of us, but yeah. It's good, Bea. We're good right now."

After talking with Hannah, I go into the powder room where I splash cold water against my forearms. I'm ecstatic for my best friend, but I'm ashamed to admit just how sorry I feel for myself.

Hannah's months ahead will include venue shopping, saying yes to the dress, planning a honeymoon, and preparing to marry the love of her life. Mine will involve MRIs and bloodwork, insurance coverage discussions, learning about MS therapies, and navigating this new world of having a chronic disease.

I know this sounds awful—especially with my lovely and (overly) supportive family sitting in the next room and a delightful dinner in my stomach—but between us?

I can't remember a Thanksgiving where I felt less thankful.

Chapter Twenty

"He was wearing a Hawaiian shirt. In December!"

That Saturday, I sit in a new waiting room at the same medical complex as Wednesday's neurologist appointment. I'm the only person here this morning, and the front desk lady must think I'm cool since she feels comfortable taking a call from her sister Jenny. They're discussing a first date Jenny went on last night.

"Well, Mele Kalikimaka to you then," the front desk woman says. I giggle because it's a good joke.

But just as the sisters are getting to the good part—Jenny went home with the guy!—a technician appears in the doorway. "Beatrix Parker?" she announces loudly, her eyes scanning the quiet space even though there's no one else in the waiting room. What does she expect? Someone to roll out from beneath a chair?

I stand, gathering my coat and purse. "That's me," I say.

"Good morning, Beatrix," the technician replies. She isn't much older than me, but she has a sort of bland look, like boxed mashed potatoes. Her pale skin matches her pale hair and her pale eyes. "Follow me."

I'm surprised to be brought to a changing room. I always dress appropriately for MRIs, usually yoga pants and a long-sleeved t-shirt, or maybe leggings and a simple dress if I'm on my way to work. And certainly no jewelry or underwire bra. As a lifetime migraine sufferer, this isn't my first rodeo.

The technician nods toward a pair of neatly folded blue scrubs. "They may be a little big, but there's a drawstring. You can store your belongings inside the locker here." She then shows me how to secure the lock. "Think of a four-digit code, type that in, and then turn it right."

"Oh, I didn't wear any metal." I gesture towards my outfit, which is a pair of joggers and a large sweatshirt that goes halfway down my thighs. Also, she expects me to create and then remember a four-digit code on the fly? Doesn't this lady know I have MS? She may as well have asked me to perform Simone Biles' signature double backflip with two twists.

"We prefer everyone to wear the scrubs," she says with a tight smile. "You can wear your shoes into the MRI room, though. I would never expect you to walk across these floors barefoot!"

And with a shrill sort of chuckle, the technician disappears.

Resigned, I change into the creepy scrubs, which are about four sizes too big for me. The drawstrings are useless. Better than four sizes too small, I guess. I decide to leave my locker unlocked and risk my Old Navy athleisure getting swiped. It seems preferable to dealing with the hassle and humiliation of being locked out. And then, I trudge toward the MRI room in my slip-on Keds, one hand holding up my pants.

"What sort of music would you like to hear?" the technician asks. "We have it all. Whatever you'd like."

I consider requesting an obscure artist or incredibly strange genre, just to see the woman's reaction, but I can feel a dull headache starting and don't want to be stuck listening to screamo rock. "Christmas music would be great," I say. It's November 28, and I'm ready to jingle all the way.

The technician helps me onto the MRI table and even covers me with a blanket, which is admittedly nice. "Ready?" she asks.

"Uh-huh." I close my eyes and am slid inside the tube, much deeper than I've ever been before.

As Perry Como and Kelly Clarkson sing their yuletide ballads, my head starts to ache and then throb with each bang, beep, and clatter of the machine. *Oh, no.* I didn't expect my morning headache to worsen like this. When I woke up with a headache this morning, I figured it was caffeine related and would resolve after my morning cup of coffee. But now, it's turning into a full-fledged migraine.

My throat feels dry, impossibly dry, and I swallow hard and repeatedly to resist coughing. I'm terrified to move just the slightest bit and ruin the MRI image. I don't want to come back next week and have to do this all over again.

Is it hotter in here than usual?

Maybe the blanket wasn't such a great idea.

Am I sweating? Is this temperature normal?

Oh God: is the MRI machine on fire? How will I even know? I'm not allowed to move my head!

As my headache pain increases and I grow warmer, I start to feel nauseous. What happens if you vomit inside an MRI machine?

Forty minutes in, the technician pulls me out to inject the contrast. She scrutinizes my teeny, tiny arm veins.

"I just had bloodwork done on Wednesday," I explain, my head awkwardly set in the stabilizing gear so I can only move my eyes. "My right arm's still pretty bruised, and my left arm veins are miniscule."

"I see that," she frowns. "Let's give the veins on your hands a try."

For thirty seconds, I feel the sharp sting of the needle as she tries to work it into a vein on my left hand. I want to scream at her to stop. I can't see *anything,* but I can feel *everything.* Tears are quickly filling my eyes and instead of swallowing coughs, I'm now swallowing sobs.

"Well, shoot. Your left hand doesn't want to work for us, now does it?" She tries to sound pleasant, but I can tell she's getting frustrated.

The technician eventually gives up and tries my right hand instead. It works, but now I'm crying. She must notice because she suddenly starts babbling about Christmas cookies and how she will head to her aunt's house tonight to make dozens of them. "Buckeyes, thumbprints, gingerbread, and sugar cookies, of course," she prattles on. "Do you have any fun plans today?"

There are tears running down my face, and I can't even move to brush them aside. I am humiliated, angry, and in so much pain. I've never felt this claustrophobic or powerless. I try to mumble a reply, but my voice is thick and muffled. I'm sent back inside the tube for the last fifteen minutes of the MRI, and this is when I truly lose it.

I have to lay there, still as a Roman statue, while inside, I absolutely crumble.

My head pain is crushing. My hands and arms are throbbing from all the needles and poking of the past few days. Even though the technician removed my blanket, I'm still boiling hot. I think I'm having a full-blown panic attack: I can no longer tell if the drumming noises are coming from the machine or my rapidly beating heart.

"Are you okay?" the technician asks every few minutes, her voice drowning out the happy holiday songs. I regret choosing Christmas music. "Everything all right?"

"Yes," I reply, my voice a pathetic gurgle, even though I am not okay. Not in the least.

This is my new normal: needles, blood tests, MRI tubes. I know medical bills are ahead of me too, big, scary, intimidating ones. Specialist visits aren't cheap. MRIs certainly aren't either. I can only imagine the staggering cost of MS medications.

I am drowning in an ocean of self-pity, gasping for air with each fresh wave of tears.

When the technician pulls me out, I sit up too fast. I'm bleary-eyed, tear-stained, and dizzy.

"Sit here for as long as you need," she says gently. "We can walk back to the changing room together."

"I'm okay. I'm fine," I lie.

I teeter off the table and stumble down the hallway. I have to get out of here.

I just want to go home.

Chapter Twenty-One

That evening, I sit at a bar morosely drinking a beer.

The book I brought sits unread beside me. Instead, I stare at the pair of television sets behind the bar, not really watching. Just zoning out. The Cincinnati Bengals are playing tonight, and I'm sure some serious football fans are glaring at me from behind, peeved this miserable woman with a book took such a stellar spot at the bar, but I don't care.

I slept away most of my Saturday.

After my MRI, I went home and immediately hopped in the shower, wanting to physically wash away the horrible experience. I stood there, beneath the pelts of scalding hot water, and rubbed rose-scented body wash into my skin, removing any lingering MRI smells. Afterward, I wrapped myself in a fluffy robe and climbed into bed. My linen sheets felt deliciously cool, while my quilt provided just the right amount of comforting weight. Tony curled against my stomach, and I looped an arm around him. The warmth of his body and the rhythm of his breathing instantly lulled me into a deep sleep.

When I woke up, the sky outside was dark and disorienting. It was half past five. Hannah had texted me, asking if I wanted to come over for a DIY spa night. A drugstore beauty aficionado, she always has bathroom drawers full of fun products to try. But I'd asked for a raincheck, not ready to face Hannah's imploring gaze or be an audience to happy wedding chatter.

The latter realization made me feel all the worse.

I decided I wanted a drink, something to sip on and numb my pain.

Drinking at home, *alone*, felt tragic, which is why I ended up here at a neighborhood bar. It's nearly seven o'clock, and the Gas Light Cafe quickly fills with lively patrons. There are families grabbing the Gas Light's famous burgers for supper (under normal circumstances, I'd order one myself), couples cozying up in the gorgeous retro booths (let's be real, even under normal circumstances, this would not include me), and sports fans of all ages huddling around the televisions, gazes fixed upwards. Holiday lights are tacked alongside framed photos of family members and sports figures, and nearly every surface is natural wood or painted green.

It's cozy and bustling, and I'm confident I'm ruining the mood with my bad vibes.

Since I'm feeling anything but spirited tonight, I've ordered an IPA. I don't even *like* IPAs, but their bitter hops sounded appropriate for the way I feel.

"Bea!" a familiar voice says, startling me. "Mind if I join you?"

I glance up to see Chris Little bounding towards me. He's wearing a red scarf and a heavy gray peacoat. His round glasses are partially fogged up, and I can hardly make out his eyes behind them. I'm surprised he recognized me with such murky spectacles.

"Oh! Hey there." I gather my worries and try to snap back into the present. "I would, um, love some company," I fib, nodding at the empty stool to my right.

Chris beams. "Great." He drapes his scarf over the stool and then covers it with his coat. He's wearing slacks and a button-up shirt, a much fancier ensemble than my leggings and sweater. Chris takes a seat and rolls up his sleeves.

"You're awfully dressed up," I say. "Big plans tonight?" Maybe he met a Sierra Club bombshell and his sister's prescribed sabbatical from dating has already ended.

"I sponsor the environmental club at school. We visited the zoo today, and they gave a presentation on their sustainability efforts." Chris gives a low whistle. "If you ever want to feel better about the state of the world, I highly recommend you check out what the Cincinnati Zoo is doing."

He pauses for the briefest of moments before continuing on. "For example, they have these massive underground tanks that store stormwater. We're talking 410,000 gallons of capacity. By 2025, the zoo is committed to becoming a net zero energy, waste, and water facility! Net *zero*, Bea! And get this: they are going to generate *more* energy for the grid than they *use*."

Chris is absolutely buzzing, speaking almost exclusively in exclamation marks, and his excitement is contagious.

"Incredible!" I smile, absolutely meaning it. "And very encouraging, too."

When the no-nonsense bartender stops by, Chris asks for a gin and tonic, which is exactly what I would have ordered if I was in a better mood.

"So, you're a teacher then," I confirm, satisfied with this new bit of intel on my cute neighbor. "Is that why you're so good at memorizing statistics?"

"Just a useless talent of mine," he says with a wry smile. "But yes, I'm a high school science teacher, currently covering Environmental Science and Biology." His chest inflates slightly. I can tell he is proud.

"Well, consider me impressed. I thought my freshman year biome project was a nightmare, and I barely squeaked by in Biology class."

Maybe if I'd been a better Biology student, I would have recognized my multiple sclerosis symptoms as soon as they started. I wouldn't have let myself gain twenty pounds. I wouldn't have allowed myself to become this weak or this fatigued. My bladder wouldn't be in the state it is, and I wouldn't be dropping things. I wouldn't be dizzy and uncoordinated. I wouldn't spend so much of my life in a brain fog. I wouldn't be so *broken*.

The thoughts are illogical, and yet, I feel that awful tightness in my chest, and my eyes start to itch. I take a swig of beer and pray, *Please don't cry. Please don't cry...*

And then I start to cry.

Chris isn't alarmed. Probably because he works with angsty teenagers all day. Instead, he calmly gets off his stool and rummages through his coat pocket for a pack of tissues. "For years I used a handkerchief, for environmental reasons, but they're just not practical when you need to lend someone a tissue."

I can't help but giggle as I dab my cheeks. "Thanks for not handing me a fistful of snot."

He stares at me so intently, I look at the televisions instead. Joe Burrow and team are at the 10-yard line, and anticipation grows inside the crowded bar.

"What made you cry?" Chris asks, oblivious to the football game.

"I was diagnosed with multiple sclerosis on Wednesday." I'm surprised how easy it is to tell Chris Little this news. I haven't even told Hannah yet! "This sounds silly, but you mentioned Biology class, and I was thinking how if I'd been a stronger student, maybe I would have recognized the symptoms and caught the disease sooner." I wave a hand. "I sound ridiculous."

"Oh, I'm so sorry." Chris's brown eyes are big and oval-shaped. He looks genuinely sad for me, which makes me start to cry all over again. "How long did you experience symptoms?"

"About a year, I guess?" I shrug, genuinely unsure when my body became so unpredictable. I wish there was a clear beginning to all of this, a memory of my brain turning a sort of switch. "It's hard to say."

"I'm no MS expert, but I do know many people suffer for *years* before their eventual diagnosis. Invisible diseases are easy to explain away," he says.

I hiccup. "That's what my neurologist said."

"If you ask me, it sounds like you were quite advanced in recognizing something was wrong with your body. Cheers to intuition and modern medicine, a true dynamic duo." He raises his glass, and bewildered, I clink mine against it.

"You're something else," I say fondly. I place my head in my hands. "I recently turned thirty, and now I've been diagnosed with this incurable disease. I just thought my life would look different at this point."

"How so?" Chris asks, genuinely curious.

"Married, kids, a house, my dream job," I admit. "I figured I would have checked those boxes, or at least some of them."

Chris's eyebrows are so thick and bushy, they touch when he frowns. "Those things happen for different people at different times," he says. "Why do we assign arbitrary ages to such important milestones? And why must they happen in a certain order? Honestly, why do they have to happen at all? For example, I know plenty of happy couples who have chosen to never marry."

"Because that's historically how they've been done?" I offer. "My parents were married in their early twenties, and they had my brother a few years later. My dad started his home-building business before he turned thirty."

"So what? I mean, good for your parents, but you aren't your mom or dad," he says. "Besides, that was the eighties, right? My dad hitchhiked across the country and my crazy aunt Cindy got into a fistfight over a

Cabbage Patch Kids doll. Things have changed a lot since then."

I laugh, wanting more details about both of those stories. "I mean, sure! Of course things were different then, but I thought my life would follow at least some of that same pattern." I poke my finger against his chest, which makes my own heart do a pitter-patter. "What about you? Are you exactly where you imagined you would be at...?"

"Thirty-six," Chris volunteers. He's slightly older than I thought. "And no. Not at all. But that doesn't bother me. I decided years ago that I wouldn't make major life decisions based on societal pressures."

"That's an awfully easy thing to say as a man," I say.

Chris sighs, "I know."

I raise my own bushy eyebrows at him. "I'm going to take a wild guess and say that thought process had something to do with your messy breakup though." Chris blushes, suddenly looking bashful. "What happened?" I ask more gently.

"We need a second round of drinks if we're going to approach that territory," he says.

Chapter Twenty-Two

We both order gin and tonics this time around, extra lime for me, and Chris asks the bartender to add the cocktails to his tab, which I think is chivalrous.

"The thing is, nothing really happened. Nothing catastrophic or dramatic that is," Chris begins, fresh drink in hand. "Her name was, *is,* Amanda, and we were together eight years, which is about five years past the time when everyone expected me to propose."

Yep. That sounds about right.

"Amanda is a perfectly nice, smart, and interesting person. She works in fundraising for a nonprofit. She has a big heart," he says. "But as the years went on, certain habits of hers started to drive me crazy. They were little quirks, and I think in the right relationship, they would have been endearing."

"Was she a litterbug?" I can't help but tease. "An anti-vaxxer? Thought climate change was a hoax?"

Chris shudders. "Oh God, no. Nothing like that," he says.

"Then what were these habits?" I press.

"She would leave lights on all over the house, and she routinely drank the last cup of coffee without making more," he says. *Do I ever do those things?* I wonder. *Probably.* "She was always running late, too. We jokingly called it 'Amanda Time,' but it became pretty annoying. And honestly, inconsiderate."

I give a small nod. I can understand how that would get old.

"The worst, though, was the DIY stuff. The home projects," he groans.

"You owned a house together?" I ask, surprised.

"Yes. Like Maria said, it was a messy breakup," he says, his voice a little quieter now. "Amanda loved that house. *We* loved that house. It was a historic home in Columbia-Tusculum that overlooked the river. We had less than 800 square feet and no driveway, but we had a view of the river and a working fireplace."

"That sounds incredible," I say.

"It was," he nods. "And Amanda loved to daydream about ways we could make the house our own. 'I've got an idea!' she would announce every other week, at least that's what it felt like, and she would be so excited. She would jump to her feet and start gesturing with her hands... It was adorable, Bea."

Chris's eyes look wistful, and I half-wonder if I'm about to witness a great reunion. Maybe Chris will ask me to drive him to the airport where he will dash past security and locate Amanda the moment she's about to disappear down the jet bridge. I'll have no choice but to cue the *Love Actually* soundtrack for them.

But no, Chris is already shaking his head.

"The problem was, she would start these home projects but never finish them," he explains. "She once stripped all the paint off the back deck with the intention of staining it for a more natural look... And then she never got around to the staining part." Chris rubs his eyes. "Or there was the time she taught herself how to do tiling so she could tackle the kitchen backsplash—which, if you ask me, was perfectly fine the way it was—and stopped halfway through."

"Yikes," I say.

"*Yikes* is right," Chris says. "When we broke up, I was relieved she wanted to keep the house. If we had decided to sell it, we would have had to bring in outside help."

"Think there's an HGTV show for that?"

Chris gives me a wry smile.

"In September, Amanda sat me down and asked if I was ever going to propose."

"Oh." My heart breaks for Amanda. "What did you say?"

"I didn't answer right away," Chris sighs. "And then I realized that... no. I wasn't. I didn't even know why we were still together. Maybe because it was easy at that point? It's comfortable being with the same person for eight years."

To be honest? I'm left pretty speechless.

I want to hug Amanda this very second. Eight years spent with a guy! Eight years of birthdays, holidays, family gatherings, vacations. Eight years of binge-watching TV shows and making chicken noodle soup when the other is sick. They'd bought a house together. They probably had pets!

And he didn't want to marry her.

"It's okay if you think I'm an asshole," he says shyly. "I'm still wondering the same thing. I definitely *feel* like an asshole. You know how Maria thinks I should remove myself from the dating scene for a while? Well, she's probably right. God forbid I do this to someone else. Maybe there's something wrong with me..."

I reach for his hand and give it a squeeze. "I've only known you for about a week now, but you don't seem like an asshole. Assholes don't carry around tissues for other people's tears," I say. "I'm sorry about Amanda. That's really sad."

"I hope she meets someone amazing and that this was all for the best."

I study him. Chris's neck turned red while talking about Amanda, but the splotches have started to clear. "Do you believe everything happens for a reason?" I ask.

"Not at all," he replies. "That's just something people say to make sense of nonsensical things. Do you?"

"No, not exactly," I say. "I believe in kismet, that God works in mysterious ways, serendipity... But I don't think every single experience happens for a reason. That's oversimplifying."

"If that ends up being the case, I'll have a lot of questions for the big man upstairs," Chris says. "Question number one: Why did I throw up on my first day of kindergarten?"

"Oh no," I giggle. "You were *that* kid?"

"It's even worse than it sounds," he replies. "We were going around introducing ourselves, and when it was my turn, instead of saying my name, I barfed straight into the sharing circle, like my name was Barf Little."

We both have a wonderful, big belly laugh at that one.

"So," Chris says, obviously trying to steer the subject away from vomit, which I appreciate. "You said you had expected to find your dream job by now. Where do you currently work?"

"I'm a graphic designer," I tell him. "I work at an ad agency called Polly Feinstein. It's down on West Fourth Street, right above that amazing French bakery everyone's always Instagramming."

"Yeah? That's cool," Chris says. "I wish I was more creative."

I smile and nod. I'm happy to be a creative type. It makes life more interesting.

"So, graphic design isn't your dream job then?" he clarifies.

"My dream job?" I repeat, before shaking my head. "No, I don't think so. Is being a science teacher yours?"

"It is," he replies simply and with such confidence, I'm left a little speechless. "I knew I wanted to be a science teacher ever since I started watching *The Magic School Bus.*"

"You're kidding me," I gape, tremendously amused. "Ms. Frizzle is why you became a science teacher?"

"Yeah, I am kidding. At least sort of," he grins. "As much as I loved *The Magic School Bus,* it was my fifth grade science teacher that lit the spark. His name was Mr. Fisco. He was passionate about climate change way back in the late 90s, when so few people were talking about it, and he got me all fired up on the issue."

I nod thoughtfully.

"I've always loved science, and I get to teach kids about the importance of the environment. I feel like I'm actually making a difference in the world. It makes me feel less helpless. And this next generation gives me such hope," he says. "High schoolers are misunderstood. They're the ones who are going to change our world, and I want to give them a solid foundation for doing it."

"Wow," I breathe, amazed and slightly envious. "I don't even know what my dream job *is,* to be honest."

"You're very self-actualized," he says. I'm flattered, even though the man hardly knows me, but I give a slight shake of my head. "I have a feeling you *do* know what it is," he continues. "It's in your head and heart somewhere. You've just got to unearth it."

Strangely, it's my tiny house sketches that come to mind.

But those are just a hobby, a craft. If anything, they're the adult equivalent of my childhood self sliding the "Barbie Fashion Designer" CD-ROM into our family's desktop computer and giddily creating Barbie a new wardrobe.

But before I can tell Chris about my tiny house drawings, my phone vibrates against the bar top. It's a text message from an unknown number.

"Probably a wrong number. Or a doctor's appointment reminder," I comment.

Except it's neither.

Hi Bea. This is John Noble, Peter and Mattie's friend. Are you free for dinner tomorrow night? Sometime around 7? I've been craving Asian! :)

"Everything okay?" Chris jostles my leg, and I feel that electric shock run through my body, every cell suddenly buzzing.

I'm attracted to my quirky neighbor, that's undeniable. But is he attracted to me?

Throw in a recent (messy) breakup, a hiatus from dating, and a contempt for societal norms, and where does that leave me? Lest we forget, Chris Little dated a nice woman for eight years and still didn't want to marry her. I don't have a decade to mess around with the wrong guy. I'm ready to find a man who will split a Costco membership with me and take Tony Soprano in for his monthly nail trim.

"Everything's fine," I smile. "If you'll excuse me, I just need to use the restroom real quick."

Sitting in the tiny bathroom stall, I text John Noble back.

Hi John! Tomorrow sounds lovely, I write, deciding I want to be a woman who uses adjectives like lovely. **Looking forward to it!**

Well, I'll be damned. Things are getting interesting.

Chapter Twenty-Three

When was the last time I had a real date?

I pour myself a steaming cup of coffee and add a splash of peppermint mocha creamer. Even though being set up by my older sister isn't exactly the equivalent of meeting a man when our dogs' leashes intertwine at the local park, it's still more romantic than all of those dating apps Hannah pushes on me. It's how she met Arthur, and while Arthur is a terrific dude and undeniably Han's soulmate, I don't want to find The One via an algorithm.

I've gone on exactly three dates generated by dating apps, and each one was progressively worse than the one before it. First was the accountant with geek chic glasses and an incredibly posh condo...and an incredibly boring personality. After that came the handsome general contractor with a chip on his shoulder. And then there was the symphony violinist with a lavish lifestyle and enormous ego, both courtesy of his doting parents.

Hannah tells me I'm being dramatic—"I went on at least fifteen horrendous dates before I met Arthur!"—but I'm the gal who yearns for the soft glow and warm beiges of a Nora Ephron romantic comedy. Smartphones and swiping right don't fit into that world.

I spread my array of tiny house drawings across the dining room table.

While tonight will be about finding love, today is about finding my *raison d'etre*. Because even if the open art director role *does* work out in my favor, I can't stop thinking about my conversation with Chris Little. Do I want to be at Polly Feinstein a year from now? Two? I don't think I do.

Holy cannoli. I've done *a lot* of these. I start to count and realize I have well over one hundred tiny house sketches. But how do I make a career out of a bunch of drawings? Where is the jumping-off point?

I flip a sketchbook to a fresh page and begin a list.

Do I combine all of my drawings into one of those quirky coffee table books they sell at Urban Outfitters? One of my high school classmates did that with sketches of puppies eating popsicles, and now she has a few children's book series under her belt. But while everyone loves puppies and popsicles, I imagine the tiny house market is a bit more niche.

I could start an Etsy shop where I sell my drawings and create custom portraits. *A perfect housewarming gift!* I imagine writing. *Happy to add family pets to your piece, as well!* But would I enjoy drawing other people's homes? Or is my pleasure derived from creating my own? I suspect it's the latter.

Maybe I could become a tiny house interior designer! *Interior designer Bea Parker specializes in stylish décor and savvy space-saving designs for your tiny house. She seamlessly melds vintage homewares with modern conveniences for a look that's cozy and convenient.*

I like that. I put a few stars beside the blurb. I'm getting warmer.

Around ten o'clock, after I've peed for the sixth time today (But who's counting?), I decide some fresh air will do me good. So, I give Janet a call.

"G'morning!" Janet answers her landline.

"Good morning to you, too. It's Bea," I say.

"What's shaking?" I hear Minnie barking in the background and the clanking of silverware. Buddy the Cockatiel is singing "If I Only Had a Brain." "Did River leave the door to the trash area open again? If I have to shoo away another racoon..."

"No, no. I haven't even seen River in a few days." River is the twenty-something dude who lives on the first floor, and he is definitively the worst. "Do you want to join me for a power walk?" I think of Billy Crystal and his friend strutting through Central Park with strong, almost robotic movements in *When Harry Met Sally.*

Janet pauses. "A power walk, huh? Can't remember the last time I did that."

"Meet you outside our doors in fifteen?" I hold my breath.

"Hmm..." I know she's trying to think up an excuse but coming up short. "Oh, why the hell not?"

Closer to twenty-five minutes later, I stand in the hallway still waiting on Janet.

I decided to keep Tony Soprano home since his little legs don't do long (or fast) walks very well. I hear Minnie whining and Janet's honeyed assurances before the door squeaks open, and Janet slips discreetly outside.

"Minnie isn't pleased with me for leaving her behind," Janet whispers. "But I wasn't sure if she could keep up."

I take in Janet's outfit, which includes a baby blue turtleneck and leggings beneath a hot pink leotard. She's also wearing pink leg warmers and vintage Reeboks. I refrain from asking, *Is that what you're wearing?* because I believe it is one of the worst questions you can ask a person. I mean, clearly that's the outfit they have chosen to wear. When people ask that question, what do they expect the person to say? *Gosh, this? No way! It's just my practice outfit! Wait until you see the real thing!*

"I like your leg warmers," I say instead, which is the truth.

Honestly, I feel a bit underdressed compared to Janet. I've thrown on a pair of tired, black workout leggings and a heavy, oversized sweatshirt with LONG LAKE, NY stitched across the bust.

"Why thank you, doll. It's from the time I was an extra in a Jane Fonda workout video. Have I ever told you about that?" Janet asks. We gallop down the stairs, and I grip the railing with a masked intensity. "I was married to a Hollywood producer. He's the one who got me the gig. All sorts of gigs, really. I did quite a bit of commercial work."

"No! You've never mentioned him or your acting career." The realistic part of me knows Janet's former lover (and former life, for that matter) stories *probably* aren't true, but I choose to believe them anyway. It's more fun. "When did you live in California?"

Janet purses her pink lips to one side. "Must have been the seventies and early eighties," she says. "It's hard to keep track. That husband's name was Stan. He had a handlebar mustache and a drinking problem."

"Ugh. No thank you," I reply in response to both. I push open the lobby doors, and we're met with a burst of cold air.

"Which way?" Janet asks, turning her head right then left, looking up and down Ridge Road. "Nothing too strenuous, I hope? My feet blister easily."

"Left?" I suggest.

Nothing gets past Janet. "You want me to do the Pandora hill?" She shakes her head, trying to fight a bemused smile. "All right then, *fine*. But

I'm only doing this because I love you and because you have MS."

"I'll take your charity," I laugh before asking for an update on the latest work drama.

Janet has been a salon receptionist for decades now, and while there is rarely friction within the staff, the clients come to their hair and nail appointments with six to eight weeks' worth of pent-up grievances.

After I hear about Marcia's gold-digging future son-in-law and the new diet Valerie is swearing by—"You can eat whatever you want, ice cream, pizza, a steak, *anything*, for exactly one hour each day"—Janet turns the conversation to me.

"So, how's work been for you? Is that manager of yours still a b-word?" she asks, though a bit breathlessly, as we head down Ashwood. "Greta? Gertrude?"

I swing my arms back and forth, trying to work my ab muscles. "Gwen," I say, wondering if Janet practices the same name-forgetting habit as my mom. "She's still...tricky, yes. Not my favorite person in the world... Work's fine, though. There's actually a promotion I'm in the running for..." I pause, thinking this next part over. "But, well, I guess I'm contemplating a career change altogether, now that I'm thirty and all." *And now that the cute, smart new neighbor suggested it.*

I love this street, where the homes have dreamy, castle-like qualities to them. Most are modestly sized but have ornate designs cut out of the shutters, fancy glass paned windows, and gorgeous stucco and brick designs. Some even boast Juliette balconies and slate roofs. The effect is cozy and charming, almost like a fairytale village.

"What do you have in mind for this career change?" We careen to the left, narrowly missing a three-year-old tricyclist.

"I'm just starting to figure that out," I say. "I'd like to continue doing something creative, but what that something is... Well, I don't know yet."

Janet is swinging her own arms and hips. "The world is your oyster, sweetie!"

Just then my legs—Is it one leg? Or is it both? I can't tell—turn weak and tingly, and I go crashing towards the cement. I take a sharp inhale on my way down and catch myself with my palms and knees.

"You're bleeding!" Janet exclaims, kneeling beside me. "Did you break anything? What did you trip on? Are you okay?"

My palms are red and scratched. I've torn the fabric of my workout pants, and my knees are covered in tiny pebbles of gravel, blood glowing red behind the gray.

"That really hurt," I admit, a lone tear escaping my right eye. I look behind me. There isn't anything on the sidewalk I could have tripped over. No raised cement edge. No rogue rock. No discarded pop can dropped by an inconsiderate litterbug.

"It's okay, Bea. Lord knows I have my clumsy moments," Janet says, trying to make me smile.

I shake my head. "It was my MS."

And the world sure as hell isn't my oyster.

Chapter Twenty-Four

*J*anet helps me hobble home, and three different cars stop to ask us if we need a ride, which is *so* Pleasant Ridge. We politely refuse each offer. Knowing my luck these days, we would probably get abducted. After a nice long soak in the tub, I bandage up my wounds and crawl back into bed for an early afternoon nap, being careful to set an alarm so I don't accidentally sleep the day away and miss my date.

When I wake up a few hours later, my stomach is growling. Since I'm pretty sure people with chronic diseases are supposed to eat healthy(ish), I squeeze a foil packet of tuna over a bowl of spinach and drizzle it all with a lemon vinaigrette. I take a bite and chew thoughtfully. It isn't bad, it just isn't my usual deli sandwich and potato chips... Or ooey-gooey grilled cheese with tomato soup... Or sushi doused in spicy mayo...

You get the picture. It's not like The Kitchn is going to be writing a feature on the flavor sensation of my spinach and tuna salad. Tony Soprano jumps on the dining room chair beside me. Mom hates that I let him sit at the table with me, but who else does she think I eat my meals with? I hand him a small piece of tuna, which he eats in a single gulp.

I scan through a few MS-specific diets on my phone while I eat. The Wahls Protocol Diet excludes all processed food, gluten, eggs, dairy and sugar, while the Swank Diet cuts out processed food, some oils, red meat, saturated fat, and dairy.

Honestly, this all sounds a lot like the way Mattie eats of her own free will and not because a disease had backed her into it.

A text message appears at the top of my screen, interrupting my research.

Hi Bea, it's Chris. I got your number from the building directory.

We have a building directory? I now vaguely remember Janet pestering everyone for their phone numbers and a "fun fact" a few years ago. What did I submit for my fun fact? **This is going to sound weird, but have you ever been on a singles retreat? Particularly one that takes place in a Catholic church's undercroft?**

I give a small wince. **YIKES!!!** I write back. **No, thank God. But I'm afraid to know why you're asking...**

Can I come up? Chris's reply is immediate and makes my skin turn warm.

Sure thing, I text, going for casual when I feel straight-up giddy.

I dispense my dirty salad bowl in the sink and am able to fluff up the throw pillows and light a candle in the few minutes before Chris arrives. He looks both sheepish and distressed. His ears are red, and he's wearing slippers instead of shoes. There's even a trail of crumbs on his sweatshirt, like he was in the middle of eating a sandwich when he found out about the singles retreat.

"Hey," Chris says.

"Hi. Everything okay?"

"I can't believe she did this," he replies, which I guess equates to *no*. Chris strides into my apartment with so much fervor, I feel like Jerry Seinfeld getting a visit from Kramer. "I mean, this *really* crosses the line..."

"Who? Your mom?" I guess, watching him pace the length of my living room. I quickly confirm that none of Tony Soprano's toys are lying in his path, because I'm sure he'd trip at the rate he's moving.

"Not my mom," he says. "Maria."

"Do you want to sit down? Have a glass of water?"

"No thanks," he replies, presumably to both.

I lean against my kitchen counter and study him more carefully. His skin is blotchy. It looked this way last night when Chris was talking about Amanda. Maybe Maria signed Amanda up for the retreat, too, in hopes of a reconciliation.

"I'm sorry for interrupting your afternoon like this. I probably should have started there. But Maria just called, and I need to vent." He sighs. "She signed me up for a weekend-long singles retreat at her church to help me 'figure things out.' What does that even mean?"

"Honestly, I have no idea," I reply. "Maybe it's an elaborate ruse to get more people to become priests and nuns?"

A wry smile tugs at Chris's lips. "I assume it's some awful attempt by Maria to get me to return to my Catholic roots and meet a nice Catholic woman in the process. She hates that I don't go to church anymore."

I shrug as I have no idea what it's like being a twin or having a sibling invested in your religious (or non-religious) life. "Doesn't Maria want you to take a break from dating anyway?"

"She wants me to take a break from the kind of women I usually date. That's my suspicion," he says. "But *eventually,* Maria wants me to meet a nice Catholic woman and have two to four kids and send them to the same parochial school *her* kids attend. She also likes the idea of me marrying her divorced friend, Beth, and becoming a stepfather to Beth's kids." He squints. "But that's a whole different topic."

Beth. I picture an adorable single mother with a sweet smile and a big heart. I feel irrationally jealous of this stranger.

"I'm sorry. I'm rambling." He runs both hands through his hair, making his thick curls stick up in comical directions. Honestly? It's pretty cute, and I decide something is seriously wrong with me considering I find this dude adorable even in the middle of a crisis. "But I'm not going on that retreat. There's no way in hell. Maria can critique my choice of clothes and music and vacation spots, but she isn't going to run my romantic life. Or my religious life, for that matter."

"I didn't realize Maria was such a zealot." It's sort of a dumb thing to say considering I've met the woman once and there are probably millions of things I don't know about her.

"Not a zealot exactly," Chris replies. "Just very traditional. She married her high school sweetheart, still hangs out with all her high school friends, is the PTA president...you know the type. And she's always seen me as her quirky twin brother who simply needs the right woman to set him straight."

"Interesting." I settle into the sofa. "And Amanda wasn't that kind of woman?" I realize I have an opportunity to probe. "Or, um, any of the women you dated before her?"

The creases disappear from his forehead, and Chris finally stops his pacing. He sits in the rocking chair (an antique, of course) across from me.

"I guess not. At least, according to Maria. Before Amanda, I dated a Buddhist mountain climber who wanted to live in a tent, and before her, I was seeing a photojournalist who eventually moved to East Africa to cover the clean water crisis."

Well, jeez louise. Color me impressed. "They both sound like incredible people," I reply, intimidated by Chris's past lovers.

He looks around my apartment in a sort of daze. I'm surprised to see him stand back up. "I can't believe I interrupted your afternoon like this. And then unloaded all of that on you." His skin turns an even deeper shade of red. "I'm so sorry. You probably think I'm a basket case."

"No matter how old we are, siblings have an amazing knack for getting under our skin," I reply, immediately thinking of Justin and the lack of effort he puts towards any group gift ("Just let me know how much I should Venmo you.") and Mattie's overzealous approach towards, well, everything. "I was actually about to turn on one of my favorite shows. *Tiny House Nation.* Do you want to join me? Maybe take a bit of a breather before you talk to Maria?" I add gently.

"I've never heard of it," Chris admits. He examines his phone, considers, and then shoves it into his back pocket. "But yeah. Okay. That sounds really nice."

I head for the kitchen. "I'm going to insist you have some water." I retrieve my sketchbook and colored pencils as well, eager to jot down notes and maybe even a few illustrations. "Don't mind me," I tell Chris, handing him the cool glass. "I doodle tiny house drawings while I watch."

"That's neat," he says in a way that's kind, not sarcastic. "Have you ever stayed in a tiny house?"

"Just once. My best friend, Hannah, and I stayed in one outside Charleston. It was right on the beach, and we each had our own sleeping loft," I tell him. The tiny home had cedar shingles and white trim. It looked like a proper East Coast beach house but in miniature. Fairy lights stretched over the patio, and there was an outdoor shower with a view of the ocean. "It was magical," I say simply.

The couple featured on this episode of *Tiny House Nation* are around my parents' age, and they're attempting to downsize from a four-bedroom ranch where they've lived for forty years. "Wow," I murmur, overwhelmed for these two strangers but also feeling a tremendous amount of respect for them. "This should be interesting."

"My mom's Precious Moments collection alone wouldn't fit into one of these tiny houses," Chris smirks.

I think of my own parents and their 4,000-square-foot McMansion. How much of that massive house do they actually use on a regular basis? The entire second floor is a sort of ghost town. My childhood bedroom, as well as my siblings', are museums of our adolescences, their only regular visitor being Tina the cleaning lady. I doubt Tina is very impressed by my *Baby-Sitters Little Sister* collection, Mattie's National Honor Society awards, or Justin's binders of baseball cards. As for the guest bedroom, its only guests are my aunt and uncle who fly in from Seattle once a year.

I stare down at my sketchpad and think about what Janet said to me earlier: *The world is your oyster, sweetie!*

It's a wonderful sentiment, but perhaps an idea that's better suited for embroidered pillows and the covers of notebooks popular with starry-eyed teenagers. How is someone like me, a person who can't manage to get through the day without taking a nap, expected to find the strength to switch careers?

I studied graphic design in school. It's a field I feel so comfortable in, I can practically create emails, social media ads, and print mailers in my sleep. But where's the fun in that? And how am I making the world a better place by helping sell one more bougie wine aerator or an overpriced smartwatch or whatever?

I watch as Zach Giffin, the master carpenter on *Tiny House Nation*, designs an innovative dining room table that slides out from another piece of furniture, almost like magic. I like how every family featured in this show has a seemingly insurmountable, unsolvable dilemma that Zach and his co-host, John Weisbarth, manage to fix.

"This sort of creative problem-solving reminds me of what my dad used to do, and what my sister does now, at Kickerville," I tell Chris. "That's the name of my family's home-building company."

I see Chris studying my notebook where I've sketched out a model with a screened-in porch and a flower box beneath each window. I'm going to color it ballet slipper pink and add dusty blue shutters for a sort of French provincial look "You're very talented," he murmurs. "Does Kickerville offer tiny homes? That sketch looks so real. Like it's a house you've seen before and know very well."

"Really?" I motion for him to follow me to the dining room table. "I want you to look at my other drawings. And please, tell me what you really think. I can handle it."

I watch as Chris flips through the dozens of tiny house illustrations I've sketched over the years. His eyes are big and curious and his brows are pressed together. It's the face of someone genuinely interested.

I bite my bottom lip. "Do you think I could turn my drawings into actual blueprints?" I ask quietly, both embarrassed and emboldened by the question.

Chris sets down one of my drawings. He studies me, a smile tugging at his lips. "I think you just found your dream job," he beams.

My heart starts to thud in my chest, and my breathing turns shallow. Could *I* be a tiny house creator? Could I make the world a better place by helping people live smaller, simpler lives? And could I do it all at Kickerville?

It's almost as though I can hear the wheels starting to spin inside my head, their movements squeaky and clunky before gaining momentum. I start to take big, confident strides across my apartment, excited energy pulsing through my body and purpose and passion in my step for the first time in what feels like forever.

"I'm going to politely excuse myself after having so impolitely inviting myself over," Chris says. "I can't wait to see what you come up with." He reaches out and gives my upper arm a small squeeze. "Good luck, Bea."

I open a voice memo on my phone, and I start talking.

It's time to dream—and plan—big.

Chapter Twenty-Five

Is that him?

I narrow my eyes at the tall man who has stopped to blow his nose in front of the restaurant. Obviously I've looked up John Noble on social media, but what if his photo is outdated? For all I know, he's gone bald and gained one hundred pounds since posing with a pal during Chicago's St. Patrick's Day celebrations.

We drove separately tonight, I insisted on it, and I sit in my sedan sipping on an espresso drink while watching every patron come and go. I want John Noble to get to our table first and wait for *me* to walk in. I want to be the one to stride through the restaurant doors, maybe the wind caught in my hair, with my hands delicately holding together the collar of my coat.

At seven o'clock sharp, a steely gray BMW pulls into the crowded parking lot, its motor so quiet, it practically purrs. A lanky man with light brown hair lumbers out of the two-door coupe. He's wearing a navy quilted jacket, army green khakis, and boots. John Noble is quite chic, probably the chicest man I've ever gone out with, which makes perfect sense considering he is friends with Mattie and Peter. I look frantically in the rearview mirror, questioning every unusual fashion choice I've made. Quickly, I pull off my satin gloves and remove the dachshund broach from my Peter Pan collar.

I stare at my reflection, starting to panic. What if he's expecting someone like my sister? Mattie would have worn dark wash jeans tonight paired with a sophisticated black top, not a 1950s swing dress and patent leather Mary Janes. I should have just stuck to this year's uniform of dark, slimming clothing beneath drapey, camouflaging accessories. Mattie would not have worn red lipstick—too garish!—or accidentally spritzed on too much perfume, like I most certainly did. I should have curled my hair or done a dramatic smoky eye or *insert beauty endeavor here!*

Most of all, I don't want to let my older sister down, to make her regret initiating this setup. I want Mattie to feel proud of me. Even if things don't work out with John Noble, I want her to think, "This is quite obviously John Noble's loss! Because my sister is hilarious and smart and wonderful."

It's three minutes past seven.

Well, it's too late now. I might be forever known as John's bizarre blind date, but I won't be known as the woman who showed up fifteen minutes late. I'll take weird over rude. I pop a breath mint to mask the coffee smell—I decided to caffeinate beforehand, beating my MS fatigue to the punch—and stride confidently into the Asian restaurant.

A hostess opens the front door for me, and I'm greeted with the scent of ginger and soy sauce. Pots clang together cheerfully in the nearby kitchen, and the decor is exclusively red and gold. Holiday jazz music plays over the speakers, and garland studded with white lights has been strung over each doorway. It's welcoming and warm, and considering John has chosen this eatery, I am instantly put at ease.

"Good evening," says the friendly hostess. "Table for one?"

I shake my head politely. "I'm meeting someone." I scan the quaint restaurant before spotting my suave date, who is reading the menu. I award him bonus points for not sitting there scrolling through his phone. "There he is. Thank you."

John is sitting at a table in the corner, and I pray my legs don't give out during the ten-second walk there. Blessedly, they comply.

"John?" I give him a big smile before extending my hand. *Exude confidence, Bea. You can do this.* "I'm Bea Parker. It's fabulous to meet you."

John pops up from his chair and promptly knocks over his glass of water. It is exactly the sort of guffaw I feared awaited me had I entered the restaurant first and been the one waiting at the table.

"Oh, God. I'm so sorry. How embarrassing," he murmurs, tossing napkins on the mess.

"It's only water." I set a hand on his arm, selfishly glad the blunder wasn't my own. "At least you hadn't already started on the sake."

He grins. "I may be clumsy, but I promise I have good manners."

We sit down at our little table, and a server comes to remove the damp napkins and refresh the water glasses. John orders us a bottle of sake to share. "Do you like crab rangoon?" he asks "I'm a sucker for it."

"I do," I reply, thinking how people tend to either love or hate the starter. I'm happy John falls into the former category. "Let's get extra dipping sauce."

John adds the appetizer to our drink order, and I marvel at how well this is going.

He clears his throat. "How have you been feeling?"

Chapter Twenty-Six

I deflate, but only slightly. I'm not sure if I'm relieved Mattie told John about my MS or disappointed. I want to be bubbly, carefree Bea tonight, and I don't know how MS Bea fits within that persona just yet.

"I'm hanging in there. Thanks for asking." I decide to keep things short and sweet. It's thoughtful of John to have asked, but we can discuss my health another night. "So! You've just moved back from Chicago. How long were you in the city?"

"Almost twenty years?" John rubs his chin. His face is smooth shaven, and he has a rather petite nose. I think of Chris Little's giant schnozzle and his eternal five o'clock shadow. Chris is probably too concerned about water conservation to shave for very long each morning. "You're making me feel old. I'm thirty-five for the record."

"I just turned thirty, so I'm not far behind you," I say. John holds up the plate of the freshly arrived crab rangoon, and I accept a toasty square. "I was only in Chicago for four years though. I came home shortly after college."

John tells me he attended Northwestern for his undergraduate degree and has worked at various financial institutions throughout the city ever since. He studied actuarial science and is now an investment analyst for the stock market.

"Do you love it?" I ask.

He frowns slightly. "It's been a fantastic career, very challenging with plenty of opportunities for advancement. I also enjoy the fast pace and ever-evolving landscape. It keeps things exciting."

He hasn't answered my question, but in all fairness, it's more than I can say about my own job.

"What brought you back to Cincinnati?" I ask. "Besides Emilio Estevez calling it 'The Paris of the Midwest.'"

"Are you serious? He said that?" John grins, and I nod. This is in fact a direct line from an interview with one of Cincinnati's celebrity residents. "That's amazing," he laughs. "I moved home because my sister had her first baby last spring. His name is Henry, and I hated being five hours away from the little guy."

It's a perfect, heartwarming answer.

"I have a niece who is all the way out in Santa Fe. Her name's Violet, and she's pretty wonderful," I say. "So, I get it. I miss her big-time."

Our server retrieves the empty crab rangoon plate and asks if we're ready to order our entrees. I ask for the veggie pad thai, and John gets the beef bibimbap.

"Mattie told me you're a graphic designer. That must be interesting work," says John.

"Yeah! Sometimes anyway, depends on the client," I say, trying to muster up enthusiasm for my career. I want John to think I'm vivacious and confident and sanguine. "I work at an ad agency called Polly Feinstein. When they offered me a job at twenty-two, I couldn't pack my bags for Cincinnati fast enough."

"Ah, okay. So, that's why you left Chicago," John says, his smile bright. "A high school friend of mine has been trying to get a job at Polly Feinstein for years now. He said it's *the* agency to work for in Cincinnati. Is it true you have nap pods?"

"It is." I refrain from telling John just how often I use them. "And our onsite gym is incredible," I add, wanting to fit into this mold of a successful woman. "Feel free to pass along my number. I'd be happy to grab coffee with your friend sometime." I blush, realizing how strange that sounds on a first date. "I meant, um, for networking—"

But John is laughing. "Already trying to get rid of me? I mean, I get it. My friend is taller and more attractive. And he definitely wouldn't have spilled water all over the table on a first date."

I smile, appreciating his self-deprecating humor.

Our main courses come out quickly, and we discuss our dogs as we sip on sake and take warm, boldly flavored bites.

"I have a long-haired dachshund with the most beautiful dapple coat," I babble, excitement probably oozing out of my pores over the opportunity to talk about Tony Soprano.

John laughs at Tony Soprano's name and agrees he has a harrowing tale. "I have a miniature goldendoodle named Wrigley," he tells me. "He's only a year old, so he's still a terror. Leather shoes seem to be his chew toy of choice."

"Fancy," I say, immediately filling my mouth with pad thai.

John doesn't share my passion for animal rescue, I think. I remind myself of Tom Hanks' golden retriever, Brinkley, in *You've Got Mail.* Brinkley was likely not a shelter dog, and that didn't make him any less sweet.

And yet, I am admittedly grateful when we shift topics to the house John has just bought in Hyde Park. "It's a four-bedroom," he says. "So, there's room to grow."

I warm, suddenly forgetting my adopt-don't-shop attitude.

"I bet it's beautiful. What year?" I ask.

"1910," he reports proudly.

"Are you close to Mattie and Peter?" My sister and future brother-in-law live in a two-bedroom bungalow in the same historic neighborhood. It's a darling house with stained glass windows and dark, moody woodwork, but they're quickly outgrowing the 800-square-foot space.

"Yep. I'm just on the other side of the square," John confirms.

I think about future holiday seasons, ones where John and I live a stone's throw from my older sister and her husband. I imagine us watching the Macy's Day Parade together with mimosas in hand, scheduling yuletide movie marathons, and taking winter strolls to admire the lights. It all sounds cozy and wonderful.

"I would love to see your house sometime," I say.

"I would love to show it to you." He studies me. "You're still renting, right?" I give him a quick nod. "Why haven't you bought a home yet?"

It's an impertinent question, and I'm left a bit speechless by the audacity of it. For all John knows, I have two bucks in my savings account and am living paycheck to paycheck. For the record, I *have* saved enough for a down payment at this point. I've just never felt inclined to buy. "I guess I'm infatuated with the idea of up and moving at a moment's notice," I reply breezily, trying to conceal my irritation. Plus, it's not entirely untrue.

"Well, give me a little notice if you decide to leave town," John teases, oblivious to my discomfort.

When our server comes to clear our plates, I'm surprised John declines a box for leftovers. "I'm weird about reheating eggs," he says, handing the young man his partially finished stone bowl.

I consider taking John's leftovers to Chris's compost bin before realizing that a) meat is not permitted in Chris's compost bin, and b) how totally creepy and bizarre it would be to request your date's leftovers.

"Everything okay?" John asks, noticing my frown.

I wave my hand, insisting that yes, everything is fine, and he grabs the check.

John walks me to my car after dinner, and I regret not tidying it up beforehand. A few online purchases that need to be returned are scattered across my backseat, and my empty coffee cup and a forgotten Diet Coke bottle are in the front cup holders.

"I had a lot of fun with you tonight," John says.

"I had a lot of fun, too."

John leans in, brushing my cheek with his lips. He smells like expensive cologne. It's a pleasant experience, and yet... There isn't any warming in my stomach. The butterflies aren't fluttering. My heart isn't going pitter-patter, pitter-patter.

"Thank you," I smile. "And thanks again for such a delicious dinner."

"I'll call you soon," he promises.

"I would love that," I reply smoothly.

But the entire way home, I can't help but wonder—would I? Would I really *love* that? My date with John was cordial and interesting. He's easy to talk to, polite, and handsome. He also adores his nephew enough to move back to his hometown, and he's clearly smart and a hard worker.

So why am I not more excited?

I park my car behind the Amelia and gaze upward. Chris's lights are on, and I can see him strolling around his apartment, a sandwich or burrito of some sort in one hand and a book propped open in the other.

I wonder what Chris's lips would feel like against my cheek.

Chapter Twenty-Seven

"Wait, so you already told the client no to this?" Hannah clarifies.

I pause the "Basic Guide to Blueprints" MasterClass I've been watching. "Uh-huh," I reply. "But it was during the kickoff call, so I wouldn't be surprised if the feedback got lost in the shuffle."

With my phone tucked between my ear and my shoulder, I pad into the kitchen for a glass of water. "If they add their logo to the front cover, inside spread, and back cover, it's going to look crowded," I continue, squeezing a lemon wedge into my drink. "Recommend two out of those three places. It's a nice compromise. And then explain you're concerned customers may be distracted from the central message otherwise."

"You're so good at this," Hannah hums. I can hear her typing. "Whenever I push back on client requests, I get all tongue-tied and awkward."

The mailer Hannah's working on is for a start-up called AllerFizz. AllerFizz will soon be releasing carbonated water drinks that treat seasonal allergies, and they are *very* enthusiastic about them.

Enthusiastic clients can be tough to reason with.

"Thank you for talking me through this on your day off," Hannah says.

"Well, thank you for covering my projects while I'm out today."

I gather the printouts, books, sketch pads, and rulers that are spread across my dining room table. The space has become tiny house headquarters as I attempt to create a dream job from my dozens of illustrations, passion for tiny living, and limited home-building knowledge.

"Oh! You know what?" I perk up. "Gwen was in that earlier AllerFizz meeting with me. I would pull her into the conversation if you run into more pushback." If there's one thing Gwen's good at, it's pushing back on client requests because she *always* knows best.

Hannah pauses. "Gwen isn't in yet."

I hold my phone away from my ear, confirming it's nine-forty. "Is she sick?" Considering Gwen's penchant for sleek, trendy outerwear, it's no wonder she's caught a cold. That woman should really invest in a frumpy parka like the rest of us.

"No, she's not sick. I emailed her about a different job this morning, and she replied that she wouldn't be in until eleven." Hannah sighs. "She got a last-minute hair appointment because she 'couldn't live with her split ends a second longer.'"

"Who gets an impromptu haircut on a Wednesday morning?"

"Well, it is December," Hannah says.

Gwen is famous for not entering vacation time from January through October, and then declaring that she must "use it or lose it" once the end of the year rolls around. (What a racket!) But December also means her annual holiday trip with her bougie college pals. They're going to Turks and Caicos this year and have hired a private chef, tra la la. Gwen spends weeks preparing for this event, and her work schedule gets overtaken by hair, nail, and exfoliation appointments.

Basically, we're used to not seeing our manager much during this final stretch of the year.

"Are you excited about wedding dress shopping?" my friend asks.

Even though Mattie and Peter's wedding is a mere five months away, Mattie still hasn't said yes to the dress. "What's the holdup?" I asked Mom back in August.

"I think she's afraid she'll feel overwhelmed by the options," Mom explained. "She's anxious she won't be able to choose, like one of those indecisive girls on *Say Yes to the Dress* who has tried on three hundred gowns."

"Hmmm..." I replied, wondering what it's like to be so beautiful, you fear every single gown will look sensational on you, and you won't be able to choose just one.

But I'm genuinely excited about dress shopping today. Mom, Mattie, and I rarely spend time as a trio, and I'm looking forward to it.

"Absolutely," I say to Hannah. "I even made these little YAY and NAY signs for Mom and me to hold. You can use them when you go wedding dress shopping, too, Han! I'll add glitter and rhinestones before your appointments though."

"Oh, how fun," she replies. "And who knows? Maybe we'll be doing that for *you* soon enough." I can just see her wagging her eyebrows.

"Now you're talking crazy, and I'm going to hang up on you." I roll my eyes.

In the few days since our date, John has texted me like clockwork. He will ask how my day is going around noon, and then in the evening, he'll ask what I'm having for supper or if I have any TV show recommendations. I can practically type up a form letter of replies:

Can't complain!

Salmon and some greens. What about you?

Depends—what are you in the mood for? Tony suggests The Sopranos! LOL

So, no. Our conversations haven't exactly been titillating, but they're text messages. It isn't as though we're sitting on opposite ends of the telephone grasping for talking topics, which would be really painful. Plus, we're still getting to know each other. Inside jokes and flirting and lively banter aren't always immediate. They might, they *will*, come. I'm sure of it.

The Old Bea would have put the kibosh on the budding relationship. If there isn't a spark, what's the point? A few free meals? But the New Bea understands that Carrie Bradshaw has confused her with all her talk of zsa-zsa-zsu. The New Bea understands that John Noble is a good guy and that affection can grow over time.

(The New Bea realizes how bizarre it is to talk about herself in third person and will stop this immediately.)

John Noble and I want the same things. And it doesn't seem so crazy that we may end up finding them in each other.

I look in the direction of Chris Little's door as I carefully make my way down the apartment stairwell. There's a construction paper Santa Claus hanging on it, a gift from one of Maria's kids I assume, and his compost bin is so full that the lid's partially lifted.

John Noble is ready to settle down, while *other guys* are comfortable leading a woman on for eight years, leading her absolutely nowhere.

Just then, my hands begin to tingle and burn, reminding me that I sure as hell don't have time to wait around for a man who doesn't know what he wants.

Chapter Twenty-Eight

I meet Mattie and Mom in the Reading Bridal District at ten-thirty. The district spans three blocks and includes wedding dress boutiques, bakeries, stationery shops, lingerie shops, florists, and photography studios. Any item or service you need for your big day, you can find it in the Reading Bridal District. It's a charming area with most of the businesses housed in hundred-year-old buildings and mature trees lining the street. Part of me expects Randy Fenoli to pop out from behind a well-manicured bush.

I park on a side street and hustle to the first appointment, which is at one of the smaller, more intimate boutiques. There's a delicate tinkling of bells when I push open the heavy glass door, and a man with an astonishingly thin mustache greets me.

"Hello. Do you have an appointment this morning?" he asks in such a way, the answer had better be yes.

"Mmhmm," I hum. "I'm here for my sister's ten-thirty. Her name is Matilda Parker."

"Ah, yes. She and your mother are already here." Of course they are. They probably both arrived twenty minutes early. "Just head back that way and take a right."

After admiring a display case that houses veils, headpieces, and belts, I round the corner to Mattie's fitting area. "Dah-dah-dah-dah! Dah-dah-dah-dah!" I sing. "'Here Comes the Bride,'" I explain, after noticing Mom and Mattie's bemused expressions. "Good morning!"

"Hey there." Mattie has her blonde hair down, the edges gently curled under. She gives me one of her soft, flimsy hugs. My sister has never hugged me tightly or fiercely. "Thanks for taking the day off. That was so kind of you."

"Are you kidding me? I wouldn't miss it!" I sit beside Mom on the blush pink sofa. She looks more excited than a kid on Christmas morning. "Work email?" I ask too brightly, watching Mattie frown at something on her phone.

"Uh-huh," she says, only half paying attention to me. Mattie slides her phone inside her handbag. "I need to be better about unplugging, but it's tough when you're running a company. You never know who needs your attention."

How does Mattie manage to take a response that *seems* self-deprecating but ultimately only makes me feel insignificant and small? I think of my tiny house notes scattered across my hand-me-down dining room table and am instantly filled with doubt.

"Hello there!" A woman with fiery red hair and funky glasses greets us. She wears purple lipstick and three-inch heels and pulls off both. I obviously think she's fabulous. "My name's Suze, and I'll be helping you this morning. When's the wedding?"

"May 20th," Mom says immediately, like this is a freaking game show.

Ten points for Eileen Parker!

"A spring wedding. Fantastic," Suze approves. I imagine she says this about all four seasons.

She then asks if we'd like water, coffee, or tea. Mom and I agree that coffee sounds nice, but Mattie requests water since she's already had enough caffeine for the day. I consider asking her what one's caffeine limit should be but figure I can google it later.

"So! What's your style, Mattie?" Suze askes. "Do you have any gowns in mind?"

I turn to Mattie, my eyes big and interested, but Mom jumps in with her own ideas of her oldest daughter's style.

"We loved watching the royal weddings," Mom gushes. I wonder if Mom and Mattie think they're creating some sort of Cincinnati version of those resplendent nuptials. "I see Mattie in something elegant like lace, maybe even a long-sleeved gown. A slight V-neck, I think, and probably an A-line shape."

Well, Mom clearly has a dream gown in mind.

"And what do *you* think, Mattie?" Suze asks, laser focusing on my sister.

"Classic, I guess. I want my look to be timeless," she says, her voice surprisingly small. "I really love satin and beading. Maybe those materials won't work for a spring wedding, but—"

Suze shakes her head. "Of course they can. Why don't we look through the racks together?"

Mattie, Mom, and I *ooh* and *aah* over the gowns. Even the ones that aren't any of our styles are still breathtaking in their own ways.

"I didn't know you were thinking satin," Mom murmurs, sounding slightly hurt. "I always imagined you in lace."

"You'll look beautiful in satin," I interrupt, giving my sister an encouraging smile. "It's just as um, princessy, as lace. Didn't Meghan Markle wear satin?"

"She wore silk," Mom and Mattie reply in unison.

Well, excuse me!

"I do recommend trying on a few gowns you wouldn't normally choose for yourself," Suze interrupts. "I've had some wild cards turn out to be winners in the past."

"*Vive la différence,*" I agree.

Suze neatly hangs the gowns inside the dressing room. "Just shout for me when you're ready to be zipped up," she says, giving Mattie some privacy.

The first dress Mattie tries on is a satin gown with a sweetheart neckline and full skirt. When she walks out, Suze secures the buttons that run up the entire back and fastens a pearled belt around the smallest part of her waist.

Mom and I both get teary eyed at our first sight of Mattie in white. She looks like a total goddess, and it honestly takes my breath away. "Oh, Matt. You're gorgeous," I squeak.

"It's a beautiful gown." Mattie twirls in front of the mirror. "But too simple, I think." She turns to us, looking for our YAY or NAY paddles.

"It's not very grand, is it?" Mom says.

Hesitantly, I raise my NAY paddle. "Next dress, Suze!"

The next four dresses Mattie tries on fall in that same middle, meh, lukewarm ground. She likes them all just fine, but doesn't love any of the gowns.

"These have all been lovely dresses, and you certainly look lovely in them," says Mom in such a way, I know there's a *but* coming. "But why don't you try on a few lace gowns now? Like Suze was saying, sometimes the frock you least suspect turns out to be the winner!"

Mattie's forehead creases for the briefest of moments and I think she's preparing to tell Mom that no, she isn't interested in lace, but a forced smile spreads across her face instead. "You're right," she says. "Of course I can try on a few lace gowns."

"What would it hurt?" Mom adds breezily.

My sister tries on three lace dresses for our mother, and each one sends Eileen Parker swooning like the ghost of Princess Diana has just entered the room.

"The sleeves! Oh, you look so elegant!" she squeals.

Or, "Now *that's* a proper ball gown."

Mom literally clutches her pearls over a cap-sleeved gown with a high collar and cathedral-length train. I think she may actually pass out from excitement over this pretty, but astonishingly fussy, gown.

"It's the one, right?" Mom waves her YAY sign with such fervor, I fear I might lose an eyeball. "I've never seen a more gorgeous dress! Bea, Suze, don't you agree? It's a showstopper. Just picture that beauty walking down the aisle!"

It's unclear if Mom is referring to her daughter or the wedding gown.

"It's a stunning gown," says Suze diplomatically.

It *is* a stunning gown, but I'm focusing on Mattie's face. While she looks slightly uncomfortable and painfully conflicted, there's certainly no giddiness or awe in her green eyes. She honestly looks a little miserable.

"I don't think it's the dress for Mattie," I say, and relief instantly fills my sister's face.

"What? *Why?*" Mom is clearly offended on the dress' behalf. "It's perfect!"

"Mattie said she likes satin and beading," I remind our mother. "Why doesn't she try on a few more dresses like that?"

Mattie nods. "I would *love* that."

"You know what? I think I have just the one," Suze says, her face lighting up with the notion. "It was returned yesterday, and I believe the bride is just about your size."

Mattie and Mom frown, and I shake my head quite ardently. "Whoa there, Suze. Why was the gown returned? We don't want to introduce any bad juju into this wedding day."

She's smiling. "We don't normally take returns, but this bride pulled on our heartstrings. She found out she was pregnant, so she and her fiancé were canceling their grand affair to do a simple celebration in her parents' backyard instead. She'll be five months along by then and knows her original dress isn't going to work. She was glowing when she brought the dress back in... She said she didn't expect any money back and just wanted another bride to enjoy it, but of course, we issued a refund."

Mom clearly isn't charmed by this story. I'm sure she's running over lost deposits in her head, plus a backyard wedding rather than a grand affair? Hot dogs and hamburgers over filet mignon and salmon? A pregnant, barefoot bride with flowers in her hair? A college professor officiating the ceremony and not a priest? This is Eileen Parker's worst nightmare. I actually catch her sneaking a quick glance at Mattie's midsection.

But my sister and I are swooning.

"That is *so* romantic," Mattie says. "I would love to try on the gown."

While Mattie changes into the gown with decidedly *fantastic* juju, I think about Hannah's playful words from earlier this morning. What if, against all odds, my best friend is right? What if it's *me* wedding dress shopping soon enough? Crazier things have happened. A woman at work met her husband on a dating app, and they were engaged within three months, married within six, and expecting a baby within a year.

She's the exception, not the rule, I remind myself.

But just like the 1990s McDonald's commercials used to say, "Hey, it could happen."

"Are you two ready for this one?" There's a twinkle in Suze's eyes as she pulls back the dressing room curtain with a flourish.

"*Wow,*" I say, goosebumps spreading across my arms.

Even Mom is blown away. "Oh, honey," she breathes.

Mattie stands there looking a bit breathless and a little bashful. She gathers the satin in her hands and walks towards us. This wedding gown has an Art Deco vibe with its straight silhouette and v-neck. It dips low in the back and fans out at Mattie's feet. The beading is exquisite, catching the light and making Mattie literally sparkle.

Mattie starts to cry. Delicate, ladylike tears mind you, but they are still tears. "It's the one," she says.

"It's absolutely the one," I chorus, excitedly waving my YAY sign with both hands and swallowing a few happy tears of my own.

"Mom?" Mattie looks over at her. I can hear the nervousness in her voice. "What do you think? I know it isn't lace, but... Do you love it?"

Mom's gray eyes are glassy as she rises from her chair and pulls Mattie into a hug. "I think it's perfect," she says, kissing her cheek. "I think it's beautiful and stunning and so perfectly you."

I jump to join our group hug.

"Well, now you've gone and made me start to cry." Suze dabs at her eyes with a lace handkerchief. I wonder if a large part of being a bridal stylist is crying on demand. Brides these days probably expect it. "Are you saying—"

I pull back suddenly. "Wait, Suze, no! Can I say it?"

"Go for it," she says.

I grab Mattie's forearms and lock my eyes with hers. For once, I feel like we're really seeing each other, our gazes held like this. Has my serious older sister ever looked this happy and hopeful? "Matilda Eloise Parker," I begin, using her full name for dramatic effect, "are you saying yes to the dress?"

"I'm saying yes to the dress!" She nods happily before pulling me close. "And thank you," she whispers into my ear.

Chapter Twenty-Nine

Mom insists on paying for Mattie's dress, and I insist on treating everyone to a celebratory lunch. It seems like the appropriate thing for both a maid of honor and a thirty-something woman to do.

We go to a cute cafe down the street where I order a round of cranberry mimosas (complete with sprigs of holly!) and spinach and artichoke dip to snack on while we peruse the menu.

"Did you want to stop at one of the lingerie shops after this?" Our mother, a proper, Catholic woman who discreetly left a copy of American Girl's *The Care and Keeping of You* on our nightstands rather than have an actual birds and the bees talk with us, asks Mattie. "Now that you have your gown, you can prepare for the wedding night."

"Oh, sweet Jesus," I mumble, hiding my face behind my menu.

Mattie's ears turn bright pink. "Um, well, since Peter and I already live together, I'm not sure the wedding night holds that same importance," she stammers, sounding uncharacteristically flustered. "I think I can handle the lingerie shopping on my own. Thanks, though."

"No need to be embarrassed, girls," says the lady who has never once discussed sex with us until this very moment. Mom turns her attention to me. I briefly panic that my own (non-existent) sex life is the next point of discussion, but as it turns out, Mom simply wants an update on my Sunday evening date.

"Mattie tells me you had a very nice date with a very nice gentleman," Mom grins.

Relieved for a change in subject, I nod. "His name is John Noble, and he obviously comes with Mattie and Peter's approval."

"Yeah? Oh, bumblebee. That's wonderful!" There is nothing Mom gets more excited about than her children finding love and opening the door to more grandkids. I once heard Mom tell her friend she dreamed she would have *twelve* of them. I sincerely hope Mom's premonitions are false, or else Justin, Mattie, and I have a lot of work to do. "Do you have a second date on the books yet?"

"Actually, yes. We're going on a double date with Mattie and Peter on Saturday," I report, not mentioning the fact that I'm slightly disappointed.

It isn't the double date aspect that's left me feeling hollow. I'm excited to spend time with Mattie and Peter and thrilled at the prospect of joining their social circle. No, it's the thought of another ordinary dinner date that leaves me wanting. Arthur took Hannah to a pierogi-making class for their second date. And God knows Janet has been on some interesting outings, including cheesemaking, a bourbon and chocolate tasting, and even sky-diving with one adventure enthusiast. (Or so she says anyway. Take those tales with a grain of salt.)

"John's pretty smitten with Bea. He told Peter how creative, charming, and beautiful he thinks she is," Mattie adds.

"Wait, really?" My heart lifts. "He said that? Why didn't you tell me?"

"I'm telling you now," she replies, sipping her festive mimosa. "Wait until you see his house, Bea. It's this beautiful Victorian with a white picket fence. And it has five fireplaces or something crazy like that."

Mom and I collectively swoon, eating it all up.

"Well! It's only been one date. No use in getting ahead of ourselves," I say, which is hilarious considering I'm now imagining John and I sharing cups of hot cocoa in front of one of his five fireplaces. I turn to Mom. "But speaking of houses, how is yours coming along? Weren't you going to do more packing over the weekend?"

My very capable mother buries her face in her hands. She's always kept her nails short and unpolished. "I'm just plain overwhelmed. We have so much stuff, and your dad hasn't been very helpful. He's distraught over the idea of the next homeowners destroying the place."

While I imagine the Beverly Hillbillies pulling into Mom and Dad's cul-de-sac, Mattie is already jumping into problem-solving mode. "How can I help?" she asks.

Mom gets a playful, somewhat embarrassed, look on her face. "Buy our house?"

"Like we could ever afford your house!" Mattie snorts.

"We would cut you a deal. An amazing deal," Mom replies, sounding more confident now, like this isn't the first time she's rehearsed this pitch. "That goes for you, too, Bea. And it would also apply to Justin if he and Katie wanted to move to Cincinnati."

I roll my eyes at my inclusion in this McMansion proposal and focus back on Mattie. "Justin is never leaving Santa Fe, and you've been complaining that your bungalow is too small for years now," I remind her.

She shrugs her shoulders. "Well, maybe. It's an incredibly generous offer... I'll talk to Peter tonight and see what he thinks. Does that sound okay?"

Mom nods, encouraged. "That sounds great. Take your time," she says.

Mattie then starts to talk about Peter's recent promotion at work, and I want to sigh, "Go ahead and tell Mom you'll buy the house already!" Lord knows it's just another perfect step forward in my perfect sister's life.

Even though I don't even *want* my parents' McMansion, and I certainly can't afford it unless they're running some sort of clearance special, I can't help but feel jealous.

Why does Mattie get everything special and dear? She has the family business and will now have the homestead. Even genetically speaking, Mattie has gotten the best: Mom's brains, Dad's focus, our maternal grandmother's dainty feet.

I envy how easily life happens for Mattie. Like my sister's many cashmere wraps, good fortune seems to encircle her. As a college student, when so many struggle to envision their futures and piece together a path forward, the Kickerville door was opened, and Mattie was ushered through. As a young professional, she bought her bungalow at a remarkably reasonable price mere months before the housing market shortage began and prices skyrocketed. And as a woman about to turn thirty, she decided she was ready to settle down and marry, and along came Peter Foster.

Whatever Mattie wants, she gets. And it's usually delivered on a silver platter.

Where's my piece of the pie, my deluxe apartment in the sky?

But these are uncharitable thoughts for a maid of honor, even one who was asked to fulfill her duties out of obligation rather than love and friendship, so I squash them.

"Another round of mimosas?" I ask brightly.

Chapter Thirty

I think of Friday evenings in my twenties and how they typically began with happy hours that trickled into late nights with my closest colleagues. But instead of downing a shot of tequila, I stand in the employee kitchen swallowing my evening supplements in big, purposeful gulps: turmeric, D3, B12, B6, and large-and-in-charge omega-3.

The juxtaposition makes me feel more like one hundred than thirty.

I won't be able to start any official MS treatment until after I see Dr. Wessels next week, but in the meantime, I can at least take beneficial supplements. I finish the entire glass of water before pouring myself a fresh cup of coffee. I do a few tidying-up tasks, tucking stray mugs into the dishwasher and running a wet paper towel over the counters. Then, I take my coffee and stand in front of a wall that's entirely window, taking in the quickly fading sky over downtown Cincinnati.

The people on the sidewalks below have transitioned from business-people to merrymakers, men and women ambling toward warm bars and cozy suppers. I can see the Fountain Square Christmas tree from here and a sliver of the crowded skating rink. Mom used to love taking Justin, Mattie, and me ice-skating there.

Most of my colleagues left hours ago. The white noise machines have been turned off, and the only sound comes from the evening janitor's vacuum. (We call him Dumbledore because of his long, white beard and kind disposition. I think he would find the nickname flattering. At least I hope so, since we mean it as the utmost compliment.) I watch him sweep around one of the company's minimalist Christmas trees, all silver and sleek with white lights decorating the branches. Even Chase, Christina's fellow art director and a self-admitted workaholic, has packed up for the weekend.

It was a pleasant day, particularly since Gwen was out of the office. (While the official reason was a bad cold that Gwen feared could be the flu, I knew she was getting lip fillers in preparation for the big Turks and Caicos trip. I overheard her making the appointment a few weeks ago.) But my sunny Friday turned cumbersome when I got saddled with a major revision for one of Gwen's projects.

"Even when she isn't here, she finds a way to rain on my parade," I grumbled. "I really wanted to get home at a normal hour tonight." I was expecting tiny house blueprints in the mail, *real* ones, and I couldn't wait to pore over them.

"Do you have plans with John?" Hannah asked. It was nearly four o'clock when the client request came in, quitting time on a Friday at Polly Feinstein, and Hannah had already slipped into her coat and packed up for the day. She faltered, shifting between her black booties. "What can I do? How can I help?"

"*You* can get going. You can't be late for your venue tour," I said.

Hannah spent most of the week gushing over the 1800s wine cellar, which sounds wonderfully moody and romantic. She and her mom are taking a quick peek at the space tonight while it's all set up for a Friday evening wedding. It's also the first venue Mrs. Nielsen is interested in seeing that isn't the family's country club, so Hannah has high hopes for the visit.

"You should just let it sit until Monday," Hannah said, looking conflicted. "This revision is Gwen's fault. She knew the client wanted to feature their CBD bubble bath line, but she didn't do it. She always thinks she knows better than the client..."

"It's fine, really. I should let Gwen clean up this mess, but I won't. Not with the promotion on the table," I said. "Now, get going and send me photos from the venue! I hope they use an astonishing amount of candles and greenery galore."

"I do, too." Hannah's brown eyes sparkled, temporarily lost in wedding dreamland. "Text me when you get home?"

"Sure thing," I said, determined to knock this work out quickly.

But my four o'clock determination ran into a roadblock: a complete inability to concentrate. I sat at my desk for hours trying to work despite my foggy mind. It took me twice as long to remember server paths, and I even had to google a few InDesign keyboard shortcuts, basic commands I've had memorized for years. It was like I was operating with only half my brain. But I wasn't distracted by visions of sugarplums and fairies dancing in my head.

It was the MS.

And I knew it was likely flaring up because I was tired and stressed.

Stress is one of MS's greatest pals. Think of MS standing in front of a full-length mirror, unsure if she feels up for that evening's soiree. Stress is her supportive best friend who says she looks *amazing* in that outfit, and that *come on,* she really must join the fun!

After taking a break with my (hopefully) energizing cup of coffee, I slump back to my desk to wrap up the remainder of the revisions. Part of me wants to just leave this mess for Gwen to clean up. An even bigger part of me wonders why I even care about the promotion. The biggest part of me wants to send out a team email that says, "I have multiple sclerosis! This is all too hard for me tonight. Have a nice weekend!"

It's strange I haven't told my teammates yet. Not even Hannah.

I've gone from "I'll tell everyone when it's definite" to "I'll tell everyone once I'm on a treatment plan." But I know the real reason I'm keeping the information under wraps: I'm afraid it will make me look weak and broken, that it will hinder my chances of getting the promotion.

And I know, *I know*—why do I even care about the promotion so much?

I believe I'm on to something big with my tiny house project, which is becoming a proposal for an entire tiny house line, and I'm spending all of my free time buried in the research. I've even been figuring out ways to incorporate my love for all things cozy and vintage, like Kickerville forming a partnership with one of those retro appliance companies.

But my tiny house dream is still just a seedling. It needs cultivating and time to grow. It needs a differentiator in a saturated market. It needs to be strong enough to stand beneath the microscope of my discerning sister.

There's a very good chance my tiny house dream will remain just that: a dream. And I am too smart to put all my eggs in one basket.

My phone vibrates with a text message. It's Janet.

Good evening! May I please have Fran's phone number? We've

been emailing a bit this week, but this question is more urgent. I **have no idea what to wear to The Nutcracker tomorrow and want to compare ensembles!**

I actually laugh out loud as I forward Fran's contact information. Part of me wants to tell Janet now what Fran will be wearing: her nice pair of jeans (the ones that have no holes, paint splatters, etc.), a peasant top similar to the one she wore at Thanksgiving (she ordered half a dozen of them from JCPenney years ago), and no-nonsense clogs.

Oh, to be a fly on the wall for tomorrow's matinee. I would pay serious money to watch Fran and Janet interact for an entire afternoon.

Finally, at seven-fifteen, I finish up the revisions. I make sure to copy Gwen and Dennis, her direct manager, on the email sent back to the client. It's slightly petty to include Dennis, but I want him to see the extent of this mishap. I consider including a lighthearted line about wanting to take a CBD bubble bath myself after working those products into the creative but figure it's inappropriate to write about bubble baths in professional emails.

Before leaving, I take advantage of the quiet office and leave my latest Secret Santa gift on one of the junior designer's desks. Natalie is a big Bob Ross fan, and I found a miniature bobblehead that speaks his calm idioms whenever you press a button.

I press the button now.

We don't make mistakes. We have happy accidents.

Ugh, now I feel guilty about my passive aggressive email. Though in all fairness, Gwen made very deliberate decisions that caused the whole debacle, not a series of mistakes. Or, err, happy accidents.

I grab my own Secret Santa gift from earlier today, a giant box of yarn, whoever pulled my name knows I love to knit, and start towards the elevators. I call an Uber, which I will absolutely be charging to my corporate card. No express buses are running at this time of day, and I'm not feeling up for an hour-long commute. That's all well and good in New York City, but this is Cincinnati, Ohio.

Three minutes later, an electric blue Nissan Sentra pulls up. My driver, Rishi, looks like he is twelve.

I shove my box across the black leather seat and enter with a heavy sigh.

"Damn, girl! Were you just fired?" Rishi asks, lowering the volume of his old-school R&B music. He gives me a wary once-over. "Want me to take you to a bar or something?"

"Well, gosh. You make assumptions awfully fast," I reply, but I'm smiling. I like this guy. I lean my head against the cold window even though it's a gross thing to do. Who knows what other passengers this twelve-year-old has taken around town? "No, it's just a Secret Santa gift. A bunch of yarn. I'm a knitter."

"I'm glad you weren't fired," he says, his tone touchingly sincere.

"You know what? Me too," I say. "That's sort of the last thing I need right now."

Chapter Thirty-One

I unlock my front door and am met with the sad sight of Tony Soprano sitting beside his empty food bowl.

"You're killing me," I sigh, setting my tube of tiny house blueprints on the kitchen counter. I fill Tony's bowl, mixing in more wet food than normal to express my sincerest apologies. I rub his ears. "I'm sorry for the delay, buddy."

I hurry into the bathroom even though I peed just before leaving the office.

I've learned my bladder problems are likely caused by a miscommunication between my bladder and my brain. Basically, the moment my bladder begins to fill up, my brain gets fed misinformation. "You're full," my brain tells my bladder. "And you've got to get to the bathroom ASAP! Hurry, hurry!"

It's about as reliable as your crazy uncle Larry's political Facebook posts.

After peeing, I leash Tony Soprano up for the long walk he so deserves. And by the time we make it out the door, a light snow shower has started.

With Etta James playing through my earbuds, I take my time walking along the peaceful streets. Christmas lights are looped between tree branches, draped across bushes, and traced along rooflines, and a few homes have elegant luminaries lining their sidewalks and driveways. I especially love catching glimpses of Christmas trees through glowing windows. There is something so magical about the silhouette of a Christmas tree.

I usually pick up a live tree at the nearby Catholic church's sale. Maybe I'll do that this weekend.

My stomach growls when I catch the scent of someone's grill. When was the last time I ate? Lunch? I pull up a food delivery app and am pleased to see the wait time for my favorite Indian restaurant is only twenty minutes. I must have missed the dinner rush. If I extend Tony's walk a bit, I'll get back to the Amelia just before my food arrives. Heck, I can even stop by the local brewery first and pick up a growler on my way. Indian food, beer, and tiny house blueprints.

A dream Friday night.

Sure enough, timing is on my side. I've just gotten to my block when I see the delivery man's black sedan pull up outside my building. I smugly accept my brown bag of mushroom matar and garlic naan and head inside.

I glare upwards at the seemingly endless stairs.

With a deep breath, I heave my bounty against my right side while holding Tony's leash in my left hand. We take a quick break on the first-floor landing and then continue upward, my breathing jagged and my limbs weak. Similar to my brain puttering out this evening, it often feels like my limbs do the same. It's like everything is hunky-dory and then bam! They're exhausted and weak and have had *enough.*

The thing is, my limbs, or my brain for that matter, don't always feel like this. Multiple sclerosis doesn't behave in regular, predictable ways. I can struggle up the stairs tonight and then feel strangely energetic and strong tomorrow.

I've just reached the third floor when I'm hit with a bout of dizziness. I press on, but the nausea quickly follows. And behind that come the light-headedness and fading vision. I lose my balance and careen to the left. I fall.

Hard.

The growler of beer shatters against the terracotta floor, and much to Tony Soprano's delight, the mushroom matar topples down the steps, splattering savory goodness all over the place. I've fallen in the same spots as my power-walking wipeout, and fresh blood begins to soak through the knees of my jeans. I don't know if it's the shock, pain, or sight of ruby red blood, but before I know it, my face has scrunched up and tears start to spill from my eyes. (How embarrassing!) I press my eyelids together tightly and try to blink away the tears, which only makes my eyes burn. Probably an effect of using expired mascara. Who knows.

Chris Little's apartment door flies open. "Bea? What happened?" Chris asks, kneeling beside me while Tony laps up my entree. *Super.* Now I'll probably have dog diarrhea to clean up later tonight.

"I'm sorry," I say, apologizing for the mess, for my crying, for my bloody knees. "I'll clean this all up—"

"You're bleeding." Chris is wearing a *Star Wars* t-shirt, this one features an illustration of Chewbacca and Han Solo with their arms around each other's necks, and jeans. "I heard a crash and... Gosh, are you okay? That must have hurt really badly."

"It did, but the blood is from an earlier wound," I wipe my eyes. "I guess I'm just the world's clumsiest person." Yes. That's easier to say than *I guess I just have an incurable disease that makes my limbs stop working and makes me dizzy and throws my balance completely off-kilter.*

"You can't be the world's clumsiest person. That's me. I'm famous for dropping the wedding rings at my uncle and aunt's wedding. No one asked me to be a ring bearer ever again."

I stop crying. "Wait, are you serious?"

"I am," he says. "The entire wedding came to a halt while everyone got on their hands and knees searching for the wedding bands beneath church pews. My new aunt and I were both crying. Even at age five, I knew it was a total disaster."

Despite my aching knees and my bruised pride, I laugh.

Really, really hard.

"Oh my God, Chris," I say, new tears escaping my eyes, though these are of the happy variety. "That's terrible."

"While there's certainly reason to cry over lost wedding bands, there's no reason to cry over spilled Indian food. Or beer." I'm surprised to feel Chris's arm wrap around me. I'm also surprised to notice how strong and well-muscled that arm is. I didn't expect him to be quite so fit. "If I help you up, do you think you can stand?"

I nod, and with a seemingly effortless lift from Chris, I am once again standing on two feet. Chris gently takes Tony Soprano's leash from my left hand, where I've continued clutching it, and nods upstairs. "I can carry you to your place," he says.

I actually snort. "Uh, right. No way," I say. "I would break your back."

Chris shakes his head. "I doubt that. But let me walk with you at least?"

"Yeah, okay." I wonder if Chris can still smell my morning perfume or if I only smell of sweat, beer, and garam masala at this point. "Thanks."

"Was it the MS?" Chris asks quietly.

I nod.

"What a sneaky disease," he replies.

I manage a small smile. "That makes it sound so playful and innocent."

Moving slowly and carefully, Chris helps me up the remaining flight of stairs and into my apartment. I flip on a light and hobble toward the hall closet. "I have a mop in here and some floor cleaner. I don't know how environmentally friendly the cleaner is, but—"

Chris intercepts me in front of my own closet.

"I'll clean up," he says. "Go relax on your sofa. I'll come back when I'm done and make you a strong drink."

I shake my head once and then twice, wondering if this is all some sort of fall-induced mirage I'm experiencing. Did I hit my head? Am I actually still splayed across the dirty stairs while Tony Soprano eats his weight in Indian food?

"Seriously. Go rest," Chris insists. "I've got plenty of cleaning supplies at my place. I'll take care of it."

"That is so nice of you," I stammer. "Are you sure?"

He nods, saying he is positive.

The moment Chris leaves, I limp to the bathroom to peel off my jeans before they stick to the bloody scrapes. I use warm water and soap to wash my freshly reopened wounds and then cover them with proper bandages. I stare at myself in the bathroom mirror, my jeans around my ankles and my face red and splotchy.

What a sorry sight.

Shiitake mushrooms—Chris is coming back! I have to do something about this. Sitting on the edge of my bed, I pull on a pair of lavender silky pajama pants and swap out my top for a crew-neck sweatshirt. Perfect. Flirty but casual. I brush powder across my cheeks and nose and manage to slide some liner on my lids. I refresh my perfume and get myself seated delicately on the sofa just as Chris knocks gently on the front door.

"Come on in!" I call.

Chris is carrying a frozen pizza and a bottle of Hendrick's. "How does a veggie pizza sound?" he asks. "And gin and tonics? I figured gin was a safe bet since that's what we had at Gas Light the other night."

Tony Soprano yips happily.

"What Tony said," I say, a little breathless. Is this why Amanda stayed around for eight years? People have certainly stuck around for far less. "Thank you. There's some Sprite in the fridge we can use instead of tonic. And limes, too."

"Don't mention it," he says, heading for my kitchen. "Pizza stone or baking sheets under the stove?"

"Pizza stone. And yep!" I say, also telling him where the drinking glasses are located. I marvel at the ease with which Chris moves around my kitchen. I'm horrifically awkward in other people's kitchens, afraid to open the wrong drawers or incorrectly use their gadgets.

After setting the pizza in the preheated oven, Chris starts on our gin and Sprite drinks.

"Watch for chipped glasses," I warn. "I'm afraid they, along with my dishware, have been another MS casualty."

"No problem," Chris says, squeezing fresh lime juice into a pair of 1960s juice glasses. They're decorated with pink, yellow, and orange stripes, and I will be devastated the day I manage to damage them. He hands me my cocktail as well as my phone. "It looks like you just got a text. Someone named John Noble?"

"Oh. Thanks." I slide my phone inside my sweatshirt pocket, not bothering to read the message.

Chris nods toward my crowded dining room table. "How's the tiny house project going?"

"Good, I think. It's starting to take shape," I say. "But it might all turn out to be nothing…"

"Or it might turn out to be something," he interrupts. "Keep me posted?"

"Sure," I reply, wondering if he's genuinely interested or only being polite. "So, did you tell Maria you aren't attending the Catholic singles retreat?"

Chris sighs. "Yes, but I can't say it was a very productive conversation. Especially since she made a comment about future retreats."

"As in maybe you aren't open to the idea now but will be someday?"

"Exactly." Chris stretches back, working his way deeper into my sofa that smells like Fritos and Febreze. "Can we watch a Christmas movie? I haven't watched a single one this season."

I'm surprised by the request, but pleasantly so. "Well, of course! Any requests?" I ask. "If you suggest *The Holiday,* I'll finally have proof that I'm in some sort of strange dream."

Chris gives me a bemused smile. "I was thinking *The Santa Clause.* Or *Elf.*"

"I vote *Elf.*" Tony Soprano jumps on the couch, snuggling right in-between us, and I scan through a few apps before finding the movie.

When Chris sets his hand gently above my knee, I actually yelp.

"I am so sorry!" He moves his hand back lightning fast, and his face turns red. "I was just going to ask how your knees are feeling. Clearly awful. And I should have asked before setting my hand there."

"Oh, no. You just surprised me," I say. *And every time you touch me feels like an electrical shock.*

The truth is I've forgotten all about my knee injuries.

I am too preoccupied with my new neighbor's extraordinary kindness.

Chapter Thirty-Two

*L*ess than twenty-four hours later, I'm preparing for a date with a different man. *The safe choice,* I remind myself. *The guy who wants to settle down. The available one.*

I've invited John Noble to my apartment for a pre-dinner cocktail, hot buttered rum, and am spending the day tidying up. Or, as Hannah would disapprovingly say, putting an Instagram filter on my life.

Sure, I've organized my tiny house research into neat piles and stowed it inside a desk drawer. And yes, I've swapped out coloring books for crossword puzzles and nightstand romance for literary fiction, but so what? I'm putting my best foot forward! John can see my pumice stone and 1990s Polly Pocket collection later.

I stare at the sofa where Chris Little and I watched *Elf* last night. I only had one cocktail and two slices of pizza before promptly falling asleep. I didn't even make it to the spaghetti breakfast scene! When I woke up at midnight, my living room was quiet, the only noise coming from a muffled television in the apartment next-door. Chris had turned off all of the lights except for one small lamp, and he'd even covered me with a blanket.

I was touched to find a note on the coffee table. Chris's printing was small and neat, and he wrote in all capital letters. *You fall asleep fast! One second you were laughing at the movie, and the next, you were snoring. It was remarkable.* I giggled. It was such a Chris Little way to open a letter. *I hope you feel better in the morning. I had fun with you tonight.*

I marveled over the final line. He'd had fun with me? He'd had *fun* cleaning up my Indian food-and-lager mess and then treating me to dinner?

Not only had Chris left the thoughtful note, but he also washed our cocktail glasses and packaged up the pizza leftovers. He had even known to turn the lock on the handle before pulling the front door shut, which I guess wasn't the craziest thing considering his apartment mirrored mine, but it was certainly considerate.

I texted Chris a quick thank-you this morning before trying to focus on my Saturday evening date. I'm quickly realizing I make a poor serial dater. Not that Chris is after my affections, but it's tough switching modes between Chris Little and John Noble.

It helps to think of Chris's last relationship and his contempt for societal norms. And then there's all of the complicated involvement from Maria… When it comes to Chris and romance, things are messy, that's for sure.

I want to get married and have a child or two. And Chris doesn't. Or, at least, it seems like he doesn't. I should get "ARA" tattooed on my wrist: *Always Remember Amanda*. Plus, as much as I admire Chris's commitment to the environment, I'm not sure I can adhere to those sorts of standards. Would he make me become a climatarian too? I think of all the foods I'd have to give up, like burritos from the nearby taco truck, and shudder.

To pull myself out of thoughts about Chris Little, I venture next door to Nativity Parish's Christmas tree sale. While Janet usually accompanies me, she has an excellent eye for which trees will *actually* fit in my living room, she'll be with Fran Bosse this afternoon at *The Nutcracker*, so I go alone.

As I walk through the rows of trees, I wonder what it's like going Christmas tree shopping with a boyfriend.

Mattie and Peter like to drive an hour east to a quaint Christmas tree farm with fields of evergreens. I wonder if Chris and Amanda did something similar. It's easy to picture Chris pulling a tree off the roof of his Subaru (especially now that I know how strong his arms are) and carrying it into an inviting living room lined with shelves of books. "Go take a relaxing soak," I imagine him telling Amanda. "I'll take care of the lights."

Because stringing the lights is the only annoying part of decorating a Christmas tree, and of course, Chris would insist on taking that pesky task on.

And then, when Amanda came downstairs after her hot bath, she'd be amazed not only by the sight of the glittering tree but by a whole spread of snazzy apps. Pigs in the blanket, shrimp cocktail, crostini, even mugs of spiked eggnog. They'd snack and sip on these goodies while decorating their enchanting tree...

Sigh.

Anyways. It must have been nice. I'm sure of it.

"Do you need help getting this back home?" Robert, a long-time volunteer at the church's sale, asks me. He gives my Douglas Fir an affectionate shake. "You got a good one." Robert says this about every tree, and he means it, too.

I start to protest, it's my Midwestern inclination to refuse help, but I think of those awful stairs and have a change of heart.

"Honestly, that would be really wonderful," I say. "Thank you."

Robert calls over another volunteer to run the checkout counter, and then he carries my tree across the street, up all four flights of stairs, and into my apartment. He gently sets the fir into my Christmas tree stand, and I hand him an extra ten-dollar donation for the church.

"You don't have to do that," he says, bending down to pet Tony Soprano, who has immediately taken to Robert's kind disposition. "Nice dog. What happened to his eyes?"

"Double enucleation," I reply matter-of-factly. I smile as Tony rolls to his back and begs for a belly rub. "But that doesn't keep him from being a ham."

After Robert leaves, I turn on a playlist of classic holiday hits like Brenda Lee's "Rockin' Around the Christmas Tree" and Bobby Helms' "Jingle Bell Rock." Because I'm not neat and organized like Mattie and Mom, my first order of business is untangling the jumble of multi-colored lights I have not properly stored. I weave them along the branches, using twice as many as necessary, before smoothing the sequined felt skirt around the tree's base. I hang each ornament with care, from my glittery ice cream cone and hand-carved dachshund to the elegant baubles my parents have gifted me over the years. I even have a nice collection of vintage ornaments, which I try to be especially delicate handling.

After a quick lunch—egg salad, nothing fancy—I launch myself into cleaning mode. And after a few hours of dusting, vacuuming, and straightening up, I have to admit, it looks pretty darn nice in here. Spirited and cozy, tidy and welcoming.

Not a moment too soon either, I think, as the buzzer rings.

I press the button. "Hello?" I say mysteriously, as if I receive visitors all the time and am not sure who this one could be.

"Hi, Bea. It's John," my date says.

"Hi! Let me buzz you in. Just head directly up the stairs. I'm on the fourth floor, 4A," I tell him. I set the *A Charlie Brown Christmas* album on the record player and give the holiday cocktail a final stir.

John arrives at my door a few minutes later, and I'm delighted to see he is carrying a bouquet of white roses. I give him a posh peck on the cheek. "Oh, John. These roses are stunning," I say, sounding more like my sister than myself.

"This must be Tony," he says, kneeling down to pet my curious dachshund. Tony hops up, leaning his head into John's hand.

"Is he the softest dog in the world or what?" I beam, standing over them like a proud parent.

"He's very soft," John agrees. "And sweet, too."

After hanging his coat, John's worn a sporty bomber jacket tonight, I set the flowers in a vase and offer him a drink. "I made this decadent hot buttered rum cocktail, but I've also got beer and wine."

"I think I'll start with a beer," he says.

"Oh, okay. Awesome." I try not to feel disappointed as I hand him a boring bottle of some boring craft beer from the fridge.

"You look gorgeous," he says, immediately lifting my mood.

I'd gone out and bought a new outfit for the evening, which includes a pair of faux leather leggings, a sleeveless black velvet blouse, and black booties. Honestly, the look is a sort of hybrid between Matie and my styles.

"Thanks! I actually found the top at Goodwill. I can't believe someone was willing to part with it," I say, before making a morbid joke. "Unless the previous owner died. And in that case, she really didn't have much choice in the matter."

John offers a weak smile. I've creeped him out. *Great.* But honestly, does he really think you find a velvet top like this at the Gap?

As I stand there behind the kitchen peninsula, I watch John take in my apartment, his gaze resting on items like Tony Soprano's Swiss chalet, my holiday snow globe collection, and the set of metallic-painted deer antlers with colorful strands of beads dangling from them. *Look at my homemade stockings,* I want to say. *I embroidered them with Tony's and my names! Admire my antique nativity set. Compliment the flattering photo of Hannah and me on the beach. I'm all tan and glowy!*

Finally, John looks back at me. "Your place is...eclectic," he says.

I know what he wants to say is *weird,* so I pretend to accept *eclectic* as a compliment.

"And very colorful," he adds.

I sip my cocktail, filling my mouth with the sweetly spiced buttered rum. I know my style isn't everyone's cup of tea, but that's the best he can do?

We only stay at my *eclectic* apartment for twenty minutes, and John doesn't even compliment the Christmas tree I spent so much time decorating. No, he talks about the current cost of a bathroom remodel, notably after using *my* bathroom, and asks if my windows are always so drafty.

"Do you put up a tree?" I ask, desperate for him to praise mine. "I just got mine today. I always get a live one from the church next door."

"Yeah? That's nice." He fingers one of the branches and pulls back immediately, apparently having been poked by its needles. "I do an artificial tree. Can't stand all the pine needles that fall with the real ones. And I'm more of a white lights guy," he adds with a good-natured grin.

Well, fiddlesticks. *That* certainly hasn't gone as planned.

I kiss Tony goodbye, blow out the balsam-scented candle, and follow John out the front door. We are heading down the stairs, moving much faster than I prefer, when Chris Little exits his apartment carrying a six-pack of beer.

"Chris." The butterflies in my stomach are fluttering erratically. I'm giddy at the sight of him, but I also feel icky to be with another man. And God, Chris looks so cute in his hoodie and jeans. And cozy, too, like he would feel really wonderful to snuggle up against. "Hey."

"Oh," he replies, some sort of conflict crossing his own face as he takes in towering John Noble. He rubs his free hand along his stubbled cheeks and neck. "Hi."

John looks between the two of us, increasingly confused as to why neither of us is saying anything more, before extending a hand. "I'm John Noble," he finally offers.

"Ugh! Where are my manners?" I say, like I'm my mother. "John, this is my..." Neighbor? Friend? Colossal crush? "...Chris. This is Chris Little. He lives just below me." I give an awkward chuckle. "Obviously."

Chris gives the smallest shake of his head before accepting John's handshake. "Nice to meet you," he says, though his voice lacks its usual upbeat politeness. "Where are you off to tonight?"

I wish I was going out with you, I try to communicate with my eyes. "We're grabbing dinner with my sister and her fiancé," I say.

"A double date then," Chris says, placing an emphasis on date.

I nod, which feels better than verbally confirming this fact, but still feel like a villainous traitor. "And what about you? What are your big Saturday night plans?"

"I'm going to watch the new Marvel movie at a buddy's house," he says, his ears coloring just a bit. I'm relieved he doesn't have his own date, which is unfair of me. "I'm glad I ran into you, though."

Chris's mood changes from deflated to purposeful. "I'm hoping to organize an electronics recycling drive after the holidays," he says. "It's a perfect time for it, what with so many people receiving new gadgets. Could you design an advertisement for me?"

"I'd be happy to," I say.

"I've never heard of an electronics recycling drive before," John chuckles, sounding condescending rather than curious. "But God knows I have a box full of old iPhones and MacBooks I've never known what to do with."

Is it just me or does John sound slightly braggy? Who has an entire box full of old Apple electronics?

"Well, it's good you never threw them in the garbage. E-waste is a huge environmental and health problem." Chris turns away from us, locks his door, and then gives a small shrug. "Enjoy your double date. I'd better get going myself."

John and I are quiet as we walk down the remainder of steps and across the shadowy parking lot. He opens the passenger seat door to his fancy sedan for me, which feels formal and unnecessary instead of sweet and sincere. John's car smells like leather, and he's quick to turn on the heated seats as well as a John Legend album.

"Your neighbor's an interesting guy," he says. "Some people have too much time on their hands."

"Why do you say that?" I ask, instantly defensive of Chris.

"Who's got the energy to organize a recycling drive?" John replies. "And during the holiday season, no less."

I stare out the window. "He's passionate about the environment," I say. "When you're passionate about something, you make the time."

I can feel John's nervous glance on me. He knows he's touched a nerve but likely isn't sure why. "Well, it's a cute hobby, I guess," he says, trying to pacify me but only bothering me more with his dismissiveness.

He must be able to tell, too, since he steers the conversation back to one of the few things we have in common: Mattie and Peter. My parents and I are throwing them a couples shower in two weeks, and John will be in attendance.

"I guess I'll be meeting your parents pretty quickly," he jokes. "Is that weird?"

"Holiday romances do tend to move at hyper speed," I tease. I'm desperate to recenter myself and have fun tonight with my handsome, emotionally available date. "Haven't you ever seen a Hallmark movie?"

"I just hope you don't throw me out with the wrapping paper and tinsel," he flirts.

I give an internal wince and an external wink.

Maybe our spark is more of a flicker...and it's windy...and raining...but that doesn't mean it can't grow into a sizzling flame.

Right?

Chapter Thirty-Three

"I'm pretty excited to try this place," I say as John turns into the parking lot of a new, trendy restaurant called Oh My, Those Thighs. The eatery is being hailed for its fancy fried chicken (whatever that means), buttermilk biscuits, and Moscow Mules. Reservations are hard to come by, but I suppose when you live in John, Mattie, and Peter's world, most everything is within reach.

John places his hand on the small of my back as we enter the restaurant, and the gesture leaves me warm. It's nice having a man set his hand there.

Oh My, Those Thighs is small and noisy, but it's also intimate and lively. The restaurant is housed in a historic building that was once a cobbler's shop, and there's a single antique shoe in a glass box as a nod to the restaurant's past. All of the walls feature striking stonework, and there's a massive wood-burning fireplace in the center of the space. Most fascinating of all? The dozens of Dolly Parton portraits on display.

"Do you think the owners like Dolly Parton?" I murmur in John's ear.

"What gave it away?" he smirks, ushering me toward the table where Mattie and Peter are already sitting. Peter happily taps his foot along to Dolly Parton's "9 To 5" while Mattie sips a glass of white wine.

"Care if we join you?" I grin as we all exchange sophisticated kisses and hellos. Mattie compliments my outfit, and I'm pleased to have her approval.

"I love your booties," she says. "Are those from Madewell?"

"You have such a great eye," I say, even though they're from Target.

John and I order Moscow Mules made with Tennessee whiskey, Peter is already enjoying one himself, and John throws in an appetizer of fried okra for the group.

"Happy Saturday," I say when our drinks arrive. We clink our copper mugs with Mattie's wine glass. "Well! We've made it through another work week," I weirdly add.

Peter gives Mattie a quick but affectionate knee rub. "Mattie nearly killed Aunt Amethyst this week," he jokes. "It would have made Christmas pretty awkward."

John laughs, Mattie blushes, and I probe.

"Why? What did Aunt Amethyst do?" I consider the likely possibilities. "Did she light a bunch of incense in her office and forget about it again? Or place crystals around the women's restroom?" Just last spring, a plumbing incident occurred when a piece of rose quartz was accidentally flushed down a toilet.

"I wish you hadn't brought that up," Mattie mumbles in Peter's direction before sighing. "Well, the first thing Amethyst did this week was order new camera equipment on the corporate account...$5,000 worth, to be exact." We all give a collective cringe. "It's not that I don't appreciate the importance of quality camera equipment, it's just that Kickerville isn't in the position right now to make those kinds of upgrades."

I frown, wondering what *that* means. I know the pandemic made for a tough few years, but Kickerville survived. Maybe naively, I assumed things were back to normal now.

"What was the second thing your aunt did?" John asks, dipping the fresh-from-the-fryer okra into an aioli sauce. "And is there a third?"

"No third, thankfully, but as for the second, I asked Amethyst to create a few Facebook ads, and she looked at me like I had two heads," Mattie groans. She finishes her first glass of wine with a frustrated flourish. "Is it so crazy to ask your Creative Director to dip her toes into digital advertising?"

"Mattie," I say, trying to hide the excitement in my voice. "I can do those Facebook ads for you. I can do display ads, targeted onsite ads... Honestly, whatever digital advertising you need, I'm your gal."

Peter brightens and John looks impressed. But Mattie is shaking her head before I've even finished.

"You already have a demanding full-time job," she says. "You don't need to worry about things at Kickerville." She attempts a breezy sort of laughter. "We all know how temperamental Amethyst can be. She'll calm down and put something together next week."

"Right, right," I say, quickly backtracking. "But if you need any design help—"

"Got it. Thanks," she says, her message clear.

Stay in your lane.

When the server comes to take our orders, I follow Mattie's lead and ask for a bed of spinach with rotisserie chicken, red onion, avocado, and a light vinaigrette rather than the chicken-and-biscuit sliders I actually want. When John offers me a bite of his own fried chicken dinner, I nearly drool at the invitation.

After supper, Mattie asks us back to their bungalow for a few drinks. Both two Moscow Mules deep, John and I happily accept the offer.

Whenever I visit Mattie and Peter's bungalow, I feel like I've been transported to a cottage tucked away in Sonoma County. The walls and fabrics are all shades of cream, and every surface is remarkably clean and uncluttered. The few framed photographs feature black-and-white snapshots, and stunning woodwork traces every window and door.

"Hey John," I call from the kitchen, where I'm standing in front of Mattie and Peter's towering stainless steel refrigerator. "Want to see something cool?"

"Always," he says, leaning against one of the granite counters.

I gently tap the front of the fridge, illuminating the inside shelf and an impressive collection of green juices, cold brew coffee, and kombucha. "Pretty fancy, huh?" I raise my eyebrows. "Want to see it again?"

John chuckles. "I have the same model at my place," he says. "And now I know what we can do for our next date."

"I was just kidding," I lie.

Sheepish, I accept a glass of (perfectly decanted) pinot noir from Mattie and retreat to the family room where a fire is crackling and Adele is singing her impassioned ballads. "I'm going to miss this place whenever you two decide to move," I say, grabbing a cashmere blanket and curling up in a corner of the deep sofa.

Mattie takes a seat in one of the buttery leather armchairs. "We aren't going anywhere just yet," she replies.

"What about Mom and Dad's house?"

"We're considering it." I see her glance toward the dining room where Peter is showing John some rare bourbon he recently acquired. "Peter's on board, but I'm struggling with the idea. You know I've always loved historical homes, plus it's so far out in suburbia. It also feels painfully unoriginal."

I squint. "You mean moving back to the neighborhood where you grew up?"

"It's more than that," she says. "I already run Dad's business, and now I'm going to buy our parents' house? It's like I can't make a single decision for myself, like I've spent my adult life following Mom and Dad's breadcrumbs."

There are so many things I want to say to Mattie.

I want to tell her what a huge honor and privilege it is that she gets to carry on Kickerville. I want to explain how much *I* want to be a part of that legacy. I want to tell her to take her time deciding on our parents' McMansion. Judging by the single box Mom's packed, Lord knows they aren't in a hurry. I want to assure her that whatever she chooses, she *is* a unique person and that she's creating her own life with Peter.

Unfortunately, Peter and John burst into the room at that exact moment.

"What do you ladies think about New Year's Day skiing?" Peter booms, picking Mattie up and settling back into the leather chair with my sister on his lap. She laughs and protests, but it's nice seeing Mattie like this. Peter has a mellowing effect on her.

"Just a day trip to Perfect North?" Mattie clarifies, referring to the slopes in Eastern Indiana. Peter and John nod. "I'm surprised our Breckenridge friend has agreed."

"I'm just eager to ski," says John, sitting beside me and wrapping an arm around my shoulder. I peek at our reflection in the sliding door and am startled to realize how much we look like a legitimate couple.

"Maybe we can go tubing, too," I suggest. Even before being diagnosed with MS, I wasn't the most talented skier.

The group laughs, and I realize they think I'm joking.

After a few hours of wine and cocktails, I start to yawn. John insists on ordering me a cab, riding with me to my apartment, and then returning to his own house.

"You can literally walk home from here," I say. "I'll be fine."

"No, no. I want to see you home safely," he says, scooting into the backseat beside me. It is probably the most gentlemanly thing a man has ever done for me. "I'll be just a moment," he tells our driver once we've pulled up outside the Amelia ten minutes later. "I want to walk my date to her door."

"Good for you," the thirty-something woman replies. "Who says chivalry is dead?" She puts on her hazard lights and pulls out her cellphone while she waits.

"She's right. You're really blowing me away with these nice manners of yours." I fold my arms across my chest, rocking on the balls of my feet in the cold night. "Thank you for such a nice evening," I smile. "And for getting me home safely."

"It's been my pleasure. I had a lot of fun," John says, enveloping me in a hug.

And then he pushes my winter cap backward oh-so slightly, tilts my head upwards, and kisses me. *Really* kisses me.

As John caresses my cheek, I try not to giggle at his touch and feel something sexual instead. A very handsome man is French-kissing me! Why aren't my hands shaking as they sweep through his feathery hair? Why aren't my knees weak? Where is that excited tightness in my chest?

What if it's the MS? What if my nerve endings are malfunctioning?

I literally gasp at the thought, stepping away from John.

"Everything okay?" he asks, looking both bashful and concerned.

"I...I..." My eyes dart around the nearly empty sidewalks. I spot a tipsy middle-aged couple walking down the street, presumably after a fun night out. "I thought I saw my junior high math teacher."

John laughs a wonderful belly laugh. "That would have been awkward."

"So awkward," I mutter. "But, um, false alarm."

With a chaste kiss on my cheek, John wishes me goodnight, and I trudge upstairs wondering what the hell is wrong with me.

Chapter Thirty-Four

"What do you mean you didn't feel anything?" Hannah sits on my kitchen counter, swinging her long legs back and forth while balancing a tray of sushi in her hands. Her nails are painted a glittery gold. "I saw his photo. John is *hot*."

It's been a few days since John and my second date, and Hannah and I are analyzing, well, everything.

I plop a piece of spicy tuna in my mouth with one hand and stir my warming soap base with the other. Hannah has come over after work to snack on sushi rolls and sip on kombucha while I finish the soap favors for Mattie and Peter's upcoming couples shower.

"It's bizarre, almost like my body is having a total disconnect. My brain recognizes how attractive John is, but my heart is all, 'Eh, he's all right, I guess.'" I remove the melted soap base from the stovetop and pour it into a pot. Then, I add the Fraser fir fragrance.

Hannah hops down from the counter and peers over my shoulder. "Smells incredible. Christmassy," she approves. "So, you felt *nothing* when that babe stuck his tongue down your throat?"

"You've really got a way with words. Has anyone ever told you to give copywriting a whirl?" I tease before letting out a long, resigned sigh. "It was like expecting a chocolate chip cookie and biting into oatmeal raisin instead."

I think of the way Chris Little makes me feel jittery and excited, how strong *that* spark is. "Maybe I'm just distracted."

Hannah raises her eyebrows. She plants herself on the couch and welcomes Tony Soprano into her lap.

"Distracted, huh? Is it the new neighbor?" Hannah knows all about Chris Little and how adorable and quirky he is.

What she doesn't know about, though, is my diagnosis. It's the real reason why I've asked her over this evening.

"I have something important to tell you," I begin, keeping my eyes on my craft as I transfer the soap into rectangular molds. "But I wanted to say it in-person."

"Bea, we see each other in the office all the time," Hannah says. She shifts on the couch, straightening her posture. Sensing the tension, Tony retreats to his dog chalet.

I bite my bottom lip. "It's too personal for the office."

"Okay," she says. Hannah gives me a hesitant smile. "You've been secretly hooking up with the new neighbor and having the best sex of your life? And now you're pregnant with his child, but actually, it's triplets?"

I shake my head sadly and take a seat beside her.

"I have MS," I say. I clear my throat. "Multiple sclerosis."

My friend shakes her head, looking disoriented and then indignant. "Wait, *what*? Since *when*? How?"

"It all started the day before my birthday, but my diagnosis wasn't confirmed until the day before Thanksgiving. I haven't known how to tell you," I admit, my eyes resting on Hannah's sparkling oval solitaire. "Your life is the bee's knees right now. You have so many wonderful, happy things happening. I didn't want to be a Debbie Downer."

"Oh, Bea," Hannah murmurs. "I hate that you felt that way."

She pulls me close and hugs me tight. "I wish you'd told me sooner. I could have been there for you. I could have helped," she says, her braids tickling my face. "Instead, I've been sending you links to bohemian wedding dresses my mother hates and complaining when Arthur leaves the toilet seat up. I feel so stupid."

I pull away. "I don't ever want you to stop sending me bohemian wedding dresses or complaining when Arthur leaves the toilet seat up!" I say. "I have a great neurologist, and she'll put me on a treatment plan soon. In the meantime, I've added a bunch of vitamin supplements to my routine. It's probably a placebo effect, but they make me feel like superwoman."

"You are superwoman," Hannah says. "Always have been."

She admits she doesn't know, or completely understand, what MS is, and I say how I didn't know much about the disease either when I first got my MRI results. I give her a high-level summary and promise we can go into more detail later.

"I'm still learning," I say. "I discover something new every day. But what I do know is that my MS was caught early. And there are so many treatments available these days. I'm pretty lucky when you consider those things."

"Keep me in the loop, okay?" Hannah looks sad again, or maybe just contemplative. It's hard to tell. "Today, tomorrow, three years from now... I want to know what's happening so I can be there for you. And in the future, don't you dare keep this sort of thing from me for so long," she adds.

"Cross my heart," I say, before getting up to open a window.

Stanley must have the heat set to seventy-five degrees, and with the stovetop having been on, it's practically boiling in here. Using a bit of elbow grease on the hundred-year-old window, I give a small "oomph" as I lift it open.

And then? Well *then*, a freaking bat flies into my apartment.

Hannah lets out a blood-curdling shriek. "OH MY GOD! OH MY GOD! WHAT IS THAT THING? IS THAT A BAT?"

"It's a bat!" I shout back, admittedly spooked. The bat flies erratically around my living room, knocking over a picture frame and making us both scream. "Shoo, shoo! Go back outside!" I encourage the bat.

Tony Soprano is growling and barking and chasing the creature, and I'm suddenly terrified that he'll end up eating our unwanted visitor and getting rabies or something horrifying.

"WE NEED HELP!" Hannah is hiding under a throw blanket now, but she's yelling plenty loud enough for me to hear her. "CALL YOUR CUTE NEIGHBOR! CALL ANIMAL CONTROL! CALL SOMEBODY!"

"Go on now!" Ugh, gentle coaxing is not getting through to the bat. "Get out of here, and nobody gets hurt!" I say, trying to take a firmer stance.

I yelp as the bat narrowly misses my head and hits a kitchen cabinet.

Okay, plan B then.

"I'll run downstairs and grab Chris—"

"DON'T YOU DARE LEAVE ME RIGHT NOW!"

And so, I reach for my phone and begin one weird SOS call.

"Hello?" Chris answers after a single ring, thank God.

"I have a bat in my apartment," I stammer, my voice all kinds of shaky. "Can you come up here and help catch him? Please?"

"A bat?" Chris repeats. "Are you sure?"

I watch the bat soar dangerously close to Tony Soprano. "Yes! I'm positive!"

There's a brief pause. "It's just that bats in Ohio hibernate from late October to—"

"Listen, I have no idea what brought this bat out of hibernation, but he's here now. In my apartment. And I could really use your help. Chris? I need you up here like *now.*"

"Roger that," Chris reports.

I hurry to the front door and watch for Chris, who arrives thirty seconds later carrying a fishing net. I swing open the front door and motion for him to hurry inside. "Thank you, thank you," I babble.

Chris waves his fishing net happily. "I'm glad to help." He watches the bat for a few moments as he darts from one end of my apartment to the other. "Fascinating. That is indeed a bat in December. Poor guy seems pretty scared."

"WE'RE SCARED, TOO!"

Chris frowns at the blanket blob that's just shouted at him.

"That's my best friend, Hannah," I explain.

"NICE TO MEET YOU!"

"Hi, Hannah," he says, like this is the most normal thing in the world. "So, I'm wondering if this bat is hibernating in that home renovation next door. I imagine there's easy attic access right now. And today was so mild, maybe he ventured out—"

"Uh-huh. Yeah, sure." The bat's chaotic movements have me completely on edge. What if he falls into my party favor soaps? "That, um, makes sense."

"My parents actually have a bat box in their backyard," Chris reports as he steps on a dining room chair. "Bats hold such ecological importance! They're imperative to our ecosystems—"

"THEY'RE FLYING RODENTS!" Hannah practically cries from beneath the blanket. "HAVE YOU CAUGHT IT YET?"

"Not yet," Chris says good-naturedly. "But did you know bats are the only flying mammals? Flying squirrels glide rather than fly—"

"SQUIRRELS ARE FINE! I HAVE NO PROBLEMS WITH SQUIR-RELS!" Hannah sputters. "BUT BATS! BATS SUCK BLOOD!"

"They only lick blood, and it's just certain types of bats. Not all of them." Chris hops off the dining room chair just as the bat nearly hits me right in the face.

"Chris, please just catch the bat!" I shriek, ducking behind the sofa.

Let's just say I'm not in the mood for a science lesson right now.

Patient as can be, Chris finally swipes his net upward—where the bat is flailing in a corner—and then gives the netting an efficient turn, securing the bat inside. "Got him!" he says cheerfully, before giving me a wink. "Well, Bea. Your apartment is so inviting, you managed to attract a bat out of hibernation."

I give him a weak smile while Hannah slowly sticks her head outside the blanket. "All clear?" she asks.

"All clear," Chris and I reply in unison.

Once Hannah has confirmation that the intruder has indeed been detained, she moves lightning fast. "Bea, I love you dearly, and Chris? Thank you. You were a real knight in shining armor. But I've gotta get home," she says, sliding into her red pea coat and slinging her backpack over her shoulder. "I need a stiff drink after *that* incident."

And with a final shudder, Hannah practically sprints down the stairwell.

We both laugh until the bat gives a fitful sort of fight, and I actually yelp. "Sorry for the dramatics," I sigh. "Why don't we get this guy back outside where he belongs?"

I grab my coat and follow Chris downstairs and out to the sidewalk, where he calmly, gently releases the bat back into the December night. We watch him fly away, his movements clumsy and unsure before hitting a smooth stride.

"Thank you again," I say quietly. "Like Hannah said, you were our knight in shining armor." Like *Hannah* said, I think. Those were Hannah's words, not mine, so it's okay to admit their truth.

"No problem at all," Chris says. "I was actually heading to my parents' house when you called. I've got lots of compost to drop off and am joining them for a late dinner. Would you like to come along?"

Chapter Thirty-Five

"I would love to," I gush.

I wait outside Chris's apartment while he grabs his own coat, a sporty parka. He nods at the two compost bins next to his front door. "I had to buy a second bin," he says, his chest puffing with pride. "I didn't expect composting to be so popular."

I pick up one of the bins and say a quick Hail Mary that I won't trip at some point and spew days-old food across the sidewalk. "Is it a very far walk?"

"Not at all. My parents live at the corner of Woodmont and Orion," he says. "Is that okay? The bins are more awkward than heavy, but we can drive."

"And emit more fossil fuels? No way," I tease. "Wait a second... The corner of Woodmont and Orion? Are they in the massive brick house with the best holiday display in town?" I always route my walks around it.

The orange brick house has vintage-style, colored bulbs that line the dramatic points of the roofline, and every yew bush out front is positively covered in matching bright lights. In the center of the yard is a wooden stable with a retro, blow-mold nativity scene nestled inside. Icicle lights are strung between trees, creating the illusion of a perpetual snowfall, and there's a wreath in every one of the nine windows.

It is definitely extravagant and absolutely magical.

Chris picks up the other compost bin and tucks it under one arm so he can hold the front door open for me. "Please repeat that to my dad," he says "And make sure my mom hears it, too. It will make her feel better about the electric bill."

The walk to Chris's parents' house is a mere three minutes, and for once, I find myself wishing the distance was much, much farther.

"So, um, did you have a nice date the other night?" Chris asks, his ears growing red. "I didn't realize you were seeing someone."

I try to decipher the emotion in Chris's voice, but I can't figure it out. Does he sound hurt? Betrayed? Or is he just genuinely curious?

"We've only been out a few times," I say, my gut reaction to minimize John's importance. "My sister set us up."

"Setups can be brutal. I've had some pretty nightmarish ones myself."

Is Chris insinuating my setup is both brutal and nightmarish?

"John's a nice guy," I say. And I'm past thirty now, have an incurable disease, and woke up with a white eyebrow hair. So, I really don't have time to turn up my nose to the whole setup scenario. "He's got a good job and a goldendoodle, and we seem to want the same things." My tone has turned defensive, and I try to rein it back in. "Anyways. We'll see where it goes."

I steal a glance at him, terrified he is going to tell me he hopes it all works out or something equally heart-shattering, but Chris only looks contemplative.

"So, if you think setups are so awful, what's your idea of a dream date?" I ask.

"A dream date?" he repeats. "I don't know. Meeting for coffee before picking up litter at a local park. Lunch afterwards, stimulating conversation…" I giggle because this is all very Chris. "I've never really thought about it. What about you?"

I hoist the compost bin higher, adjusting my grip. It really is awkward.

"Easy. My beau would bring home pizza and hoagies, and then we'd watch Anthony Bourdain reruns and drink too much red wine. Life-chat deep into the night. And then dance to a romantic song on the fire escape before slipping into bed."

Chris raises his eyebrows at me. "It's like you've thought about this before."

"I've been single most my life," I point out. "I've had a lot of time to mull it over."

"Tell me how your tiny house project is going," he says, his breath visible. "I've heard you pacing around late at night. I can tell they're the footsteps of focus and hard work."

"How do you know they aren't the footsteps of restlessness or anxiety? Or an insomniac?"

"I just know," he says in such a way, I grow all warm inside. "A lot of people think best when they're moving. Many of history's most brilliant minds believed in the importance of long walks... Einstein, Wordsworth, Thoreau..."

"I imagine walking around Walden was more inspiring than pacing the length of my one-bedroom apartment," I say.

"So, have you told your sister yet?" Chris asks. "Or maybe your dad?"

"No, they don't know about it yet." I stare down at my feet, which are quickly turning red in the evening's cold. As usual, I'm wearing flats since they're easier to get on and off than boots. "I want to have a complete project proposal before I present anything to Mattie. I figure we can make revisions from there."

I don't mention how impenetrable Mattie becomes whenever I offer to help at Kickerville, afraid Chris will tell me my project sounds like a lost cause. I'm already filled with plenty of self-doubt.

Chris is quiet, thinking this over. "That makes sense," he says before stopping in front of his parents' house. "Well! Here it is. The Little residence."

I notice the artificial poinsettias in the flower boxes for the first time and a little sign along the front sidewalk that reads "All Are Welcome Here." Two Toyotas, a 4Runner and a Prius, are parked in the driveway, and a winter-themed flag flies from the front porch featuring an illustration of a kitten popping out a gift box.

Chris must notice my stare, because he says, "Mom loves cats, but Dad's allergic. And yes, she does have a few of those creepy fake cats that look like they're curled up and sleeping in armchairs."

"Fabulous," I reply, following him up the steps.

Chapter Thirty-Six

Chris pushes open the glass-paned front door, and I'm greeted with the smell of oregano, butter, and roasted tomatoes. The most perfect Christmas tree I've ever seen stands proudly in the family's foyer beside a dramatic oak staircase. The tree is decorated with the same colorful lights as outside and heavy with handmade ornaments and gumdrop garlands.

"Christopher! There you are." A woman, presumably his mother, greets him. She has short, tight curls and the most massive bosom I've ever seen. "Wow! That's a lot of compost," she laughs. "Hello there. I'm Colette."

I set the compost bin on the hardwood floor. "Hi! I'm Bea. Chris's upstairs neighbor."

"Ah, so *you're* Bea," Colette winks, which makes Chris immediately blush and mumble, "*Mom.*"

Oh, God. What does that mean? Chris's mother probably knows me as the poor lady who spilled mushroom matar and beer all over the apartment stairwell. Tragic!

"Bea?" I'm surprised to see Maria striding down the hallway, a cardboard box in her arms. "How have you been?"

My heartbeat picks up, and my voice turns shaky. Holy cannoli, I feel nervous around Chris's sister. "Just dandy!" I reply, proving I say the weirdest things when I'm anxious. Is Maria going to suggest I attend the Catholic singles retreat? Or maybe straight-up tell me I'm an inappropriate choice for her twin brother? "Um, how are you?"

"Good, good. Just navigating through the holiday hubbub." Maria nods at the cardboard box. "I'm in charge of the giving tree at the kids' school, and my parents grabbed a whopping ten ornaments."

"I wanted to take more," Colette says.

Maria studies me carefully—*wears flats instead of boots in winter weather; is clearly a moron,* I imagine her thinking—but before she can say anything, Colette suggests a glass of wine.

"Christopher and his dad can take the compost out back," she says. "Ron's already out there messing with some Christmas light fiasco."

"But I was going to show Bea the composter," Chris begins.

"Another time. Show her when it's warmer outside," Colette says. "Maria? Call me tomorrow when you know what time Simon needs to be picked up?"

Maria gives her mom a kiss on the cheek. "Of course. Thanks again for grabbing him." She narrows her eyes at Chris before giving me a small smile. It's not an unkind smile, but it's definitely suspicious. "Great seeing you, Bea. Take care."

Before I can dissect *that* interaction, Colette is leading me down the warm hallway past folk art prints and family photos. "Now then, I've got a bottle of merlot open. How does that sound?"

"Fantastic," I beam, thinking I'll take a glass of anything that gets me away from Maria's scrutinizing stare.

I stop in front of a picture of Chris and Maria. They must be only five or so, and Chris is riding a bike. Maria is clapping behind him and mid-shout. They both look exuberant.

"Isn't that a great shot?" Colette sighs. "Ron snapped that the evening Maria taught Chris how to ride a bike. She's always been the leader of those two, tugging Chris along on new adventures before he's ready." Colette smiles. "It's *usually* a good thing."

My eyes move to Maria's wedding day portrait, her hair pulled into an elegant bun and her lips painted a deep red, followed by a picture of Maria, her husband, and their three kids.

"Maria and Ryan have their hands full right now, but it's a happy chaos. Simon is in kindergarten, and Madelyn is in preschool. Little Joey is only two. He's a grandma's boy, always wanting to snuggle. I hope it never ends."

A happy chaos. It's the very term I use when daydreaming about my own bustling household someday, and I bask in the thought for a few moments.

I follow Colette into the kitchen where tomato bisque is simmering on the stovetop, and the windows are fogged up with steam. Colette has Brandi Carlile playing from a CD player mounted beneath a kitchen cabinet, and a half-eaten charcuterie spread is sitting on the butcher-block countertop.

"Help yourself," she says, nodding toward the assortment of meats, cheeses, and olives. "We're actually making grilled cheese tonight, so I apologize for doubling down on the dairy, but I'm a bit of a cheese fiend."

"I could live on charcuterie," I admit, accepting a full glass of red. "Thank you. Thank you so much for having me over on such short notice."

"I love guests." Colette busies herself over a wooden salad bowl. "The more the merrier. Judging by your love of charcuterie, I think I already know the answer to this question, but..." Colette holds up a zip-top package of plant-based cheese. "Do you want this fake mumbo jumbo on your sandwich like Chris? Or the real deal?"

"The real deal," I laugh. "And what can I do to help?" As awkward as I feel working my way around someone else's kitchen, I don't want to be the oaf slogging wine and gobbling up the entire charcuterie board.

Colette nods towards an attached sitting room. "Take off your coat and set your purse in there," she says. "Stay a while."

Chris and, presumably, his father trek in through a side door. "The backyard Frosty has been fixed!" his dad proclaims, hanging a flannel Stormy Kromer hat and shrugging out of a down coat.

"Thanks be to God!" Colette says, rolling her eyes towards me.

"And more importantly for Mother Earth, the compost has been taken care of," Chris smiles, his glance landing on me. "Bea, I'd like you to meet my father, Ron."

Ron Little is a slight man with thin wisps of hair combed over a shiny bald head. "It's a pleasure to meet you, Bea," he says, shaking my hand. Ron has kind, blue eyes and a big smile. "Thanks for helping Christopher get the compost over here."

"Well, thank you for having me for dinner," I reply. "This is such a treat." Especially since most of my meals these days consist of a lean protein and lots of vegetables. "And I absolutely love your Christmas display. It's one of the best in the neighborhood."

Ron's eyes light up. "You're my new favorite friend of Christopher's," he says, and I try not to feel hurt over the use of *friend,* which is stupid. Of course I'm just Chris's friend. I'm lucky Ron didn't simply call me his neighbor. "Did you hear that, Colette?"

"I'm not deaf, sweetie," she replies before shooing Chris and me into the dining room while she finishes the salad.

The Littles' dining room is elegant and formal, with maroon wallpaper dotted with gold flowers and a giant cherry table that seats twelve. An elaborate holly display runs down the center of the table with a large candle votive in the center. Chris holds out a middle chair, and I graciously take a seat.

"Grilled cheese and tomato bisque! Coming right out!" Colette announces, bursting into the dining room with the tray of sandwiches and soups raised like she's Rafiki presenting Simba to Pride Rock. Ron follows behind her, carrying the salad bowl and a bottle of red.

Colette divvies up the cozy crocks and plates of warm, gooey grilled cheese while we serve ourselves from the salad bowl. I marvel at how easy it is to be around Chris's parents.

"Are you from Cincinnati originally?" Ron asks.

I swallow my buttery, cheesy bite. *Mmmm.* "Yep! I grew up on the west side of town. My parents still live over that way."

Ron nods approvingly. "West siders are hard workers," he says matter-of-factly.

"I think so, too," I smile. "We're hardy stock."

"What do you do for work, sweetheart?" Colette asks.

"I'm a graphic designer," I say. "I work at an ad agency called Polly Feinstein."

Colette wags her forkful of salad in my direction. "I knew you were a creative the second I opened the door."

Before I can accept Colette's compliment, my spoon randomly drops from my hand, splattering tomato soup across the cream tablecloth. "I am so sorry!" My face burns hot, and I quickly try blotting the red stain with my napkin and water. "I..." Instinctively, my mind scrambles to come up with a polite excuse for such impolite behavior, but then I stop.

"I have MS," I say instead, "and sometimes things literally just drop out of my hands."

Colette reaches across the table, setting her warm hand on top of my cold one. "Tablecloths are meant to get messy, that's their job." She gives my hand a comforting pat. "One of my childhood girlfriends has MS. You have no explaining to do."

My throat tightens at her kindness. "When was she diagnosed?" I ask. "Is she doing all right?" I hold my breath, waiting for Colette to tell me her friend is wheelchair-bound or partially blind. Maybe both.

"She was diagnosed in her thirties, and she's in her late sixties now. She's an avid cyclist, and there's no puzzle she can't piece together. She's doing *great*," Colette emphasizes. "She was able to raise a family, four kids, no less, and after some trial and error, found a medication that works for her."

I swallow and nod, overcome with hopefulness. "Thank you for telling me that."

Colette nods back, giving me the world's warmest smile.

We eat for a few moments in silence before I take the conversation in a lighter direction. "What was Chris like as a child?" I ask, which immediately makes Chris blush, which is completely adorable. "Was he always so into science?"

"He was," Ron says fondly. "I own a dry cleaners over on Montgomery Road, and when Christopher was little, he was fascinated by the whole process. He wanted to know exactly *what* was in the cleaning solutions and if it was safe for the environment, how the mechanical racks worked, how far down the laundry chutes went..."

Colette covers her face with her hands. "I *hated* how intrigued he was. It made me a nervous wreck. I was always afraid he would get into the chemicals or take a ride on the clothing rack because, trust me, he tried!"

We all laugh.

"But that was Christopher. Always so curious," Colette says. "He got into *Star Wars* when he was about seven, and I bet he was Luke Skywalker for three Halloweens in a row. Does that sound right, Ron?"

"At least three," Ron confirms.

Chris waves his hand. "I'm right here, you know," he says. "For the record, it was five. You're both wrong."

"He was always capturing box turtles and caterpillars outside," Colette continues, enjoying this stroll down memory lane. "And he treated them right, too, being gentle and kind. He never kept them longer than a day or two before letting them go."

"That's very sweet," I say, resisting the urge to place my hand on Chris's thigh...his arm...anywhere. I just want to touch him. I want to squeeze his hand, to give him a silent signal that I think he is someone special.

"I'm sure you have plenty of sweet childhood stories," Chris says. "I bet you were knitting and building birdhouses by age five.”

“More like finger paints and Play-Doh,” I say. “I wasn't *that* cool.”

And then he looks at me in such a way, my entire body feels like a warm plate of brownies.

Chapter Thirty-Seven

*T*hanks again for coming last night. My mom insisted I ask you this, so sorry if it's weird... Did you know Beatrix means "she who brings happiness"? P.S. It's true. ;)

How can a little, smudgy phone screen deliver so much joy? I beam downward, simply staring at Chris's words.

I also have a text from Hannah that simply says, **Forget John! I am Team Chris now, and you should be, too! He is ADORABLE! And BRAVE! Can we call him Batman???**

"Is this *People* magazine neurologist specific?" Mattie interrupts my happy thoughts. I watch her flip through the glossy pages, her forehead creased in a frown. She examines the front and back covers for some kind of clue.

I feel vindicated. "Right? Since when do they write articles about soap opera stars who suffer from migraines? And there isn't a single celebrity hookup mentioned. I looked the last time we were here."

Mattie and I are sitting in Dr. Wessels' waiting room, ten minutes early for my two o'clock appointment. This afternoon, Dr. Wessels will review the MRI scans of my neck and spine, and we'll choose a medication route. Mattie is filling in for Mom, who's attending the funeral of a distant relative. "Oh, he was a curmudgeon of a man, never a very warm uncle." Mom waved away my condolences. "No need for hysterics, but family is family."

Mattie sets the magazine back on an end table. "How are you feeling?" she asks, leaning forward in her chair. "Are you nervous?"

"A little bit, yeah." I *am* nervous, both for the results of my scans and for another barrage of probing medical questions from my sister. I told Mom I'd be fine coming to today's appointment alone, I am thirty years old and all, but when Mattie found out, she insisted on joining.

I stare as a woman exits the elevator out in the lobby. She's probably in her forties, with dark, limp hair that hangs at her shoulders and a sallow complexion. She looks tired and sad, and who can blame her? She's using a walker and having to drag along the entire left side of her body. I grip the arms of my chair, ready to jump up and help somehow, when I see a caregiver exit the elevator behind her.

Mattie clears her throat. "Don't forget, you're already starting this marathon miles ahead," she says, noticing the situation I'm watching unfold. "They caught the MS early, *so* early, and there are *so* many more treatment options available today than fifteen, ten, even five years ago."

An image of myself running Cincinnati's Flying Pig marathon immediately comes to mind. I think of myself sprinting up one of the city's famous hills as the MS monster, a decidedly green, slimy creature, chases behind me, struggling to keep up.

"Thanks for coming today. I know you're swamped at work. Or, um, I assume you are," I fumble. Because between us? I guess I am pretty relieved that my older sister is here with me. God knows bad things don't happen on Mattie's watch.

"That never changes, though." Mattie gives me a forced smile. "I'm glad I could come. Besides, Fran's got things under control."

Now that I do not doubt.

"Did you know Fran and my neighbor Janet are cooking their way through a Julia Child cookbook together?"

"*Really?*" Finally, a genuine smile from Mattie. "I thought Fran was more of the *Moosewood Cookbook* type. And she's always been such a lone wolf. Besides her brother and his family, and our family, of course, I don't know if she hangs out with many people."

"Trust me, I'm just as baffled. But I think it's a good thing." I pause, not quite sure how to venture down this next path. "Um, I would love to stop by Kickerville sometime soon," I finally say, sounding like the most random person in the world.

Mattie has pulled her phone out and is typing an email. *The client insists she ordered a red roof and we sent green instead. Now she's asking for a complimentary screened-in porch,* I read over her shoulder.

"Why?" Mattie asks, and it takes me a moment to realize the question is for me and not regarding the disgruntled customer.

"Oh, well," I scramble for the right words, quickly losing confidence. "Visit with Fran, see what you're all up to..."

"Well, sure. Stop by whenever," Mattie replies, only half-interested.

Our old friend, Donna, is the nurse who calls me back. She seems *slightly* softer but mostly still bothered by us, especially when I joke, "Can we get a room with a view?" Though funny enough, Donna does take us to an exam room with a window. Sure, the view is of the crowded parking lot and interstate, but the natural light's nice.

After taking my blood pressure, Donna leaves us with the promise that Dr. Wessels will be in shortly. In addition to an exam table and blood pressure equipment, this room also includes a large desk with two chairs sitting opposite of it. Mattie and I settle into the seats.

After the standard double tap, Dr. Wessels opens the heavy door. "Hi, Bea," she smiles before extending her hand towards Mattie. "Hi again, Mattie."

I'm impressed Dr. Wessels has remembered my sister's name, but then I remember how Mattie went all *Dr. Quinn, Medicine Woman* on us the last time, so I'm sure she left an impression.

Dr. Wessels flips through the papers on her clipboard. "So, Bea. How have you been feeling?"

"I've been okay," I say, wondering if the MRI technician told her about my meltdown inside the tube, which now feels embarrassing and immature. "I looked up the Wahls Protocol and Swank Diets. They're *tough*. Though, maybe I can finally drop this extra weight if I give either a real try."

"They're certainly not for the faint of heart, huh?" Dr. Wessels smiles. "There's always the Mediterranean Diet, which I think benefits just about everyone."

I imagine myself sitting in a beach chair beside the Mediterranean Sea with a generous Greek salad in my lap—juicy tomatoes, salty feta, crisp cucumber—and a glass of wine beside me. Maybe a bowl of pistachios to snack on...

"Now then," Dr. Wessels says, taking a seat behind the desk. She jiggles a mouse and coaxes a computer screen to life. "Let's have a look at these scans."

Dr. Wessels pulls up the images from my recent MRI. It's strange seeing my skeleton from these new angles. Mattie immediately takes out her notebook and pen from her oversized purse, and even though I know she's only trying to be helpful, I feel annoyed. This is *my brain,* not the test material for an upcoming exam she's trying to ace.

"I didn't find any lesions on your neck or spine," Dr. Wessels says.

Mattie writes this info down. "That's fantastic news," she says, an edge to her voice that seems to communicate, *And don't tell me otherwise.* "Don't most MS patients have spinal lesions in addition to brain lesions? It's fairly rare that Bea doesn't, correct?"

"Correct," Dr. Wessels confirms. Mattie pats my knee, and my heart feels a little lighter. "Bea, I cannot emphasize how early we caught your MS."

Dr. Wessels takes a piece of paper from one of the desk drawers and draws a pyramid. She lists the MS medications with lower risks and lower efficacies at the bottom of the pyramid. As she moves up on the pyramid, the efficacy rates improve, but so do the risks.

"It's about where you feel comfortable," she says. "And it's important you understand the risks involved with each."

Mattie studies the chart intently, sucking her bottom lip in deep concentration. "So, there are three categories: injectable, oral, and infusion?"

"Yes, exactly," says Dr. Wessels. "Again, it's what the patient is most comfortable with."

I cringe. "I can't imagine sticking myself with a needle every day."

"What's the cadence for the self-injecting drugs?" Mattie wants to know.

"It varies from every day to once a week," she says.

I'm still not interested. What if I faint and conk my head on the clawfoot tub? "Even if it's only once a month, no thank you," I say, resolute. "That's not for me."

Ultimately, I'm stuck between a twice-daily pill and a twice-yearly infusion. They fall in the upper middle of the pyramid, effective but with moderate risks.

"The twice-yearly setup would be fantastic," I say. I hold out my arm, which is *still* bruised from all of my recent blood work. "But an infusion... I don't know. It sounds intimidating and scary." The only infusions I know about are related to cancer treatments.

Dr. Wessels is quiet, but she nods gently. She understands.

"How do most patients feel after the infusion?" Mattie asks, not even looking up from her notebook. She's filled an entire page with her neat handwriting. "I assume they feel better in the long term, but are there any short-term adverse reactions?"

"It's common to feel nauseous and tired, maybe even a bit achy, a week after the infusion, sort of like you have the flu. But those symptoms are only temporary. They subside."

Both Dr. Wessels and Mattie stare at me as I trace a finger up and down the pyramid, hedging my bets and considering my options.

Ultimately, I choose the twice-daily pill.

After Dr. Wessels goes over the scary PML warning, a very small number of patients contract the rare-but-fatal brain disease, she tells me about the medication's most common side effects, which are flushing and stomach issues. "The flushing and stomach problems generally go away after a month or so," she says. "But some patients do find those side effects intolerable."

Flushing sounds like an ailment from a Jane Austen novel. I picture proper ladies in petticoats clutching hands against their foreheads and proclaiming how flushed they are. As for the stomach issues, I figure I can manage those, too. I was a carsick child who grew up puking into plastic grocery bags during long road trips, so I can handle nausea and whatever else comes my way.

"I can deal with that," I say. "Let's try the twice-daily pill."

Since I've already had a very robust set of blood tests done, including my blood cell count to check my liver and kidney functions, my only task now is to wait for the pharmaceutical company to call.

"I'm starting to feel better about everything," I tell Mattie after the appointment. We stand beside my car in the parking lot, our butts and our backs against the cool metal. "I've got an action plan. I don't feel so helpless anymore."

She hugs me, the intensity of her embrace taking me by surprise. Has my sister ever held me like this before?

"Can you take the rest of the day off?" she asks, surprising me further. "I was thinking we could grab coffee and check out the conservatory."

I nod happily, not needing a second to consider. "I would love that!"

Chapter Thirty-Eight

The Krohn Conservatory is magical any time of year, but especially during the holidays. Located in Eden Park, the greenhouse was designed at the height of the Art Deco era. There are thousands of plant species to admire in addition to a twenty-foot indoor waterfall. The conservatory's holiday show features a live nativity out front, poinsettias galore, and the most spectacular train display.

As girls, it was always Mattie and my favorite holiday outing.

I hop in my Corolla and follow Mattie's sporty Lexus toward Eden Park, making a quick stop at a local coffee shop along the way, where we both order peppermint lattes.

The parking lot at Krohn Conservatory is full, and Eden Park Drive is lined with cars. It doesn't matter when you visit during the yuletide season, this Cincinnati landmark is a happening spot. I find an open stretch of street close to the Eden Park entrance and pull off a near perfect parallel parking job.

"Impressive," Mattie comments, walking up the sidewalk. She parked farther away, not possessing my same parking skills. It's probably the one thing I'm better at than Mattie. How lame.

"Thanks again for coming to my appointment." We walk down the sloping sidewalk, my flats squeaking with each step. Mattie's questions and commentary were genuinely helpful today. "It would have been overwhelming making that sort of decision alone."

"I'm happy I could be there. And for the record, I would have chosen the pill, too," she says, which is the best thing she could tell me.

We pass the sheep grazing outside the nativity scene and duck inside the crowded stable. Ever since I was a child, this space has felt sacred. They keep the lighting dim and play solemn, spiritual music. The figurines of Mary, Joseph, Jesus, and the shepherds are made of wax and look so real, they always manage to startle me.

I say a little prayer in front of the Baby Jesus. *I want to feel better. I'm tired of operating in survival mode. I want to thrive.* It's a vague prayer, so who knows if it has any chance of being answered? Maybe higher powers require details.

We walk inside the crowded vestibule of the conservatory, where the greenhouse windows are fogged and condensation drips down the glass. The air is delightfully warm and humid, a sensory winter respite.

"How was your cake tasting on Sunday?" I ask Mattie.

"You didn't hear about that drama?" she asks, sounding both tired and amused.

I shake my head, wondering how various combinations of airy cake, ganache, and sweet frosting can be anything other than delightful.

Mattie pulls off her knit hat and runs a hand through her hair, coaxing volume at the roots. "Right, so you know how Mom is set on that bakery on Bridgetown Road?"

"Of course," I say. Mom describes this woman's red velvet cake as a transcendental experience, which is not small potatoes coming from our Catholic mother. "What's the name of the place again? Buttercream Betty's?"

"Uh-huh. So, Buttercream Betty is baking Stephanie Stooplemeyer's wedding cake, too," Mattie begins. Oh, boy. This can't be good. "And Stephanie *just* asked Betty for a groom's cake and two-hundred cupcakes. In addition to the three-tier wedding cake she already ordered."

"Whoa." That's a lot of cake. "But how does this translate to drama for you?"

"Betty is a one-woman operation. She can't handle that massive order as well as Peter and my wedding cake, and since Stephanie Stooplemeyer reserved hers first..."

"No way," I say. "You're down a wedding cake baker now?" For once, it's me who jumps into problem-solving mode. "I can make your cake, Matt! You've seen the cakes I've made for bridal and baby showers. I'm pretty good!"

But am I Mattie and Peter good? I falter.

"No, no," Mattie says, but she's laughing. "I mean, you *are* pretty good. You're a fantastic baker, Bea! But I don't even like cake all that much. Mom's in an absolute tizzy, but I think this is a blessing in disguise. Maybe we can do the gelato bar Peter and I wanted from the get-go."

Mattie and Peter want a gelato bar? Well, gosh. That's fun.

"Remember how we took that big trip to Italy a few years into dating?" she asks. "We thought it would be a thoughtful nod to that. It was such a special time for us."

I smile. "Thank God for Stephanie Stooplemeyer then."

We shuffle through the throngs of visitors and into the greenhouse that holds the train display. I adore this holiday display of a miniature Cincinnati. It's far from traditional, flawlessly incorporating the surrounding plants and natural materials, like sticks, lush greenery, and tree bark. The result is a woodsy, whimsical version of the Queen City, one that seems fitting of a fairy tale.

"Don't you think Dr. Wessels has the most amazing job?" Mattie asks, a sort of dreamy look across her face as she studies a model of Union Terminal.

"Not really," I say "She has to give people terrible news. Plus, can you imagine the sort of pressure she's under? If I botch up something at work, a client gets upset. If she messes up, someone could *die*."

Mattie isn't deterred. "Well, sure. It is a tremendous amount of pressure. But she helps people feel better. She gives them their quality of life back. She *heals*."

"Like Mom does as a nurse." I stand in front of the slanted tracks of the former Mount Adams Incline and watch the cable car move up and down.

"Yes, exactly." Mattie nods, a glimmer of something in her green eyes. "Like Mom. Like a nurse. I think it's incredible."

"Well, you help provide people with shelter and warmth. Safety from the elements. Comfort from the anxieties of everyday life," I point out. "That's nothing to snuff at."

But Mattie snuffs anyway. "What I do is hardly altruistic." She sits down on one of the benches nestled throughout the greenhouse. "You know the big holiday show NBC puts on before they light the Rockefeller Christmas tree?"

"Sure. I watched it last week," I say. "When does Savannah Guthrie sleep? I mean, same goes for Hoda Kotb, but Savannah covers politics, too."

"I missed this year's show," Mattie replies. "But the year of the pandemic? Well, this country music star sang 'I'll Be Home for Christmas' in front of a New York City hospital. He thanked all the healthcare workers, a handful of them were circled around him, and Bea... It hit me *hard*." She holds a hand against her heart.

"They sacrificed everything when so many Americans weren't willing to stop their normal activities. Or even wear a mask."

"They were, and still are, superheroes," Mattie says, her eyes looking damp. She takes a deep breath. "Sorry. I guess I'm just emotional because of..." She gives a vague hand wave as her cheeks turn red. "...the holidays."

"No, I get it," I say, desperate for my sister to keep sharing, to not feel embarrassed about confiding in me. "I remember feeling prouder than ever having a mom who's a nurse."

"Me too," Mattie smiles.

We mosey around the train display a bit longer before venturing back to the lobby. We walk down the main pathway and stop in front of the towering waterfall where we watch kids toss pennies and make wishes. "Want to make a wish?" Mattie asks me, fishing in her wallet like I don't have a penny to my name.

"I already said a prayer outside," I tell her.

She hands me a penny anyway, and with my eyes closed and my breath held, I toss it over my shoulder and into the water. *I just want to feel normal again*, I wish.

We pop into the conservatory's gift shop next.

I pick up a delicate cardinal figurine and watch Mattie examine a jar of bath salts. Before I can lose my nerve, I ask, "Hey Mattie, do you remember that tiny house we passed on our way to the Adirondacks? Not last summer, but the one before? We were still on the thruway, between Buffalo and Syracuse."

"I do, yes," she says, before grinning. "Honestly? I remember you and Dad sticking your noses against the window more." That's right! Dad was equally enamored. "What about it?"

"Do you, um, think those are cool?" I ask, sounding like a ten-year-old boy comparing baseball cards with a friend.

Mattie sets the bath salts down and folds her arms, looking pleasantly pensive. "Yeah, absolutely. I find the whole movement fascinating."

Oh my God—she does? My heart races in my chest, and my mouth goes dry as I think of the dozens of things I want to say to her.

"So do I," I stammer instead.

Smooth, Bea. Real smooth.

But before I can say anything else, the delicate figurine drops out of my palms and shatters against the floor. Mattie's eyes lock with mine. She knows why the bird fell.

I bend down, gathering the tiny, sharp pieces in my unreliable hands.

Mattie kneels beside me. "Are you okay?" she whispers.

"Yeah! I'll buy my broken cardinal and use the pieces for an art project." I try to smile bravely. "It's all good."

As we stand in line at the register, I make bright chit-chat about how the broken cardial will be perfect for some made-up mosaic project. But inside, I'm crumbling. I was just given the most opportune moment to tell Mattie about my tiny house project, and MS ruined it.

"Are you sure you're all right?" Mattie murmurs.

My voice turns small and squeaky. "It never gets any less upsetting when that stuff happens. It makes me distrust my entire body."

She grabs my trembling hand and squeezes it tight.

Chapter Thirty-Nine

I'm chewing on a pen cap and reading my horoscope when the pharmaceutical company calls the following morning. (I'm a Sagittarius, if you're curious. Mattie is a Capricorn, which isn't surprising at all, is it?)

"Just give me a second to move someplace quieter." While I knew the pharmaceutical company would be calling me today, I wasn't expecting them to call so early. I knock over my page-a-day calendar with my sudden, awkward movements. "*Shit.* Sorry, not shit to you, shit to my clumsiness."

Hannah is wearing her giant noise-cancelling headphones and tuned in to her work. She doesn't even notice me standing up. As for the rest of my colleagues, they are equally transfixed on their computer screens. Only Gwen sees me scurrying away with my phone, and she glares in my direction. As if taking a personal call is somehow against the rules!

I slip inside the first empty privacy booth and lean against the cool, white wall. "Hi. Sorry about that," I exhale. "So! Would you like my insurance information? Home address? How do I go about getting the goods?"

The woman chuckles. "Let's start with your financial information and see if you qualify for our copay assistance program."

Dr. Wessels prepared me for this conversation, explaining that as long as I'm not a billionaire, I will qualify. ("Even I would qualify," Dr. Wessels explained, which was all the evidence I needed of the program's generous threshold.) The pharmaceutical company associate goes over the terms with me, you can't be on the program if you are on any sort of government insurance, which I think is backwards as hell, and I say a solemn "yes" to every question asked of me on the recorded phone call.

"So, I'm good to go then?" I say at the end of the conversation.

I watch Gwen and Chase walk by wearing their coats, presumably off to grab coffee. I haven't considered it before, but Chase will likely have a significant say in choosing Christina's replacement. I'm thankful I have a good rapport with him. We also tag-teamed an extensive redesign for a major client last spring, which certainly won't hurt my case either.

"Oh, sweetie no," says the woman. "We've only just begun. Now you'll wait to receive a call from the specialty pharmacy."

My mood deflates. "Oh, okay. Well, when should I expect that?"

"Lord only knows," she replies, which is about the least scientific response you could expect from a pharmaceutical company. "Hopefully soon," she adds, sensing my disappointment.

I return to my desk and spend the remainder of the morning hopelessly distracted as I glance down at my phone every few seconds.

"Want to go for a quick walk? Grab soup and sandwiches?" Hannah asks around noon, after I've effectively wasted ninety minutes making the same client revisions on repeat. "I was going to stop by the drug store, too. Check out that new eye cream the Internet's been raving about."

"I packed today," I say, thinking how much better hot broccoli cheddar soup sounds than the kale salad in my backpack. I lower my voice to a whisper. "Plus, I'm waiting for the specialty pharmacy to call me about my MS medication."

"Got it." She gives me two swift nods. "Text me if you think of anything you want me to pick up? I think the deli finally has their peppermint bark out."

"Thanks, Han," I smile. "But I'm okay."

At twelve-thirty, the specialty pharmacy finally calls. When I answer, I think I'm crossing the finish line, but as it turns out, this is only the start of the phone tag marathon that will consume my entire afternoon.

For *hours,* I field calls from the pharmaceutical company and the specialty pharmacy, who have seemingly endless questions for me. The pharmaceutical company wants to be absolutely sure I qualify for the copay assistance program, and the specialty pharmacy wants to be absolutely sure I qualify for the medication itself. It doesn't help that my office building has unreliable cell phone service, and a handful of these calls randomly drop.

"*No!* No, no, no." I audibly groan, knowing it will take nearly ten minutes to get reconnected with the associate I was working with.

While everyone I speak to is friendly enough—strangely, each person also has a Southern accent—the sheer amount of phone calls and conversations is draining. Every time I think this *has* to be the last person I'll speak to, I'm transferred to another department. It's like I'm on a hamster wheel, the pharmaceutical company and specialty pharmacy dangling my MS medication on a stick just out of reach.

"Everything okay?" Gwen asks around two o'clock, intercepting me as I hurry towards a privacy booth for the umpteenth time. She doesn't sound concerned, though. She sounds suspicious. "You've been taking an awful lot of personal calls today."

No shit, Sherlock, I think.

"Sorry about that," I say instead.

Is this the pot calling the kettle black or what? Gwen routinely takes calls from her friends and family members. She once infamously spent an entire hour gabbing to a boyfriend about their rental in St. Lucia. We knew all about the private infinity pool, fully stocked fridge, and king-sized bed by the end of it.

"I was hoping to assign Lauren her first job today," Gwen says, referring to the junior designer I've been onboarding. "It's an email and some social ads for that new kombucha client."

"That sounds straightforward enough," I reply. "Yeah, I think she's ready for it. It's been a smooth transmission." Gwen glares at me, and I immediately know I've slipped up an important word. I shake my head. *"Transition,"* I correct myself, despising this MS quirk. "It's been a smooth transition."

She studies me carefully. "A new hire's success is directly tied to her trainer," she says.

And an employee's happiness is directly tied to her manager, I think. "Yes, I agree," I say instead. "And I think Lauren's onboarding is going well."

"Good," Gwen says coolly, before taking the subject in a different direction. "I don't need to tell you how difficult it is getting all of our client deliverables out the door before the holidays. You've been here what, five years now? This isn't your first December in the agency world."

"Almost eight, actually," I say. *Three years longer than you've been with the company,* I think.

"Right." She gives me a tight smile, her thin lips spread even thinner.

"Well, then you know it's all hands on deck. Be a team player and keep the personal calls to a minimum."

I swallow tears as Gwen glides away. It's one thing to have my wrist slapped for taking too many calls, but to be accused of being selfish? Of bringing the entire team down? That stings. *I have MS!* I want to shout behind her. *I'm trying to secure medication for my incurable disease!*

I glue myself to my seat for the next hour, ignoring the barrage of calls and voicemails and trying not to cry. Once Gwen leaves for the day—at four o'clock, an entire hour early—I slump back to a privacy booth.

A poor nurse named Dottie is the final person I speak to, and I can only imagine how miserable I sound.

"Did your doctor go over the common side effects?" she asks.

"Uh-huh," I mumble.

"Please answer yes or no."

"Yes." I stare at yet another blank white wall. I still have so much work to complete before I leave the office today. I'm going to be here until eight at this point. Dumbledore the Janitor will probably get to leave before me.

Dottie then goes over all the side effects *again* with me, the common ones as well as the terrifying rare ones. "All right, Beatrix. It looks like your first shipment will arrive on Monday, December 14th," she says.

"Wait, so I'm finally finished with all of this?" My voice must sound hysterical. I shake my head. "You're sending the medication now? Like, I am good to go?"

"Yes. But it won't arrive until Monday."

"Monday's great! That's perfect!" I rejoice. "I'm just so thankful it's on its way, and I'm done talking to you people! No offense, Dottie."

"Well, be sure to call if your prescription doesn't show up on the 14th," she says. "We can't have missing medications wandering the streets."

I imagine a pill bottle with legs, sunglasses, and a baseball cap slinking down the road. I laugh with delirium. "Right. I'll be sure to call if there's a problem," I promise.

After hanging up, I wander back to my desk in a sort of daze.

"You okay?" Hannah asks, lowering her headphones.

"No," I sigh, collapsing into my swivel chair. "But I will be soon."

Chapter Forty

Just as Dottie promised, my medication promptly arrives on Monday. I feel like Gollum clutching it to my chest, nearly whispering, "My precious." I tuck the rest of my mail beneath my armpit and practically sprint up the stairs.

Chris Little opens his apartment door as I race past. "Did you leave the stove on?" he frowns, noticing my haste.

I hold up my prized delivery. "My MS medication arrived!"

"Oh!" He gives me a high five, which is silly and unexpected and makes me laugh. "That's great news. I've been doing quite a bit of reading on MS. Is it a self-injectable?"

Chris has been studying MS? *He's probably curious from a scientific perspective,* my brain tells my heart.

"A twice-daily pill," I swallow.

"Well, right on," he says, locking his door and sliding his modest key ring inside his coat pocket. He must be heading out for the evening. "I'm thrilled for you, Bea."

I notice his button-up and dark slacks beneath his heavy pea coat. "You look nice. Where are you off to?" I ask, trying to sound casual.

"My nephew's Christmas concert. It's over at St. Mary's," he says. "And then Dewey's afterward to celebrate. Between us? I'm more excited for the pizza than the performance."

My heart warms. "Oh, you don't mean that. School holiday programs are the best! Violet hasn't had any yet, but when she does, I'll probably be hopping on a plane to Santa Fe."

"They're very sweet, but I don't think I'd travel across the country for one," he laughs. "Have a good night, Bea. And good luck with the medication."

We start to go our separate ways when I remember something from my morning that I feel strangely inclined to share. "Chris, wait!" I grab his wool sleeve.

"Yes?" He raises his bushy eyebrows, looking amused.

"Did you know Cher's real name is Cherilyn Sarkisian?" I ask. "It was a clue in this morning's *New York Times* mini crossword puzzle, and I can't stop thinking about it."

Chris doesn't find this tidbit weird or random. He's just as tickled as I felt. "You're kidding! That's marvelous, Sarkisian... Armenian, I think?" he ponders, getting lost in his own head for a moment. "I can't wait to tell my family at dinner."

"Your parents probably already know," I say. "At least my mom did. But it sent me down this bizarre rabbit hole where I looked up celebrities' real names for a solid twenty minutes. Do you think you would change your name if you became famous? Or just shorten it a bit like Cher?"

"I'm not sure much shortening can be done to Chris," he smirks, before looking me square in the eyes. "I love the way your mind works."

And with that, Chris waves goodbye for the evening, leaving my heart rap-tap-tapping. He loves the way my mind works? Chris sees something good in *my mind*, a place where scary lesions have been hiding? It's such a kind sentiment.

After letting Tony Soprano outside and feeding him dinner, I make myself a cup of green tea and curl up with the cheerful welcome packet that came with my medication. It reminds me of the one I received when I first started birth control as a teenager. (It was for treating acne, as there was no way I was having sex in high school, and there was also no way Mom would have approved the prescription otherwise.) The welcome packet includes glossy booklets with bright images of happy, healthy MS patients and weirdly chosen branded materials, like pens and a cosmetic bag.

One of the photographs is of a woman in a yoga class doing a headstand. My heart lifts. That can be me again.

Since I'm going to the Cincinnati Zoo's Festival of Lights with John tonight, I will start my medication bright and early tomorrow morning. My self-revolution is on the horizon.

In a burst of optimism, I decide to open the not-so-small pile of medical bills I've been routinely shoving behind the kitchen fruit bowl.

As each new one arrived, I only grew more anxious about opening *any* of them.

I have a high-deductible HSA account, an appropriate choice for the healthy twenty-something I was when I elected the coverage. But of course, now I'm a thirty-something with a chronic disease. And fighting a disease isn't cheap.

I've already paid the bill for my day-before-Thanksgiving MRI, an even $600, and I know my current HSA account balance hovers around $1200. It isn't pocket change, but it also isn't going to go very far in the world of multiple sclerosis.

I open the first bill, which is for the seemingly endless amount of blood tests Dr. Wessels ordered for me. The amount comes in at...$91.62. Okay. *Phew.* That isn't bad at all! I neatly set the bill in the new "opened" pile and toss its envelope into the trash.

The second bill is for my initial neurologist appointment with Dr. Wessels. Specialists are expensive, and I won't fare as well as I did with the blood work. With one eye open and the other squeezed shut, I pull out the neatly folded piece of paper. Sure enough, my first visit costs $227.62 after insurance.

"We're still in the green," I remind Tony.

Tired of Christmas music but still in need of some uplifting tunes, I cue up a Shania Twain playlist. Shania Twain always makes me feel sassy and confident. Maybe the country star can get me through these medical bills one brassy ballad at a time.

Instead of opening my neck and spine MRI bill, I skip ahead to my second neurologist visit and confirm the same amount, $227.62, which puts my total at $546.86. That means I still have over half of my HSA amount left, and since I know MRIs cost around $600, maybe I'm going to squeak by after all.

Shania begins to croon "Man I Feel Like a Woman," one of my all-time favorites, and I sing along.

It's been a close call, but I'll at least make it through December without having to dip into my savings or checking accounts. Next year, I'll enroll in a more appropriate healthcare plan.

I tear open the final bill, this one for my most recent MRI, and my jaw falls open at the number. The amount is just shy of $1300. This single MRI costs more than the balance of my entire HSA account.

"Man I Feel Like a Woman"? More like man, I feel *broke.*

This must be some sort of mistake, I rationalize. I immediately call the imaging center's billing department, hoping to catch someone before the office closes at six. I quiet Shania while I wait on hold.

"Hello, this is Shelby speaking. How may I help you?" A woman answers after I've spent ten minutes listening to the holiday edition of fuzzy elevator music. Shelby sounds remarkably like my fifth-grade teacher, which I find disorienting.

"Hi. My name is Beatrix Parker, and I have a few questions regarding a recent bill I received," I say.

"Can you give me the bill number?" Shelby asks. I recite the numbers as clearly and slowly as my quivering voice can manage. "Great. I've got it pulled up now," she confirms. "What questions do you have?"

"I guess I only have one," I say, staring at the half-finished needlepoint of a Ruth Bader Ginsburg quote I'm giving Hannah for Christmas. "I'm wondering if there's been a mistake."

"You think the cost is incorrect?" Shelby clarifies.

Feeling self-conscious, I babble, "Well, yes. I think it's too high. Maybe. I don't know. It's just that I've had an MRI before, a lot of them actually, and the cost has never been this much."

"Well, let me take a closer look," Shelby says patiently. "We imaged two areas, your neck and your spine, and we used contrast. Did any of your past MRIs include those factors?"

"Yes to the contrast," I reply, feeling sick at the realization that this bill is not a mistake. "But I hadn't considered the fact that I was having images taken of two areas. I guess that explains why it's double the price."

"I'm sorry," Shelby says, and I can tell she means it. "We do have payment plans available."

"I've never had to do that before." My apartment feels uncomfortably hot, and I move to open a window. "Can I call you back tomorrow? I have a date tonight, and I still need to get ready. We're going to the Festival of

Lights." Why am I telling this woman from the billing department about my date? Is this some sort of involuntary attempt to sound less pathetic?

"I love the Festival of Lights. My husband actually proposed to me there," she replies, surprising me with the personal detail. "Of course you can call back tomorrow. We open at eight." Shelby pauses. "And Beatrix? It's not unusual to use a payment plan for a medical bill. Our healthcare system doesn't exactly set us up for success, does it?"

"No. It doesn't," I say, Shelby's kindness bringing me close to tears. "And thank you. I appreciate it."

I'm touched by Shelby's sympathy, but that tenderness is quickly replaced by anxiety and stress as I ponder the bigger picture. I think of all the dumb purchases I've made with my HSA account in the past, like multiple pairs of Warby Parker glasses (even though I have only the slightest prescription) and a food sensitivity test to determine the cause of my GI issues (during a time when my diet largely consisted of fried foods and alcohol).

My current pile of medical bills is scary and overwhelming, but it isn't the reason why my body is practically pulsing with a low panic. It's the pile of *future* bills that overwhelms and terrifies me. I'm only at the very start of a lifelong battle with this disease, and I only have the tiniest understanding of what lies ahead.

"Maybe we can move to Canada?" I say to Tony, trying to cheer myself up. "Universal healthcare *and* Justin Trudeau? Sounds pretty sweet right about now."

Tony's stare seems to say, *We both know that's not as easy as it sounds.*

I take a few deep breaths and try to steady my trembling hands. I can't let myself get worked up. I can't let the stress in. Stress will only pour gasoline over the fire of my miserably unreliable body.

I am on the up and up with this disease, not the down and down.

I will handle the bills tomorrow.

Chapter Forty-One

John Noble's house is truly a stunner.

The three-story Victorian is painted white with elaborate trim work that puts the finest gingerbread houses to shame. With a wrap-around porch and a bright red door, it looks like something plucked from a movie set. Even the elaborately laid brick driveway, where my little sedan's currently rumbling, is impressive.

Sophisticated white lights trace the roofline, and a large wreath with its own twinkly lights hangs in the center of the second story. Swirls of white lights circle the manicured yew bushes, and there's a single Bethlehem star at the top of a mature pine tree. The display has the sort of neat uniformity that makes me guess John hired a company to do the work.

I don't have much time to admire John's home, or will my hands to stop shaking, before he strides out the front door. He's wearing a black knit cap tonight and one of those wildly expensive goose feather parkas all of Mattie's friends have.

John slides inside my car and kisses my warm cheek. "Hey! Thanks for picking me up," he says.

"Your house is gorgeous. Does Wrigley approve?" I give him my best smile. "And sure thing! Now you get to experience the extraordinary performance and engineering of my 2009 Toyota Corolla. Why, I bet it has the horsepower of a single horse."

John laughs, and it's a good laugh, too. "Yes, Wrigley loves his fenced-in backyard. I also think he has a crush on the Bernese Mountain Dog next door," he says, and I wonder if this date will be different. Maybe this is when we'll hit our stride. "I know it's dark, but you look very pretty tonight,"

John adds, feeding this hope of mine. "You smell nice, too."

Since we'll be outside most of the evening, I've chosen a heavy turtle-neck in emerald green, dark jeans, and two pairs of wool socks beneath my fur-lined boots. I even hung little Christmas trees from my ears and gave myself sultry eye makeup.

My motto for the night? Feel shitty, look pretty.

I take a deep breath, trying to put my medical bill anxiety to bed, and ask, "Did you know Cher's real name is Cherilyn Sarkisian?"

I peek over, excited to catch John's reaction, and am immediately disappointed. He looks more confused than charmed. "That's random," he says. "What made you think of that?"

"It was in my morning crossword puzzle," I reply, fumbling to remember another recent fun fact or riddle. "Okay, listen to this one: Guy who's always getting lost in a book?" John raises his eyebrows. "A bookworm?"

"That was my first thought," I say quickly. "But the answer was Waldo. Isn't that clever?"

John nods and hums along with the overplayed Christmas song from pop music's latest and greatest star.

"It's how I start every morning." I find myself babbling. "I like to do the *New York Times* Mini Crossword and read my horoscope while I drink my first cup of coffee. I almost always do the Wordle, too. Um, what about you? How do you start the day?"

"Yeah? I begin mine with a run and a green smoothie from that natural foods shop in the square." He gives me a wry smile. "I guess it's an expensive habit, but if it helps me live longer, then I'd say it's worth every penny."

Not only is John's morning ritual unrelatable and snobby, but it also brings my financial anxieties top of mind. *Don't talk about money,* I silently beg.

"So, I haven't been to the Festival of Lights since I was in elementary school," John chatters, much to my relief.

I try to picture John as a child and am surprised when I can't. I can't imagine him wearing character clothing, no Mickey Mouse ears or Super-man t-shirt for him, or even giving a goofy grin after losing his front two teeth. All I'm able to picture is a smaller version of this polished man.

"Has it changed much?" John asks.

"Well, sure," I say, thinking that's a pretty dumb question. It's also a touch rude. Does John think Cincinnati is so ho-hum? "But I bet it will still feel a lot like those childhood memories of yours," I quickly add.

"I was thinking of taking Henry before the holidays are over," he says. "Or is that dumb? He's just a baby..."

I shake my head, this question quickly redeeming my opinion of him. "No, it's perfect for a baby. He'll have all of those lights to ogle. As long as he's snug as a bug in his stroller, I bet he'll love it."

John's encouraged by this idea.

We exit off the highway and head down Martin Luther King Drive. There are a lot of hospitals and medical office buildings in the Clifton neighborhood, and the sight of them makes my stomach lurch.

I am going to need a payment plan to pay a single medical bill.

A payment plan. For a single medical bill.

How often will I need a $1300 MRI? Once a year? Twice? Are there even more expensive procedures in my future?

What if I'm forced to funnel all my money into my treatment? I'll never be able to buy a new car or place a down payment on a house. Maybe I won't even be able to afford my current apartment. What if the bills that lie ahead are so staggering, I'll need to move back in with Mom and Dad?

John says something, maybe about Mattie and Peter's couples shower, but it's suddenly becoming difficult to listen. "I'm sorry. What was that?" I ask, blinking a few times.

My vision starts to cloud on the peripherals. The street lamps turn blurry, and I struggle to focus on the road ahead. Cars seem to flash by at impossibly fast speeds.

"Damnit, people need to slow down," I murmur.

"Bea?" I hear John say.

Pedestrians on the sidewalks look like dark, menacing figures. I squint as hard as I can, but it isn't helping. Shit, shit, shit. What is *happening* right now? My skin is cold, and my heart is beating in a rapid panic.

I make a right turn onto Burnett and then immediately a left onto Piedmont.

"Is this some sort of shortcut?" John asks.

The question is so simple, and yet I suddenly have no idea. I no longer know which side of the road I should even be driving on. It's like the information is there, somewhere, but my brain can't access it.

I begin to hyperventilate.

Chapter Forty-Two

"Is everything okay?" John asks.

I spot an open stretch of street ahead with no parked cars.

I pull over too fast, the car's erratic movements matching my body's, put the sedan in park, and lean back against the headrest. I close my eyes and try to turn my shallow breaths into measured, deep ones. I can hear a car alarm up ahead and a fire engine in the distance, but they all sound far away. So far away.

Instead, my racing heartbeat thunders loud and angry through my ears. Everything else sounds like it's being fed to me through a tunnel.

"Are you all right?" John asks, his voice small and tinny. "What happened?"

I blink away tears. I do not want to sob in front of this man I hardly know, this man who only sounds mildly concerned and not entirely panicked. He should be more panicked.

"I don't know," I say, which is the absolute truth.

"Was it something caused by your MS?" he guesses.

"Yes," I croak, my throat now scratchy and dry. "It must have been."

But there are so many other things I want to cry, want to shout.

I forgot where I was going! And for a second, I couldn't figure out if I was driving on the correct side of the road!

My vision was fading! What if I had gone completely blind?

My brain was malfunctioning!

What if my disease is worse than Dr. Wessels suspects?

Scariest of all, what if I'd hurt someone? Oh thank God I haven't hurt anyone.

"I see." John nods quietly, but he doesn't ask for further elaboration.

How is he satisfied with such a vague answer? Why isn't he squeezing my hand and asking me more? "Would you like me to drive the rest of the way?"

What I would like is to go home and call my mom.

"I think that would be safest. Thank you," I reply instead, my voice still trembling.

My legs feeling like Jell-O, I stagger to the car's passenger side. I watch John adjust the driver's seat to accommodate his long, runner's legs and then settle in with too much calm.

I think of Chris Little and how kind he was after a simple staircase stumble.

John Noble is decidedly done with the topic of my MS and what's just gone down on the dark side street. He talks about a family white elephant exchange for the remainder of the drive, eager to leave whatever *that* was behind us. At the zoo, we nibble on spiced nuts and sip hot cocoa. We walk arm in arm through the Instagram-worthy rainbow tunnel and watch the music-and-lights show on Swan Lake.

But it all feels so hollow.

"Excuse me," a dewy-cheeked girl smiles shyly. "Could you take our picture?" She and her boyfriend are standing near the towering Christmas tree decorated with red bows and white lights. They can't be more than sixteen. One of their parents may have even dropped them off.

"Of course," I say, hoping my shaking hands don't result in a blurry snapshot.

When I hand the girl her phone back, she beams at the screen, her entire face filled with joy. Maybe it's young love, but will I ever gaze like that at a photo of John and me?

"Did you have a high school girlfriend?" I ask him.

"Sure. Her name was Rachel," he says. I'm bothered by his *sure*, like it's just assumed someone like him would have a high school sweetheart. "We broke up before college, though. I was going to Northwestern, and she was heading to Vassar. We didn't want things to get messy."

"Wow. That was very mature of you," I reply, wondering if the situation was really so clean and simple.

"What about you?" he asks.

We duck into the penguin display, my favorite, and watch the birds glide through the icy water. Before tonight, I would have joked about the unrequited crushes that dominated my teenage years. But now I feel vulnerable around John. I don't want him to know yet another embarrassing fact about my life.

"Of course," I say, mimicking the confidence of his *sure*. "I dated a guy named Kyle for a few years. We tried to make it work after I moved to Chicago and he went to New Haven..." I let the Connecticut town, yes, *that* New Haven, sit for a few beats. "But the distance was too much. We still keep in touch, though. He's a scientist now." Oh, yeah. That sounds good. "He's actually one of the scientists at the forefront of the climate change crisis."

John's eyes widen. "That's important work," he says.

"Some would say the *most* important work," I can't help but add.

When our hands and feet begin to feel the winter chill and our noses start to run, we decide to head home. John doesn't ask me to grab coffee, drinks, or a light bite at one of the charming nearby restaurants. I drive us back to his Hyde Park Victorian. He doesn't ask me inside his elegant house with five fireplaces.

He gives me a chaste kiss goodnight. "Are you sure you're okay driving home?" he asks, a question normally reserved for someone who's been drinking versus the diseased.

"Absolutely. I'll be fine," I reply, trying to sound more confident than I feel.

John falters, chewing his bottom lip. "I guess I'll see you at the couples shower then."

It's a simple sentence that insinuates so much more. John doesn't plan on asking me out between now and Saturday. He has a better understanding of my disease, and he's decided I'm not worth the hassle.

The John Noble fairy tale has come to an end.

And even though I don't feel a spark for the guy, I can't help but feel rejected. Plus, I've let my sister down. No wonder Mattie's never set me up with one of her friends before, and she certainly won't be after this fiasco. The *one time* she decides to pair me off with someone special, I have to go and have a terrifying medical episode and ruin everything.

Once I'm safely back outside my apartment building, I call Mom.

I sit in my car, staring at Chris Little's countless bumper stickers, and listen to the telephone ring. *Protect Our Environment. Give Bees a Chance. Love Your Mother* beside an illustration of the Earth.

I give a small whimper when I get her voicemail. *Hi, this is Eileen. Leave a message after the beep. Thanks!*

I press end, remembering Mom and her friend are at an immersive nativity experience tonight. "We'll be walking through a recreation of Bethlehem!" Mom excitedly told me. "Apparently, you have to sign a waiver in case one of the Roman soldiers roughs you up."

Considering Mom is either knee-deep in hay as she admires the manger scene or possibly even detained by soldiers of an ancient civilization, I take a deep breath and call the second most capable person in my life.

"Hey," Mattie answers, her voice warm. I can hear a television in the background, a laugh track. "How was your date? You guys went to the Festival of Lights tonight, right?"

"Can you come over?" I ask, starting to cry. "Something scary happened with my MS."

"I'll be there in ten," she says. "And don't google anything in the meantime."

Chapter Forty-Three

Seven minutes later, Mattie is standing outside the lobby door.

She looks remarkably put-together in chic lululemon joggers paired with a fitted hoodie. The only indications of a frazzled departure are the whitening strips on her teeth and the messy bun on her head.

As soon as we enter my apartment, I break into heavy sobs. I haven't cried like this in front of Mattie since we were kids, but once the floodgates are open, the tears feel big and endless.

"I'm going to be poor and sick, and no one is ever going to want to marry me," I stammer, sounding nasally with my nose all stuffed up.

I no longer care if my perfect older sister sees me as a disaster. What's the point in hiding it? I forgot which side of the road to drive on tonight! Who knows what scary things are ahead for me?

"My brain is breaking. *I'm* breaking," I say.

"None of those things are true, and they aren't going to be either," Mattie says, leading me towards the sofa. She wraps a blanket around my shoulders and tries to push the hair away from my hot face, as strands have started to stick to my wet cheeks. "I won't let them happen."

I hiccup, thinking if anyone can stop a disease in its tracks, it's my sister.

Mattie purchases the Hallmark movie app, makes us a pot of chamomile tea, and suggests we escape to the fictional world of small towns, idyllic professions, and yuletide romance. It's the calming distraction I desperately need, and I fall asleep within the hour.

The next morning, I wake up to the sound of coffee percolating and the warmth of sunlight against my face. I blink a few times, surprised to find myself on the living room sofa. I am even more surprised to see Mattie preparing a fruit salad in my kitchen.

"Mattie?" I say, my voice weak and toadlike. "Did you stay the night?"

"I did," she confirms. She sets down the chef's knife and pours me a hot cup of coffee, which she brings over to the sofa. She sits on the edge of the coffee table. "And I swear I'm not a monster who stole your bed. You fell asleep here, so I just tucked you in as best as I could."

"And *then* you stole my bed," I say, taking a grateful first sip of java.

"Exactly," she smiles. "How are you feeling?"

"A lot better than last night," I say, rubbing my eyes. "Has Tony Soprano been outside? What time is it?"

"It's only seven-thirty. Mr. Soprano hasn't come out of his chalet yet."

Tony sticks his head outside his front door at the sound of his name. We both laugh.

"Let me take Tony out. You get your bearings. Dr. Wessels' office opens at eight. We can call her then," Mattie suggests. She eyes me somewhat sadly, her expression a mixture of compassion and encouragement. "It's going to be okay. I promise."

While Mattie takes Tony outside, I fill his food bowl and help myself to some fruit salad, which includes pineapple, strawberries, and honeydew. My favorites.

At eight a.m. sharp, Mattie and I sit at my dining room table and call Dr. Wessels' office. "What's all this?" Mattie asks, taking in my mess of loose papers, sketchbooks, pencils, and tape measures. She delicately lifts the cover of one of the notebooks.

Alarmed, I swat the notebook shut, concealing my tiny house scribbles and sketches. "A surprise," I say, my hand placed over the phone's receiver. "For, um, Christmas. So don't look."

"Hmm... I'm intrigued," she says, before nodding towards the phone. "Make sure you put the call on speaker."

Is she bossy or what? I roll my eyes but do as I'm told. I watch Mattie take out her own little notebook and pen, the same ones she had at my previous neurologist appointments.

The main receptionist puts us on hold, and a few moments later, we're greeted with a gruff voice. "This is Donna," the not-so-delightful nurse says.

I widen my eyes and Mattie returns my grimace.

"Donna," I try to sound bright and cheerful, like the kind of friend you want to chat with at eight a.m. on a Tuesday morning. "Hi. This is Bea Parker. I'm, um, one of Dr. Wessels' patients?"

She sighs. "Yes, I know who you are." And judging by her tone of voice, that isn't a good thing.

Despite all the anxiety and fear of the past fourteen hours, I have to stifle a giggle. I catch Mattie also smirking.

I take a deep breath. "Something scary happened to me last night," I say. "I was driving, and my vision started to blur, and I..." This next part is hard to talk about. "I forgot where I was going. And for a split second, I even forgot which side of the road I should be driving on."

"Oh." Donna instantly softens. "Oh, I'm sorry." She pauses. "Let me grab Dr. Wessels. It'll only be a moment."

"Whoa," I mouth to Mattie, who looks equally surprised.

Dr. Wessels is just as sympathetic as Donna. "I'm glad you called," she says. "It's important you keep us updated regarding any new symptoms." She explains that cognitive problems are common in people with MS. "A lot of my patients call these moments 'cog fog' for short," she said. "Makes them sound a little less scary, doesn't it?"

I know about cognitive and concentration issues related to MS, and I certainly experience them, too. It can feel downright impossible to think straight some days, especially when there's any distraction, and I'm constantly forgetting words, misusing phrases, things like that. But last night's episode was so unlike these more mundane nuisances.

"I didn't realize cog fog could happen to such an extreme," I say.

"Confusion and disorientation are certainly parts of cog fog," Dr. Wessels says. "Let me ask you this, were you experiencing high levels of stress prior to the episode?"

I think of how I sat on the edge of my bathtub for a solid ten minutes crying before last night's date, my anxiety having brought me to tears.

"I was, yes." I refrain from telling Dr. Wessels that my stress was related to medical bills sent from *her* office. I don't want to sound accusatory. Plus, it's not her fault our country's healthcare system is such a mess. "When it happened, the driving episode, it was like the information was there, but my brain couldn't get to it. It started off feeling like a panic attack and turned into something much worse. It was...well...terrifying."

"I'm sure." She takes a deep inhale. "What are your coping mechanisms when it comes to stress?"

I shrug. "A hot bath and a glass of wine?"

Mattie rolls her eyes, but she's smiling.

"Right." I can also hear the smile in Dr. Wessels' voice. "As enjoyable as those may be, a bathtub and wine aren't always available on the fly. I'd like for you to work on some relaxation techniques. Since it's impossible to eliminate every stressor from your life, you need to equip yourself with a few reliable rituals. Do you do any meditation or yoga now?"

Mattie looks up from her notebook, where she's been frantically scribbling.

I shake my head. "I used to do yoga. Twice a week, actually. But I've been too afraid to go ever since balance became such an issue. There may have been a bloody nose involved."

Dr. Wessels encourages me to get back in the saddle. "Or, I guess I should say, mat," she says. "I cannot recommend yoga enough for my MS patients. As you're aware, it not only relieves anxiety but can also improve your strength, flexibility, and balance."

I know all of this, of course. *But it's embarrassing, I think. It's embarrassing having once been so darn good and now looking like an amateur.*

"As for meditation," she continues, "there are a lot of great apps you can download. They're wonderful because you can access them whenever anxiety strikes."

"Unlike a hot bath and a glass of wine," I can't help but add.

"Exactly," she says. "You can just pop in your earbuds and do a five- or ten-minute calming meditation."

Dr. Wessels then tells me more about optic neuritis, which is the inflammation of the eye nerve and a condition about half of people with MS experience. She thinks my temporary blurred vision was more of a response to my panic, but she wants me to be aware of the condition and how it fits into the bigger picture.

"Good luck on the medicine," she says. "And call the office if you experience any more cog fog episodes, or any new symptoms for that matter."

"Got it," I confirm.

After the call, Mattie and I stare at one another, unblinking and at a loss for words.

"I'm so glad you're okay," she finally says.

"Me too," I breathe. I shuffle up from the table and pop my very first pill in my mouth. I wag the bottle in Mattie's direction. "It's only up from here."

She gives me a small smile, undoubtedly thinking, *You've said that a lot these past few weeks.* "I'd better get to work," she tells me. "I hope you don't mind, but I helped myself to your personal care products."

Personal care products? *Really?* Why, after having held me as I sobbed and having stroked my hair, does my sister feel the need to be formal?

"Of course I don't mind," I say hurriedly. God knows I've taken quite a few liberties with Mattie's own "personal care products," from quick swipes of deodorant during summer barbecues to routinely trying her expensive makeup products. "Do you need to borrow any clothes for today? I know they'll be a bit baggy, but—"

"I would love that," Mattie immediately replies. "Thank you."

Oh. Well then!

I rummage through my closet until I find three contenders for Mattie: a sophisticated (and never worn) cream sweater Mattie herself gifted me paired with skinny jeans I haven't been able to squeeze into since I was twenty-five (Why do I still have either?), a red buffalo plaid dress, and a vintage wrap dress with remarkable range. Trust me when I say it works for sizes six to twelve.

"The buffalo plaid dress is pretty," she says, surprising me with her choice.

"Hey, can I come with you? To Kickerville?" The idea escapes my mouth the moment it enters my brain. "I was going to work from home today anyway, and I would love to work from Kickerville instead. I think a change of scenery might be nice."

Mattie pauses, considering my question, and then shrugs. "Okay. I mean, why not? Fran will be ecstatic to see you."

Chapter Forty-Four

Kickerville Cabin Co. is located in Guilford, Indiana, which is a nearly forty-five minute drive from my apartment. Mattie turns the heat on high, and combined with the familiar sound of my favorite NPR reporters, I'm nearly lulled back to sleep.

"I don't think John will be calling after last night," I say quietly, before I lose my moxie.

She glances over at me, her hands compliantly placed at the updated nine and three positions. "Why do you say that? Because of your cog fog episode?"

"Partly. He wasn't exactly Dr. McDreamy when it happened." I pull my backpack tighter against my middle. I will never forget the way John looked at me last night, more bewilderment in his gaze than concern. Honestly, he made me feel like a freak. "But even before that, there wasn't much of a spark anyway. I'm sorry. I've probably embarrassed you."

"Embarrassed me?" Mattie repeats, looking incredulous. "Oh, Bea. The only person who should be embarrassed is John. I'm sorry we set you up with a dud."

My heart swells at her loyalty. Speechless, I simply shrug. "No, it was fun. Or, you know, it had its fun moments. While it lasted. And John isn't a dud. We just aren't compatible."

"Do you want Peter to beat him up?" she teases.

I giggle at the thought of my mild-mannered future brother-in-law doing anything of the sort. "What would Peter do? Wipe his hard drive? Give him a virus?" Peter works in IT.

"That's some pretty devastating stuff if you ask me," says Mattie.

The Kickerville parking lot is nearly full by the time we arrive at nine-thirty. The Kickerville headquarters has always been quite grand. Even in the company's early days, it was important to Dad that his home business had an impressive home base. "Our customers need to feel confident working with us," Dad would say. "And our headquarters is a reflection of our craftsmanship."

This most recent building, the most spectacular of all, looks like a traditional log cabin. The structure is constructed of hewn logs and has a green metal roof. A towering stone fireplace greets you when you first walk in, and there's always a fresh pot of coffee brewing behind the front desk. Dad used to insist on burning a fire whenever a potential customer visited, no matter if it was a humid August afternoon or a crisp January morning, and Mattie has carried on this tradition. Thankfully, it's a gas fireplace, so they aren't burning through copious amounts of firewood.

Fran Bosse is outside circling red ribbon and garland around the entryway columns.

"Fran!" I exclaim.

She whirls around, startled. "Bea Parker? It's about time you come and pay us a visit out here!" she shouts back. "I thought you'd gotten too good for your Kickerville pals."

I practically sprint across the parking lot, and Fran engulfs me in a tight hug. "Never," I say. "Besides, I was just here in October. It hasn't been *that* long." I joined Mom and Dad for the annual Kickerville pumpkin-carving competition.

"How have you been feeling?" she asks.

I step back. "It's sort of a crap shoot right now, but I just took my first dose of MS medication this morning."

"You're a tough gal. You'll be okay." She kicks at a box of garland. "Carry that inside for me?"

I do as I'm told. "Hey, I heard you and Janet are cooking partners now," I say, my boots crunching against the gravel parking lot.

"She's something else, all right," Fran says, but I can hear the fondness in her husky voice. "On Sunday, I woke up with a God-awful sore throat, and do you know what Janet did? She drove all the way to my house to drop off matzo ball soup! Like I haven't been taking care of myself since I was ten years old."

Fran gets cagey whenever she speaks of the past, but we know her mother left when she was just a girl. Fran's father was a good dad, kind and gentle with an excellent sense of humor, but he was stretched thin running the family's farm. In addition to her farm chores, Fran stepped in to do most of the cooking and cleaning for their family of three. She is truly the hardest worker any of us has ever met.

"Well, sure, but wasn't it nice having a friend bring you some delicious soup?" I ask.

"Yeah, yeah," Fran mumbles. "But I could have microwaved a bowl of Campbell's just fine, and Janet could have saved herself a whole lot of time and gas money."

We head through the heavy front doors and stop in the employee kitchen where Mattie and I refresh our tumblers of coffee. The corner TV is set to a morning news program and Gary, one of the engineers, is enjoying a breakfast sandwich.

I open the fridge and am delighted to find a mason jar of unpasteurized milk from Fran's dairy cow. I hold it up excitedly. "What a treat," I say, using all my strength to unscrew the lid. *Ugh.* Lids. Yet another MS nemesis.

Gary swallows a large mouthful of biscuit, bacon, and egg. "Hiya Bea," he says. "What's happening to your skin?"

"I'm sorry?" I close the black fridge door and reach for the toaster instead.

Clutching the metal appliance, I watch as red splotches begin to cover my face and my neck. Even my hands and arms are turning red, a furious rash overtaking my epidermis. Heat radiates in my cheeks, and even the pressure in my head increases. *Thump, thump, thump.*

"Flushing," Mattie and I say, the realization hitting both of us at the same time.

"Is that some sort of allergic reaction?" Fran frowns. "Do you need a Benadryl?"

I explain that it's a side effect of the medication. "Once my body gets used to the drug, it should stop happening," I say.

Holy cow, *this* is flushing? My entire body burns hot and itches. It is far from the image I conjured of old-timey women clutching handkerchiefs. If Jane Austen's characters experienced anything like this, she sure wouldn't have written about it.

"Um, but maybe I'll grab a cold glass of water instead of coffee," I say.

"Good idea," Mattie approves.

Mattie and Fran share a large office. Both women have L-shaped desks on either end, and there's a sitting room setup in the center. I settle into one of the armchairs and prop my computer on my lap, praying Gwen won't notice my nearly ten a.m. sign-on. Lucky for me, she's scheduled yet another last-minute beauty service.

She put a podiatrist appointment on the team calendar, Hannah explains over chat. **But then I overheard her confirming a pedicure in the kitchen.**

Tricksy! I write back.

"People are asking about the party," I hear Fran say, as Mattie sorts through a large stack of papers.

"Is this the November financial report?" Mattie gives a low hum. "And what did you say when the party came up?"

"I said to stop gossiping," Fran replies, which makes Mattie smile sadly.

"What's going on with the holiday party?" I ask.

Fran walks over to the office door and pulls it closed. "It's cancelled," she says.

"Wait, what?" I sit up straighter. "Why?"

Mom used to tease Dad that his favorite part of running a company was throwing the annual holiday party. While it was held in the Kickerville lobby, Dad had the space completely transformed with a soaring Christmas tree, an elaborate train set, and evergreen out the wazoo. He brought in a caterer to serve a proper feast and a live band to play cheerful tunes. Everyone dressed up for the evening—most especially Dad, who dressed up as old St. Nick himself. At the end of the night, Dad made sure every employee left with a Christmas bonus and a spiral-sliced ham.

While Mattie no longer hands out hams, a lot of people prefer turkey and there are apparently three vegetarians on the payroll these days, she keeps all of the other holiday traditions afloat.

"I suspect everyone would prefer a paycheck over a party." Mattie rubs her temples. "I think we can still make a small Christmas bonus happen, but the party is a huge cost. We just can't justify it, not after the year we've had."

My stomach sinks. "Kickerville isn't doing well?"

Fran raises her eyebrows. "Oh, honey. That's an understatement."

"We're still recovering from the pandemic. When lumber prices rose as sharply as they did, few people could afford to build." Mattie sighs. "But we'll work things out. We always do. Or Dad always did anyway..." She turns to her computer screen, anxiety creased into her forehead.

I glance back at my own laptop, understanding that the conversation is closed.

But how am I supposed to focus on my Polly Feinstein work with this newfound knowledge? I want to toss my laptop aside and finish my tiny house project instead. Because what if it's my tiny houses that can help save the business?

Maybe I'm giving myself too much credit, but there's something here. I can feel it in my bones.

And just like that, my little passion project carries more weight than ever.

Chapter Forty-Five

I blink at the unfamiliar number displayed on my phone: *5:00*

For a split second, I think I've set the alarm by mistake. Excluding early morning flights, when have I ever set an alarm for five a.m.? And then I remember.

Why did I agree to go swimming with Janet at this ungodly hour?

I certainly didn't help myself by staying up until midnight researching composting toilets, but who knew there were so many models and price points to choose from? I fell down the rabbit hole of YouTube reviews trying to figure out which throne was king. But after learning about Kickerville's financial situation, a new sense of determination is pulsing through me.

Before I'm able to press snooze, my cell phone rings.

It's Janet. Calling from her landline.

"No flaking out on me now, girlfriend," she clucks. "Grab your gym bag and meet me in the hall in ten minutes."

Bleary-eyed, I empty my work backpack of my laptop, notebook, and collection of stray power cords and toss in a swimsuit, flip-flops, and a beach towel. I tangle myself out of my flannel pajamas and into sweatpants and a hoodie.

"Do you want to go outside?" I ask Tony Soprano after brushing my teeth. "Or sleep for another few hours?" He burrows deeper under the covers, and I feel irrationally jealous of my four-legged friend.

The Mayerson JCC is only five minutes from Janet's and my apartment building. Janet slides in a Tina Turner CD—yes, Janet still uses CDs—and sings along like it's eight o'clock on a Saturday night. "I call you when I need you, my heart's on fire... You come to me, come to me wild and wired," she croons. "Oh, you come to me, give me everything I need..."

Janet turns down the volume as we make a left into the JCC parking lot. "One of my ex-husbands was a record producer for Tina. Have I ever told you that?"

I shake my head, but a grin manages to break through my grogginess.

"Fran didn't even know who Tina Turner *was*." Janet is scandalized by this. "Do you think she's just pulling my leg? How can someone not know about Tina Turner? Fran said she'd heard the music before but never knew the artist's name."

This tidbit actually makes me giggle, a true miracle considering the time of day. "I think Fran only listens to her dad's old record collection," I reply. "So, you may have to fill her in on everything that's come out since 1975."

We both grip our parkas tighter as we walk toward the building's entrance, the wind stinging our bare hands and cheeks. The sky is pitch black, and the temperature's only in the teens. Hopping into a swimming pool, even an indoor one, sounds ludicrous.

"Morning, Janet." A middle-aged woman with short, cropped hair greets us. She sits at the reception desk nursing a cup of coffee. "Who have you got with you this morning?"

"This is my friend, Bea," Janet offers. "She made me go power walking a few weeks ago...*dreadful*...and I've been telling her she needs to try swimming instead."

"Wait, is this a punishment?" I interject.

"It's payback," Janet says. "But trust me, you're going to love it."

The woman hands me a clipboard and asks me to fill out the basic information required for a guest pass. I look around, admiring the welcoming vestibule, which is currently decorated for Hanukkah. There's even a small cafe and a courtyard that must be lovely in nicer weather. I like it here.

"Can I ask a stupid question?" Janet and I peer through the windows of the workout area. A few people are on treadmills and ellipticals, mostly watching local news stations, and a spinning class is happening in a separate room.

"The answer is no, you don't have to be Jewish to join the JCC," she smiles at me.

Well, that's nice to know.

The women's locker room reminds me more of a spa than a gym. Everything is clean and tidy, and there's even a steam room. "We can hit the steam room after our swim," Janet says. "It helps improve circulation, open up your sinuses... All sorts of benefits, hon."

I use one of the private changing areas to get into my swimsuit, which is tight around the middle and doesn't cover as much of my tush as I'd prefer. In my morning stupor, I stupidly grabbed a one-piece with a giant pink bow across the bosom. I'm going to stick out like a sore thumb compared to the Speedo-clad swimmers out there.

"Do I look ridiculous?" I moan, exiting the changing room.

Janet is wearing a maroon one-piece and has pulled a swim cap over her frizzy blonde hair. She even has sporty goggles propped on top of her head! For once, she looks much more understated and appropriately dressed than me. "Not in the least. I love your bow," she says. "Let's get out there before the lanes fill up."

As it turns out, I didn't need to bring a beach towel. The JCC offers their own towel service, and I grab one of their fluffy, white towels instead. Again, I wonder if this place is a secret spa disguised as a community center.

The indoor aquatics center is deliciously warm and humid. The tiled floor consists of various shades of aqua, and I'm careful as I walk across it. Two of the lanes in the lap pool are already taken by an extremely athletic man and woman, both of whom glide through the water like Olympians. I swallow.

"Just have fun. Let it all go. The water can be a healing place." And with that, Janet lowers her goggles and disappears beneath the waves.

I sit on the edge of the pool for a few moments, watching the swimmers and their graceful movements. There's something beautiful about the lines their strokes cut into the water and the ripples they create. I loved swimming as a child but became self-conscious as a curvy teenager. I went from being the kid who could spend hours in the water to the fourteen-year-old who sat on a beach chair wearing a sarong or gym shorts to camouflage my expanding hips. "I just can't put this magazine down," I would lie. Or, I'd throw out the tried-and-true, "I don't want to get my hair wet."

I feel sad for that girl and even sadder when I realize how much of her remains in the woman I am today. With a deep breath, I press my feet against the wall and propel myself forward.

I start with a simple breaststroke. I'm rustier than I would have thought, but I give the backstroke and butterfly tries anyway. I've also forgotten how, well, *difficult* swimming can be. My arms aren't as strong as they once were, and my breathing quickly turns jagged.

I swim far, far beneath the water's surface. It's so peaceful down here, blue and astonishingly quiet. Since I'm not wearing goggles, my view is distorted, but the effect is freeing and pleasant. I feel weightless under the water. It *is* healing, just as Janet said. I don't have to worry about my balance in the water. I don't remember my incoordination. My MS simply doesn't exist in this underwater world. I feel strong and capable. My mind feels at peace.

Maybe this is a workout I can continue.

After thirty minutes, I follow Janet's lead and head toward the hot tub. "Time to soothe our joints," she says.

The hot water and jets feel marvelous, and I lean my head back. This really isn't such a bad way to begin the day. Our fellow swimmers, who look to be husband and wife, join us. They are about my parents' age, maybe a little older, and in far better shape than me.

"Hi, Janet," the man says.

"How lucky are we to spend a cold December morning in a place like this?" says the woman, her serene gaze resting on me.

"I'm a guest of Janet's. This is my first time here." My obnoxious pink bow bubbles to the surface. I push it down. "But it's amazing."

"Well, hopefully it won't be your last," says the man.

The woman pulls her beautiful, steely gray hair into a ponytail. "Isn't this so much nicer than a typical gym?"

"So much nicer," I agree.

Back in the locker room, Janet and I rinse off before sitting in the steam room for a bit. I inhale deeply, letting the humid air fill my lungs, and watch the droplets of water slide down the aquamarine tiles.

After the steam room, we towel off and change into our dry clothes. Since Janet wore a swim cap, her burst of curls is still bouncy and dry. I, on the other hand, leave the JCC with a head of sad, wet hair.

"Did you have fun?" The sun is just rising for the day, and we both pull down our sun visors in the car. "Was it worth the early alarm?"

"Yes and yes," I say, the apprehension obvious in my voice.

"But…?"

"It was tough putting on a swimsuit. I've managed to avoid it since I put on all of this weight." I watch the rearview mirror's fuzzy pink dice swing with the turn. I stare out the window, avoiding Janet's eyes. "I feel pretty lousy about myself," I admit. "Especially after everything that happened with John. It's like, who is going to want to deal with all of this baggage? Not only am I carrying around twenty extra pounds, but my body is literally malfunctioning. Who wants to deal with *any* of that?"

"This doesn't need to be said, but I'll say it anyway—you are a beautiful person, Bea. Inside and out. And at any weight." Janet tightens her grip around the steering wheel. "And your baggage is lovelier than many people's strong suits. It's what makes you *you*. Baggage is a part of all of our stories."

I nod quietly, touched, but also not entirely believing Janet's kind words.

"You're too hard on yourself, kiddo," she says, glancing over at me.

I give a noncommittal shrug.

Janet snaps her fingers, excited by an idea. "Why don't you get a snazzy new hairdo? That always gives me a bit of pep. I can get you in at the salon this Saturday."

I push aside the sun visor's mirror protector and stare at my mop of hair. I've been getting trims to my shoulder-length locks for years now. When was the last time I did something different?

"Even just a few caramel highlights could be fun," Janet says encouragingly.

"Do you really think you can get me an appointment the Saturday before Christmas?" I know how slammed salons are during the holiday season, so what Janet is suggesting sounds fun but highly improbable.

"I've been managing the front desk for nearly fifteen years now," she reminds me. "I can work my magic."

"Well, okay." I let myself get excited by the idea. "Thanks, Janet. I would love that." Maybe I *will* do a few caramel highlights. Or even a short, sassy bob.

We make it back to the Amelia by six forty-five, leaving me plenty of time to blow dry my hair and get ready for the workday. But as misfortune has it, we run straight into Chris Little in the lobby.

"Oh, God," I breathe, pulling my hood over my head and trying to conceal my tragic appearance. I look only slightly better than an overfed wet mouse.

"Hey there!" Chris has a canvas messenger bag slung over his shoulder and is much too happy for this hour of the morning. Or, you know, for someone on his way to work. "Why were you two out and about so early?" He glances at his smartwatch as though to confirm it is indeed quarter until seven.

"We fit in a morning swim at the JCC," Janet eagerly volunteers.

"Trying to get that BMI down," I say feebly, though who knows if anyone can even hear me from deep inside my hood.

Chris frowns. "You do know BMI is both racist and sexist, right?" he says. "The whole system is based on northern and western European men. I'll send you a few articles later. It's a largely inaccurate metric for people who don't fit inside that small box."

"Oh," I breathe, feeling as though Chris has delivered the famous Mark Darcy line. *I like you very much. Just as you are.*

With a cheerful wave, Chris Little goes off to work.

Janet wags her eyebrows at me. "And he's a science teacher," she reminds me. "So, he would know."

Chapter Forty-Six

True to her word, Janet somehow finds me a last-minute hair appointment the Saturday before Christmas. It also happens to be the day of Mattie and Peter's couples shower, and I'm excited to have my hair fixed up for the soiree. Particularly since I'll be seeing John for the first time since the Festival of Lights catastrophe.

I haven't even *heard* from John since then.

For some stupid reason, I sent him a *Home Alone* meme on Wednesday. I guess I was desperate for one instance of normal dialogue before seeing him at the party. But John didn't reply. I didn't even get a single pity emoji.

He's ghosting me.

The thought makes my cheeks burn hot. It doesn't matter that there isn't a spark between us. I'm embarrassed by John's rejection, his complete lack of regard for me, and it stings. He'd gotten a behind-the-scenes look at my disease and declared, *No, thank you! This is all too weird and messy for my posh life!*

As if finding The One isn't difficult enough, now I have to saddle around multiple sclerosis.

I'm toast.

An adorable stylist rounds the corner to the waiting room. "Beatrix?" She's wearing a reindeer antler headband and is so cute, she could even pull off a red-painted nose.

I set down my magazine and jump up with too much enthusiasm. "That's me," I say. "But you can call me Bea." Even though I'm only 5'4", I tower over the petite woman.

"Hi! I'm Madison. I'll be doing your hair today," she says brightly.

"Thank you so much for fitting me in," I tell her. They've scheduled me for a nine-twenty appointment, and I know Madison is doing me (and Janet) a favor. Every chair in the waiting area is taken, as are all the recent issues of *People Magazine*, and the salon is humming with happy holiday chatter.

"Happy to! I graduated from cosmetology school back in the summer, and the holidays have been awesome for all of this extra experience," Madison says. "I'm still in the process of building a solid client base."

Everyone needs to start somewhere, I remind myself, a smile plastered across my face. And besides, it isn't like Madison walked out of cosmetology school yesterday. She said summer, so for all I know, she's been here for six months already.

"Well, thanks again," I say, this time a bit weaker.

Madison props a hand on her tiny hip. "What are you thinking today?"

I stare at my reflection in the mirror, fingering the edges of my dark hair. "Janet suggested a few caramel highlights. That sounds nice." Madison nods eagerly. "And, well, I've only gotten trims for years now. Maybe I'm ready for a cut? I was thinking of a neat bob, just above my shoulders."

"Love the caramel highlights idea! Your natural hair color is gorg, and they'll only make it pop even more." Madison examines my reflection with such intensity, I feel slightly awkward. "You have killer cheekbones. Do you have any Native American in your ancestry?"

"I do?" I reflexively place my hands there. "And no. I don't think so. But I've never taken one of those DNA tests..."

"Totally." Madison sucks in both of her lips as she nods some more. Her own features are so delicate, I wonder if she has fairy in her ancestry. "I'm thinking pixie cut."

Well, I *have* always daydreamed about a daring pixie cut...

"Do you really think I could pull it off?" I ask, doubtful.

Another confident nod. Madison puts her hand in my hair and gives it a little shake. "Your hair has this great curl, too. I bet you'll look like Audrey Tatou once we're done."

I'll look like Amélie? My eyes widen, and I practically swoon over the possibility. "Let's do it," I reply, my mind already far off in the hills of Montmartre.

"Yeah?" Madison's blue eyes are big and excited.

"Yeah! If it looks awful, it's not like it won't grow back," I say, before quickly backtracking at Madison's hurt expression. "But it won't look awful! I was only speaking hypothetically."

For the next few hours, as I'm ushered between Madison's stylist chair, the processing lamp, the shampoo bowl, and back to the stylist chair, I day-dream about my new look. Strangers will think me chic and adventurous, daring. My colleagues will be reminded of how smart and creative I am. Men will go weak in the knees over my head of gentle curls as their minds spin, wondering I remind them of.

"Audrey Tatou?" I'll then offer innocently. "Better known as Amélie?"

"YES!" these men will exclaim. "That's it! You could be her twin."

Maybe I'll take up French again. It was my favorite class in high school, and people swear by that Duolingo app. Better yet, I can find an in-person class that meets at a bohemian coffee shop. There, I will meet a sophisticat-ed man ready to embark on a year-long work assignment in France. We'll fall madly in love, and as crazy as it will sound, he'll ask me to join him, a sort of reverse Mr. Big and Carrie Bradshaw situation, if you will...

"Bea? Hello?" Madison is waving her hand in front of my face. Her nails are red with tiny Christmas trees painted on them. How did the manicurist manage such tiny Christmas trees? "What do you think?"

"Sorry, I was daydreaming." I take a deep breath and look up at my reflection, ready to bask in my new glamorous identity.

Mon Dieu! Quelle horreur!

I do not look like Audrey Tatou.

I look like a brunette Little Orphan Annie with chunky caramel highlights.

"So, your curls got a lot tighter than I would have thought..." Madison carefully pulls one out, and we both watch it snap back to my scalp. She lifts a strand of her own poker-straight hair. "I don't have much experience with curls."

I'm not sure if I want to laugh or cry. Or sob.

"But look how it emphasizes those cheekbones of yours!" Madison says excitedly, hopefully.

"It, um, absolutely does," I squeak. And because it's too late to do any-thing now, or maybe because Madison is all of twenty years old and has the best of intentions, I swallow and tell a very big lie. "Thank you so much. I love it."

"YAY!" she exclaims, literally jumping up and down with glee. "Oh, I am so glad!"

And because I'm a total chump, I tip Madison 25% and leave with my horrible haircut. I walk back to the Amelia, my mood plummeting in the winter cold. I have to go to Mattie and Peter's couples shower looking like this! I have to live life looking like this!

An attractive young couple pushing a stroller nearly collides with me at the intersection of Ridge and Montgomery roads. "Excuse me, sir," says the husband before realizing my true gender. "Oh! I mean, ma'am. Excuse me, ma'am!" he corrects himself.

"It's a bad haircut. It's fine," I murmur.

By the time I get back to my apartment building, I'm ready to have a proper sob. Time is of the essence. I have to squeeze it in fast so I have time to soothe my puffy skin before tonight's party.

Naturally, Chris Little is arriving home just as I am. Because God is determined for Chris to see me at all my worst moments. He's carrying a large terrarium of sorts, though it's difficult to tell through my bleary eyes.

"Bea?" He frowns, carefully setting his armful on the floor. He breaks into a smile. "Wow! What a haircut. It's quite efficient. You'll require so much less water to wash it, too. Very green of you."

I burst into wonder peals of laughter, happy tears actually running down my face. "With compliments like that, it's a wonder you shared a womb with a woman for nine months," I gasp between giggles.

"Touché," Chris winks, making my stomach flutter.

"It's horrible," I sigh. "I think I'm going to have to wear a hat for two years."

To my amazement, he reaches out and gently touches one of my curls. He moves it between his fingers, the gesture making every cell of my body tingle. "You have the softest hair," he says quietly.

It's suddenly hard to breathe. "Thank you."

We both jump at the sound of skittering on the floor.

"What is that? Did you just carry in a live animal?"

"Oh. *Oh.*" Looking bashful, Chris lifts up the terrarium. Inside is a hermit crab. "This is SpongeBob. I rescued him from my nephew's friend."

"I'm sorry, but *what?*" I laugh.

"I'm going to give him a miniature beach setup." Chris holds up a bag from a local pet supplies shop. "The goal is to make him comfortable while also including lots of sensory details that I'll rotate to keep him stimulated."

I'm surprised at how cute SpongeBob is with his big, almost cartoonish, black eyes and beige-colored shell.

"He's adorable," Chris agrees fondly. "But people really shouldn't keep hermit crabs as pets. They thrive in the wild, often living upwards of thirty years, but only live a fraction of that time in captivity. I have SpongeBob since my nephew's friend's parents didn't want this little guy any longer. Unfortunately, it's too dangerous to release him back into the wild at this point, so I'll do my best to give him a good life."

I kneel down and watch SpongeBob mosey around his terrain. "Better days are ahead, little guy," I tell him. I ask Chris if he'll take SpongeBob to his classroom.

"Yep, eventually. After I've gotten to know SpongeBob better, I'll start letting the students take turns taking him home." Chris smiles at the hermit crab.

"Well, I better get going. My mom and I are throwing a couples shower tonight for my sister and her fiancé." I briefly consider inviting Chris, but how weird would that be? Besides, he would probably think it was all so silly when you consider his views on milestones in general and marriage in particular. And he definitely wouldn't approve of Mom's use of plastic party-ware. "Thanks for making me laugh about this crazy head of hair. I'm going to try washing it. Maybe I can at least get the curls to lay more normally."

"I think it looks beautiful on you," Chris says so sincerely, I well up all over again. "It's fun and different. No one has hair like that."

"Yeah, probably for a reason," I quip.

I scamper up the stairs before my heart flutters straight out of my chest.

Chapter Forty-Seven

The couples shower is off to a smashing start.

I've placed small votive candles on nearly every flat surface, giving the evening a warm glow and scenting the air with cinnamon and vanilla. The playlist is a dreamy mashup of John Legend, Otis Redding, and Van Morrison with the perfect amount of holiday tunes mixed in. Mistletoe has been hung in every doorway, and my parents' glittering Christmas tree is getting plenty of *oohs* and *ahhs*.

Mom took down their stockings for the night, and instead, we draped a banner of charming childhood photos across the mantle. I sprinkled more recent pictures of the happy couple throughout the first floor, including their engagement photos which look straight out of a J. Crew catalog. (Mattie and Peter had them taken on a summer trip to Cape Cod, and there is more seersucker than you can imagine.) There are gold balloons filled with confetti, lots of them, and I've been making the rounds with trays of warm appetizers and bottles of wine.

"May I top you off?" I ask with a smile.

This first hour of the party is blessedly busy, and my hostess obligations distract me from worrying about, or interacting with, John Noble. But at the top of the second hour, my medication-induced stomach issues decide to strike. I set down the bottles of pinot noir and sauvignon blanc I've been carrying and sprint upstairs.

Fifteen minutes later, I gently close the upstairs bathroom door with a grimace.

Well, jeez. I wasn't expecting *that*. Since I started taking the medication on Tuesday, I've only experienced cramps and diarrhea in the late morning or early afternoon, but oh no, not today. Of course they decided to make their evening debut tonight of all nights.

"Oh shit!" I exclaim, nearly colliding with Mattie. I cover my face. "Seriously. Oh *shit*—do not use that bathroom."

"Thanks for the heads-up." Half of Mattie's mouth tugs upward. She's wearing lipstick tonight, which makes her look overly done-up. "Are you feeling okay?"

I lean against the freshly painted greige wall, lowering myself to the ground. "Remember those stomach problems Dr. Wessels warned me about?"

"Oh." Understanding floods Mattie's face. "Is it just pains or—"

I hold up my hand. "Let's not discuss the specifics."

"I'm sorry," Mattie says. "Can I get you anything? Considering the way Dad eats, I'll bet he has a killer stash of Pepto-Bismol."

Our father harbors a serious love for takeout food, salty snacks, and pop.

"I'm okay, thanks. It usually only happens once. And at least the party is here, where I can get to a private bathroom ASAP." I stare up at Mattie, who seems impossibly tall in her heels. "What are you doing upstairs anyway? Surveying your future estate? Going all 'everything the light touches is our kingdom' on us?"

"Oh, please. You know we haven't decided yet." Mattie neatly takes a seat beside me on the carpeted floor. "The west side is just so different from Hyde Park. Did you know Mrs. Carothers and her husband bought the ranch a few doors down?"

I try to place the familiar name. "Are you talking about your Girl Scout leader? *That* Mrs. Carothers?"

She nods, half-amused, half-perturbed. "I guess I should get used to that. Running into Girl Scout leaders, first-grade teachers..."

"The girl whose house you puked at during her *101 Dalmatians*-themed birthday party," I add, which makes Mattie audibly groan. "Remember her? Julia Paulson? She bought a house one subdivision over."

"Super." Mattie rolls her eyes.

I falter, wondering if I've been wrong about Mattie's attitude regarding Mom and Dad's house. Maybe her trepidation isn't all part of some holier-than-thou act. Maybe it's genuine.

"Anyways. I'm up here hiding from Mom," she divulges. "She wants us to open presents in front of everyone even though I asked—no, *begged*—her not to."

Even for extroverts like me, opening gifts in front of a crowd is an uncomfortable, anxiety-inducing activity. Are you showing enough enthusiasm? Or are you showing *too much* enthusiasm? Will the giver think you're being phony? Are you conveying the appropriate amount of gratitude? Will your face be forever contorted after forcing a smile for so long?

There's a lot to worry about.

"Are you hoping she'll change her mind if she can't find you?" I ask.

"That's the plan." Mattie pats my knee. I'm wearing a violet swing dress paired with lace tights, and Mattie's hand feels warm against my skin. "How have things been with John?"

"Nothing to report," I say. "Turns out we are fabulously in-sync when it comes to avoiding each other. Although, maybe he doesn't even recognize me with this horrible haircut."

"I like your haircut! It's fun!" Mattie insists. "And you're trendy enough to pull it off, too."

I eye her warily. "I look like a baby bella mushroom."

Mattie bursts into laughter. "I'm sorry," she says, wiping her eyes. "Maybe you do. Just a little bit. But a very cute baby bella mushroom."

We hear footsteps coming up the stairs. "Girls?" It's Mom, hot on the trail. Mattie gives a long sigh, her grin turning into an exasperated frown. God, our mother is fast. "Why are you two hiding up here?"

"Stomach problems," I say, quickly clarifying, "From my medicine. Not the catering."

"Oh no, sweetie. We have plenty of Pepto-Bismol if you think that will help," she says, which makes Mattie and I smile. "Do you want to lie down in the guest room? It's nice and quiet up here. And I just changed the sheets."

Mom looks great tonight in a blue sheath dress with snazzy buttons down the back. She had her short hair trimmed and styled this afternoon and is wearing more makeup than usual, though it looks pretty on her.

I shake my head. "Thankfully, these side effects are usually one and done," I explain. "And after a month or so, they should disappear completely."

"God willing," replies Mom, which I think is a tad dramatic. She moves her gaze to Mattie. "Amethyst is asking when you and Peter are opening gifts."

Mattie gives Mom a dubious sort of stare. "Since when do you care what Aunt Amethyst thinks?"

"It's rude not to open the presents people have brought for you," says Mom, now conveniently avoiding eye contact.

Mattie and I dutifully follow our mother back down the winding grand staircase with its gentle curve. Mattie and Peter take their seats in the two oversized armchairs beside the gift pile, and I perch on the brick fireplace next to them.

Chapter Forty-Eight

"I had secretly hoped Peter and I could open our presents tomorrow morning while enjoying coffee and scrambled eggs," Mattie murmurs. "Doesn't that sound relaxing?"

"Keep dreaming, sista." Mom is all about proper etiquette. Starting Monday she will start badgering Mattie about writing thank-you cards. I pull my iPhone out from one of my dress pockets. "The least I can do is take notes. It will make writing those thank-yous a little easier."

Mom has her own iPhone out and is snapping photos left and right. I know Mom is being overzealous with the wedding, but you should see how happy it makes her. Since Justin and Katie eloped, Mattie and Peter's engagement has taken on an extra level of importance. Mom cherishes every one of these moments. Throw in my recent MS diagnosis, and the wedding's become an even stronger ray of light in Eileen Parker's world.

"Here's a plate for the bouquet!" one of my aunts shouts, throwing a paper plate in my direction. There's a slit cut in the middle for me to thread gift ribbons through. This will serve as Mattie's bridal bouquet during the rehearsal. "And Mattie, don't forget the ribbon rule..."

"No! Please forget it!" Mom laughs, hoping that superstition rings true and lots of broken ribbons will result in lots of grandchildren for her.

Mattie tries to grin, but it looks more like a grimace.

"Start with our gift," Mattie's best friend, Ivy, says gently, handing them what appears to be artwork. The package is large and rectangular and wrapped in brown kraft paper. She's added a red bow to one corner, which is a sweet touch.

"One of your fine masterpieces?" Mattie guesses, carefully unwrapping the package.

About three years ago, Ivy started her own home-flipping business, and she's become a bit of a local Joanna Gaines. Her signature touch? A piece of her own artwork, usually an oil painting, but occasionally something more dramatic depending on the clients. (Ask her about the giraffe sculpture she made from twigs. Now *that* was a sight to see.)

"Charley Harper!" Mattie and Peter both exclaim.

It's a framed Harper poster that reads "A Day in Eden." There's an illustration of Cincinnati's famous Eden Park gazebo surrounded by Harper's classic animal illustrations, including a chipmunk, a cardinal, and even a mischievous raccoon.

"It's a print of the poster they used for a 1984 festival," Jocelyn, Ivy's wife, says.

"And it's perfect," Mattie beams. "Thank you both! And thank you, Milo."

We all watch adoringly as Ivy and Jocelyn's toddler waves his chubby hand. Gah. Milo is seriously the cutest. He's going to be Mattie and Peter's ring bearer alongside Violet, and I have a feeling those two will steal the show.

"When we first started dating, Mattie and I spent a lot of time in Eden Park," Peter explains to the group. "I was renting a place in Mount Adams, and we used to take Sunday runs there." He wraps his arm around Mattie's petite shoulders. "It's actually where we had our first kiss."

Everyone sighs. Oh, such perfect love!

Peter then opens a heavy Le Creuset Dutch oven. He waves toward his colleague, Andrew, who has his new girlfriend on his lap. You should see these two; it's like neither has touched the opposite sex before!

"Thanks, Andrew," Peter says. "Appreciate it, man."

"Thanks so much. This is so generous," Mattie adds graciously.

I type these details into my phone. *Fancy schmancy Le Creuset Dutch oven that you will use for a bone broth or a sourdough bread phase.* I know Mattie will laugh at this blurb. She's one of the busiest people I know, and most nights, it seems she only has time to nuke a frozen meal or settle in with a cup of Greek yogurt.

I, on the other hand, have never been too busy to miss a meal.

The next present Mattie and Peter open is a piece of wall art. It's their last name, *Foster*, spelled out in wine corks. You know, because everyone needs their last name spelled out in wine corks!

"What a special gift," Mattie tells Aunt Amethyst, her voice sounding robotic.

"I made it myself," she says, before looking out onto the crowd. "And I'm taking orders, too. You can find me on Etsy." She elbows Thomas Buchanan. "Pass out the business cards, sweetie."

Her dutiful boyfriend jumps up, but no one asks for further details. I see Mom suppress a fit of laughter.

The happy couple then receives a three-tiered serving piece, a set of red wine glasses, dishtowels, a very expensive-looking chef's knife, a marble cheese board, and a Smeg toaster in pastel green. They also receive a few sets of their dinner plates—white, so boring—and a cake platter with a heavy glass dome. The living room looks like a Williams Sonoma exploded.

"Open mine next," I say to Mattie, handing her a heavy, white envelope and a small box. "Envelope first, please. This one is for the both of you."

I bought Mattie and Peter a "Brush in Trunk Package" from the Cincinnati Zoo. Basically, they will get to choose a date to go and watch an elephant paint them a piece of art. Insanely cool, right? After picking out two paint colors, the zookeeper will hand the elephant a paintbrush. From there, Mattie and Peter will be awed and amazed as their elephant artist gets to work. And while I suspect the elephant's artwork won't make it into Mattie and Peter's curated collection—there's no way my sister is hanging elephant artwork on her clean, white walls—it'll be a fun outing for the love birds.

"This is *awesome*," Peter says. I've printed out the specifics on a piece of cardstock, and the two giggle as they read the details. "How did you think of such a thing?"

"I have a friend who works at the zoo. She clued me in," I reply proudly.

Mattie laughs, "I love this. It's so thoughtful and totally unique."

"As if we could expect anything less," Peter adds.

"There's one more small thing for you, Mattie. It's sort of silly." I nod toward the box in Mattie's lap. "But I thought you could use it at your bachelorette party or maybe your honeymoon."

The watermelon clutch I've sewn Mattie is made out of cotton and has been cut into the classic, semicircle shape. I attached pink, green, and black beads to it and included a strap for her wrist. I even found a fun little pom pom to add to the zipper pull.

"This is so cute!" she exclaims, giving me a hug. She holds the watermelon clutch up so everyone can see it. "Bea made this!" she announces.

"Pass it around!" Mom demands.

"Do you get it? The watermelon?" I ask Mattie, while the watermelon clutch travels around the room.

"Are you kidding me?" she says. "Of course I get it!"

When Mattie and I were little, probably only five and eight, I swallowed a watermelon seed at the neighborhood block party. An older girl named Alexis whispered in my ear, "Now a watermelon is going to grow inside your belly," and Mattie and I believed her. For weeks, Mattie would measure my stomach each morning to track the watermelon's progress.

"I'm really happy a watermelon never grew inside your stomach," Mattie says.

"That Alexis Walter was such a jerk. What do you think she's doing now?"

Mattie's green eyes sparkle. "Working for Newsmax? Spreading false information to the masses?"

We both burst into laughter. I forget how funny my sister can be.

"But seriously, she was in my Facebook list of suggested friends a few months ago, and I think she's a preschool teacher," Mattie says.

"Now that's a terrifying thought."

She gives a good-natured shrug. "People change…"

I hold her glance. *I've changed,* I so badly want to tell her. *I want to be a part of Kickerville. I want to work with you. I want to help.*

"Well anyway! We survived the public gift opening," she says, the moment lost. "Thank God that's over."

I watch as Dad and Peter stuff garbage bags full of wrapping paper and tape while Mom and her sisters inspect the housewares with such care, you would have thought Mattie and Peter received a slew of diamonds and rubies.

"Yeah, thank God," I echo.

Chapter Forty-Nine

An hour later, I sit on a barstool sipping a gin and tonic and feeling like an extra cast in some sort of reality show. "Place the normal-looking girl there!" I can practically hear a director shout. "Yes, by the bagel dip. God knows she'll be eating it."

All of Mattie and Peter's friends are impossibly glamorous. They're fit, thanks to the Peloton bikes they purchased during quarantine, and attractive, the women with just-colored hair and just the right amount of makeup, the men with chiseled jawlines and broad chests. Their clothes are simple and sophisticated, and they're definitely not covered in dog fur.

John Noble fits in flawlessly. He could be the commander of the Beautiful People Army.

"Long time no see!" I attempt to joke when we finally meet around a slow cooker of Teeny Cocktail Weenies. Mom found a catering company that specializes in quirky miniature takes on classic dishes, like Lil Piggies in a Blanket and Itsy Bitsy Brie Bites.

"Oh! Wow! Hey there, Bea," he says, pretending like this is the first time he's noticed me. We've been orbiting each other for hours now, and even though Mom and Dad's house is big, it isn't *that* big. "Fantastic party. You and your parents did such a great job. How have you been?"

How have I been? I just saw the guy on Monday! Is John going to pretend that disastrous night never happened? That *none* of our dates ever happened? He's probably embarrassed by me, especially now that I look like a mushroom.

I load my appetizer plate from a nearby veggie tray, pretending I haven't been camped beside the deviled eggs instead.

"Just super busy with work this week. A big client request came in from L.A." It isn't true, but it sounds important and interesting. "Apparently, Meghan and Harry are attached. I'd say more, but we all had to sign NDAs."

"Whoa. That should be interesting work." I watch him take furtive glances at my hair. After washing it and properly styling my curls, it isn't nearly as bad as when I left the salon, but it's still rather shocking. "So, um, about Monday..."

Stop the presses! He wants to have the breakup talk *here*? In the middle of the Beautiful People Army?

"It's fine," I say hurriedly. "Seriously, it's fine."

He blazes onward. "I had a lot of fun on our first few dates, but I realized we may be more different than I appreciated. I think we could be looking for—"

"Really, it's no big deal. I get it." I set one of my hands on top of his. "No need for further explanation. We both have a lot of stuff going on right now."

He looks visibly relieved to be freed of the girl with the disastrous haircut and the chronic disease. "I'm glad things won't be weird between us, especially with all the wedding events we have ahead."

Ugh. I forgot that John is one of Peter's groomsmen. At least he isn't Peter's best man. I can only imagine the gossipy whispers if John and I had to walk down the aisle together. *Can you believe he went out with her? It was only for a few dates, but still! He is so out of her league.*

"Not weird at all." Maybe I should have pursued a career in acting. "It'll all be fun."

"I'm so glad we had this talk." John's eyes are already moving to Sarah Marsh, and who can blame him?

Sarah Marsh is Mattie's running friend and a certifiable goddess. Tonight, she's wearing a red dress with a high neckline and lots of intricate embroidery. Her hair is pulled into a chignon, and her makeup is so perfect, it looks professionally done. Though, when you're working with a face like that, you can probably smear peanut butter and jelly across your cheeks and look like a million bucks.

I feel a warm hand on my back.

"Hey, Bea? Can you help me with something on the patio?" It's my dad.

I nod eagerly, never so happy to assist my father with a chore.

Once we're outside, Dad hands me a bottle of Great Lakes Christmas Ale and settles into one of the Adirondack chairs he built himself. Space heaters have been placed around the patio, and they're keeping the area comfortably warm despite the below-freezing temperature.

"What's this?" I stare down at Dad, who is leisurely sipping our favorite seasonal beer. "I thought you needed my help."

"It was a coverup. I had to rescue you from that Chris Hemsworth wannabe." Dad grunts, as if to provide further evidence of his opinion of John Noble. "You're too interesting for a guy like that."

My heart swells. How does my dad always manage to look out for me? I tackle him with a hug, nearly knocking the beer out of his hand. "First of all, thank you," I gush. "And second, how do you know who Chris Hemsworth is?"

"I've seen the *Avengers*," Dad shrugs, playing it cool.

"Right. Well, that makes one of us." I should really expand my movie repertoire.

We're quiet, staring up at the clear night sky, not a single cloud in sight. There are a brilliant amount of stars, and my parents live far enough outside of the city to really see and appreciate them.

"You're lucky you found Mom in the seventies," I mumble. "The dating world is a scary place these days."

My parents' love story, particularly its beginning, could have been pulled from the sort of romantic film starring Diane Lane and Billy Crystal. Mom was waiting at her neighborhood bus stop on a cold, rainy day when Dad pulled up in his dad's Oldsmobile. Mom was crying (dramatic!) because she'd missed her bus and was going to be late to class. As a first-year nursing student, she was trying to make all the right impressions.

"I'm heading that way now," Dad fibbed. "I could give you a lift."

Despite the fact that it was the 1970s, which sounds like the heyday of serial killers, Mom recognized Dad from the local Catholic church (very west side of Cincinnati) and decided that she'd rather risk her life than be late to class (very Eileen Parker). It was only a twenty-minute drive to campus, but that was all the time those two needed to fall in love.

Dad was ultimately late for his own job, he'd been apprenticing with a plumber, and he likes to say, "I lost a job that day but gained a wife."

Sitting out here now with Dad, I give a large exhale to see my breath, to remind myself that I'm alive, that I'm still here. We can hear the happy scuffle inside, laughter, people exclaiming, chairs scraping across the floor, but the party feels far away.

"John wasn't the one for you," Dad says matter-of-factly. "A parent knows when his kids have met their person. I knew it when Mattie introduced us to Peter, and when Justin brought Katie home for the first time."

"But what if I don't have a person? What if I end up all alone?" This never crossed my mind before my MS diagnosis. I've always had a lot of fun being single and embraced the freedom of only reporting to myself, so to speak. But now that I have this disease? The thought of being alone, *forever,* sounds terrifying. It suddenly feels overwhelming in a way it didn't before. Because between us? I would love to have a partner to share this load.

Dad frowns at me. "You aren't alone."

"Please don't say I have Tony Soprano..."

"No, no. It's more than Tony Soprano." He smiles, shaking his head. "You have Mom and me. You have Justin and Katie, Mattie and Peter. You have Violet, who thinks you're the coolest aunt in the world. And you have friends and colleagues and neighbors who all love you. You're surrounded by support, honey. And considering the sort of person you are, you always will be."

I stare over at Dad, tears in my eyes. "Thank you for not lying and saying that you know I'll find 'The One' someday," I say.

"I wish I could promise those things," he replies.

I scoot my chair closer and reach for his hand.

My dad is right. I'm not alone. Far from it.

Chapter Fifty

The next morning, I meet Hannah for brunch downtown.

"I'm sorry it's so early. This was the only reservation they had available," she says, nearly snatching the freshly brewed cup of java from our server's hands.

I gaze around Cincinnati's latest breakfast spot, Books & Nooks, which is part cozy bistro, part bookshop. Housed in an 1800s brownstone, the owners managed to keep the home's historic charm while integrating smart modern touches, like a stunning skylight that sends shimmery sunlight across all three floors. The original greenhouse off the back of the brownstone was also preserved and is now part of the café, meaning diners get to munch and brunch among fig trees, ferns, and flat-leaf parsley.

Basically, I completely understand why an eight-thirty reservation was the only one available. I'm surprised there were *any* open spots at a place as magical as this.

"You're probably exhausted from the couples shower," Hannah continues.

I shake my head, stirring creamer into my coffee. "Nah. I only had a few drinks since I had to drive home. Plus, I didn't want to overindulge and say something embarrassing to John Noble."

Hannah rubs her eyes. She and Arthur are night owls, routinely turning on a movie at ten p.m. or deciding to run out for a nightcap before the bars close. "Like what? 'I curse the day you were born?'" she grins.

"I think Charlotte York proved that line doesn't pack quite the punch one would hope for," I smile back.

I watch Hannah dig in her purse and pull out a small box and envelope.

"Here. I knew I'd get all choked up, so I wrote everything down."

Curious, I open the lavender-colored envelope and pull out a piece of paper decorated with borders of cheerful flowers. I know Hannah must have drawn them herself. "You could start a stationery business, you know," I say, before beginning to read Hannah's elegant cursive.

Dear Bea,

You know I'm an easy crier, so I took the letter route. I hope this isn't awkward, you sitting across from me, reading a letter FROM me, as I gaze at you adoringly. (And let's be real, I'm probably crying anyway.) Will you be my maid of honor? I promise to love and cherish you, in good times and in bad, in sickness and in health, and when Gwen is a real pain in the butt. You're my best gal pal, and I can't imagine standing up there without you by my side. Thanks for being the kindest, most fun, most loyal friend anyone could hope for. You're the bee's knees!

Love,

Hannah

"Well, I'm keeping this letter forever." My bottom lip quivers as I reach across the table to give Hannah a hug. "And I would be honored to be your maid of honor. Obviously."

"You've got to put on the ring first!" she says.

"You got me a ring?"

"I *made* you a ring," Hannah says, nudging the box toward me. "I hope you like it."

I open the small cardboard box to find a polymer ring with a bumblebee illustration carved into its face. "It's *perfect*," I say, marveling at its simplicity, its beauty, its dash of quirkiness. "Thank you, Han. But are you sure you want me up there?" I falter. "What about your cousin Monica? You two have always been so close…"

"Monica is wonderful, but she's not the girl who stood outside the bathroom stall on my very first day of work asking if I was okay," Hannah says with a smile. "The girl who not only handed me tissues and found me touchup makeup, but refused to go away until she knew for absolute certain I was all right. The girl who insisted we walk back into the office pretending to be in the middle of a hilarious conversation, so that everyone could see me laughing."

I know the memory well. My sweet Hannah. It makes my heart hurt.

"Well, that was an especially awful situation. You had every reason to cry. I just wish we had reported that guy to HR." A middle-aged man (who, thank God, no longer works at Polly Feinstein) asked Hannah if her Afro was "business appropriate." The memory makes my blood boil. "Do you think it's too late? I bet we could find him on LinkedIn, notify his current employer…"

Hannah shakes her head. "I believe in karma," she says. "Let her handle him."

I raise my cup of coffee. "I hope she's got a doozy up her sleeve for Greg from Finance."

As we giggle about funnier work stories, like the time I lost my grip on a kettlebell during a lunchtime workout class and nearly sent the weight into the instructor's crotch, and brunch on our quiche and fresh fruit, I can't help but think how different it was when Mattie asked me to be her maid of honor.

Mattie had mailed me a box—yes, she had shipped me a box via FedEx, even though she lives ten minutes down the road—filled with all sorts of fancy things. There was a monogrammed robe inside and matching slippers, a bottle of champagne, and even a wedding cake-scented candle. And buried at the very bottom? A card from the Etsy seller that said, "Will you be my maid of honor?" with "Love, Matilda Parker" typed at the bottom, almost like a form letter.

It was a generous gift but so…*impersonal.* Disingenuous even. Honestly, I felt a bit awkward calling Mattie afterward to say yes, wondering if this was a decision my sister would prefer in writing and notarized.

I reach across the table and give Hannah's hand an appreciative pat. "Thank you, Han," I say.

"For what?" she asks.

"For being you," I tell her, "my sensationally sweet best friend."

Chapter Fifty-One

I'm home before eleven and spend the remainder of my Sunday morning and early afternoon buried in my tiny house work. But after three hours and an entire pot of coffee, I'm still stumped on a few important factors. How can I keep the weight of my tiny house line low? The dry weight—that's the weight before you fill your tank with water or toss in any of your belongings—of the average tiny house is 10,000 pounds. While 10,000 pounds doesn't sound like much for an entire home, towing that sort of weight requires you to own a serious automobile.

I'm also stuck on how I can make my tiny houses shine in the environmental space. I know that many people choose tiny living to have a smaller footprint on the earth, and while I've thought of rain-catching systems and compostable toilets, I don't have the best understanding of how solar energy works.

Lucky for me, I have an older brother who works for a solar energy company.

"Hey there, Beezus." I hear the *Bluey* theme song in the background and know it will be stuck in my head for the rest of the day. Why is it so darn catchy? "What's shaking?"

"I need you to explain solar energy to me," I say, pulling up a blank Word document on my laptop and preparing to take notes. "Specifically how it can be used for tiny homes."

"I'm going to need a fresh cup of coffee for that one." I listen as Justin fumbles around his kitchen, cupboard doors clambering and ceramics clinking. My brother has a knack for making the simplest tasks loud and clumsy. He comes by it naturally by way of our father. "Are you considering living tiny?"

The question catches me off guard.

"Actually, yes," I admit to myself for the first time. "It's a possibility. Someday, anyway. But this question has to do with an entire tiny house line." I pause, taking a deep breath. "Designed by me." Another deep breath. "For Kickerville."

Justin whistles. "Kickerville doing tiny houses? That's an incredible idea! Are you doing work for them now? How did I miss this?"

"You think it's a good idea?" Justin's enthusiasm gives me a desperately needed boost of confidence. "And, well, I'm not working for Kickerville. At least not formally. This is a passion project of mine. I'm trying to get all my ducks in a row before presenting it to Mattie."

He hums. "Gotcha. Yeah, it's worth fleshing out the details before you show Mattie anything." I've always hated that saying. It feels so grotesque. "She's scrupulous, that's for sure. But your secret is safe with me. And between us? I really do think it's a good idea. It's a great way to diversify the business and reach a new segment of customers."

Over the next fifteen minutes, Justin gives me a crash course in solar energy. He suggests I make it an optional feature, so potential buyers can decide if it's worth the cost for their situation. Justin explains how solar panels can provide not only electricity but power heating and cooling systems, too. "As I'm sure you've already discovered, solar power is *huge* in tiny living," he tells me. "It gives people the ability to live off-grid."

I think of all the awing photographs and videos I've seen of tiny houses nestled in stunning remote locations, like deep within forests or perched beside crystal-clear bodies of water.

"This is going to sound dumb, but the system stores energy, right?" I ask. "So, even if you have a cloudy day, you can still have power as long as you have the energy stored?"

"Correct," he says. "But you want to use those reserves smartly, of course."

"Of course." I type all of this into my document. "This is very cool. Why doesn't everyone use solar?"

"Trust me, I agree." I hear the smile in Justin's voice. "But the upfront cost can be pretty intimidating. And not everyone's home is situated in such a way that it works. You have to consider tree cover, power lines, roof obstacles… There are a lot of variables."

We talk a bit more about solar energy followed by Violet's ever-growing Christmas list and the advent calendar she sent me in the mail. "She wants to know when you enjoy your daily piece of chocolate," Justin says. "She gets hers after dinner."

"Uh, yeah." I glance over at the red advent calendar poking out of my trash can. I finished the twenty-five chocolates within days. "Me too."

Then, I ask Justin a question I've wondered about for years.

"Why did you leave Kickerville?"

There's a beat of silence as my convivial brother turns quiet.

"Come on, Bea. You know why I left Kickerville," he finally says, sounding exasperated, maybe even a little guarded.

I know Justin wanted to move out west, but is there more to the story? It was such a big thing to leave behind. He had worked at the family business for years with the intention of one day taking it over.

"Listen, I've got to go. Katie has a snowman craft she wants us to do with Violet." Justin sounds impatient with me, but just as quickly, his voice softens. "Let me know if I can answer any other solar questions, okay? You should visit an RV dealership to get some ideas on keeping your dry weight low. Tour the travel trailers in particular."

I clearly touched a nerve, but I attribute Justin's shortness to his sleep deprivation rather than any ill feelings. Poor Violet's been suffering from night terrors lately, and no one in that house is getting much rest. But another part of me wonders if Justin leaving Kickerville wasn't as black and white as I've always believed. What if Mattie *pushed* Justin out? What if my sister decided my brother didn't fit into her idea of what Kickerville should be?

I've never known Mattie to be cruel, but she is ambitious.

"Okay, thanks," I say, deciding to let the topic drop. "That's a great idea."

"Sure thing, Beezus."

"Don't let Violet open her presents from me until Christmas morning," I remind him. "One of them is an Easy Bake Oven. Remember how much fun we used to have with ours? Those cakes were terrible."

"Mattie would get upset and say it was our fault for not following the recipe," Justin reminisces.

"But Mom ate them anyway." I think of her gingerly taken bites and overly enthusiastic smiles. "Anyways. Maybe take a video when Violet opens my gifts? I'm going to miss you guys on Christmas. We all will."

Justin assures me he will, and we say our goodbyes.

I open a new tab and type in "RV dealerships + Cincinnati, OH."

Well, this should be an interesting afternoon anyway.

Chapter Fifty-Two

I arrive at Walt's RV at half past two.

The sales office is a small building with a slanted glass panel facade. I wonder if it was originally a car dealership or even a gas station. The building looks especially tiny surrounded by the dozens of gigantic RVs. There's something intimidating, even beast-like, about the massive motorhomes.

A portly man wearing a Santa Claus tie greets me. "Welcome to Walt's RV, Southwest Ohio's most trusted source for recreation vehicles!" he booms cheerfully. "My name's Howard. How may I assist you?"

Up until this moment, I assumed I'd tell the truth, that I was doing research for a tiny house line. But standing here now on the checkered linoleum floor, I realize how silly that sounds.

"Hi! I'm Bea. And, um, I want to surprise my husband," I say. "He's always dreamed of owning a travel trailer, and I figure, why not knock his socks off on Christmas morning?"

"Wow!" Howard is impressed. "That's some Christmas present!"

"Well, he is some husband," I reply. "He brings me fresh flowers every Friday after work, and he cooks supper every night. His specialty is seafood linguine." This is fun creating a marvelous pretend life for myself. "Plus, a lot of people say he looks like Hugh Jackman."

Okay, Bea. Reel it in.

Howard beams, and I can tell he is genuinely happy at the thought of some random stranger having such a happy marriage.

"Are you married, Howard?" I ask, suddenly wanting the same for him.

He holds up his left hand, showing off a silver wedding band. "It was twenty-two years in June. We have three kids, all girls, and a basset hound named Susanna."

I like Howard very much. And I find this information satisfying.

"Can I get you a coffee before we head out to the lot?" he asks.

"That sounds nice. Thank you," I say. Howard asks me if medium roast is fine, I say it is, and I watch him pop a K-cup pod into a Keurig machine.

"So, was there a travel trailer you had in mind?" he asks, as I follow him through the crowded parking lot, the paper coffee cup warm in my hand. "Or a certain length or sleeping capacity?"

I scramble to remember brand names and typical trailer lengths. "I would love to see your lightest weight travel trailers," I finally say. "My husband drives an older truck, and the towing capacity is only 3,500 pounds."

Howard nods, his bald head shining a sun ray into my eyes. "Not a problem. Many of these modern travel trailers have remarkably low weights."

"And, ah, how do they keep the weights so low? The manufacturers, that is." We stop in front of a travel trailer and Howard opens the door for me. The inside is surprisingly spacious, with a kitchenette, dining booth, full-size bed, and even a pair of bunk beds.

"Aluminum framing, for one," Howard says. I write this detail down in the small notebook I've brought along. "And a fiberglass exterior."

"Great to know," I say, adding the second piece of intel.

"Do you have any kiddos at home?" He points to the bunk beds. "This one is only twenty feet long but comfortably sleeps four."

I contemplate imaginary children, giving them my very favorite baby names—Pippa and Grover, if you're curious—but that seems to take this act too far. I'm not aiming to be the subject matter of a Lifetime movie.

"Hopefully someday," I say instead, which is the absolute truth.

Howard shows me three more travel trailers. I'm surprised to find a bathtub in one and *two* sets of bunk beds in another. "These are remarkably efficient," I marvel. Howard takes the time to show me special space-saving features, like netted areas to hold odds and ends, shelves that flip down, and dinettes that convert into sleeping spaces. All of the travel trailers also include a decent amount of storage beneath the vehicle, ideal for bulky and outdoor items.

"Watch this," says Howard, pressing a button outside one of the trailers.

I watch an awning automatically extend outward. How neat would that be for one of my tiny homes? "Such a breeze. It used to be a pain setting up these awnings. I grew up camping in my family's 1961 Shasta Airflyte, and the awning always got my dad swearing. It used to be this whole song and dance that involved stakes and rope."

Howard is showing me how a ceiling air-conditioning unit works when I feel the now unmistakable heat starting in my face. I pull up the sleeves of my coat and watch fiery rashes spread across my skin.

"Are you all right, Bea?" asks Howard, genuinely concerned.

I'm frustrated that my flushing is cutting the appointment short, but I'm also relieved, appreciative for the easy escape it provides. How else did I intend to get off this sales lot without purchasing a travel trailer for my dreamy husband who cooks and looks like Hugh Jackman? Christmas is only a few days away!

"I'm okay. I have multiple sclerosis, and this is a side effect of my medication," I say, inexplicably feeling the need to be transparent about this aspect of my life. Or maybe it's because Howard has made me feel so comfortable. He's the very opposite of a pushy salesperson. "I'm afraid we'll have to pick this back up another time."

"Absolutely. No worries at all," Howard says. "Can I get you a bottle of water on your way out?"

I smile but shake my head. "No, thanks. You've already been so much help."

More help than Howard will probably ever know. I decide to name a tiny house model after him. Probably the one with the automatic awning.

Chapter Fifty-Three

"Oh!" I startle at the sudden vibrations of my phone against my desk, accidentally deleting an entire line of Pinterest ad copy in the process. "Oh, jeez." I immediately press the Undo button and am relieved to see the text reappear.

I glance downward, expecting a message from Mom or Justin, and am pleasantly surprised to see Chris Little's name on my screen instead. Intrigued, I close my InDesign file, not wanting to introduce any more errors, and open his message.

HUGE favor to ask!!! And I wouldn't ask if it wasn't an emergency. We're taking a group of freshmen to volunteer at a food bank this afternoon, and one of our chaperones just went home sick. Any chance you could take the afternoon off and help?

All sorts of warm, fuzzy thoughts crowd my mind.

Of course Chris is one of the teachers to volunteer for such an event. That isn't surprising. But of all his friends and acquaintances and family members, Chris asked *me* to cover for the sick chaperone.

Me!

Does he think I have an altruistic spirit? Assume I'm good with teenagers? Or does he simply want to spend more time with me?

Although, judging by his overuse of exclamation marks, maybe he's just desperate.

"Pssst! Han!" I poke my best friend's shoulder.

"This day is dragging," she complains, removing her headphones. "All of my projects were due last Friday, I haven't received a single piece of client feedback this week, and I think I've done every BuzzFeed quiz out there. And it's only eleven."

"Yeah, this week is a bore. But check this out." I hold up my phone screen so she can read Chris's message.

"Batman's sent you the Bat-Signal!" Hannah squeals. "You have to go!"

I'm conflicted. "I *want* to go. Work's slow, and we have those volunteer hours to use every year."

"Which we are both admittedly bad about using," Hannah reminds me.

"But I feel like I've already taken off a bunch of weird time this month for my doctor's appointments," I say. "And worked from home maybe more than I should have... I know Gwen gets weird about that."

Even though Gwen isn't permitted to discourage remote work, her glares and curt emails make it clear how she *really* feels about the setup. She's the master of impromptu video calls on her subordinates' work-from-home days, and considering I have a penchant for working from bed, these surprise meetings always send me scrambling.

"I wish they would just make the promotion announcement already." I reach for my ball of stress therapy dough, which smells like lavender and feels like Play-Doh. "I'm so afraid I'll make one wrong move and *poof.* There go my chances."

"Oh, I doubt it's as simple as that." Hannah picks at the fibers of her oversized sweater. The colorful sleeves fan over her hands. "Just be super transparent," she says. "Tell Gwen it's a volunteer opportunity, and that you'd like to help your friend. Maybe add how *handsome* that friend is... and brave..."

I swat at her. "I get it. I'm making a mountain out of a molehill."

Since Gwen's on a phone call, I send her an instant message.

Me: Hi Gwen! So, my friend is a high school teacher, and he just texted me that they're down one volunteer for a trip to the food bank this afternoon. Is it okay if I put through volunteer hours for this PM? All of my projects are in good shape.

"And now we wait," I whisper to Hannah, as we both watch my screen for Gwen's reply.

Gwen (approximately three minutes later): That's fine.

"Well, that was anticlimactic," Hannah giggles.

Grinning, I text Chris back, **No problem—I'll be there! Send me the address, and I'll see ya this afternoon!**

Holiday season volunteer work plus extra time with Chris Little?

I'd call that a win-win.

Chapter Fifty-Four

I arrive at the food bank fifteen minutes early. I feel jittery and excited, like I'm going on a date rather than volunteering with a bunch of teenagers.

I mosey around the lobby, trying to look cool and immensely interested in the little plaques I'm reading about the food bank's history. I'm surprised at the amount of food, resources, and even jobs the food bank provides the community. Why haven't I volunteered here before? The distribution center is only a five-minute drive from the office. It couldn't be more convenient.

New Year's resolution, I think. *Be less selfish.*

I catch my reflection in the glass of one of the black-and-white photographs. I've pinned a red beret over my curls and am surprised at how much I like the look. Sure, it probably isn't a good sign that the first day I appreciate my new haircut is when it's partially hidden beneath a hat. And no, I certainly haven't achieved Audrey Tatou doppelgänger status.

But I feel pretty today.

At exactly one p.m., the front doors burst open and a sea of high schoolers floods through them. Good God! They are like a herd of cattle! Suddenly self-conscious, I pull down the hem of my tunic and try to brush away any stray dog hair from my leggings.

Where is Chris? I scan the boisterous crowd, starting to feel a bit panicked.

These kids look straight out of the early 2000s sitcoms that were on TV when *I* was in high school. There are lots of baggy jeans and cargo pants (yes, cargo pants!), plus hoodies and cropped sweaters. Most of the girls are wearing Ugg Tasmans or Doc Martens, while the boys are sporting New Balance and Nike sneakers. It is all very Y2K with the addition of Stanley cups and belt bags.

The group is loud and giggly and loud.

I swallow. Why are teenagers so scary?

"Bea! Hey!" It's Chris Little! Thanks be to God. He's making his way through the crowd of twenty teenagers that feels more like two hundred. "You're my hero. Thanks so much for coming today." He smiles. "I like your beret."

Instinctively, my fingers go to its felt edges. "Oh, thanks. And sure thing! Happy to help."

He lowers his voice, moving his mouth close to my ear. "This is a great group of kids. I promise there's nothing to be scared about."

"I'm not scared," I stammer, my cheeks growing red.

"I know teenagers can be intimidating, but they're a misunderstood group," he says. "You'll love them once you get to know them."

"Bonjour." I'm surprised to see a gorgeous woman suddenly at Chris's side. Where has this goddess come from? She has a proper pixie cut, the kind I *expected* to leave the salon with, and striking blue eyes. We're talking Nicole Kidman-level blue. "I'm Sabine, Mademoiselle Lavigne for this afternoon. It's a pleasure."

Sabine Lavigne? Are you kidding me?

"Hi. I'm Bea." I clear my throat. "Or, um, Ms. Parker? Is that what the kids should call me?"

"Yes, you're Ms. Parker today," says Chris. "Mademoiselle Lavigne is one of our French teachers. She moved to Cincinnati last year but spent most of her life in Nantes."

"Nantes! Wow!" I say, realizing I know nothing about Nantes. I assume it's a town in France, but who knows? My beret suddenly feels immature and stupid. I want to stuff it inside my purse. Or a garbage can. "That's awesome."

"The kids adore her," Chris adds.

Mademoiselle Lavigne smiles at him. What's the expression in those big, beautiful eyes of hers? Fondness? Lust? "That's funny to hear from the school's most popular teacher," she says, her accent thick and enchanting.

Am I going to have to sit here and listen to them argue over who is more adored?

Thankfully, a food bank employee breaks up their little love fest.

"Good afternoon! Hello!" The employee is short but has a big voice. She reminds me of Fran Bosse. For extra measure, she sticks two fingers between her lips and gives a good whistle. "Thank you for donating your time this afternoon to help your community."

To my surprise, the high schoolers immediately quiet down.

After giving a brief history of the food bank, which I already know from having read all the plaques and photo captions, the employee explains what we'll be doing this afternoon. "You'll be sorting through donations and discarding any expired or compromised items," she says. "This will help us clear out the food we can't distribute and organize the items we can."

I wonder if Chris brought his compost bins. But when I go to murmur in Chris's ear, I see Mademoiselle Lavigne already has it. Is it really appropriate for her plump lips to be so close to his ear?

"You'll want to keep your coat on. It's chilly in the processing area," Chris tells me once we've been dismissed. He hands me a pair of gloves. "I brought you these in case you didn't have your own."

I do have my own gloves, but I accept Chris's pair instead. They look hand-knitted and are definitely an upgrade from my drug store mittens. "Thanks," I tell him. "Do you do this every year?"

"Ever since *I* was in high school, if you can believe that," he says.

Chris, Mademoiselle Lavigne, and I disperse ourselves evenly among the students. I end up standing between three girls, Ava, Abby, and Sophie, and am thankful I haven't gotten stuck with a bunch of boys. As a gal who went to a Catholic, all-girls high school, I have very little experience with teenage boys and am incredibly awkward around them.

"Hi! I'm B–" I stop, catching myself. "Ms. Parker."

"We love your beret," Abby gushes, her mouth full of braces with tiny, pink rubber bands. I forgot how teenage girls often speak as a group. We love this. We hate that. "How do you know Mr. Little?"

"We're neighbors," I tell them.

"Well, Mr. Little is the best," says Sophie. "He's sort of a dork, but he's the nicest teacher in school. He lets you retake a quiz or test if you don't feel good about your grade."

"And you get extra credit if you listen to Science Friday," says Ava. "I'm not sure if you're familiar, but that's a show on NPR."

"I listen to Science Friday sometimes," I smile.

We receive our first load of canned goods and pantry items and begin the discarding process, carefully reviewing the dates listed by the food bank. While any canned goods with pinched metal and pantry items that are partially opened or damaged must be tossed, we learn all about "best if used by," "sell by," and "use by" dates. As it turns out, there is more wiggle room than I would have thought.

Chris briefly pops over to check in on us. "I'm just thrilled we were assigned this task today." He's practically buzzing with excitement. "Think of all the food waste we're avoiding!" he tells the group. "We can apply this to our daily lives, too."

"Mr. Little is obsessed with food waste," Ava says. Girlfriend, tell me something I don't know! "He runs the compost program at school."

Jeez louise. How many compost programs does Chris Little operate?

"What do you do for a job?" asks Sophie. She has her long, blonde hair tied into a ponytail.

"I'm a graphic designer," I say, glad I have a somewhat cool career to chat about. "What do you girls want to do someday?"

Sophie is considering business school, she wants to work in marketing, Abby's interested in fashion design, and Ava wants to be a lawyer. "Whatever I do, I want to live in a big city," clarifies Sophie. "Probably New York. But maybe London."

"Oooh. Go to London," I say, suddenly nostalgic for my teenage years, when anything felt possible. What changed between then and now? "Or Paris!"

"Have you watched *Emily in Paris*?" Abby asks. "It's on Netflix."

I toss an expired can of green beans into the discard pile. "Yep. I couldn't stop swooning over the outfits."

"Have you ever been to Paris, Ms. Parker?" Sophie wants to know.

"Just once. On a high school trip actually," I reply. "Does your school offer anything like that?"

"Uh-huh. Mademoiselle Lavigne leads it. I think Mr. Little might go next summer," Ava says, which makes Sophie and Abby giggle.

Why do I suddenly feel like I'm on the outside of an inside joke?

"What's so funny about that?" I ask.

The girls exchange knowing looks before Ava whispers, "We think Mademoiselle Lavigne and Mr. Little are secretly in love. Even though Mr. Little is sort of nerdy, and Mademoiselle Lavigne is so pretty."

"And French," Sophie adds. "French people are so chic!"

Immediately, my stomach sinks. I watch Mademoiselle Lavigne toss a box of pancake mix in Chris's direction. He raises his eyebrows at her. They laugh.

"Why do you think that?" I need some hard evidence.

Ava purses her lips at me. She looks like my mother with an expression like that. "They eat lunch together every day, and they laugh *a lot,*" she explains.

"Plus, they're the only two semi-cool teachers in the entire school,"

Sophie says, as if this designation means they are destined to fall in love. "A girl in my algebra class said she saw them at the movies once."

"Oh my God, really?" Shit. That's pretty damning. "Are they, like, allowed to date?"

Ava shrugs. "They're both single. It's a free country. I don't see why not."

Because I like Mr. Little! I want to shout. *That's why not!*

"And it's not like they do anything weird at school," Abby clarifies, like I'm picturing them making out against the lockers or something. Which I totally am not!

The girls startle when Chris appears behind us.

"Everything going okay over here?" he asks, an easy-going smile across his face.

"Uh-huh! Yep! Yeah!" the girls all chorus, giggling as they pretend to be intently focused on the donations pile once again.

Chris pulls me aside. I want to ask him all about Mademoiselle Lavigne. I want to know if he is in love with her. What if Mademoiselle Lavigne is the real reason why Chris and Amanda broke up?

"What do you think?" he beams. "Aren't these kids amazing?"

Amazingly informative, I think.

Chapter Fifty-Five

etween my bus running late and an impromptu stop at William's French bakery, it's nearly nine o'clock by the time I arrive at my desk on Wednesday morning.

"No pain au chocolat today," I inform Hannah, sliding the pastel pink-striped box of confections onto our desks. "I went for sugar cookies instead. They felt more festive."

And reminded me less of Mademoiselle Lavigne.

"Yum!" Hannah nods toward the expansive, high-top table where we hold impromptu meetings and review print projects. "I brought Buckeyes." Buckeyes are an Ohio specialty, little balls of powdery peanut butter dipped in chocolate. "There are also donuts and brownies." The last day in the office before the holiday break is always treated like a little party.

I have also arrived bearing gifts: a heartfelt present for Hannah (the RBG needlepoint), a final surprise for my Secret Santa (a journal where you sketch a doodle a day, plus a set of colored pencils), and an obligatory gift for Gwen (an uninteresting bottle of white wine for an uninteresting lady).

"Awww Bea! You shouldn't have!" exclaims Hannah as I hand her the awkwardly wrapped gift. Circular items are tricky to gift wrap. She pulls out a gold foil bag from beneath her own desk and hands it to me. "Merry Christmas."

We open our presents at the same time. "I love it!" we both declare at the exact same time. We giggle, especially as we catch a few eye rolls around the office.

"Haters gonna hate," I say, making us laugh all over again.

Hannah's gift to me is a gorgeous hardback planner. It has

inspirational quotes and whimsical illustrations sprinkled throughout and places to write to-do lists. It even includes a sticker collection (so fun!), and Hannah has thoughtfully decorated special dates for me throughout the year, from St. Patrick's Day and the Fourth of July to her wedding day (officially October 6) and my birthday.

"Nothing like the possibility of a new planner," Hannah says brightly, before lowering her voice. "Next year's going to be one for the books. I just know the most amazing things are ahead for you, Bea."

"You really believe that?"

She nods, and I give her a quick hug. Hannah's confidence in my future is the best gift she could have given me.

"Cute outfit, by the way," Hannah says, eying my ensemble.

I've woven gold tinsel around a headband and am wearing an oversized holiday vest—knit with boughs of holly and Santa's sleigh, including all nine reindeer—over a red turtleneck and black jeans. My earrings are even little candy canes that light up when I shake my head with enough Christmas spirit.

"I couldn't help myself," I say, ever a sucker for costumes, themes, and special occasions. Any reason to dress out of the ordinary, really. "You should have seen the looks I got on the bus."

I can't say we get a tremendous amount of work done that morning. It's the day before a holiday break, and we are *wound-up*. All of my colleagues are, from the junior designers to the copy directors. It's like that three o'clock on a Friday feeling but given four shots of espresso. We're excited, and we are beyond distracted. The office is whirring with anticipation: *Are you traveling? Have you bought anything super cool for someone special? Which holiday delicacy are you most excited to eat?*

Polly Feinstein always closes its offices between December 24 and January 3, giving its associates nearly two full weeks to celebrate and spend time with family and friends. I love this tradition as it makes me feel like a schoolgirl again, preparing for a cozy break with my family.

Around eleven a.m., Hannah sends me an instant message: DENNIS IS HERE!!!

I spin around in my chair just in time to see Dennis slip into Gwen's office. He's wearing charcoal slacks, a crisp white button-up, and a jolly red tie. I eye Gwen and realize she's also more dressed up than usual in a simple, black sheath dress and heels.

It's a Christmas miracle.

They are going to make the announcement today, right before we all take off for break!

"It's marvelous timing," I tell Hannah before pointing excitedly at the bar cart being rolled in. Jeez louise! They've brought in champagne! "This is *so* exciting."

We share a little squeal.

"I'm going to pee real fast," I tell Hannah, feeling the beginning of that uncomfortable urge.

"Good idea," Hannah says. "You don't want to be standing in Gwen's office with your legs pressed together during such a major career event!"

"Be back in a flash," I say.

I grab my cosmetics bag so I can freshen up my makeup while I'm in the restroom and hurry off.

But when I return to my desk a few minutes later, I'm surprised to see Hannah's chair is empty and her monitor still on. Unlike me, Hannah always remembers to lock her computer when she leaves her desk.

I look around, my breathing turning shallow and my heart beginning to race as my body realizes what's happening before my brain catches up.

I watch my best friend walk towards Gwen's office, where Gwen and Dennis are both standing to receive her with big smiles. I see the hand-shakes, the look of surprise on Hannah's face, the hug from Gwen.

I will not be receiving the promotion.

The promotion is going to Hannah.

Sure enough, the team email goes out just moments later.

We are pleased to announce that Hannah Nielsen has been promoted to Art Director, backfilling Christina Chambers' vacant role, effective January 1. Join us for congratulatory champagne to toast Hannah's success!

Oh my God. This hurts.

I train my eyes on my computer screen until I'm sure the tears have passed.

Don't cry, don't cry, don't cry.

The rejection hits me in unrelenting waves. I can't catch my breath.

You aren't good enough, a mean, little voice sneers somewhere inside my head. *You've fallen short in yet another aspect of your life. You just keep failing.*

I'm desperate to leave—all I want is Tony Soprano and my bed— and for a split second, I nearly grab my coat.

But I stop myself.

I can't do that to Hannah. She's a brilliant graphic designer, and she deserves to be showered with congratulations. She should be celebrated, most of all by her best friend.

I'm the first person to whistle the moment Gwen's office door opens. "Congratulations!" I shout, leading our creative group in a round of applause. I see the way Gwen studies me and notice her thinly veiled satisfaction over my disappointment.

I envelope Hannah. We're both shaking but for wildly different reasons. "You are going to be an amazing art director," I tell her. "The best."

She pulls back, her brown eyes big and conflicted. I know she's happy and surprised and thrilled, she has every right to be, but I also see the apprehension there, the apology. "I am so sorry..." she starts to say.

"You deserve this," I say, as Hannah is whisked away by more hugs and warm wishes.

I talk with Chase, Hannah's fellow art director, while nursing my flute of dry champagne. It's bubbly and crisp. They've splurged on the good stuff. I wonder how long I can keep my hot tears at bay. Is there a point where they will suddenly gush out of my eyes, my entire head exploding with despair?

"I thought it would be you," Chase says. He's an office gossip, always saying more than he should, particularly for someone of his level. "You're our digital design guru, and with more of our projects moving in that direction... Well, it made the most sense. Plus, you've been here the longest out of the senior designers. I know tenure doesn't mean everything, but it's important. That's where my mind was at. I just thought you should know."

I want to roll my eyes. He just thought I should know? *Right.*

I shrug, choosing to be a loyal friend and avoid taking the bait. "There must be a lot of factors that go into a promotion. Hannah was a great choice," I say breezily.

Chase takes a swig of his champagne and tries to backtrack. "Definitely!"

he echoes. "I know you and Gwen aren't close, but I hadn't realized…" But before Chase can elaborate on just how much Gwen loathes me, his eyes widen. He looks quite concerned, quite shocked actually.

"Um, Bea, don't freak out, but your skin is turning red," he says. "Very, *very* red. Are you okay?"

Chapter Fifty-Six

Oh, God. My flushing!

Instinctively, my hands go to my hot cheeks.

"It's just a medication side effect," I assure Chase, now wanting to cry at the humiliation of this timing. "But if you'll excuse me, I'm going to go and try to tame it."

I move quickly and quietly through the rowdy crowd, trying to smile and look happy despite the fact that I've been passed over for the promotion and now my skin is actively breaking out into angry rashes. I grab my backpack from beneath my desk, wondering if a spray of rose water might calm my skin. My grin is so forced that my mouth begins to ache. I wonder if I look more like the Joker than a gracious loser.

I can only imagine what my colleagues are whispering about me.

Did you see her face? It was bright red!

She couldn't leave the celebration fast enough.

You'd think she would be happy for her best friend, but her face said otherwise.

Once safely in the bathroom, I splash water all over my arms. I wet a paper towel and hold it against my chest and face, trying to calm the inflammation. I take deep breaths and try to center myself. I gasp at my reflection in the mirror, a woman covered in giant red splotches, my eyes big and hysterical.

I look like a monster.

The only thing this stupid medication has done is make me feel like more of a freak. It's not like I've noticed any alleviation of my symptoms. It's only uncovered even more terrible ways my own body can betray me.

Unable to stare at myself a second longer, I slip into the handicapped stall and lean against a corner where it will be difficult for anyone to come in and see my feet. This is where I belong anyway. Even if I'm not physically handicapped now, I probably will be someday. Nerve damage is probably happening even as I cry here in this cold bathroom stall.

Hannah is my only coworker who knows about my MS. I chose not to tell anyone else, particularly Gwen, because of the stupid promotion. I didn't want my colleagues questioning my capabilities, wondering if I could pull off the director role with a chronic disease.

And yet, maybe it *is* the reason they passed me over.

What if my MS has affected my work more than I've realized? I know I'm not as sharp or quick-witted in meetings as I once was, and I almost always need my headphones to focus, the bustling office suddenly too distracting. I don't work as fast anymore, and there are many afternoons, especially when the fatigue sets in, when the most basic tasks feel insurmountable.

It's no wonder the promotion went to Hannah.

But had I even wanted it?

I start to pace the length of the bathroom stall, the heels of my suede booties tapping quietly against the concrete floor. As I walk, my self pity and doubt begin to wane.

Was it the job I was after or simply the accomplishment? Did I want to be an art director, or did I want a prestigious title?

Was I simply desperate for something to go right? Was I determined to tell my family and friends a piece of happy, encouraging news? *I may be thirty and recently dumped and diagnosed with a chronic disease, but I have this shiny new promotion!*

I exit the bathroom stall, grimace at the sight of my aggravated skin, and make a split decision to head for the elevator corridor instead of the celebratory office, where holiday tunes are now playing and the chatter and laughter have grown louder. I don't want to have to explain my flushing, and I certainly don't have the energy to tell everyone about my multiple sclerosis. Besides, it isn't the time or place for such news. Hannah deserves to be the center of attention, to bask in her colleagues' glow.

I lean my head back against the cool metal of the elevator wall and close my eyes, feeling the sensation of dropping, dropping, dropping.

My heart hasn't been in graphic design for a while now. Maybe months, maybe years.

But my heart has found a place in my tiny house project. I have a project I'm passionate about, a project that could turn into a career.

And that's something. It's something big.

I take a deep breath, exiting the elevator on the ground floor.

I'll go home and let myself have a proper cry. Even if the position hadn't been right for me, even if I hadn't wanted it deep down, the snub still hurts.

But then I'll order my favorite takeout food and dive headfirst into my tiny house project. The holiday break will serve as a much needed refresh, a time to clear my mind, focus on what matters, and press the "restart" button.

Congratulations, Han! You DESERVE this!!! Soak in every moment! I text my friend.

And then I walk toward the bus stop, my head held high.

Chapter Fifty-Seven

It's always been my belief that Christmas Eve, not Christmas Day itself, is the most magical day of the year. Growing up, Christmas Day was merry and bright and bustling with activity. But Christmas Eve was different.

Christmas Eve was quiet. It was full of wonder and awe. It was when we attended evening mass, and Mom made us all dress up in our fanciest outfits. "Does Jesus really care what I look like?" Dad routinely grumbled while fumbling with his necktie. Christmas Eve was one of the rare days when Mom pulled out her curling iron and sat Mattie and me down in front of the bathroom vanity. We nicknamed the tragic result "Christmas Hair," an erratic hairstyle that involved ringlets, lots of hairspray, and a large bow.

After mass, we would drive around the neighborhood and admire our favorite holiday lights displays while listening for Santa Claus sightings on the radio. Once we were back home, Mattie and I quickly ditched our itchy frocks and pinchy shoes for flannel pajamas and slippers while Justin moseyed around outside, spreading reindeer food across the lawn.

Mom would make her chicken pot pie casserole, and then we'd watch *Home Alone* together in front of the fire. It was nearly impossible to fall asleep that night as my mind buzzed with the anticipation of Santa visiting and I wondered what he would be leaving beneath the tree. Eventually, exhaustion would get the better of me, and I'd drift off, my last sight the little aluminum Christmas tree on my nightstand.

Christmas Eve was special all right.

So, it seems fitting that this unexpected snowstorm of a century has blown into Cincinnati today.

I spend the morning wrapping presents while listening to a Carpenters' holiday album. Each time I glance out a window, I'm surprised to see the heavy flakes continuing to fall. Cincinnati doesn't get big snows as often as we once did. Are we finally going to get a white Christmas? It seems too lucky.

But at noon, there are already three inches of snow on the ground. I know because when I take Tony Soprano outside, the snow brushes against his belly. I clear a small area of grass for Tony to do his business, but he still isn't pleased about the ordeal.

Mom calls an hour later. "Well, isn't this something? I can't remember the last time we had a real snow on Christmas Eve," she says. "Though, I'm afraid this might jeopardize tonight's plans..." I can hear the conflict in her voice. The snow is beautiful, magical, and so wonderfully Christmassy, but it also means she won't be seeing her daughters for mass, chicken pot pie, and *Home Alone*.

"We'll see each other tomorrow," I say brightly.

"But honey, what will you do tonight?" It's *me* Mom is worried about. Mattie has Peter. I have no one. I'm the one who will be spending Christmas Eve alone. "Do you want me to send Dad out?" Mom is encouraged by this idea. "Yes, I'll send Dad over to get you, and you can stay at our house for the night."

Dad is a skilled motorist with four-wheel drive, but this is the sort of storm no one should be driving in unless of an emergency. "That's nice of you to offer, but I'll be okay," I assure her.

"What will you do?" Mom presses. "To celebrate?"

"I don't know," I admit. "But my apartment is warm and decorated, and I have just about every Christmas movie at my disposal. Plus, a very soft, very snuggly dog. So, I think I'll be all right. There are a lot worse ways to spend Christmas Eve, you know?"

"Hmm..." Mom gives her signature hum of apprehension. She isn't convinced.

I suddenly imagine my mother pulling a Mrs. McCallister and hitching a ride across town with a polka band. "We'll see each other tomorrow, the whole family," I tell her. "If the roads are still rough, *then* you can send Dad over to get me."

Mom is satisfied, or satisfied enough, with this response. We exchange "I love yous" and I press the end button.

So, Christmas Eve all on my own.

What should I do?

-∗-

I decide to take a gingerbread-scented bubble bath paired with a glass of sparkling CBD water. I apply a calming face mask and turn on the annual airing of David Sedaris' "Santaland Diaries." Escaping into the hilarious world of a department store elf is the sort of dark humor I need. I laugh as I refill the tub with hotter water, thinking that this singleton Christmas Eve is actually quite sublime.

After my relaxing soak, I snuggle into my cool sheets and take a two-hour nap. When I wake up, I pad to the bay window above my bedroom desk and inhale at the sight of a snowy Pleasant Ridge. The neighboring homes' Christmas lights are dim orbs beneath the snowfall, the gaslights shining only a bit brighter. *What a storm,* I marvel, watching in awe as the snow seemingly pours from the sky. It looks like someone has turned a box of instant mashed potatoes upside down. I picture myself below, holding out a bowl and collecting the flakes, stirring them with butter and milk. The thought makes me smile.

Even though it will only be Tony Soprano and me for the evening, I take care styling my hair—I'm finally figuring out how to get the short curls to lay just right—and doing my makeup. I even give myself glossy, ruby-red lips. "Why, you look like Rosemary Clooney with lips like that," I tell my reflection. I change into the blue velvet jumpsuit I planned on wearing tonight and slip into a pair of leopard-print kitten heels.

In the kitchen, I stir myself a Peppermint White Russian before rummaging through the contents of my fridge and freezer. I won't be having Mom's chicken pot pie casserole tonight, but that doesn't mean I can't make myself something special. I'm delighted to find a jar of summer pesto hiding in the back of the freezer. I set it out to defrost, as well as a large piece of salmon.

Knock, knock, knock, someone taps on my door.

Chapter Fifty-Eight

*M*ust be Janet, I think.

She's been badgering me for Christmas gift ideas for Fran. No matter how many times I tell her that Fran would love nothing more than a gift certificate to Ace Hardware, Janet insists there must be something else Fran might like, something with "more pizzazz."

I swing the door open.

"Chris." My heart's the first to react, immediately picking up its pace, and my skin follows with a wave of chills. "Hi."

I watch Chris's eyes take me in, his appreciative gaze leaving me warm. "Wow," he says. "You look beautiful."

"Well, you look very nice, too," I deflect. Chris is wearing corduroys and a red-and-green flannel, his hands folded politely behind his back. "It's sort of silly, but I wanted to feel fancy tonight. Even though I knew it would just be Tony Soprano and me," I explain, feeling bashful, like a girl caught playing dress-up. "It is Christmas Eve, after all."

"I assume you're snowbound, too?" He looks down at the scuffed hardwood floor. "Or, um, is your boyfriend coming over? John, isn't it?"

"John isn't my boyfriend. He wasn't *ever* my boyfriend," I say quickly. "But he's out of the picture now. He got a proper look at what my disease is like and got the hell out of Dodge."

Chris lifts his gaze. Is it wishful thinking, or does he look relieved? It's hard to tell because his immediate reaction is quickly replaced by one of outrage. "Are you kidding me? *That's* why it ended?"

"Yep." I would add the baby bella mushroom haircut to the mix, but since it happened after John ghosted me, I know it's innocent in the matter. "Anyways, it's fine, really. We didn't have a lot in common."

"It's his loss," Chris says. "But what an asshole. The worst kind of asshole."

I want Chris to say more, but I'm also afraid of what that more could be. My greatest hope is that he continues into a declaration of love for me.

Ever since I met you, I believe in happily ever afters! he could proclaim. But what if instead, he suggests I check out some new dating app? Or recommends a book about the science behind adjusting to a life spent alone?

"I'm surprised you haven't snowshoed to your parents' house," I say, guiding the conversation to safe territory.

"Ah, well…" He sighs. "My family all traveled to Ann Arbor last night. It's where I'm supposed to be now, but that obviously isn't happening."

"I was just about to sit down with a holiday cocktail," I say. "Care to join me?"

"I would love to."

He follows me inside, and I watch him admire my tree for the first time. He carefully examines the dried orange garland I threaded before bending his face toward a balsam candle. Chris then carefully lifts a vintage snow globe, gives it a gentle shake, and smiles contentedly.

"When did you get interested in antiques?" he asks, watching the snow fall on the cottage nestled among tall pines. The water solution has yellowed a bit over the decades, but the effect is of a warm glow.

"I've loved old things for as long as I can remember," I say, handing him an icy glass. "My dad used to repurpose a lot of reclaimed materials in his home builds. He constantly made us stop at roadside antique malls and flea markets to search for smaller interior stuff. Kitchen sinks, light fixtures, things like that. My brother and sister hated it. Justin was bored, and Mattie thought everything smelled funny. But I felt like I was a part of a big treasure hunt. Every item felt magical to me."

Chris gives me a big smile. "Does the company still use reclaimed materials?"

"Actually, no. Not at all. Once Dad changed his focus to modular, pre-fab homes, Kickerville became a sort of big, well-oiled machine." I take a long sip of my drink. "But maybe my tiny houses could…"

"I think your tiny houses *should*," Chris says. "Think of the cost savings and environmental impact."

My mind starts to whir, and I immediately jot this down on my fridge notepad before I forget. "This is good," I murmur. Then, I hold up my glass. "Well then! Cheers. Happy Christmas Eve."

"Happy Christmas Eve," Chris choruses, and we clink glasses. Our eyes lock as we take our first sips. I wonder if he's as excited about this twist of events as I am. "I can't remember the last time we got a true blizzard."

"It's pretty magical," I reply. "So, who lives in Ann Arbor?"

"My aunt and uncle. They both work at the university. They've got this historic home right in Kerrytown on a cobblestone street." He looks down at his feet. "I've been kicking myself today for not leaving sooner. It's such a wonderful place to spend Christmas. Although..." He takes another admiring look around my quirky apartment. "This is pretty great, too."

I can tell he means it, and I am touched.

Chris and I stare at one another, all dopey and happy, for a few moments before he reaches into his back pocket and pulls out a small box.

"Merry Christmas," he says shyly. Curiously, I accept the gift, which is wrapped in the same material as a brown paper grocery bag. The "bow" has been drawn on with a black Sharpie. "Sorry it's not a real bow. Or real gift wrap. That stuff is all—"

"Very wasteful. Yes, I agree," I say, suppressing a smirk. "But I think this gift is wrapped beautifully."

I glide my fingertips beneath the tape. Inside is a cardboard box and a pair of earrings featuring James Gandolfini's, the real Tony Soprano, face. "Oh my God!" I exclaim, bursting into laughter. "Where did you ever find such a thing? These are absurd!"

Chris looks anxious. "Are they stupid? I'm sorry, I—"

"They are the opposite of stupid," I immediately secure the studs in my ears. "They are weird and wonderful and so very perfect. Thank you!" On impulse, I reach for Chris, enveloping him in a hug. Our very first hug, to be exact.

I feel his body tense and then relax, every muscle in his shoulders and back seeming to exhale. I wrap my arms around his neck while his arms weave around my waist. His hair smells like dandruff shampoo, but his skin smells woodsy and clean. I want to nestle my face into his neck and then to his chest.

"I found them on Etsy," he mumbles into my hair.

"Etsy is the best," I reply, still not pulling away, still hoping Chris will lift my chin, that he will bring his lips to mine.

"They're made from recycled plastic," he adds, his mouth sending shivers down my spine.

Since this is getting weird, I finally let go of Chris Little. We're both breathless and rosy-cheeked. Has a hug ever affected me like that? Good God, that isn't normal.

"I actually have something for you, too." I stumble toward my bedroom. "One second."

I've crocheted Chris three Star Wars figurines: Baby Yoda, Luke Skywalker, and Princess Leia. But where is a cute gift bag I can put them in? I trip around the room, tossing dirty laundry, half-finished crafts, and long-forgotten novels aside. *Aha!* I spot a reusable bag I got for free at a local grocery store. There's an illustration of a pack of green vegetables—broccoli, brussels sprouts, and green beans— all wearing leather jackets and sunglasses and looking tough. The text below reads: Lean & Green Fighting Machine.

"Here we are," I announce, startling Chris. He's standing in front of my living room window. "Is the snow still coming down out there?"

"Remarkably, yes." He shakes his head in disbelief. "I pity any motorist on the road tonight."

"Especially when you consider what rotten drivers we Cincinnatians are." It's a joke that only works between two Cincinnati natives. Because a transplant sure as heck isn't permitted to comment on our driving abilities (or lack thereof). I thrust the grocery bag in Chris's direction. "Merry Christmas. Sorry for the random bag."

Chris sits on my sofa, and Tony Soprano hops beside him. I settle into the floral armchair that still smells like my late grandmother's perfume and squeaks with the slightest movement. The wind howls outside, and I reach for a blanket to wrap around my shoulders.

"Well, I love the bag. So don't be sorry," Chris says, grinning at the trio of veggies.

And then, as Chris pulls out each of the crocheted characters, I watch as his face positively lights up. Even his eyes seem to be smiling. "Bea!" he says, examining Baby Yoda. "Did you make these?"

I nod proudly. "I did."

"Wow!" he says. "Just...wow! Thank you. I don't know if anyone has ever made me anything so cool. These will look great in my living room."

His living room? Yikes. I was thinking more like his classroom or maybe a corner desk.

"I'm so happy you like them," I say.

I'm so happy you like them because I like you.

We both drink our cocktails quietly, broad-but-shy smiles on our faces.

"I don't want to keep you on Christmas Eve," Chris says.

"Would you like to stay for supper?" I sputter, before I can lose my nerve. "I'm going to warm up some pesto and serve it over salmon. I also make the most amazing roasted potatoes, all buttery and peppery. It's nothing fancy, especially compared to what you probably eat at your aunt and uncle's, but...."

"That sounds incredible," he says. "I would love that."

"The salmon is wild-caught," I quickly add. "Everything is organic, but I don't know the origins of the butter...or the parmesan I used in the pesto, come to think of it..."

"I think I can make an exception for Christmas Eve," Chris the Climatarian smiles.

We work in the kitchen side by side, our movements comfortable and in sync. While I take care of the salmon, pesto, and potatoes, Chris throws together a kale salad. I open a bottle of champagne to enjoy with our dinner and light the candlesticks on the table. It's the most unconventional Christmas Eve supper I've ever prepared, but it's also the most delicious.

"This is somehow even better than my mom's chicken pot pie," I hum, licking the oily pesto off my lips. "But don't ever repeat that to her."

"I'm sworn to secrecy," he replies, and I marvel at the implication. Will Chris one day meet my mom? My parents? His eyes catch mine in the candlelight. "Those earrings look wonderful on you."

Instinctively, I touch my earlobes. "Yeah?"

"Yeah." He takes a big bite of the leafy salad. "You can see them better with your short hair, too."

I never want to take them off. They are ridiculous, which makes me love them all the more.

"I actually showed them to Sabine, to see what she thought," Chris says. My stomach sinks at the mention of her name. *Mademoiselle Lavigne.* And suddenly, my earrings don't feel so special after all. "But she had never seen

The Sopranos, so I can't say she completely understood the joke. Maria thought they were hysterical though."

A storm cloud begins to gather in the blue skies above my happy heart.

"Oh." I look down at my plate, pushing a potato around. "Did you two exchange gifts? You and Sabine?"

Chris nods, oblivious to my disappointment. "She got me one of those reusable coffee pods for the breakroom Keurig machine and a batch of my favorite coffee beans," he reports matter-of-factly. "Can you pass the salt?"

I take an aggressive swig of champagne, burning my throat. "And what did you get her?"

I hand him the saltshaker. He shakes it over my perfectly seasoned potatoes.

"I made her a succulent garden." Chris dabs the corner of his lips but still misses a smear of green pesto. "Her classroom is in a depressing part of the building—it hasn't been touched since the 70s and is really, well, *brown*—so I figured some plants would brighten things up."

I want to reach out, to wipe the pesto away as well as any thoughts of sophisticated Sabine and her succulent garden.

"That was so thoughtful," I say, deciding that a succulent garden is superior to earrings featuring a mobster's face. Chris's gift to me was something silly, a joke between friends. His gift to Sabine was special and heartfelt.

Oh, God. Maybe the high school girls were right. Maybe Mr. Little and Mademoiselle Lavigne *are* in love.

Chapter Fifty-Nine

I open my eyes on Christmas morning, struck by the cold and stillness of my apartment. I eye the empty spot beside me, feeling immensely lonely.

After dinner last night, Chris stayed to watch *Home Alone*, but my holiday cheer had been dashed by the succulent garden revelation. It was silly that a little garden, one that likely included prickly cacti and too much aloe, had soured my mood, but I just couldn't shake my disappointment. Judging by Chris's concerned glances, he knew something was wrong, but he probably chalked it up to my MS, assuming I was tired, disoriented, or *insert MS symptom here.*

I shift to my right and carefully pull Tony Soprano out of his cocoon deep within the blankets and covers.

"Merry Christmas, buddy," I say, kissing his head.

Caught halfway between slumber and wakefulness, Tony nuzzles against me, making a satisfied whimper that sounds more like a purr.

With bleary eyes, I leash up Tony and take the two of us outside. The sidewalks are untouched, the snow hitting just below my knees. The roads are a mess of packed-down snow and ice, and I wonder if Dad will be able to pick me up after all. What if I have to spend Christmas Day all by myself? It isn't like I can hang out with Chris Little again. Besides, he's probably taking his Subaru out to fetch Mademoiselle Lavigne. He got stuck with me last night, but I'm sure he'll find a way to see his *true* beloved today.

Back inside, Tony Soprano receives a proper holiday breakfast of canned meaty morsels over plain white rice, and I make myself a pot of peppermint mocha-flavored coffee. I take my coffee to the sofa and turn on *Rick Steves' European Christmas* to lift my spirits.

Christmas as an adult always makes me nostalgic for Christmas as a child.

I miss waking up at dawn, deliriously excited to run down the steps with Mattie and Justin and survey our spread. A French toast casserole would already be baking in the oven, filling the entire house with the scents of vanilla and cinnamon, and the hardwood floors would feel cold against our bare feet.

I should have made myself a French toast casserole this morning.

As I drink my warm coffee and watch Rick Steves traipse through a European Christmas market, I try to conjure some of those warm and fuzzy feelings from Christmases past. I'll never forget the year I got my American Girl Doll (Kit Kittredge, a Cincinnati gal!) or when Dad wheeled in Justin's first bike and my brother performed the most bizarre celebration dance, complete with fist pumping. (I'm happy to report this was all caught on Mom's camcorder.)

I feel a sudden pang of longing for those simpler times. Then, I feel an even deeper sadness at the realization that Christmas will never be like that again. Mom and Dad are moving to a condo. Justin, Katie, and Violet are thousands of miles away in Santa Fe. Mattie and Peter will soon start their own family, only dropping into ours when it's convenient.

And what about me?

My gaze rests on the binder sitting on my dining room table, the binder where my ideas are beginning to take shape and my dreams are starting to resemble a possible path forward. I think of next year's Christmas. What if the Kickerville line is launched by then, and I have my own tiny house? I imagine it parked in Mom and Dad's new driveway, wherever that may be, or even in front of Justin and Katie's white stucco ranch.

I feel a rush of comfort, a thrill of hope.

Maybe my own weary world will soon be rejoicing.

-*-

As it turns out, Dad doesn't need to drive all the way from the west side to get me because Peter and Mattie insist on swinging by instead.

"My heroes!" I exclaim, nearly slipping on the ice and thinking how refreshing it is to have almost fallen for normal reasons. I neatly stack my gifts in Mattie's trunk. "Thank you so much for picking me up!"

"No problem," Peter says, looking jolly in a bright red sweater.

I'm glad to see my future brother-in-law is behind the wheel. Mattie is an excellent driver, but she gets too tense in inclement weather.

"How was your Christmas Eve?" Mattie asks, turning around in her seat. She's wearing a pair of diamond earrings that seem to catch every ray of sunlight. I wonder if they were a Christmas gift from Peter.

"It was better than expected," I say, which is mostly the truth. "Chris, my neighbor, came over for dinner and a movie. He couldn't make it to his family's gathering either because of the storm."

Mattie and Peter exchange wide eyes. Ugh. "Now *that* sounds romantic," my sister says. "A Christmas Eve date during a snowstorm."

"Very cozy," Peter adds.

"I'm pretty sure he's involved with someone else," I say, sounding like my mother. "And she's French."

Mattie narrows her eyes. "Why are you so sure of that?"

"That she's French? Because—"

"No. That he's interested in her."

Because a group of high school girls told me, I think. Plus, Mademoiselle Lavigne is gorgeous. And Chris gifted her a succulent garden.

"I just know," I reply.

Remembering my mobster earrings, I pull them out of my lobes, stowing them safely in the smallest pocket of my handbag. I don't feel like explaining my James Gandolfini studs to my sister, or God forbid, my mother.

I decide to turn the tables on Mattie. "So, will this be your final Christmas in Hyde Park? Will you be hosting us all in your west side McMansion next year?"

Mattie grows quiet, but Peter sneaks a wink at me. "I hope so," he says. "It's your sister that's the holdup here."

"I don't know if I can give up the walkability we have now," she says, her grip tightening on her handbag. Mattie and Peter can walk to shops, bars, and restaurants in Hyde Park. The streets are lined with towering, old trees, and the neighborhood has a lively square. "There aren't even sidewalks in Mom and Dad's neighborhood."

"I guess because they don't get much traffic," I muse. "But did you hear about the new coffee shop? A girl I went to high school with is opening it."

"Wait, really?" Mattie looks intrigued. "Where?"

"Just down the road from Mom and Dad's on Weber Lane," I tell her. "So, you could walk there. It sounds like they're planning to revitalize that little strip of shops. As of now, it could include a pho restaurant, pet supply store, and 1930s speakeasy-style bar."

Peter raises his faint eyebrows towards my sister. "What do you think of that, Matt?"

"I think you need to send me your sources," she says to me, though a smile is tugging at the corner of her lips.

Chapter Sixty

"Hey, honeybee." Dad greets me at the door, wrapping me in a big hug. "How are you feeling, kiddo?"

"Good. I've already had my morning flushing, so no one has to watch my skin turn all red and scary." I poke the polar bear on his stomach. "Love your sweater," I say.

Dad's worn the same wool sweater with a fluffy, white polar bear drinking a bottle of Coca-Cola for as long as I can remember.

"Wouldn't be Christmas without it."

Mom nearly knocks me over with the force of her hug. "I hate that you spent Christmas Eve alone," she says.

"She didn't," Mattie reports. "Her neighbor *Chris* joined her."

"Oh?" Mom eyes me curiously.

"We're just friends, err, neighbors," I say.

"Well, friendship can blossom into romance," says Mom, which makes me crinkle my nose. She wipes her hands on the smart, white apron tied neatly around her neck and waist. "Coffee, hot tea, or a cranberry mimosa?"

"I overdid it on the coffee this morning," I say. "A cranberry mimosa for me, please."

"Did you see Mary Ellen Stooplemeyer's Christmas display?" Mom trills, filling a crystal champagne flute with champagne. (She always refers to Mrs. Stooplemeyer by her first name, even though the women have essentially known each other for their entire lives.) I shake my head. "She dressed Santa and Mrs. Claus up as a bride and groom! Like she's the only one planning a wedding this year!"

"That sounds cute," I say, which almost gets my mimosa confiscated before I've even taken a sip.

"What can I help with?" Mattie asks, surveying the tidy kitchen. "Want me to set the table?"

Naturally, Mom already set the table days ago, and she insists we all simply relax. I can smell the egg casseroles baking and the salty, savory scent of bacon and sausage patties roasting in the oven. There's a big bowl of fresh fruit set out and a basket of warm, flaky croissants. Mom never lets Mattie or me bring anything for Christmas brunch. "It's a day I want to spoil my children," she says.

We eat within the hour. Mom and Dad sit at opposite ends of the table while Mattie, Peter, and I sit in between. The three empty chairs glare at us, the absence of their rightful occupants felt most heavily on Christmas.

"Did I tell you guys Justin had me write a letter to Violet on behalf of the stork?" I ask. Talking about my brother and his sweet little family always helps in times like these. Everyone shakes their heads, looking amused. "I guess Violet has been asking for a baby brother or sister."

Mom, Dad, Mattie, and Peter all laugh.

"Let me guess, Justin wanted the stork to let her down gently," Mattie says, spooning more fruit on her plate. Mom inherited her own mother's Spode Christmas tree china, and she gets the entire set out for Christmas Eve and Christmas Day.

"I hope you did no such thing," Mom says. "I want more grandchildren."

I explain how I danced around the topic. I did as Justin asked, saying how all families were different, but I also included a note of encouragement. "I told her that you just never know when the stork will change her mind."

After brunch, we settle into the family room. Dad lights a proper fire while Peter turns on TBS' twenty-four-hour marathon of *A Christmas Story*. I play the role of Santa Claus, parceling out the assortment of gifts nestled beneath the two-story-tall Christmas tree.

I can't help but think of the Littles' Christmas tree with its colored lights and mismatched ornaments. I would never tell Mom this, but I prefer their spirited spruce over Mom's silver-and-gold bauble-filled tree. It looks like a decoration from a department store, too formal and too uniform. Too perfect.

Mom loves the plum-colored sweater I knitted her. Mattie adores the matching earrings and necklace I beaded. Peter thinks my carved bottle opener is awesome (the oak piece is engraved with his last name and easily mounts to a kitchen wall), and Dad says the log cabin-style birdhouse I crafted is incredible.

"It looks like our camp in the Adirondacks," he marvels, referring to their Kickerville-constructed lakeside cottage. It was Dad's final project before he retired, and he and Mom are looking forward to spending more time there once Mom's retired as well.

"That was the point," I laugh.

The jaunty notes of "We Wish You a Merry Christmas" surprise us all. Someone is at the door, ringing Mom and Dad's holiday-themed bell.

"I bet it's Mr. Watson," Mom says. "He hasn't dropped off the fruit basket yet."

Mr. Watson always hand delivers a fruit basket on Christmas Day.

"I'll get it." I hop up from where I've been sitting on the floor, smoothing out my accordion skirt. Mr. Watson is the sweetest old man, and he has the bushiest mustache I've ever seen. You can barely tell he has a mouth beneath the wiry, gray sheath.

But when I swing open the front door, it isn't Mr. Watson and his fruit basket.

"OH MY GOD!" I squeal, the happy tears immediate. "JESUS CHRIST!"

Mom, Dad, Mattie, and Peter scramble to their feet. Either Mr. Watson's brought one heck of a fruit basket, our Lord Jesus Christ has returned on Christmas Day, or something else entirely is going down on the front porch.

"Beezus!" Justin grins. Katie stands beside him, a huge smile across her own face, and Violet holds her tiny hands over her cheeks, delighted by this giant surprise. "Merry Christmas," Justin is able to say before he, Katie, and Violet are nearly tackled with hugs, kisses, exclamations, and tears.

Jeez louise, there are a lot of tears!

I sweep Violet in my arms. She smells like peanut butter and sugar cookies. "How did you ever keep such a big secret?" I ask her.

"It was *so* hard, Aunt Beezus," she says bravely.

"Yes, it's been a very hard twenty-four hours for Violet." Katie rolls her eyes, kissing my cheek. Her thick, black hair is woven into a gorgeous braid, and her eyes look bright despite cross-country travel. "We didn't tell her until we were leaving for the airport."

"My sweet Violet!" Mom exclaims, taking her turn loving on her only grandchild. She gathers Violet in her arms and kisses her cheeks, her nose, her forehead. "Look how much you've grown." My parents haven't been out to Santa Fe since August.

"Gramma! Are you crying?" Violet asks, alarmed. All of our eyes follow as our mother is decidedly *not* a crier.

"I'm just so happy to see you." Mom dabs at her wet eyes. "This is the best Christmas present we could ask for."

"Did you hear that?" She looks at her parents. "I'm a Christmas present! The *best* Christmas present!"

"You're the best Christmas present I've ever received, that's for sure," I tell her.

"All right, folks. Let's not give the child a complex," Justin teases before lowering his voice. "She's already an only child, so we're treading lightly here."

Dad and Peter help Justin with the family's luggage, and we all traipse inside, finally feeling whole.

"We were supposed to be here last night, but then the storm blew in," Katie explains.

"A once-in-a-century blizzard," Justin sighs. "What dumb luck."

"But you're here now," I say. "And you get to enjoy a rare white Cincinnati Christmas." Mattie makes everyone hot cocoa, the adults' mugs spiked with Bailey's, and we all gather around the fire. Violet climbs into my lap, resting her sticky head of hair on my chest. Only a few minutes later, I can feel the happy hum of Violet's light snores. A small smile is spread across her face.

"Look at Violet," Katie says, looking content herself wrapped in a blanket and tucked into an armchair. Justin is sandwiched between Mom and Dad on the sofa, and I think it's taking all of Mom's willpower not to hold him the way I'm hugging my niece. "I don't think she's slept that soundly in months."

"Tell her doctor we've found a cure to the night terrors," Justin says. "We just need her aunt to move out to Santa Fe."

I may never meet The One.

I may never have my own children.

But I have this wonderful niece of mine, this most interesting, most marvelous little person who will grow up and become a most interesting, most marvelous big person.

And maybe that's enough.

Chapter Sixty-One

I end up spending the night at Mom and Dad's—Janet is a saint and takes care of Tony Soprano for the evening—and Mattie and Peter do, too. It's the first time all eight of us have slept under one roof. Even though we've had a few family vacations since Violet was born, Justin and Katie tend to rent a separate space for their little brood.

It's disorienting to wake up in my childhood bedroom the next morning, my polka dot-patterned sheets wrapped around me and a constellation of glow-in-the-dark stars stuck on the ceiling above me. I stare over at my workbench, a Kickerville hand-me-down Dad transformed into a makeshift art studio for my fifteenth birthday. He added nooks, hooks, and shelves for all my supplies and hung wire over the workspace so I could display my artwork. "Do you think I'll be a famous painter someday? The next Mary Cassatt?" I'd asked him, deep in an Impressionist phase. Even though I'm pretty sure Dad had no idea who Mary Cassatt was, he smiled, "I think you'll do something creative, that's for sure."

Maybe that something creative is a tiny house line for Kickerville.

The notion is perfect and satisfying, like that final puzzle piece clicking into place.

I pull a high school hoodie over my head and give a good yawn and stretch before heading downstairs. I'm surprised to find the first floor empty and quiet. I expected to find Mattie already up for the day ("I can't sleep past six!" she would say brightly), dusting a chandelier and preparing a frittata.

In that same spirit, I quietly gather forgotten wrapping paper and place dirty mugs in the dishwasher before starting a pot of coffee. I turn on instrumental holiday music, setting the volume to low, before pulling out the ingredients for lemon-blueberry pancakes.

Mom is the second person up. She practically floats into the kitchen already showered and dressed for the day in a pair of jeans and a burgundy sweater.

"Are you wearing perfume?" I ask, catching the faint scents of wildflowers and bergamot.

She kisses my cheek (Has my mother ever done that first thing in the morning? Who is this woman?) before pouring herself a steaming cup of coffee.

"A mother never sleeps as well as when all of her children are under one roof," she says. "And I used the new shower gel Justin and Katie got me," she adds.

Violet tumbles down the stairs a few minutes later, and the three of us enjoy a leisurely breakfast before the rest of the family wakes up.

"What happened to all your hair?" Violet asks, her mouth full of pancakes.

"I got it cut off," I say. "Didn't you notice last night?"

"I was distracted," she replies, reaching for her milk.

I hand her the plastic cup. "By all the presents?" I tease.

Violet frowns. "No. By all the love."

My mom literally presses her hands against her chest, and I wonder if the both of us are going to faint from this tender moment. "There's no way she's Justin's child," I murmur into Mom's ear, which makes her laugh out loud. Violet pouts, not quite following the joke.

Mattie and Peter give me a lift home later that morning, and from there, I throw myself deep into my tiny house project.

I switch my phone to "Do Not Disturb" mode, plop down at the dining room table, and get to work. For hours, I scan illustrations, transcribe notes, and create colorful charts. All of the information is there and complete, I just have to compile it into a narrative now. I have to bring it all together and show why Kickerville Cabin Co. should be interested in Bea Parker's tiny house line. I think of a college Rhetoric class and realize I'm making the most important argument of my life.

Around two, I take a break for a late lunch and an afternoon nap, no longer able to focus through the MS fatigue, but I pick back up later that evening. I keep going.

And so, at half past seven, I find myself staring at an impressive stack of printouts. Part of me is afraid they might simultaneously combust, like they'll be hit with a wayward Harry Potter spell if I look away for just a second. Another part of me worries they don't exist at all. What if I'm dreaming?

I slowly run my fingertips along the edges.

No, this is real.

My tiny house proposal is complete.

I decide I'll present my project to Mattie tomorrow evening. Our family is having a proper Sunday dinner and cooking Grandma Hazel's fried chicken recipe. Considering the Parker family's satisfied stomachs and happy hearts, I figure I'll have a receptive crowd. And what marvelous timing having my brother in town! Sure, Justin left Kickerville years ago, but I bet he can offer smart feedback and help smooth any wrinkles in my proposal.

I had hoped to finish my project by the end of the year, but I didn't know how doable that was when I first started. And now here I am, with a binder full of crisp paper and big ideas. Ready to rock.

I pick up the proposal and hug it against my chest. *Done.*

When was the last time I felt this proud of a project? It certainly wasn't at Polly Feinstein. My projects there all involve designing advertisements to sell people items they don't *really* need, like overpriced face creams and Bluetooth speakers for your shower. My work is occasionally fun, but it never feels rewarding. And while my crafts make me happy, it isn't like I've ever finished a macramé planter and thought, "My life's work is complete!"

No, I don't think I've ever felt so satisfied with something that I, Bea Parker, created.

This tiny house proposal required me to do careful research, from learning the history of the tiny house movement to gaining a better understanding of popular vehicles' towing capacities. I taught myself how to sketch a proper blueprint, something that wasn't as simple as they made it look in the movies.

I forced myself to look at the project from a marketing point of view, and I had to poke holes in my own proposal to make sure others could not. I studied every Kickerville brochure at length to understand the company's current offerings and capabilities. I went the extra mile to ensure my tiny homes are as environmentally sound as possible, that they'll help ease the human burden so many of us are placing on Mother Earth.

And I did all of this despite my multiple sclerosis.

The fatigue, the difficulty focusing and just plain *thinking*, the distracting tingling in my limbs, the frequent trips to the bathroom, the dizziness, the clumsiness...even the uncomfortable flushing...none of that had stopped me.

I can do hard things.

And I will continue to do them, too.

Chapter Sixty-Two

I turn on a Taylor Swift playlist and pull Tony Soprano out of his dog chalet. I hold one of his paws out while cradling his warm body against my chest, doing a little celebration dance with my dachshund.

We're dancing like that, with lots of twirls and hops, when someone knocks on my door. "Coming!" I shout over Taylor's 2006 hit "Our Song," a tune that always brings me back to my teenage years.

I pad to the front door, turning the music down on my way. When I open the door, my heart practically soars outside my chest at the sight of Chris Little.

"Hey, Bea. I hope this isn't a bad time. I tried texting you a few hours ago, but I'm sort of desperate." Chris's face is bashful, and he's clutching a pair of dress slacks. "Do you know how to sew on a button?"

"You came to the right place," I say, wondering if he could be any cuter. I motion him inside.

Visibly relieved, Chris smiles and follows me into my apartment.

I set Tony back on the hardwood floor, and he wiggles in Chris's direction, eager to properly greet our neighbor. "Sorry I missed your text. I spent all day finishing my tiny house project." I break into a huge smile, my voice nearly cracking. Instinctively, I reach for his forearms, giving them an excited squeeze. "It's ready, Chris! It's done!"

Chris is sitting on the ground while Tony Soprano bombards him with dog kisses. "That's fantastic news!" he says, and I can tell he is just as excited as I am. "Tell me everything! I want the full proposal, the entire presentation!" He pauses, maybe noticing my nerves. "Please?"

"Yeah! Of course," I say, thrilled but also anxious over the prospect of someone hearing my full proposal for the first time. What if Chris thinks it's stupid? What if he's quick to point out its flaws, proving it isn't such a strong concept after all?

I take my binder and stand in front of the kitchen counter while Chris takes a seat at the dining room table.

"I present to you Beahives," I say with a flourish. "A new tiny house line specially designed for Kickerville Cabin Co."

Chris is already clapping. "Beahives!" he repeats.

"Beahives," I confirm. "You know, like beehives... Safe, little spaces..." I place a hand on my chest. "*Bea...*"

"I understood it immediately." His grin only grows larger. "I think the name is brilliant. Very clever."

I flip to the first page, starting with a brief overview of the tiny house movement. This section is a result of dozens of interviews with current tiny house owners and countless hours spent watching tiny house shows. I read three different books on the topic and did a whole bunch of googling.

"I can skip the marketing analysis," I say, turning past the slew of pages that include pie charts and trend graphs. "That part's probably pretty boring..."

Chris shakes his head. "No, please don't. I want to hear all of it."

And so for the next thirty minutes, Chris intently listens to my Beahives proposal. It's easy to imagine what a star student he must have been by his bright eyes and quiet nods. It's even easier to imagine what a marvelous teacher he is now. I can picture him sitting in the back of a classroom during his students' presentations, giving them encouraging smiles and looking at them like what they have to say is of immense importance.

"I can't believe you have models with dry weights under three thousand pounds," he says as I'm going over the specs.

I explain how I turned to the camper world for help. "There are a lot of lightweight travel trailers on the road, many of which have small kitchens and bathrooms, so I knew it was possible." I turn to one of the models I've sketched, pointing out the aluminum in the bathroom and the vinyl flooring. "Just because these materials are lightweight doesn't mean they can't look nice. You only have to get a little more creative."

I move on to some of the pet-centric features, my personal favorite part of the proposal, and Chris chuckles at the model that features a Photoshopped Tony Soprano enjoying the yard space outside a tiny house. I've designed a retractable fencing system that can be set up within five minutes, keeping your dog safe and contained no matter where you park. Naturally, I've chosen a stunning beach setting for the Tony Soprano photo opp.

"Are you and Tony Soprano leaving me for the ocean?" Chris raises one of his unruly eyebrows.

Leaving me. I turn those two words over in my head, feeling a low thrill in my stomach.

"I think I have too many arts and crafts for full-time tiny living myself," I say, dodging the question. I don't want anyone, especially Mattie, thinking I designed myself a future home. I did this project with Kickerville in mind, and if I end up going tiny myself, so be it. "But maybe a vacation home someday. You know, when I'm middle-aged and rich."

"Ah, yes. Middle-aged and rich." Chris nods, still smiling. "Exactly what this high school science teacher will be."

"So, this is the part of the proposal I think you'll be most excited about." Proudly, I turn the page. "Sustainable living." His eyes widen, and he sits up a little straighter. (It's adorable.) "Okay, Mr. Environmental Superhero. Here we go."

I went to all lengths to make my Beahives shine in this sector. And while I told myself it was because I was catering to tiny house enthusiasts' desire to live off the grid and leave a smaller impact on the earth, my heart knows I did it to make Chris proud.

"Remember how we talked about reclaimed materials on Christmas Eve?" I ask. He nods enthusiastically. "Each Beahive will include a minimum of 25% repurposed goods. Whether that's lumber from a torn-down barn or a vintage cabinet turned into a bathroom vanity, I'm excited to be more eco-friendly *and* inject a bit of old-world charm into such a modern concept."

"Did I tell you how brilliant you are?" Chris grins. "I think I already did, but it deserves repeating."

Brilliant. Chris thinks I'm brilliant.

When I conclude my impromptu presentation, I give a small bow for dramatic effect. Chris leaps out of his seat and applauds, which is much appreciated. Tony Soprano yips and spins around, picking up on the excitement.

"Bea!" Chris exclaims, walking toward me so there are only a few inches between our faces. I want to hug him, to smell his skin and feel his hair against my face. "You're extraordinary. The proposal is incredible... It's smart, innovative, and thorough. You've thought through every detail."

"Well, thank you! I hope Mattie thinks so, too." I blush, looking down at our feet. Chris is wearing sneakers, while I'm wearing my outlandish French bulldog slippers. "It was fun." *It was fun?* I'm not good at accepting compliments and quickly try to change the topic entirely. "So, what about this button?"

Chris stares at my face for a full five beats, making my entire body radiate with heat.

Finally, he gives his head two small shakes. "Yes, the button that brought me here," he says. "But Bea? The tiny house proposal. It's stellar. You should know that."

"Thank you," I say, this time adding, "I worked really hard on it."

"I know you did," he says. "And it shows."

Chris pulls a round tortoise button from the front pocket of his jeans and holds up a pair of black slacks. "I only own one pair of nice pants," he explains. "And I'm supposed to wear them to my family's Christmas celebration tomorrow. My mom is insisting on hosting a small redo now that they're back from Michigan."

"My sewing supplies are in my bedroom." I think of my bed, which is also located in the bedroom. "Can you grab us two glasses of water? I'm feeling a little parched."

While Chris rummages through my disorganized kitchen cabinets, I do a quick scan of my sleeping quarters. My bed is made (admittedly, a rarity), and there's nothing embarrassing sitting out, like my mouthguard or a half-eaten chocolate bar.

"Here you go." Chris enters my bedroom, looking like he's always belonged there. He hands me a glass embossed with a vintage Coca-Cola logo. "I chose this glass for you because you're classic, cool, and bubbly."

I stand there beaming like a fool, too touched to use actual words.

"This is an amazing space," he says.

I love my bedroom. Every piece of furniture is a flea market find, and the walls are a pretty lavender. My bedspread is soft and embroidered, and my curtains are decorated with colorful tassels. My sewing machine lives on an antique desk in front of the window, making it a perfect spot for early-morning coffee while working on projects.

Chris stares at the oil painting above my dresser. "Awesome still life," he says. The painting features an assortment of fruit, bread, and cheese resting on a butcher block. The window in the backdrop is open, its curtain rustling in the breeze, and a storm blows in over a blue-gray sea.

"It might be why I'm always hungry," I realize.

I motion for Chris to sit on the bed behind me. I set his slacks in my lap and reach for my sewing basket. "Normally, I would use my sewing machine, but all you really need is a needle and thread," I say. "Even my brother can sew on a button, so I'm confident you'll get the hang of it quickly."

Chris leans forward, and I can hear his breathing. Am I imagining it, or are his breaths quicker, shallower? Does he feel as unsteady as I do? All I want right now is to turn around and crawl on top of him.

Steadying my hands, I reattach Chris's button, detailing the process as I go, and return his sole pair of dress slacks to their former glory.

"And there you have it," I say, my shaky voice betraying me. "There are a ton of YouTube tutorials out there, but, um, I'm always happy to help. And I've always got sewing supplies."

Chris holds up his pants and eyes them with a newfound wonder, as though I'm the girl in Rumpelstiltskin who can turn straw into gold. "You're incredible, a tiny house creator and seamstress extraordinaire. Thank you so much," he says. "I don't think my mom would have appreciated me wearing jeans to Christmas. Even if it is a redo."

I feel proud that I was able to help Chris with his minor wardrobe dilemma.

"No problem! All in a day's work," I reply.

But between us? I am pleased as punch.

Chapter Sixty-Three

"Would you like to come to my place?" Chris's words come out so quickly, it takes me a few seconds to comprehend what he's just asked. Before I can say *you betcha*, he adds, "I owe you a drink. And while your Peppermint White Russians are a tough act to follow, I do make a mean spiked eggnog."

"I love spiked eggnog," I say.

"Me too."

We sit there like that, Chris on the edge of my bed, me turned around in my sewing chair, just smiling at one another, before Tony Soprano barks from the living room.

"Does Tony want to come?" Chris asks.

"No, Tony will be fine." I look down at my French bulldog slippers. "Just let me put on a pair of real shoes, and I'll be right down."

I tell Chris I'll be there in five minutes, and you can bet I make the most of those three hundred seconds. I'm able to pee, brush my hair, brush my teeth, and put on some makeup. Then, I swap out my slippers for a pair of mules and practically sprint out the front door.

Janet sticks her head outside her front door while I'm locking mine.

"Bea!" she whispers, her heavily lined eyes wide. "I just spotted Mr. Geek Chic leaving your place! What's the sitch?"

"He needed a button sewed on," I say, smiling at the thought that Chris came to me for help. "And now he's invited me down for a spiked eggnog."

Janet pumps a fist into the air. "You go, girl!"

I scramble down the flight of stairs and then take a deep breath before knocking.

"Come on in!" Chris calls. "The door's unlocked."

I push the door forward and walk into the apartment I've wondered so much about. Logically, I know it must be set up just like mine, but I can't wait to see the books that line Chris's shelves, the artwork he displays on the walls, and if he keeps his place messy or neat. My first thought is that it smells like quesadillas, which is probably what Chris had for dinner, and my second is the realization that he has David Bowie playing.

Chris is standing in the kitchen, a tea towel draped over one shoulder and two short glasses in front of him. The countertops are remarkably empty with the exception of a coffee maker, green compost bin, and knife block. Above the sink is one of those clocks that looks like a cat, its tail swaying back and forth while making a satisfying *tick-tick-tick* sound.

"Welcome to Casa de Chris," he says, giving the milky drinks a rapid stir. "Take a seat. I'll bring these over."

I survey the living room setup, which includes an olive green canvas loveseat and two rocking chairs. An unexpected combination. I choose the comfier-looking couch and sit down, crossing my left leg over my right. There's a brass, 1980s-style floor lamp with a yellowed shade and an Ikea bookcase stuffed with so many books, I fear it might collapse at any moment. The only holiday decoration is the tabletop Christmas tree. It rests on the entertainment cabinet, partially obstructing the TV screen.

Between us? Chris's apartment has major starving-grad-student-meets-bachelor-pad vibes.

"I know it's pretty hodgepodge," he says, making me instantly regret my internal critiques. "I left most of my furniture behind after Amanda and I split. This is all from my parents' basement."

"What? No! Your place is great." I shake my head, accepting the cool glass. There's an image of Princess Leia on the front. "Give me a tour of the rest of your apartment? I've only seen Janet's unit, and I'm so curious."

We grab our drinks, and I follow Chris into the dining room. First, he shows me SpongeBob, who now lives in a large, blue-topped terrarium. There's a miniature beach scene set up for the hermit crab, which includes a few fake palm trees and a sun chair alongside real plants, seashells, and pieces of bark.

It's definitely an upgrade. "This little crab sure got lucky scoring you as his new owner."

Chris then shows me the bathroom. It matches mine exactly, down to the vintage pink and green tiles, and I'm pleasantly surprised to see how clean he keeps it. No toilet bowl ring or strange hairs (ick!) sticking to the shower wall. He keeps a bottle of Listerine on the sink as well as an electric toothbrush.

Chris's bedroom is just as tidy. He has a queen-sized bed, two oak nightstands, and a tall dresser. There's a movie poster for *The Empire Strikes Back* above his bed (yikes) and a Yoda-themed alarm clock (double yikes). The comforter looks like something out of an L.L. Bean catalog with all of its navy and green plaid, and I appreciate the generous stack of books on one of the bedside tables. I picture pulling Chris over to the bed this very instant, sending the books toppling over in our urgency, and the thought sends a shiver down my spine.

A very noticeable shiver apparently, since Chris asks, "Brain freeze?"

I swallow. "Yep. I must have been drinking too fast..."

"I know just the solution." Chris reaches for my empty hand and pulls me toward the kitchen.

We're holding hands, we're holding hands, we're holding hands, I buzz.

Once in the kitchen, Chris opens various cabinet doors, grabbing a box of graham crackers, Andes mints, and jumbo-sized marshmallows. "Mint s'mores," he says. He finds two metal skewers more likely intended for shish kabobs and hands one to me. "My mom used to do this with us when we were kids."

With a flick of his wrist, Chris ignites the first burner on his gas stovetop. He suspends his marshmallow just over the blue and orange flame, gently charring its edges.

With the exception of the floor lamp in the living room, it's dark in Chris's apartment, and I love watching the way the flame illuminates his face. He has the beginnings of a dark, coarse beard, and his nose is big and slightly crooked. I determine Chris has one of the most handsome faces I've ever seen.

"Come on. Give it a try," he coaxes.

I hover my marshmallow over the flame, though not as expertly as

Chris. My marshmallow immediately catches fire.

"Rookie mistake," Chris teases.

I quickly blow out the flames before smooshing the blackened piece of fluff between a pair of graham crackers and a single Andes mint. Chris holds my gaze as I take a bite of the gooey creation. "Delicious," I say, sounding garbled. "A combination as timeless as PB&J."

The corners of his mouth lift, but his eyes don't look playful. They spark with a sudden intensity, a subtle sensuality. Quietly, Chris lifts his thumb to the corner of my mouth, wiping away a piece of marshmallow.

"Thanks," I murmur.

"Did you know you have three freckles on the back of your neck?" he asks.

I shake my head, instinctively reaching for the area just below my hairline.

"They make a sort of pattern. There are two small ones with a larger one in the middle," he says. "I think they're beautiful."

Now hardly able to breathe, I find myself moving towards Chris.

Oh my God: is this finally happening?

But then Sabine's beautiful face flashes in my head.

Damnit.

"What about Mademoiselle Lavigne?" I whisper, unable to help myself.

Chris steps back, looking bemused and slightly disturbed. "What about her?"

I've probably ruined the moment, but I'm not about to add boyfriend stealer to my resume. I am in no position to mess around with karma.

"Your students told me you two are in love," I say, stepping backward and feeling the countertop hit against my back. "They said you've been spotted at the movies together, and, um, you gave her that succulent garden. Plus, I saw her, and she's gorgeous. And French. I mean, I totally get it! I'm just a boring American, from the Midwest no less, and my legs certainly don't go up to *here*, and—"

"Bea, no." My entire body goes hot as Chris gently lifts my chin. "It's not like that. Honestly, I'm pretty sure it's illegal in most states."

I shake my head. "I'm sorry, but *what?*"

"Sabine is my mom's cousin's daughter. What does that make us— third cousins? I don't know. Something like that." He shrugs. "But I can assure you, Sabine and I are not romantically involved. This isn't a Roosevelt situation."

"Holy cow," I marvel, trying to wrap my mind around all of it. Also? Maybe I shouldn't have considered a group of high school girls the most reliable source of information. "But you don't even look alike!"

"Do you look like your third cousins?" Chris asks.

"I don't even know who my third cousins are," I admit.

"Sabine's dad took a work assignment in France when she was a toddler. Her parents moved back to Cincinnati years ago, and our mothers rekindled their friendship. So, when Sabine returned, my mom asked if I would grab coffee with her and see about any French teacher openings in my district," he explains. "Sabine and I have become great friends, but I can assure you, there's nothing romantic between us."

I take a deep breath, my entire body shaking with amusement and just plain relief. "You have no idea how happy I am to hear that," I say.

"Yeah?" Chris's voice turns low and gravelly.

"Yes," I whisper.

He bends his head down towards mine—finally, *finally*—and our lips brush. Chris wraps his arms around me, his hands moving from my lower back to my sides before pulling me even closer to him. I run my hands through his thick, curly hair and bury my face in his neck, wanting to take in every touch, every scent. His five o'clock shadow bristles against my own cheeks; it's a sensation that feels masculine and thrilling. I'm literally pulsing with pleasure and anticipation, and the area between my thighs grows warm. Have I ever physically wanted someone this badly? I'm desperate for Chris's hands to keep exploring me, and I want to discover every part of him.

"Is this okay?" he asks. His eyes are big and dark. They're full of lust, but there's also a gentleness there, too.

I swallow. "Uh-huh. It's okay."

Obviously, I am more than okay with this.

Our mouths open, and we make out in the kitchen before moving towards the living room, running into the corner of the countertop and then knocking over a stack of textbooks in our fervor. We giggle between kisses, and I determine this is absolute ecstasy, total bliss.

Chris lowers me to the loveseat, graciously setting a throw pillow beneath my head. He kisses my neck and my chest, which makes me go wild, but just when I think he's about to go further, he abruptly stops.

"Is everything all right?" I ask, breathless and flushed. Chris is braced over me.

He leans on the backs of his calves.

His eyes turn apologetic.

My heart falls.

Chris rubs a hand along his neck. "I'm sorry," he says. "It's just..."

I study his face, he's clearly at a loss for words, and I stupidly try to supply them. "Is this too much?" I ask. "Are you not ready to start something new?"

Every physical insecurity runs through my head. My bizarre haircut. My wide hips. My short, unmanicured nails. My rough, calloused heels. The cellulite on my butt and thighs. (I mean, not that he's seen it, but maybe he just assumes?)

Oh, yeah. And that little thing known as the disease of my central nervous system.

Please tell me I'm wrong, I think. *Please say you only want to go brush your teeth or something ridiculous.*

Chris falters, and it's all I need to know.

"I'd better go," I say, standing up too quickly and losing my balance. How humiliating.

Chris scrambles to his feet. "Bea, I'm so sorry. I'm just really confused right now..."

I snort. "Obviously. You dated a woman for eight years and still couldn't make a decision on her." It's unfair of me to bring up the situation now, to throw it in his face like this, but I can't help myself. "And you're still letting your twin sister run your dating life," I add. "Honestly? My life is complicated enough right now. I'm not sure this is right for me either."

Chris turns red in the face, but I can't tell if he's angry or embarrassed.

"I'll see you around," I murmur.

I turn to leave, having to use every bit of my willpower not to break down and cry.

Chapter Sixty-Four

Chris doesn't text or call me that night or the next morning, which only solidifies what's happened between us. I wipe away a stray tear while reheating the previous day's coffee, and then I have a complete meltdown in the shower where the water drowns out my sobs.

At least this all happened now and not eight years down the road, I rationalize.

It still hurts, though.

I feel foolish for having fallen for a guy who was so disastrously unavailable. I think of all the red flags I brazenly breezed past: recently out of a long-term relationship, alarmingly codependent relationship with twin sister, disregard for societal norms. But then I think of all the encouraging moments along the way.

All of the kindness, the thoughtfulness... He always knew how to turn my lowest moments around, usually making me laugh in the process.

Has anyone ever made me laugh like Chris does?

I shake my head. *Stop thinking about all of that. He isn't interested in you.*

But if it hadn't been for Chris, would I have ever landed on my tiny house idea? Maybe that was the universe's reason for introducing him into my life. Perhaps Chris was just an emissary of sorts, shepherding me in the direction of my dream job, and I foolishly developed feelings for him along the way.

Only I would go and fall for my envoy from the heavens.

I decide to take Violet to the grocery store with me to grab a few items for my tiny house presentation tonight: a bottle of nice champagne, goat cheese, fancy crackers, and red pepper jelly. Maybe the champagne is presumptuous, but I feel good about this. My relationship with Chris is completely wrecked, but that doesn't mean my tiny houses are toast. This hope keeps my heart afloat.

"Aunt Beezus?" Violet tugs on my coat sleeve. "I hate goat cheese." She points at the offending log of soft cheese.

"It's definitely an acquired taste. I don't think I liked it until I was in college," I acquiesce. "What kind of cheese do you like best?"

"String cheese." Per her request, I've braided her fine hair into two pig-tails. She chews on the end of one, her brown eyes big and curious.

"Then we'll get some string cheese," I reply, to which she claps happily. "And some sparkling apple juice so you can make a toast with us."

"Apple juice on my toast?" Violet crinkles her nose. "Gross! Mama puts butter and cinnamon on my toast. That's my favorite."

Jeez louise, this child is a delight. And she's exactly who I need to bring me out of my Chris Little despair. "This is a different kind of toast, where you raise a glass of something fizzy and celebrate a special occasion," I explain, trying not to giggle. "Are you interested in participating?"

"What are we celebrating?" Violet asks, as I guide her past a display of holiday-flavored Oreo cookies.

"Well, we're celebrating your family being in town," I say. "And we're celebrating a big idea of mine."

"What's your big idea?"

I have to hand it to this girl. She wants all the intel before committing to a plan. If she keeps this discernment up, she'll save herself a lot of grief in her twenties.

"You'll just have to wait and see," I reply.

Violet may have been able to keep the surprise Cincinnati trip under wraps, but I'm not about to have my four-year-old niece spill my tiny house beans. Feeling slightly guilty for my distrust, I nod back towards the Oreos.

"Grab the double-stuffed ones," I say.

-*-

That evening at Mom and Dad's, I watch as Mattie and Peter take a formal tour of a home where Mattie once lived. Which is, you know, bizarre.

"But so much has changed," Mom insists. "We had a California Closet system installed in our bedroom. Did you know that?"

"I just put in a new ceiling fan, too," Dad boasts. "Top of the line. Feels like an ocean breeze."

"Really?" I interrupt, but no one seems to notice.

Wordlessly, Mattie gives a small shake of her head and follows them toward the primary suite. Justin hands Peter a beer. "You might need this, pal," he winks, as the foursome disappears around the corner.

"I could never live here," my brother comments, stealing a goat cheese-smeared cracker. "It would be too weird."

"It's a spectacular house," I say. "I think I could get past the weirdness, but it's so giant. There are too many places for murderers to hide. I don't think I'd sleep very well."

"You really need to cool it on the true crime podcasts," Justin says, reaching for another cracker.

I swat at his hand. "Stop eating my appetizers. They're for my tiny house line reveal."

My brother raises his eyebrows. "You're doing that tonight?"

"Yeah, and I've got approximately four hours before I take my next dose of medicine and my face turns into a giant rash. So, please keep all questions and comments to yourself until *after* the presentation. Time is of the essence."

He looks at me sadly, which I hate, so I wave him toward the family room. "Start a fire?" I ask. "I want to create a cozy ambiance."

"Sure thing," he replies.

Ten minutes later, Mom, Dad, Mattie, and Peter stroll into the kitchen, looking more like a museum tour group than house hunters. "Genuine walnut cabinetry." Dad taps against one of the doors. "You certainly don't see this very often."

"Or custom cabinets done by your father," Mom says fondly.

"It's a beautiful home," Peter says, his voice earnest. "We would be so fortunate to be its next owners."

Mattie offers a small smile. "You didn't overlook a single detail."

"I thought we would be here forever," Dad says, sounding much less boisterous than usual and more introspective. "I used to tell Eileen they'd have to carry me out feet first."

"*Dad,*" I frown, hating the very thought.

"But I didn't consider these lousy knees of mine or how much damn work it is to keep up this place," he sighs.

Mom slings her arm around his lower back. "Those knees aren't lousy. You've just put them through a lot," she says. "But this is a house for a family. Not two empty nesters. There's so much space... That backyard needs a playset."

I find this sentiment funny considering my family moved here well past the playset days.

"Soon enough," Mattie says, starting to look agitated.

"I'm just saying, after the wedding—"

"Soon enough," Mattie repeats.

I clear my throat, desperate to alleviate the tension that's quickly filling the kitchen. I do *not* want Mattie to land in a bad mood before my grand reveal. "If everyone would please join me in the family room, I have an exciting, ah, prospect to present to you," I announce.

"Sweetie, you didn't get involved in one of those pyramid schemes, did you?" Mom touches my arm, looking concerned. "Multi-level marketing takes many forms—"

"God, Mom. No," I reply. "Just go into the family room, please."

Katie and Violet, who are curled in an armchair with a coloring book, perk up. "Gramma, Aunt Beezus has a big idea she wants to tell us about!" Violet reports. "And then we're going to toast."

"It has to do with Kickerville," I preface, as my family all shuffles to their respective seats. My nerves are setting off my dizziness, so I grip the cold edges of the granite countertop and take a few centering breaths. The last thing I want to do is fall over or faint during my presentation. "Justin? Could you please grab the appetizer?"

My brother gives me an encouraging smile and carries over the tray of small bites.

I reach into my oversized bag and pull out my binder, which suddenly feels small and ridiculous. Why didn't I make a slideshow or even a quick movie? My binder is going to feel like a children's story hour in front of the group.

"I'm sorry," I start, which is probably the worst way to begin a presentation. "I should have made a poster board or something. You can pass around my binder once I'm done, though. And hopefully, my words will suffice."

Channel the Bea from last night, I encourage myself. *She only had the binder and presented just fine!*

Mattie sips on a glass of water. She looks so chic today in a pair of high-waisted jeans and a cream sweater, with simple gold hoops hanging from her delicate ear lobes. In my attempt to look like a serious but sophisticated businesswoman, I've worn a black turtleneck and black jeans, essentially turning myself into a chubby Elizabeth Holmes. But at least I'm wearing my bumblebee ring from Hannah. I twirl it around my finger, reminding myself it's there.

"Okay, so like I was saying, this is an idea...an opportunity...for Kickerville." My hands shake fiercely, and my legs begin to tingle. *Don't stress,* I warn myself.

Sensing my anxiety, Justin jumps in with his big, easy-going smile. "You're all going to love this," he says. "It's genius. Very forward-thinking."

Mattie's serious face turns into a disgruntled frown. "You told Justin about a Kickerville idea before me?" She sets her glass down on an end table. I see Mom and Dad exchange worried glances. "Why would you do that?"

I haven't heard this tone of voice from my older sister since our high school days, when we'd fight over the bathroom or argue over who could borrow Mom's vintage cowboy boots for a Friday night outing.

"I needed his advice," I say. "Oh, you'll see—"

Mattie holds up her hand, flustered. "So, wait. You want to be a part of Kickerville now?"

This isn't going at all like I expected.

"I mean, maybe... I don't want to assume anything, but..." I stammer, looking down at my pointed-toe flats, now afraid to even look my sister in the eye. "I would love for you to listen to this pitch first."

"I thought you loved your *glamorous* job in advertising," Mattie says, exaggerating glamorous in a not-so-kind way. She presses her fingertips against her right temple, looking like she has a migraine.

"Do you feel bad for me or something? Kickerville isn't a charity case. We don't need your pity."

"No! I've never thought of Kickerville as a charity case," I exclaim, my voice sounding scratchy. My thoughts are turning foggy, and I struggle to grasp them, to think of the correct words and string them into sentences.

"But, well, let me just backtrack a bit. After I was diagnosed with MS, and I'd just turned thirty, I started to re-evaluate my life. Maybe that sounds dramatic." I give a little laugh, but no one joins in. "I realized maybe graphic design isn't my dream job..."

Mattie abruptly stands up. "Kickerville doesn't have a revolving door. You and Justin don't get to come and go as you please," she snaps.

"Mattie, come on," Peter says. "Let's hear Bea's idea."

"You have no idea what it's like to run a company," she continues, her eyes moving from me to Justin. "Neither of you do."

"She's not asking to run the company, Mattie," my brother interrupts. "Will you just hear her out?"

Mattie moves her gaze back to me, looking absolutely furious.

"I think you have this idyllic vision of working at Kickerville. It isn't building birdhouses with Dad or visiting Fran's dairy cow when the weather's nice," she says. "It's dealing with unsatisfied customers, making difficult financial decisions, operating under the crushing pressure to keep a family business afloat..." Mattie's own voice cracks. She looks upward, centering herself. "You could never deal with the sort of stress that's involved."

My heart sinks. My mom audibly goes, "*Oh.*" And my dad sighs heavily. Katie excuses herself, carrying Violet out of the family room and away from the drama. "But I wanna toast!" I hear Violet whine.

"Bea doesn't deserve to be associated with my shortcomings," Justin says, his voice sharp. "This has nothing to do with me."

"She isn't talking about your shortcomings." I close my binder with a sharp *snap* and stalk toward the kitchen, where I shove my supposed "great" idea back inside my tote. "She's talking about my MS and how I could never do a job like hers because I couldn't handle it. My brain is broken, and she knows it." I think about the night I spent sobbing into her shoulder as Hallmark movies played in the background. "Mattie knows it better than anyone."

Mattie's face goes pale. She hurries towards me. "No, that wasn't—"

"It was, though." I cut her off. "And you aren't wrong."

My legs are tingling now, and before they can give out beneath me, I grab my coat and leave out the side door. Refusing to look back, I get into my car and drive away, my hands shaking and my breathing jagged.

I feel like such an idiot.

Chapter Sixty-Five

The next days pass in a sad sort of blur.

I get myself out of bed to spend time with Violet, but seeing my niece is the only thing I have energy for. I put on my happiest face as we admire the holiday train display at Union Terminal. I wear opera gloves, a floppy hat, and a floral-printed frock for afternoon tea at the BonBonerie. I hold Violet close as we watch Scuba Santa swim with the sharks at the aquarium. Understandably afraid of the whole spectacle—"But will Santa be safe?"—she only sneaks glances from behind her hands. I decide it's a pretty messed-up setup, showing kids the jolly guy in red navigating shark-infested waters, but maybe that's just the sort of headspace I'm in.

When I'm not with Violet, I'm sleeping. And when I'm not sleeping, I'm ignoring texts and calls from Hannah, Janet, and Mattie.

Why the radio silence? You haven't asked me what my crazy Auntie Diana bought me for Christmas! Hint: It has an "as seen on TV" sticker.

Earth to my sweet neighbor! What's shaking, girlfriend? I have some BIG news to share!!! Cosmos soon?

Please call me. We need to talk.

But I don't know what to say to any of them, least of all Mattie.

I feel devastated. Crushed. Like someone died.

The tiny house project was *everything* to me. My tiny houses, my Beahives, were a bright spot in an awful series of events. They were a north star of sorts, a glimmer of hope, when so many other aspects of my life had gone to shit. I'd been diagnosed with an incurable disease. I'd been tried on for size and then rejected by a guy, who by all accounts, was a catch. I'd been passed over for the big promotion at work. And then! I'd been rejected by another guy, one I had actual feelings for and really, *really* liked.

And now my older sister's rejected me, too.

Mattie was so disinterested in my idea that she hadn't even cared to hear about it. What was I thinking, springing something of that magnitude on her, on my entire family, like that? Why hadn't I typed up a business plan, emailed it to Mattie, and then asked to meet for coffee so we could discuss it? I went about everything wrong. I screwed up.

Had I really thought I could save my family's business with my silly tiny houses? How naive! How immature! How embarrassing!

When I'm not wallowing in my sadness, I'm anxious for the future.

Maybe Mattie is right. No, Mattie probably *is* right. Mattie is always right. With my MS, I can't handle the stress of a job at Kickerville. I don't have the stamina to launch a new initiative.

Maybe I'm doomed to stay a mid-level designer for the rest of my life.

Maybe I should just be grateful.

Why do I think I deserve bigger and better things? There are plenty of people who would be thankful for a job like mine. I'm simply another delusional millennial who fancies herself someone special.

Just as I feel like my head will explode from the questions, from the sheer worry of it all, my limbs start to tingle. Sometimes, I'll get dizzy and lightheaded, and my vision will begin to cloud. And then the fatigue hits. It hits *hard*. I crawl into bed where I sleep for hours. My sweet Tony Soprano understands, the way dogs somehow always do, and he stays snuggled against my side until the darkest moments pass.

God, I am tired.

I am so exhausted.

I'm tired of trying, tired of fighting. I can't shoulder another disappointment.

I am spent.

Chapter Sixty-Six

I decide to spend New Year's Eve alone.

I wanted to go to my parents' house and watch Disney movies with Justin, Katie, and Violet. I wanted to make homemade pizzas and light sparklers at ten o'clock before Violet conked out for the night.

But Mattie and Peter are going to Mom and Dad's tonight, and I have no interest in seeing my older sister.

Instead, I stand in my cluttered kitchen microwaving a quartet of White Castle sliders. I bought them from the freezer section at the grocery store, which feels especially pathetic. I've never been the type who can't stomach food during sad or stressful times. I am the type who can't get enough of it.

Forget the Mediterranean Diet. Forget Dr. Wahls and her diet, too, I think bitterly, tearing into a hamburger. I bet when Dr. Wahls first presented her protocol, it was met with applause and praise. My sister hadn't even allowed me to speak!

I gather the empty White Castles box, plus my overflowing container of other recyclables. The contents are positively tragic: ice cream pints, wine bottles, macaroni and cheese boxes. I stick a baseball hat over my oily hair and head to the basement where my building's garbage and recycling bins are located.

The sound of music and laughter inside Chris Little's apartment cracks my heart in two. The construction paper Santa Claus is still hanging on his door and is now joined by a drawing of Baby New Year.

Chris is having a party.

While I've been watching romantic comedies and sleeping and crying and binging, Chris has been planning a New Year's Eve gathering. One I wasn't invited to attend.

I hear kazoos, and Maria exclaim, "Beth! Where did you find those? Cappel's?"

I press my eyes shut, but a tear manages to escape anyway.

Beth. The single mother who Maria believes is perfect for her twin brother.

"Exactly! I popped in during my lunch hour," Beth replies. She sounds like a southern belle with her accent and twinkly laugh. I imagine Reese Witherspoon parsing out colorful noisemakers to the kids. Adorable. "Wait until you see the mini bottles of champagne I picked up. They're darling!" She's fun, too.

The basement is damp and lit by a single bulb. Each tenant has a small storage closet with a plywood "door," and thousand-leggers routinely crawl up the stone walls. Stanley stashes his "end of the world" supplies down here: expired canned goods, bottled water, flashlights, you get the picture. The space is like a scene from a horror movie, and I use this as another reason why I should move next year. Even if Mattie thinks my tiny houses are stupid, maybe Dad will help me build my own. "It'll be like building that treehouse," I imagine Dad saying, and I wonder if that's all my tiny houses were supposed to be, a fun sort of project. A hobby or craft. Why did I have to go and make them into a career?

As is typical these days, I'm hit with an overwhelming wave of embarrassment.

After I unload my pathetic assortment of recyclables, I trudge back up the stairs. I am moving at a comically slow rate, but I can't muster the energy to go any faster. When I finally arrive outside my apartment door, my breathing is struggled and jagged. I think I'm having some horrible combination of panic attack, MS flare-up, and heartbreak.

"Bea Parker?" I turn around to see Fran Bosse exiting Janet's apartment. "Kiddo, what's going on? You look terrible."

Fran Bosse is probably the least soft and fuzzy person I know, and still, I want to collapse into her arms and cry. Thankfully, Janet walks out of the apartment just then—her blue eyes matching her blue shadow, both of which perfectly match her blue sequined dress—and curiosity beats out despair.

"I know I look awful." I may as well own it. "It's my MS. My symptoms have been rough these past few days." *In a pinch, I treat my MS as a sort of scapegoat,* I'd read on an online discussion board for MS sufferers. *This disease is enough of a burden, I may as well get some benefit from it!*

"Oh, sweetie. You poor thing," Janet coos. "Why don't I grab you some of my matzo ball soup? I have a Tupperware of it in the freezer."

I'm touched by Janet's offer, but I need a heck of a lot more than matzo ball soup right now. "I'll be okay. Thanks, though. Where are you two heading tonight?" Janet looks quite fancy compared to Fran's peasant top and flared jeans.

"A dinner cruise! On BB Riverboats," my neighbor nearly squeals. "I've always wanted to go on one, and Fran surprised me with tickets for Hannukah."

Fran moves the collar of her leather jacket aside and delicately lifts a pendant necklace. "Janet gave me this necklace, and it was a tough act to follow." The necklace features a small emerald square set in sterling silver and definitely has "more pizzazz" than the hardware store gift card I suggested. "It's my birthstone. It was my Dad's birthstone, too."

"They're both Taurus bulls," Janet volunteers. "Stubborn as H-E double hockey sticks."

I smile, trying to make sense of all that is unfolding in front of me. Are Janet and Fran *romantically* involved? Excluding a lackluster boyfriend named J.T. in Fran's early thirties, I've always assumed Fran is asexual or simply has no patience for men. And as for Janet, well she has dozens of past lovers, but none of them were female. At least not to my knowledge.

Fran wags her thumb. "I'm going to get the truck started."

"Thank you," Janet says. "You know how much I hate a cold seat against my tush."

The moment we hear the lobby door click shut, I turn to Janet. "Are you and Fran dating?" I whisper, even though I know my long-time family friend is outside and can't hear us.

Janet blushes. "I can't explain it," she says.

But even if Janet can't put her thoughts into words, her feelings are evident by the smile spreading across her face. And the weirdest part is that it doesn't feel weird at all. If anything, it feels like the most natural thing in the world, like these two (very different) women were always meant to find one another.

"I've never met anyone like her before," Janet says. "I thought she was intimidating at your family's Thanksgiving, but then we went to *The Nutcracker* and she made me laugh. She made me laugh harder than anyone has in a very long time. Maybe ever."

I nod encouragingly. "Fran is very funny, even when she's not trying to be."

"When I grew up, people didn't talk much about being gay," Janet murmurs. "But maybe that's why love's never worked out for me before. Maybe I was looking at the wrong gender."

I reach for her hand and give it a squeeze. "Or maybe you like both genders," I offer. Janet looks both overwhelmed and intrigued with this concept, so I add, "Which is perfectly normal. What matters is that you've found someone special."

Janet gives me a quick nod and a big smile. "I've been trying to tell you for the past week or so, but you went radio silent on me, girlfriend," she says.

"I'm sorry about that," I sigh, swallowing a few times to keep my voice from cracking. "I haven't been my best self lately."

Janet pulls me into a hug, and I immediately know she understands a lot more is happening than an MS flare-up. "Tomorrow's a whole new year, a whole new start," she murmurs. "And honey, you're gonna be okay."

Chapter Sixty-Seven

I don't want to go hiking.

Particularly not on a January morning when the projected high for the day is a mere twenty degrees.

But Justin guilted me into the activity. "It's my last day in town," he reminded me.

"I have terrible balance. It's part of my disease," I reminded him. "And I'm out of shape. Can't we do something else? Why don't we check out that new coffee shop in Silverton?"

"Let's go to French Park. We can do a beginner's trail. It'll be fun."

Fun. I roll my eyes at the thought as Justin pulls up outside my apartment building. He's driving Dad's truck.

I've paired fleece-lined workout pants with my heaviest coat and pulled a knit cap over my three-days-since-it's-been-washed hair. All of my clothing feels tight, and my skin is starting to break out from the sugar and stress. I feel like I'm beginning the new year as the worst version of myself, both on the inside and out.

"Get in, loser. We're going hiking," Justin grins. It's a reference to *Mean Girls*, a movie I watched approximately one million times while I was in high school. "Nice hat," he says.

I smirk, touching the spirited pom-pom on top of my noggin. "Nice face," I counter.

He laughs, and we drive the few minutes to nearby French Park. Cincinnati is known for its beautiful parks, and French Park is no exception. Located in Amberley Village, just a stone's throw from Pleasant Ridge, French Park boasts rolling hills, wooded trails, creek beds, and even a stately two-story manor house, which is a popular wedding venue.

True to his word, Justin chooses a beginner's trail, and we head into the wintry forest. I forgot how magical the woods can be this time of year, the spindly tree limbs stark against the gray sky. There's still frost on the ground, and our boots make a satisfying *crunch* with each step.

"What's Violet up to today?"

"Mattie took her to one of those paint-your-own-pottery studios," Justin says.

"That's nice," I say, because it is.

We both turn quiet and inward. I focus intently on the trail ahead. While I can't always control my balance, I can at least keep an eye out for exposed tree roots and large rocks. I try to soak in the serene nature around me rather than yearn for my bed. I can already feel the fatigue building, and a haze is settling around my brain.

I am so tired.

"Should we talk about the elephant in the room?" Justin asks. He's slowed down his usual pace, which I appreciate. Not only is my brother fit, but he's also a foot taller than me.

"Which elephant?" I ask, thinking of all my recent failures.

There's a whole herd of elephants in my room.

"Kickerville. Your tiny house line," he says. "I was looking forward to hearing about it."

"Well, that makes one of you."

Justin looks at me sadly.

"Are you happy you left Kickerville? Just tell me I dodged a bullet," I say. "It will make me feel better."

We veer right, past a wayward tree branch. "I wanted to move out west, sure," he begins. "That was always my dream. But..." Justin pauses, giving me a curious sort of look. He wrinkles his nose and narrows his eyes, like he's trying to figure something out.

"But what?"

"I hate reliving this," he says quietly. He starts moving again, but his steps are more measured. Slower. "Are you messing with me, or do you really not know why I left Kickerville?"

I stare at him blankly. "I swear I'm not messing with you," I say. "What are you talking about?" I think of the anger in Mattie's voice last Sunday, the absolute fury in her eyes. I will never forget the awful things she said to me. "Mattie pushed you out, didn't she?" I snort, shaking my head. "I've wondered about it before, but..."

"What?" Justin spins around so fast, I walk right into his chest. He looks disturbed. "*No.* It was nothing like that. Bea, Dad asked me to leave Kickerville," he says, looking me straight in the eyes. "I didn't leave voluntarily."

"Wait, *what*?" I'm shocked by this revelation. And I can't picture it either. My cheerful, laidback brother was fired? By our own father? How has no one told me this before? What in the world did Justin do?

"Can we please keep walking?" he asks. "It's easier to talk about this when I'm moving."

I nod quietly and stumble to catch up, both literally and figuratively.

"I was twenty-three. A young and immature twenty-three," he clarifies.

Justin worked at Kickerville part-time throughout high school and college. He enjoyed working with his hands and had shown an early interest in Dad's business. Growing up, both Mattie and I assumed it would be Justin who would one day take things over. And after graduating college with a civil engineering degree, Justin appeared to be doing just that.

"I was a God-awful employee," Justin says. "I showed up late. I fell behind on projects. I didn't submit important documents on time, and when I finally did turn in my work, it was sloppy and half-assed."

"Oh," is all I can say.

It's difficult to think about my older brother acting that way. Sure, he's always been a goofball, but he knows when to take things seriously. I wouldn't have thought Justin could act so irresponsibly at Kickerville, at the business our father tirelessly built from the ground up. I didn't think Justin was capable of acting like that *anywhere.*

"I still get embarrassed when I think about the morning Fran Bosse chewed me out. She said I was breaking my dad's heart and to get my shit together." Justin gives me a small smile, and I return it. "Unfortunately, I didn't take her advice. And a few weeks later, Dad called me into his office. He said I had some serious growing up to do, and that he was disappointed in me. He said he would reconsider hiring me in the future, but for now, the arrangement wasn't working."

Ouch, I think, my chest aching at the thought. I want to hug both my brother and my dad.

"It was the kick in the butt I needed," Justin continues. He tells me how he deeply regrets his behavior but not the end result. "I don't know if I would have made it out to Santa Fe otherwise. And if I hadn't made it out to Santa Fe—"

"You wouldn't have met Katie," I say, relieved for a happy turn in this story. "Or created my perfect niece."

"Or discovered a passion for solar energy," he adds. "It's terrifying to think of the person I would have become if Dad hadn't set me straight."

"That twenty-three-year-old wiener dog would now be a thirty-six-year-old wiener dog?" I guess.

Justin cringes. "Now that's a scary thought."

We're quiet for a few moments as we admire a nearby cardinal perched high in the trees, its red feathers striking against the muted backdrop.

"Does Mattie know?" I ask.

My brother stares at me in disbelief. "Of course Mattie knows. She was still in college and had to overhaul her life because of me," he says. "Kickerville wasn't the original end goal for her. She was debating between a finance degree and nursing school, but running a home-building business? That wasn't in the cards." Justin studies me. "You must have known that."

But I didn't know that. I hadn't known *any* of this.

I shake my head. "I must have just moved to Chicago, right?" I was so excited to attend DePaul University and start a new life in a big city. I certainly hadn't called home much during my college days. And at age eighteen, I wasn't especially chummy with either of my siblings. We were too close to our adolescence, where we'd fought over the remote and focused on our small differences rather than our huge similarities.

"That's right. You were in Chicago." Justin adds this piece of the puzzle to our family's history. "But I can't believe Mattie wouldn't have told you since. Or Mom and Dad. It wasn't like I begged secrecy from anyone."

My head is spinning. I can remember bragging to my roommates about my cool older brother moving out west. I assumed Justin was being a rebel without a cause, leaving behind the family business for the open road. It was adventurous and bold, I'd thought. *Brave.*

And as for Mattie, my perfect sister, I figured the opportunity couldn't have been more ideal. I knew she'd changed her major a few times already, and here she'd been given a clear end goal on a silver platter. Growing up, Mattie's passions seemed more centered on excelling than the activities themselves. Did my sister really love being on the volleyball team, or was she enamored with the quest for a state championship ring? Did she lose herself in her history books and the latest political news because the material excited her, or did she simply want to be on the winning mock trial team?

Mattie should *run our family's company,* I'd rationalized at the time. She was a winner. And this was the ultimate prize.

"I wish I'd known all of this," I mumble.

Justin stops walking. We both take a seat on a massive fallen tree. "I honestly thought you did know," he says.

"Do you think Mattie is glad she took over Kickerville?" I stare up at the cloudy sky. "Do you think she's happy?"

My brother sighs. "I think you have to ask her that yourself."

Chapter Sixty-Eight

I shoot up, my heart racing and my skin wet with perspiration.

It's a few minutes past eight. I must have fallen asleep on the sofa, my blinds left open and my television left on. *Are you still watching?* Netflix wants to know. I can see the sun beginning to rise in the east, its amber burst warm against the pale gray sky.

I was dreaming about Mattie.

We were in Chicago, back in my freshman-year dorm room. I'd been assigned a triple in DePaul's Seton Hall, a glove factory-turned-dorm with astonishingly high ceilings and an open, airy feel. I'm not sure any of us realized how lucky we were at the time.

Doors open on the right at Fullerton. This is a red line train heading for downtown! The "L" operator boomed. My dorm was located directly beside the train tracks, and the rumble quickly became a constant, its vibrations going from a nuisance to a dependable lull. Even the operator's voice became a sort of comfort in its reliability.

"Is there a good time we could talk?" Mattie was standing in front of me now. She was college Mattie with her hair trimmed just below her chin and too much eyeliner. It was a version of my sister I hardly knew. She may as well have been a stranger.

"I don't know," I replied. "I'm just so busy." I was also the college version of myself, with a tangle of long hair and over-plucked eyebrows.

"I only need ten minutes," Mattie pressed.

I shrugged, more focused on choosing an outfit for that evening's outing than the trepidation in my sister's voice. "Give me a call on Saturday morning," I said. "I'll be around."

She looked anxious and unsure. "Things have gotten sort of weird at Kickerville," she said. "I could really use your advice. You were always more of a natural there than me. You can actually tell the difference between pliers and wire cutters." She gave a small laugh.

This was a real conversation, I realize now.

It transpired over the phone, but all of these words were said. I even remember Mattie's joke about pliers and wire cutters. But our Saturday conversation never happened. I drank too much that Friday night and slept through the next morning's ten o'clock call. I'd been too hungover to talk to my sister.

"It's fine, don't worry about it," she said when I reached out later that afternoon.

And I'd been too selfish, too wrapped up in my own world, to insist we reschedule.

I need to talk to Mattie *now.*

Since I slept in yesterday's clothes, if you can call leggings and a hoodie proper "clothes" that is, all I have to do is brush my teeth and apply a quick brush of powder to my inflamed skin. I trip a few times as I hurry down the stairs but am able to catch myself on the wall or railing each time, avoiding any serious falls.

Though as it turns out, I don't even need to leave the building to see my sister.

She's already here.

"Mattie?" I frown at the bottom of the steps. She's waiting outside the glass door, pressing my buzzer. I throw open the door. "I was just heading to your house."

"You're kidding." She's carrying an elegant orchid and a small, gift-wrapped box, her purse slung over one shoulder.

"Come upstairs. I'll start a pot of coffee," I say.

Back inside my apartment, I feel self-conscious. I haven't cleaned in well over a week, and it shows. Tufts of dog hair have gathered in the corners, there are empty candy wrappers and half-finished crafts spread across the coffee table, and the sink is full of dirty dishes. "I'm so sorry for the mess," I say. "I haven't been my best self lately."

"No, it's fine," says Mattie, trying to pretend like it's normal to live so slovenly. She takes a seat at the dining room table, likely because she's found a rare clean surface to sit on. I notice a few blemishes on her own usually flawless skin.

I hand her a cup of black coffee, and she basically thrusts the flower and small box in my direction. "What are these for?" I ask. The orchid is purple and in a terracotta pot. I unwrap the box to discover a Jo Malone candle inside. "Thank you so much, Matt. But why?"

"The candle felt like a small indulgence. I don't know. I once took a test that said my love language is gifts." I think of the maid of honor box, now realizing the package was more genuine than I appreciated. "But the orchid, well, it reminds me of you. And I hope it reminds you of yourself, too."

I shake my head, not quite following.

"Please don't think I'm being cheesy," Mattie says. "But orchids go through periods where they lose their petals, right? And they're just green stalks? So, maybe they don't look like they're thriving on the outside, but they're just resting before their next big bloom."

"Oh." I understand immediately. "Thank you," I say, my mouth quivering. "I don't deserve such nice gifts, though. I am so, *so* sorry. I'm pretty sure I'm the worst sister ever."

And it's not just the giant Kickerville misunderstanding either. I'm feeling pretty confident that I've misjudged my older sister in almost every aspect of our lives.

She frowns, blinking a few times. "Sorry for what? I'm the one who should be sorry. I promise I'm not a horrible person. There's a reason why I acted the way I did last Sunday, though you have every reason to think I'm awful."

"You aren't awful. *I'm* awful." I push my coffee mug away and grab us two glasses of water instead. My mouth feels impossibly dry, and my heart is racing while my brain tries to keep up. "Justin told me the real reason why he left Kickerville, how he got fired. And he told me how *you* got stuck picking up the pieces."

"The worst part is, I now realize you tried to talk to me about it, right when it was all happening," I continue. "I was too selfish to help...or even listen to what you had to say. I am just so sorry, Mattie."

Mattie takes a long drink of water, mulling this over.

"You had a lot going on. You were getting your start in Chicago, in the big city," she says, not unkindly. "And please don't think of me as getting stuck with Kickerville. I chose it."

My sister explains how upset our parents were about Justin's irresponsible behavior followed by his cross-country move. Mattie volunteered to work at Kickerville part-time, to help with the more secretarial tasks Justin left behind. "It wasn't like Justin left, and Dad handed me the key to the city," she explains.

My cheeks grow hot, as that is exactly what I've imagined all of these years, my sister eagerly accepting leadership of the family business. And of course, in my more uncharitable moments, I wondered if Mattie *pushed* Justin out. It is such a ridiculous thought now.

"Mom and Dad were crushed, but especially Dad," she says. "And I guess the parent-pleaser part of me wanted to do whatever I could to help. Really, it was like a series of small 'yeses' that eventually led to this. And I was appreciative of the opportunities. It definitely gave me direction," she says. "I really did believe, I *do* believe, it's an honor to carry on a family business. But..."

Mattie stops talking. She looks at me with a mix of hopefulness and uncertainty.

"But what?" I ask gently.

"I don't think I'm the Parker child meant to carry on Kickerville either," she says.

My heart lifts, but it also aches for my sister. What does that mean for her?

"Just because you've had a lousy few years doesn't mean—"

Mattie crosses her arms over her chest, shaking her head. "It's not that. Every small business will have its rough patches, particularly following a global pandemic." She looks away from me, focusing on the orchid instead. "I've been restless for a while. Unsatisfied. It's not that I'm miserable... I just don't feel fulfilled. I want something more."

"That's how I feel at Polly Feinstein," I say.

I'm amazed my sister and I have been grappling with the same existential crisis. And I feel foolish for never taking the time to notice it. It takes two to tango, and I'm realizing I'm not innocent in the friction that exists between Mattie and me. My guard's been up just as high as hers. I didn't even tell her about my possible MS diagnosis the night she visited me before my birthday. And how immature and dysfunctional is that?

It's time to be honest.

It's time to finally share my more vulnerable side with my older sister.

"I've wanted to be a part of Kickerville for years, to help in some small way, but you haven't exactly made me feel welcome," I say. Mattie's brows press closer together. She doesn't understand. "Every time I offer to do design work, you turn me down. Pretty adamantly."

"Oh," Mattie says.

"Why have you always pushed me away like that?" I want to know. "Is it because of how I acted when I was nineteen? Because I promise I've changed…"

"No! No, of course not," she says. "Honestly? I resented you and your posh ad agency job," she admits. "I was jealous. You've always seemed happy and confident in your career, as if you ended up *exactly* where you hoped to be, and I assumed you only offered to help at Kickerville out of pity. 'Oh, let me lend my fabulous design eye to my family's country bumpkin home business out in Indiana.'"

"I'm sorry, but country bumpkin home business? You really thought I'd say something like that?" I start to laugh, and Mattie joins in. I wipe the happy tears away from my eyes and sigh. "I can't believe you were jealous of me in *any* way. You've always been my perfect older sister who has every part of her life figured out."

"That's kind of you to say that," Mattie says. "But I don't feel that way. Although, I wonder if anyone ever feels like they've got every part of their life under control?"

"Maybe Oprah," I muse.

"Maybe Oprah," Mattie agrees.

Tony Soprano jumps at my chair, resting his two little paws neatly on its edge, and I pull him snugly into my lap. "So, what would you do if you weren't running Kickerville?" I ask quietly.

"That's a great question," Mattie says. "I know I want to help people in a more meaningful way." Her gaze drops down to her feet. I can tell she feels shy about what she's about to say next. "I think maybe...maybe I'd like to become a nurse."

"Mattie." I set an encouraging hand on her forearm, which is covered in goosebumps. "Then apply for nursing school, you nut."

She looks back up at me. "In my thirties? I can't imagine starting all over now."

"Trust me," I say with a smirk. "I know the feeling."

"I'd be the oldest one in my class." Admittedly, it is a strange thought. Matilda Parker, the woman who's always crossed the finish line of Life's Great Accomplishments first (And with such class! Such grace!), doing another lap. Starting over. "You don't know that," I say. "But who cares if you are?"

Mattie shrugs before breaking into a big smile. "Tell you what, come into Kickerville first thing tomorrow morning," she says. "I want you to present your tiny house idea to Fran and me. Formally."

I jump out of my seat, nearly tackling her with my embrace. "Wait, really?"

"Absolutely," she says. "And I promise to be a much better audience this time around."

I hold her close. "I promise to be a much better sister this time around."

"Oh, Bea," she sighs. "Me too."

And then, just the sweet end to a Hallmark movie, we hug and shed a few tears in the glow of the Christmas tree.

Chapter Sixty-Nine

I insist on driving by myself to Kickerville.

For starters, I have my real full-time job to hurry to afterwards. But I also want the nearly hour-long drive to practice my Beahives pitch. I spent all of last night creating an actual PowerPoint presentation this time around, and I ran through it seven times to make sure I had it down pat. Finally, there is the simple fact that Mattie and Fran might think my proposal is totally lame, and I sure as heck don't want to stick around (or be stuck in a car with Mattie afterward) if that's the case.

I feel more like myself today, not only since the Parker Family Sunday Supper Massacre, but even since I was diagnosed with MS on the eve of my thirtieth birthday. Honestly, I feel more like myself than I have in *months*, maybe even years.

Instead of sleeping until the last possible moment this morning, I set my alarm for five o'clock and went swimming at the JCC with Janet. I remembered a pair of goggles and a swimming cap this time. My bathing suit still featured its ridiculous bow, but I was done being embarrassed about it.

Once I was back at the Amelia, I took Tony Soprano for a longer-than-usual stroll, and I took my time getting ready for the day. I conditioned my hair. I shaved my legs. I rubbed extra-healing moisturizer into my skin. I applied a mild acne treatment to my blemishes and drank a full glass of water before brewing a pot of coffee.

I gave my body the love it deserves.

I applied my red lipstick that always gives me an extra boost of confidence, and I didn't try to manufacture a posh, businesswoman outfit. No, I'm wearing a pair of plaid, 1970s straight-legged pants, a white turtleneck, and a green blazer. I look spunky and smart.

I look like *me*.

I grip the steering wheel now, tossing around my own New Year's resolutions. It's a clear, sunny morning, and the sky is a citrusy orange above the barren trees and frosted hills of eastern Indiana. I quiet NPR and take a sip from my traveler's mug.

What do I want to accomplish this year?

I want to find a new job, maybe an entirely new career. Even if my Beahives pitch tanks this morning—God knows Fran Bosse will tell me if she thinks it's a junk idea—I don't want to stay at Polly Feinstein. My relationship with Gwen is too toxic, and I don't want to work at a place where my happiness is dependent on that next big promotion. Maybe I should take a cue from the advice I gave Mattie yesterday. I could go back to school. I could start my own second act.

Sure, it's an intimidating thought, but do you know what's even scarier to imagine? Thirty more years spent in a career where I'm unhappy.

I turn left into the crowded Kickerville parking lot and find a spot close to the entrance. I turn off my car and take a deep breath. I have so many happy memories here, from playing with my Barbie dolls beneath Dad's desk to pizza dinners in the employee break room on nights when Dad had to work late. Mom was a stickler about us eating as a family, and if that meant takeout shared over a wobbly folding table, then so be it. Of course, my favorite moments are the famous holiday parties. I think of Dad dressed as Santa Claus and hope Violet can experience a Kickerville holiday party someday. She deserves to see her Papa dressed as jolly old St. Nicholas and skip around the giant dance floor.

I'm willing to go back to school, to take the long road towards happiness, but I hope Kickerville works out. I hope my Beahives are a sensation, that they not only impress Mattie and Fran, but invigorate the entire company.

My heart is here.

I say hello to Doris, Kickerville's long-time secretary, and she tells me Mattie and Fran are in their office. "How are you feelin'?" she asks. "Mattie told me about your diagnosis. I was so sorry to hear."

"I've been okay," I say. "I'm still figuring out a lot of things."

Doris nods vigorously, but since she has her hair professionally set every Saturday, her curls stay remarkably still. "Well, I've been praying for you every night," she says.

My chest tightens at the thought. "Thank you," I say, genuinely touched. "Can you say one more prayer for me now?" I point toward the end of the hall. "Before I go in there?"

"Absolutely. I've got the Big Man Upstairs on speed dial," she winks.

Mattie and Fran's door is closed, so I take the opportunity to fit in a few more deep breaths and calming mantras. I knock twice.

"Come in," Fran calls.

"Hi," I say. Fran and Mattie are huddled at Mattie's computer. "Is this, um, still an okay time?"

"Of course it is," Mattie says. She and Fran take their seats in the armchairs that sit in the center of the office, between their two workspaces, and I set down my backpack with a clunk.

"You still have that pull-down projector screen, right?"

"Yep, yep." Fran points to the area above the door. "It's a stupid place for it, but with all of the windows, there isn't a better spot."

"And we'd give up just about anything before the natural light," Mattie adds.

I smile at them both, suddenly shy around two women I've known my entire life. I awkwardly pull on the circular tab at the bottom of the projection screen and unroll it into place. My hands shake as I set up both my laptop and the projector, which I've borrowed from my local "Buy Nothing" group. I'm glad I've delayed taking my pill. I can't deal with the flushing this morning, and I definitely don't want to risk any stomach emergencies.

"Would you like a glass of water before you begin?" Mattie asks.

I shake my head. "I brought a water bottle." *Inhale. Exhale. Inhale. Exhale.* I pick up the remote that will allow me to flip between slides and promptly drop it. "Just my MS. All good," I say, surprised to find strength in taking ownership of my disease.

"Thank you both for having me here today," I begin. "I'm delighted to present Beahives, an exclusive tiny house line designed for Kickerville Cabin Co." I click to the next slide, which shows a rather impressive blueprint and rendering of my favorite tiny house model. This one features a rooftop deck and the retractable fencing system.

Fran's eyes widen, and Mattie smiles. I can tell she's proud of me.

For the next hour, I walk the two women through Beahives, starting with the blueprints and estimated manufacturing times, and working my way to the fun pet-centric features and sustainability components. They both love the vacuuming system I've envisioned, which was inspired by a tiny house owner who said while cleaning a tiny house may be fast, it gets dirty even faster. And Mattie and Fran think my kitchen layouts are especially smart. "One of the models actually includes an outdoor kitchen setup, too, which is super fun," I tell them.

"I want that one," says Fran. "I want all of them!"

I can tell they are both impressed, and honestly, a little shocked when I get to the market analysis portion of my presentation. Between us, I can't think of the word "analysis" for a few moments, my brain substituting "research" and "study" instead, but I recover the correct term without Mattie or Fran noticing.

Slow down, deep breaths, I tell myself. *The correct word will come. There's no rush.*

"There are a lot of tiny house builders out there, so how do we differentiate ourselves?" I say. "This is also a market saturated with DIY folks, people who are handy enough to make their own tiny houses. How do we prove to them that our models are worth the extra cost?"

"You've thought through everything," I hear Mattie murmur.

At the end of my presentation, I clasp my hands across my stomach and give a small nod. I'm surprised to see Mattie and Fran stand from their seats, both women clapping and Fran even giving a good whistle.

"I think this is just the sort of spark Kickerville's needed," Fran says.

My heart pounds. "Really?"

"Really," Mattie says. "It's brilliant. And you've done all of the preliminary work for us. I'm blown away. Truly blown away, Bea. This is the sort of proposal it would take an entire team months to put together."

"When can you start?" asks Fran.

I laugh, delirious with happiness and pride.

My sister's smiling face turns serious. "No, really," she says. "When can you start?"

We decide on two weeks from that very day, and as much as I want to drive straight to Polly Feinstein, push over a chair, and declare, "I quit!", I do no such thing. I'm too much a coward to make a scene like that. Instead,

I drive home shout-singing Taylor Swift, power up my laptop, and work remotely for the remainder of the day.

Chapter Seventy

The next morning, I wake up to the opening chords of "Do You Believe in Magic." Someone is calling me at seven a.m., and that someone is my sister.

I cough into the receiver, which is disgusting. "Sorry," I answer, clearing my throat. "Is everything okay?"

"Yes, of course it is," Mattie says, sounding like she's been awake for hours. "I just finished my morning run," she continues, confirming this suspicion. "And I wanted to share some exciting news."

I blink a few times, staring at the familiar crack that runs through my plaster ceiling. "Are you pregnant?"

I can't claim to have the most original thoughts first thing in the morning, that's for sure.

"Negative," she says, her voice happy, breezy even. When was the last time my sister sounded so light? So carefree? "We're buying Mom and Dad's house. We decided last night."

I'm thrilled for Mattie and Peter, but does this really warrant a seven o'clock telephone call? I figured my sister would eventually land at this decision. It's nice to hear how content she feels about it, though.

"That's awesome news. I'm excited for you guys." I close my eyes and snuggle back into my pillow. "I think you'll be very happy there. You'll make it your own. Just don't paint the kitchen cabinets white, or Dad will kill you."

"There's some other news," she says.

"Yeah?" I yawn, wondering if she'll next tell me they're ordering a new sectional or installing wainscotting.

"We're cancelling the wedding."

I shoot upwards so fast, I feel dizzy. "Excuse me?" I say. "You're buying a house but calling off your wedding?"

"That probably wasn't the right way to say it." Mattie laughs. "We're cancelling the extravagant Catholic wedding Mom orchestrated."

"But...*what?* Why?" I ask, thinking of all the careful planning that has already gone into the day.

The debate between a spring or fall wedding! The argument over bridesmaid dresses: should they all match in style and color or *only* color? Were reception favors passé or a must-have? Should the meal be plated or served family style? Lord knows a buffet wasn't even a consideration in Mom and Mattie's worlds.

Honestly, I could write a book on the planning of Mattie and Peter's wedding.

"I thought this was the wedding of your dreams," I say.

Mattie is quiet.

"It was the wedding of *Mom's* dreams," she finally says. "Well, Mom and Mary Ellen Stooplemeyer. I've been having panic attacks at the thought of walking down the aisle in front of hundreds of people, most of whom I don't even know."

"I want a wedding with only our closest family and friends. Maybe even an outdoor ceremony, in a garden or a forest," she continues, her voice softer now. "And I want to have a nice supper afterward instead of a reception. With absolutely *no* dancing."

I'm speechless.

"Are you there?" Mattie asks.

"Roger that. I'm still here," I say slowly. "I'm just...surprised? Okay, honestly? I'm shocked. But I think that all sounds wonderfully romantic. Really, I do."

"Yeah?" I can tell she wants my approval, and I'm happy to give it.

"Yeah," I say. "Seriously! It sounds perfect."

We talk about the specifics a bit longer. They have a few Cincinnati parks in mind for the ceremony, and Mattie hopes they can keep their same May wedding day.

"I'm finally figuring out what I *actually* want and what I've done just to make Mom and Dad happy," Mattie says, absolutely buzzing. "I guess it's about time."

I hesitate before asking the next question. "How does nursing school fit into this equation?"

"I'm not sure yet," she says. "But I think a lot is about to change."

"In the most amazing ways imaginable," I reply.

-*-

I sip on my coffee as the bus rolls down I-71 towards downtown. Food and drinks aren't permitted on the bus, but since Cliff is driving today, I know he won't scold me. (But Debbie? Don't mess with Debbie.) I want to soak in every moment of one of my last morning commutes. I want to remember and appreciate every detail. I'll be driving to Kickerville, and I know I'll miss these bus rides full of interesting characters, cat naps, and dog-eared novels.

My heart sinks when I get to my desk and realize they've moved Hannah closer to Chase and Gwen's workspaces. *A lot is about to change.* I think of my response to Mattie's revelations, and this lends me perspective. *In the most amazing ways imaginable.*

"I have ten minutes before my first meeting."

"Ahhh!" I yelp, which is just about the worst way to greet your boss. Even though Gwen is petite, she towers over my desk in a pair of heeled knee-high boots. "Oh! Oh, um, yes," I bumble. "Just give me one second."

Can we chat sometime tomorrow? I don't have any client meetings, so I'm flexible! I emailed Gwen yesterday. I assumed she would reply via email and set up a meeting time, but it looks like she's in ambush mode.

As quick and discreetly as I can manage, I send an instant message to Hannah: **I'm resigning. Promise it's a good thing. Will tell you more ASAP.** I don't want my best friend to be blindsided by the news, and I don't want Gwen to be the one to tell her.

"The art director decision wasn't easy," Gwen says, taking off with long, measured strides. I hurry after her, my coffee spilling over the edge of my mug in the process. "But Hannah seemed like a safer, more even-keeled choice."

"Oh." I shake my head. "No, that isn't what I wanted to talk about. Hannah's going to be an amazing art director."

Gwen abruptly stops walking. She glares down at me. "Then what did you want to discuss?"

Here it is, the moment I've dreamed about. Every time Gwen put me down in front of a large group, every time she gaslighted me, every time she made a snide comment about the quality of my work, I thought of this very moment.

I want to say dozens of mean and awful things to Gwen.

I want to knock her unethical professional behavior, like the way she sneaks out early and takes too much credit for her subordinates' work. I want to make petty personal comments, too, like how she conveniently forgets to donate to group gifts and makes passive aggressive remarks to put others down.

But if my MS has taught me anything, it's that you have no idea what people are dealing with behind closed doors. Diseases can be invisible. Sadness, anger, frustration, and anxiety can be, too. Some of life's nastiest monsters are beasts that cannot be seen. I have zero idea what Gwen's life is like outside work. For all I know, she's got much bigger problems than I do. Maybe someone bullies her, and she takes it out on us. Not that it excuses her behavior, but it makes it a little more understandable.

"I'm putting in my notice," I say, my smile big and sincere. "I'm going to be launching a new tiny house line at my family's home-building company."

"What?" I've taken Gwen by surprise, and as a result, she seems rather speechless. "You're resigning?"

"Yes. And I'll miss working here." I mean it, too. I think of all the late-afternoon happy hours, the brainstorms that drove us to loopiness before finally hitting all the right notes, the hours spent in deep concentration, and the satisfaction of a job well done. Plus, I met my very best friend in these offices. "I would like next Friday to be my last day."

Gwen continues to stare at me, looking both shocked and disappointed, if you can believe that. "If you'd been given the art director role," she begins, "would that have changed anything?"

My response is immediate.

"No," I say. "It wouldn't have."

The truth of the statement brings me peace. It's like a salve on both my heart and my ego. I'm relieved I didn't get the art director role.

As it turns out, the universe has something much greater in-store for me.

325

Chapter Seventy-One

"Come on, just one more flute of champagne!"

After work, Hannah and I traipsed through the winter cold to the Netherland Plaza Hotel. It's a fabulously fancy hotel in downtown Cincinnati known for its splendid Art Deco design, and the Orchids at Palm Court bar felt perfectly special for our celebratory happy hour.

I smile but shake my head, zipping up my parka. "Sorry, Madame Art Director. I'm researching garage door walls tonight and want to have a clear mind."

Hannah gives me a hug with so much force, it nearly topples me over. "I'm so happy for you," she says. "And so proud of you, too."

"I'm so happy for *you*, Han," I tell her. "And so proud, too."

Hannah slips into her own coat. "I should honestly get home myself," she smiles. "You know how my dad's been in that same bowling league for decades? Well, he asked Arthur to sub for one of his teammates tonight, and I can only imagine how nervous Arthur is!"

"Even if Arthur's an atrocious bowler, I'm sure his sense of humor will keep your dad and his teammates entertained," I beam, understanding what a significant victory this is.

"Yoga on Saturday morning?" Hannah asks.

I chew on my bottom lip. "Do you promise we can choose spots in the back row?"

"I promise."

I tell Hannah yes, that I'm in.

Once home, I roast a sheet pan of veggies and boil a pot of fettuccine. Then, I turn on the *Little Women* soundtrack—I've determined its instrumentals are my favorite to work alongside—and pull up an article I've bookmarked about garage door walls in tiny houses. While it's neat when a garage door opens to an open-air deck, I'm curious to explore the possibilities of one opening to a screened-in porch or even a sunroom.

For the first time since being diagnosed with MS, it's difficult to sleep. My mind is constantly brainstorming interesting, innovative, or just plain fun features to include in Kickerville's Beahives line, and many nights, it feels nearly impossible to turn my ideating off. It's the best form of insomnia.

I've only taken two bites of pasta and read approximately three paragraphs when there's a knock at the door. Curious, I set down my fork and quiet Tony Soprano's barks with a treat before greeting my visitor.

It's Chris Little.

And he looks as awful as I felt on New Year's Eve. There are dark circles beneath his eyes, his normal five o'clock shadow has turned into a full-on beard, and even his clothes are wrinkled in a sad state of surrender.

"What are you doing here?" I ask, more guarded than giddy.

Chris is carrying a pizza box and a brown paper bag from Goodfella's, our local pizza place, and there's a bottle of red wine cradled in the nook of his arm. Is he going to ask me to borrow a corkscrew? Or lecture me on how greasy pizza boxes can't be recycled? Instinctively, I close the door slightly.

Chris swallows, his Adam's apple prominent. He starts to say something, clears his throat, and then begins again.

"I'm here to eat pizza and hoagies with you," he says. "And then watch Anthony Bourdain reruns and drink too much red wine. I'm here to life-chat until late in the night and then dance on the fire escape together."

My heart feels caught in my throat.

"But first, I'm here to say I'm sorry." Chris sets the pizza, hoagies, and wine down at his feet. He sticks his hands deep inside his pockets. "Bea, I am so sorry. I *was* confused that night in my apartment. I didn't want to hurt you the way I hurt Amanda. I was worried there was something wrong with me, that I had some terrible flaw that would just keep repeating itself."

I nod, quietly stepping outside my apartment and leaning against the closed door. Tony Soprano slips out behind me. I can sense my little dachshund is on the defensive, and I give him a quick rub of affection.

"But I no longer think that's the case," Chris says. "You aren't Amanda.

You're Bea. And I'm crazy about you. I've overthought everything for so long that I didn't realize when I had the real deal standing right in front of me."

"You think I'm the real deal?" I say, my sight turning blurry with tears.

"You are the most real deal I've ever met," Chris grins. "You're smart, interesting, and fun. You're creative and kind. You're beautiful. I think you're my favorite person in the entire world."

I look down at my leather mules, hiding my own huge smile.

But there's more to discuss.

"I walked by your apartment on New Year's Eve," I say. "It sounded like you were having a party." *You didn't seem very torn up then,* I think. *And Beth was there with her kazoos and mini bottles of champagne.*

"Maria said she was stopping over with the kids," he sighs. "And surprised me by having Beth and her children in tow. After taking one look at me and my apartment, I'm pretty sure Beth was horrified my sister had ever thought to set us up. If you think I look bad now, you should have seen me a few days ago."

I actually start to laugh, and Chris joins in.

"Can we switch up the order to your perfect date?" Chris asks. "Because I'd really like to dance with you now."

"I think I can be flexible," I say.

Chris pulls out his phone and turns on Journey's "Don't Stop Believin'." What is it about this intro? Note by note, my heart swells and picks up its pace, my anticipation growing. Chris extends his hand, and with a deep breath, I place my clammy palm inside his. He pulls me close, and I rest my head against his chest.

"Why this song?" I murmur.

We're dancing in the middle of the hallway, right between mine and Janet's apartments, and somehow, it feels just as romantic as a fire escape set against a sparkling city skyline.

"Honestly?" I can feel the vibration of Chris's deep voice against my cheek. "I think it's the most romantic, most hopeful song in the world. Plus, it's the song they play during the final scene of *The Sopranos*. I thought you and Tony Soprano might like that." He pauses. "Is this...weird?"

"Totally weird. But I've always thought this song was wildly romantic and hopeful, too. Especially as a teenager at high school dances," I tease, before pulling him closer against me. "So, I guess we're pretty compatible."

Chris looks down at me, his brown eyes hopeful.

"I'm crazy about you, too," I whisper. "Just so you know."

He stops our swaying and lifts my chin. "Can I kiss you now?"

Tony jumps at my knees, which I take as his blessing.

I nod. "Please."

Chris presses his lips against mine, and the fireworks are so explosive, my nerve endings forget all about my multiple sclerosis.

They feel every, single thing.

Epilogue

The Following December

We walk through the Santa Fe Plaza, marveling at the holiday lights twirled up tree trunks and spun between branches. There's a dusting of snow on the ground, and I wonder if I've ever been to a place so magical, so delightfully Christmassy. Even the lamp posts around the Plaza have snowflake- and Christmas tree-shaped lights adorned to them, and the shops are festooned with plenty of their own lights and baubles.

"So, we're going to tell them tonight?" Chris Little reaches for my hand. "I hope your dad doesn't kill me."

"More likely my mom," I say before noticing Chris's pale face. "I'm kidding! They're both going to be thrilled. It's not like we're teenagers. Think of how Hannah reacted!"

"Hannah is the happiest person we know," he says fondly. "You could tell her that you organized your inbox or won twenty dollars in scratch-offs, and she would be thrilled."

"Well, she was *especially* thrilled over this news," I smile, remembering how Hannah hopped off the sofa and spilled Arthur's beer in her excitement.

It's our last evening in Santa Fe, and I want to share our big news before we head home tomorrow. Chris's winter break is coming to an end, and we want to give ourselves enough time to journey back to Cincinnati.

Since this has been our first cross-country trip towing our tiny home, we're trying to be patient with ourselves.

We start the short walk back to Justin and Katie's house.

"Maybe we can come back during your spring break?" I suggest. I'm not ready to leave yet, and I suspect Chris feels the same. This has been his first trip to New Mexico, and it's easy to see he's enamored.

"I'm open to the idea," says Chris. "How does that time look for you at work, though? Would you be able to handle everything from the road?"

I nod. "Our next model doesn't launch until June, so I think the timing would be perfect. Plus, Mattie will still be around."

When Mattie started nursing school in the fall, she stepped down from her position at Kickerville, making Fran Bosse and me co-owners of the company. Fran hadn't been expecting the promotion, and I certainly hadn't deserved it, not yet anyway, but Mattie felt confident in our dynamic duo. Mattie is still working at Kickerville part-time as she helps Fran and me get up to speed on all things business ownership, but her heart is in nursing.

"I thought Santa Fe would be warmer than this," I admit, snuggling into Chris's side. He loops an arm around me. "Whenever I imagined us all coming out here for the holidays, I thought we'd be sipping mai-tais by the pool." While Santa Fe is a touch warmer than Cincinnati, we haven't made it out of the upper thirties yet.

"I sent you that article about Santa Fe's climate. They have a true winter with many nights below freezing between December and February," Chris replies. "Remember? It was when I warned you about nosebleeds because of the altitude."

"You send me approximately ten articles every day," I say. "I can't keep up."

Back at Justin and Katie's, we're met with the smell of Katie's famous tuna noodle casserole and the sound of wood crackling in the fireplace. Violet sits in Dad's lap, flipping through a new storybook Santa Claus brought her, while Mom quizzes Mattie for an upcoming exam.

Mom has become Mattie's best study partner, and the two women spend hours together each week poring over diagrams and shuffling through flashcards. It's certainly helped mend their relationship after Mattie put the kibosh on Mom's big, Catholic wedding dreams.

"Nice timing," Justin says. "We were going to give your dinners to Tony

Soprano if you didn't get home soon."

"He's lying!" Katie calls from the kitchen. "I just pulled the casserole out of the oven."

Tony yips at my feet, excited over the possibility of handouts. Since we've taken our tiny house with us to Santa Fe, bringing along Tony Soprano has been a breeze. And lucky for us, Justin and Katie welcome him into their home whenever we aren't in ours.

Our home.

Oh, I can't wait to tell you about it.

Chris and I moved out of the Amelia in October and into our very own Beahive. We chose the most environmentally friendly model of the fleet. (Of course!) Our tiny house runs on solar energy and includes a compostable toilet and rainwater-gathering system—plus an old farmhouse sink, reclaimed cabinetry, and an antique chandelier. Our home is exactly two hundred and fifty square feet, with two lofted bedrooms, a two-sided fireplace, and the world's most darling kitchen. Of course, we also opted for the pet-specific features, like the retractable fencing system and a hidden slot for Tony's food and water bowls.

It's the perfect mix of our two personalities.

Janet's already been over four times to visit. She thinks our little house is "cute as a button" but says she could never live tiny herself. "I don't have the wardrobe for tiny living," she claims. "My costume jewelry alone wouldn't fit in this space." Janet also moved out of the Amelia this past fall and into Fran's farmhouse. The two women drive each other crazy ("Our couple name could be Franet," Janet recently proclaimed. "Good God, *no*," Fran immediately replied), but they are also crazy in love. I've never seen either so happy.

As for Chris and me, we purchased fifteen acres of land in Harrison, Ohio, a town that's about halfway between Cincinnati, Ohio and Guilford, Indiana, and park our tiny house there. Chris dreams of planting a giant vegetable garden which could eventually become a neighborhood co-op, and don't even get me started on his composting ambitions.

Peter and Mattie sit down at the dining room table, followed by Mom and Dad.

My parents will be staying in Santa Fe for the entire month of January.

After selling their house to my sister and brother-in-law, they ended up in a condo that overlooks the Ohio River. Dad's adjusted quicker than any of us could have expected, appreciating their new life without a gigantic house or sprawling lawn to maintain. He also likes that he can visit his masterpiece of a mansion whenever he feels like it, though I'm not sure the newlyweds enjoy the impromptu visits quite as much.

Despite Dad's surprise drop-ins, which he swears he's going to be better about, Mattie and Peter love their new house. Ivy St. James, Mattie's design guru best friend, helped them make it their own. It's amazing what new paint colors and furniture can do to a space. Honestly, Mattie and Peter's décor feels a lot like their May wedding: simple and elegant, with no fussy details.

Oh, and a coffee shop *did* go in down the street from their west side Mc-Mansion. Even better? So did a satellite branch of Mattie's nursing school.

Is that kismet or what?

"Aunt Beezus, can I sit on your lap?" Violet asks, starting to climb on me before she even finishes her question.

"You're a big five-year-old now, Vi," Justin says.

"And it's poor table manners," adds Katie.

"Maybe later," I wink, as she slumps into her own chair.

I finger the ruby that now rests on my left ring finger. Even though Chris and I got engaged back in July, I still marvel that it's there. After a mere six months of dating, Chris decided he wasn't against marriage after all. He just hadn't met the woman he wanted to marry yet. Even crazier, it was Chris's life-chats with Mattie that helped him reach this point. "Your marriage will be just that: *your* marriage," she apparently told him. "You'll do things your own way. Don't worry about what other people have done or think you should do."

Yep. My older sister actually says things like that now.

And speaking of sisters, while Maria doesn't understand why Chris and I wouldn't want to get married at her parish's grand church—we're doing a small ceremony at the observatory—she's learned to be more of a spectator than a coach in her twin brother's life. "But I'm never going to stop teasing you about your amount of *Star Wars* t-shirts," she recently told Chris. And on that point, I wholeheartedly agree.

Katie holds a bottle of white wine above my glass. "We're going for a high-low vibe," she says. "Tuna noodle casserole and Sonoma's very best chardonnay."

"None for me, thanks," I reply, before whistling for everyone's attention. I hold Chris's hand. "We have an announcement to make."

"Are you starting a new treatment? The infusion?" Mattie asks, referring to the MS therapy that involves a twice-yearly infusion. I came off my twice-daily pill back in February after a miserable few months of flushing and stomach issues, but I haven't started a new medication since. "That seems like a great option."

Between diet, exercise, supplements, and stress management, my MS is in a good place. Multiple sclerosis is a disease that changes every day, and while some days are certainly harder than others, overall, I'm doing pretty darn well.

I've found techniques to alleviate certain symptoms—like writing to-do lists and reminders, scheduling afternoon power naps, and making time for meditation—and I'm working on being patient with myself. I've found talking about my disease and taking ownership of it give me a sense of control over an otherwise unpredictable illness.

My most recent MRI was in June, and it was a stable scan with no new lesions. It was, it *is*, the hugest relief. Dr. Wessels is keeping a close eye on my disease progression, and now more than ever, I know I'm one of the lucky ones. My disease was caught early, and it's slow-moving. I have a lot to be thankful for.

"The infusion does sound like a great option," I reply to Mattie. "But the thing is, I won't be on any MS treatments for a while." Even better, this most recent change to my body has nearly eliminated my MS symptoms, a pleasant surprise I discovered many women with MS experience during this time.

Mattie frowns, but I can see the understanding, the hopefulness, flicker in Mom's eyes.

I look over at Chris, who smiles and nods at me. It's amazing how much can change in a year. My downstairs neighbor is still my environmental superhero, but he's no longer my crush. Chris is now my fiancé and... *wait for it...*

"We're pregnant," I announce, as everyone shrieks and clambers to their feet.

Because who says you have to do things in a certain order? The Pope?

Life is messy and complicated. It's occasionally devastating and defeating.

But jeez louise, it sure can surprise you in all the best ways.

Acknowledgements

I often doubted if this book would ever see publication.

I finished its first draft in 2019. The story was told from both Bea and Mattie's perspectives, but it took place over a single evening—during Mattie and Peter's engagement party—when a snowstorm blew in and left the guests stranded for the night. I was trying to make a chick lit version of Ann Patchett's Bel Canto—yes, I really was!—and let's just say I failed miserably.

I was diagnosed with multiple sclerosis later that year, just a month shy of my 30th birthday. After (many) more failed drafts—I just couldn't get to the heart of the story, which is a pretty big problem for a rom com—I finally realized it was my MS story I wanted to tell. And Bea Parker was the perfect heroine for it.

Thank you to Aura Lewis, my designer extraordinaire. I had no idea how polished and professional a self-published novel could look, and it's thanks to Aura that this book looks as downright lovely as it does. When I saw Aura's sketch of the book cover, I actually cried because she had gotten it all so right. I feel privileged to have worked with you, Aura. Your talents are extraordinary.

Another big thanks to Cincinnati author, Jessica Booth. I was having a nervy-b over the thought of self-publishing when I saw an Instagram post from a local bookshop called the Bookery. Jessica's romance, A Match Made in Autumn, was the store's second best-selling novel of 2023. When I did more digging and realized Jessica was an indie author, my spirit got a much-needed boost of confidence. Jessica, thank you for your generosity, expertise, and kindness during this entire process. You are my indie author guardian angel. Thank you to my beta readers as well, Chelsea, Jackie, and Lizzy, who gave me gut checks and helped me spot oversights. If you can believe it, Chris was even quirkier in early versions. And Bea and Mattie's relationship was even more awkward! Thank you to Sierra Hollabaugh, who not only owns my favorite bookstore in town (the Bookery!) but also champions local authors. Sierra, you have showed me such patience and kindness during this entire process, and I cannot tell you how much I appreciate it. Cincinnati and its entire community of readers and writers alike are so lucky to have you.

Is it weird to thank my neurologist here? Because I must! I am fortunate to be a patient of Dr. Michelle Bowman, a brilliant and caring doctor in the Cincinnati area. Dr. Bowman is a true advocate for her patients, and knowing she is in my corner has given me tremendous comfort and confidence these past four (almost five!) years. She's smart and empathetic with a talent for translating complex medical jargon into every-woman speak. Dr. Bowman is one of my heroes.

Huge hugs to my nearest and dearest family and friends. Mom and Dad, in addition to fostering a love of books and reading, thank you for the stacks of computer paper you gave me to write my very first storybooks. Thank you for making Adam, Marigold, and my lives so much easier through all the little and big things you do. Grandma Betty, I wish everyone had a granny like you, because I think it would make the world a better place. You inspire me every day, and I hope I can be half the person you believe I am. Thank you to Meg, Libby, Kelsey, Clare, Rachel, Rachael, Emily N., Emily H.S., Kim, and Sue—my gal pals who keep me honest and keep me hip. (Just kidding on the latter point. I am not hip!) I am a girls-girl, and I'm lucky to be surrounded by a network of strong, smart, funny, and kind women. Extra big hugs here to my MS ladies: Courtney, Mary, and Patricia. You are all bright and beautiful, and you make me feel so much less alone. Also? Special shoutout to Meg for all your unparalleled "come to Jesus" talks, which are famous for pulling me out of the funkiest funks.

Speaking of Meg, we have a new mantra I would love to share with you, reader. Build the shelf. If you don't see the space for your book, write it anyway and build the shelf yourself. You don't need anyone to tell you that you're "worthy" of that space. Build the shelf. Make space for yourself. This applies to all of your big, beautiful ideas.

My last thank-you is the most important thank-you.

Adam, thank you for never giving up on me and my dreams. You've always believed in me, even when I didn't believe in myself, and that confidence helped keep me going when times got tough (and all I really wanted to do was cry and feel sorry for myself). You've encouraged my writing and helped make it a reality by cooking us incredible meals, taking on extra household chores, keeping an eye on Marigold...really, just swooping in however you could to make writing time a reality. (Which is hard with a toddler, three dogs, and full-time jobs.) I am so darn lucky to have such a steadfast and caring husband. You've never once made me feel like a burden because of my MS, and you've so lovingly shared the emotional and physical loads of this unpredictable disease. Thank you for everything you do for our little family. I love you.

About the Author

Jenna Beall Mueller lives with her husband, toddler, and three dogs in Cincinnati, Ohio and Adirondack Park. She is the author of *Fairy Tales as Told by Clementine*, a children's series which includes twelve picture books. This is her first women's fiction novel. Jenna enjoys antique-shopping and all things colorful and cozy.